Praise for the CAT CRIMES series!

Cat Crimes
"Scary, funny, clever and traditional, each story has its own special flavor. . . . This is a grand collection indeed."
—*Mostly Murder*

Cat Crimes 2
"Offers an even livelier selection of cat tales for reading and rereading pleasure."
—*Mystery News*

Cat Crimes 3
"Tales from some of the best writers in the business."
—*The Washington Times*

Danger in D.C.
"Lighthearted and pleasant . . . Cat-loving mystery buffs . . . will lap up the offerings."
—*Publishers Weekly*

FELINE AND FAMOUS

Cat Crimes Goes Hollywood

Martin H. Greenberg and Ed Gorman

IVY BOOKS • NEW YORK

Ivy Books
Published by Ballantine Books
Copyright © 1994 by Martin H. Greenberg and Ed Gorman

Library of Congress Catalog Card Number: 95-94900

ISBN 0-8041-1362-9

This edition published by arrangement with Donald I. Fine, Inc.

Manufactured in the United States of America

First Ballantine Books Edition: February 1996

10 9 8 7 6 5 4 3 2 1

Contents

Author Notes

Terry Black is the author of *Dead Heat*, a detective/horror film starring Treat Williams and Joe Piscopo, now available on home video (at an absurdly low price). He's also written for *Dark Justice*, a crime series on CBS, and *Tales from the Crypt*, HBO's acclaimed horror series. Terry's first *Tales* episode was directed by Richard Donner, and won a Cable ACE Award for Best Dramatic Teleplay.

Edward D. Hoch first began publishing crime fiction back in the late 1950s. Since then, he's become a master of his craft, a writer just as comfortable with a locked-room puzzle as he is with a light-hearted piece of whimsy. His has been a most distinguished career.

Rochelle Majer Krich has swiftly made her name as a major writer of suspense novels. Her books are lauded for their pace, mood and humanity, qualities amply on display here.

Barbara Collins's short stories distinguish any book in which they appear. She writes in a style and voice all her own. We felt we needed one cat-hater in every book—to keep us from getting all icky-poo on the subject of felines—and we decided to make it Barbara. She hates cats with such grand high style.

Barbara Paul is one of today's best suspense writers. She has mastered virtually all the forms of mystery, putting her own very individual stamp on each. *Mystery Scene* called her a "true master" and heartily recommended all of her novels.

Bill Crider is one of the most underpraised writers in mystery fiction today. He's able to handle every form of the crime novel, and to do so with genuine distinction. *Blood Marks* is one of the best suspense novels of this decade, and the Sheriff Dan Rhodes books are prose versions of "Andy of Mayberry," sweet but with bite and wisdom, too.

John Lutz's "Ride the Lightning" is one of the finest short stories ever produced by a mystery writer, a slice of real life that engrosses, shocks and saddens the reader each time he comes to it. The amazing thing is that Lutz has been able to reach this same level many times, in both his short stories and his novels. He is a modern master.

Tracy Knight is a young psychologist just now finding his own voice and slant on fiction. He writes a simple but elegant prose invested with a lot of humanity and sly humor. This is one of his best stories.

Jon L. Breen is known first as a fine writer of fiction and second as an equally fine critic of mystery fiction. Here we see Breen in his writer guise, and he's rarely been better.

Les Robert's fiction is smooth, observant and forceful. He's done for Cleveland what Raymond Chandler did for Los Angeles—given us not just a map but also a psychological profile of a city. Roberts is at last finding the larger audience he deserves.

Jill M. Morgan has written a number of novels in a number of genres but no matter which form she chooses, she always brings polish and solid craftsmanship to the task. Here she takes some liberties with the traditional mystery—and has a good time doing it.

Author Notes

Jan Grape's short fiction has won her an audience that eagerly awaits the appearance of her first novel, which is being completed as this book is being put together. Jan has a great good feel for everyday people and the sad little twists and turns that sadden them. As here, in this bittersweet tale.

Ted Fitzgerald here reveals not only his skills as a storyteller but his fondness for the *noir* fiction of the fifties. Fitzgerald is one of those rare writers able to mix comedy and drama, a facility that makes his fiction distinctive and eminently readable.

We forget that the movie industry actually began on the East Coast. Yes, indeed, the trek to Los Angeles came later. **P. M. Carlson** takes us back to the original Hollywood—the East Coast one—in a tale rendered in a prose style that approximates the slapstick style of the first movie comedies.

Catherine Dain's novels are quickly winning her a large following. Here we see her in a playful but sage mood, one her many readers know from her books. Enjoy.

Livia Washburn and **James Reasoner** are a rarity—a husband-and-wife writing team who work together all the time without ever imperiling their marriage. Yes, they do books separately, too, but they are also able to work together on the same piece—and remain good friends. If you think this is easy, ask anybody who's ever had a collaborator.

Bruce Holland Rogers's last story for this Cat Crimes series won him an Edgar nomination and no small amount of attention. He's back with a story that is equally daring and equally clever. Maybe lightning *will* strike twice.

Introduction

When I was a youngster growing up in the Midwest, no pleasure ever equaled that of going to the movies. Usually this was Saturday afternoons, but every once in a while my parents would surprise my brother, sister and me by taking us to a double feature at night. Upon occasion, we even went to the drive-in, which was a special pleasure because the movies there ran to James Stewart westerns (which hold up very well today, especially those directed by Anthony Mann) and the Universal monster films with Karloff and Lugosi and Chaney (which also hold up very well).

There was a holy darkness inside a movie theatre. On the screen was a race of giants—of operatic giants, for all their griefs and joys were far larger than most of us would ever experience, just like the griefs and joys in opera. And with a bag of popcorn in one hand and Good n' Plentys in another and the *Looney Tunes* musical theme blaring from the speakers—well, life just didn't get any better.

While this is a collection about cats, it's also a collection about Hollywood—both the nostalgic one I've recalled here, and the real one, which wasn't always so much fun.

Gaudy, shallow, cynical as it frequently is, Hollywood is, nonetheless, the most creative city in the world. From Chaplin and Keaton and Mary Pickford to Tom Hanks and Charles Grodin and Winona Ryder, Hollywood has probably given more people more pleasure than any other town on our planet.

We hope to bring you a little bit of that same pleasure in this book of ours.

—ED GORMAN

Dying for Dollars

•

Terry Black

"**D**amn it, Greg, you didn't *die!*"

Taylor Trumbull's bullhorn baritone shook the walls of the frail soundstage. No one had ever accused him of being soft-spoken (least of all, the actors), but this current outburst was earsplitting even for him—a measure, perhaps, of how badly things were going.

"The shot was perfect, the timing was perfect, the squib was perfect," he roared, reddening with anger. "It was a great death scene, only you didn't die!"

Greg Newbury sat up, groping for a towel. "Sorry, Trum," he said, dabbing at the blood-colored syrup on his forehead. "I thought this was just another rehearsal."

"Then why did the cameraman say, 'rolling'?"

"Why'd he mumble it, you mean."

The debate continued, but I was no longer listening. Greg's unfatal head wound was easily correctable, but the head-butting between star and director brought everything to a dead stop. Greg and Trum's off-camera skirmishes had become a daily routine, as *Creepy Tales* fell further behind schedule and the budget soared skyward, threatening to capsize our modest production.

The only upside was that while they traded slurs, the stand-ins could relax, since there wasn't much to do.

Except seduce the script girl.

"You and me, Alyssa," I whispered, nodding offstage, "behind the morgue in five minutes, what do you say?" I gave her a sunny smile, not really expecting it to work but hoping (ever the optimist) to lay the groundwork for future tomfoolery.

Alas, she wasn't buying.

"Sorry, Felix," she said, not even looking up from the dogeared screenplay where some (but not enough) of Page Twelve was crossed off. She blew a strand of hair from her forehead—strawberry blonde, my favorite—and said, "Can't do it. I have to be ready if the battling egos over there need a line change. Besides . . ." she scratched the ears of the coal-black Persian, nestled cosily in her lap, ". . . you wouldn't want to disturb Fauntleroy here, would you?"

Perish forbid, I thought, but only shook my head.

In a way, Fauntleroy and I had the same job. I'd been hired because I was roughly the same size and shape as Greg Newbury, our star, the man who gets shot in the scene just filmed (albeit badly). My job was to stand there and be tape-measured and light-metered while Greg browsed the pages of *Daily Variety* and blew cigar smoke into the director's face.

Fauntleroy was also a stand-in, of sorts. They needed two cats on the set of "Dying for Dollars," *Creepy Tales'* thirteenth episode. The story involves a man who gets a gland transplant from a cat, and promptly inherits its nine lives. He joins a carnival and gets famous, dying right onstage, a trick he can manage eight times. But he miscounts somehow, and winds up buried alive with no lives left—while a cat dances on his grave.

Fauntleroy was to be the grave-dancer. Actually, he was one of six animals supplied by our local cat wrangler, a long-suffering character named Greaves. The extra cats were there, Greaves explained, because cats are tough to train; they differ from dogs, monkeys and horses in that a cat could care less what its trainer expects. You're lucky if one in six follows orders, even for a mountain of Kal Kan.

True to form, Fauntleroy had escaped within minutes of arriving at Soundstage B, and would probably have been halfway to San Pedro by now if he hadn't taken a fancy to Alyssa's lap—a place I wouldn't mind settling myself.

"Keep him there," Greaves had said, not even trying to recapture the beast. "Maybe he'll calm down in time for Wednesday's shooting."

So Alyssa had gained a lapcat and I'd had to get used to it, at least until His Lordship was carted off to another assignment. I sighed and tried to pet the little guy, but he sniffed at my fingers the way you'd smell something green and lurking on your refrigerator's bottom shelf.

"I think he likes you," she said.

Then Alyssa went back to her script, recording which takes were slated for printing and noting the timing on each one. She had an eye for detail that Sherlock Holmes would have envied. Fauntleroy watched with great interest, as if he wanted the job himself someday.

Furry little bastard.

"Break for lunch," Trumbull announced, and the first assistant director (the loudest mouth on every set) repeated it for him. The cast and crew vanished like smoke, headed for the craft service table, where a beefy ex-weightlifter named Murphy was unpacking a jeepload of takeout Chinese. Only the finest for the men and women of *Creepy Tales*.

First in line was Greg Newbury, never one to miss a meal, chomping his trademark stogie and leaving the stench of Havana all over the dim sum pork. He took a generous helping, doused it with soy sauce and was just settling down to his first sloppy bite when a shrill voice yelled, *"Don't eat that!"*

All heads turned to find Millie Swanson, *Creepy*'s costume designer, stalking forward with fists clenched and brows furrowed and (you'd swear) steam coming out of her ears. "*Mister* Newbury," she began, "what did I tell you about eating in costume?"

"I forget," he said, forking down some rice.

"Then I'll remind you. This little drama calls for you to die nine times. Specifically, you have to be shot, stabbed, drowned, hanged, electrocuted, pricked with poison darts, mangled in a car crash, flung from a trapeze and, finally, buried alive—all in the same costume!" She put her face inches from his. "Can you guess why that upsets me?"

"I dunno," he said, wiping his chin.

"Because it's all filmed *out of order*, you moron! We have to have nine outfits, including the one you're wearing now, each with a different damage pattern. There's the shirt with bullet holes, the shirt with bullet holes and blood-stains, the shirt with bullet holes, bloodstains, burn marks and mud splatters, and so on—but none, I repeat, *not one of the shirts in your wretched wardrobe has food stains!*"

"So what you're telling me," he said, through an open mouthful of garlic shrimp, "is that you think I'm a sloppy eater?"

Millie's comeback was probably scathing but I never heard it, because Trumbull picked that moment to tap Alyssa's shoulder and say, "Come on, let's see the dailies." Taylor Trumbull liked to work through lunch, viewing yesterday's footage with a skeptical eye and a growling stomach. Alyssa tagged along, grabbing a quick plateful of egg foo yung—not for herself, but for the four-footed spectator who followed her everywhere. Sure enough, Fauntleroy trotted right alongside, trying to coax a tasty morsel out of his shapely surrogate mom.

"Lucky devil," I muttered, reaching for a paper plate.

Lunch was a tedious affair. Most of it was spent listening to Timothy James, esteemed author of our tale-in-progress, griping bitterly about credit jumping and failed Guild arbitrations. Timothy had few previous writing credits, but he'd taken an extension course at UCLA and, apparently, he was the brother of somebody famous. I hoped his dialogue was more riveting than his conversation.

I was looking for a way to sidestep his company when a secretary did it for me.

"New script pages," she said, handing him a bundle of Xerox sheets. You could tell how much the script had changed by what color the pages were. First draft pages were printed on white, second on blue, then pink, yellow, green, buff, salmon, cherry, and tan. These pages were a color I'd never seen before, possibly chartreuse.

"I thought the script was finalized," he said feebly, thumbing through the revisions. His face turned the color of the page he was reading. " 'SCENE 17—OMITTED'? Whose idea was that?"

"Mine," said Greg Newbury, scarfing down his dessert. "I was looking over the script last night, and suddenly it came to me: Scene Seventeen is unnecessary. It doesn't have what every great scene needs."

Timothy frowned. "What's that?"

"Me. I'm not in the scene anywhere. Nobody cares about the story here, kid. They want stars, they want to gawk at some famous faces. Like (ahem) mine." Greg offered his popular three-quarter profile, the one *People* magazine used in their "Who's Hot" issue, disturbing the chiseled features only to shovel in one last bite of cherry cheesecake.

"But, uh—" Timothy's objections went unvoiced as Greg clapped his shoulder and departed, stage left. I followed; it was time to get back to work, if what I do can really be called that. Standing-in isn't a glamorous profession, but it pays the bills for lots of would-be actors.

I headed for the set, but I didn't get far.

"Take a look at this, would you, Felix?" It was Hal Brennan, the property master, a fidgety veteran of countless productions, who guarded his props like the crown jewels of London and went haywire if you moved so much as a paper clip on a hot set (one where shooting is still unfinished).

"Hold this," he said, handing over a severed head.

Not a real one, of course. The thing was made of rubber, from a plaster mold of an actor's features—Mel Davies, one of Tinseltown's best-known faces, forever typecast as the sneering heavy. Davies gets decapitated in Scene Thirty-One; his head appears in Scene Thirty-Two. And that's what Hal was upset about.

"They can't just put the head on the floor, in a pool of its own blood," he groused. "No, that would be too easy. It's got to *drop* into the frame, like it's tumbling from Mel's

5

own shoulders. But there's a problem." He signaled me. "Drop the head."

I did. It hit the floor and bounced back, right into my hands.

"The damn thing's made of rubber! It *bounces*! How are we supposed to make the head look real when you can dribble it like a basketball?"

I shrugged. "Can't you tell Trumbull—?"

"It's not Trumbull's idea," Hal said. "It's that bastard Greg Newbury. He wants the head to land at his feet, part of this big dramatic reveal. Me, I wish he'd mind his own business." Gus started raving about Newbury's shortcomings, but I chose that moment to make my exit.

I showed up just in time for Trumbull's next tantrum. "Everybody, *off my set!*" he snapped. "I want this quick and simple, no problems, no distractions. Everyone who doesn't need to be here, scram. Not you," he added, pointing at me, before I could make my getaway.

Alyssa gave me a weary smile as she left the set, with Fauntleroy padding in her wake. Practically everyone followed her, grips and gaffers and P.A.s in headphones, the set dresser and makeup artist and production coordinator, all the extras and members of the crew who gather when the camera's ready to roll. But not this time. The only ones left on the set (besides me and the cameraman) were Taylor, Greg Newbury, and Mel Davies—whose job it was to blast Greg with a .38 caliber blank cartridge.

Out of sight, I knew, was a hired marksman with a rifle that shot only paint pellets, called squibs. At the precise moment when Trumbull yelled "Action!", Davies's gun would roar but hit nothing, while a paintball would strike Greg's forehead where the unshot bullet would have.

"Get Felix in there for a trial run," Trumbull said. I stepped forward, but Greg waved me off.

"We did all that before lunch," he said impatiently. "You want to shoot this thing, let's do it." He climbed onto the stage—a mock shooting gallery, where Greg himself was the target—and got in position, with a final puff of his cigar. Davies went to his mark and stood fingering his gun butt. Trumbull nodded.

"Rolling," said the cameraman.

"Speed," said the sound man's voice.

"Action," said Trumbull.

Davies drew his gun and fired. The roar was deafening in the small space. A red spot blossomed on Greg's forehead; his eyes went glassy and he slumped to the floor, slack-jawed.

"Cut and print," said Trumbull triumphantly. "Much better, Greg! Couldn't have been more convincing. Hell, I'm ready to send for the morgue wagon."

Which is exactly what he ended up doing.

"Let me get this straight," said LAPD detective Julia Rheingold, hastily summoned when Greg showed no signs of reviving. "He died from getting shot with a paintball?"

Trumbull looked flustered. "He was also shot with a .38 caliber blank. Sort of like . . ." he shuddered, ". . . Brandon Lee."

I recalled the incident, and perhaps you do too. Brandon Lee, son of Bruce, was making a film called *The Crow*, where he's shot to death and comes back from the grave. Unfortunately, the gun was loaded with real bullets for a closeup, then reloaded with blanks. The lead tip of one bullet had come loose in the cylinder; when the blank behind it fired, it shot the leftover slug and killed Brandon as dead as any live bullet would have.

"I'll need that gun," said Rheingold. She was dark-haired and sort of pretty, if you like authority figures, but there was nothing feminine about her now.

"It's right here," Trumbull said, pointing to the spot where Mel Davies had dropped it in dismay. "The last man to handle the gun before filming was Hal Brennan. He loaded the cartridges."

Rheingold turned to the highly strung property master, who couldn't have looked guiltier if they'd caught him on a flight to Rio. "Are you licensed to handle firearms, Mr. Brennan?"

Brennan's head bobbed up and down, like the rubber one in his prop trailer. "I was real careful," he insisted. "I don't see how this could have happened—"

"Maybe someone didn't like this Greg Newbury," Rheingold surmised. "Did *you* like him, Mr. Brennan?"

Well, no one in Soundstage B could answer "yes" to that question, so it was no surprise when she took Brennan's arm in a grip that wasn't friendly. "Perhaps you'd like to answer a few questions," she suggested, "down at the station . . . ?"

"You want to do *what*?" Alyssa looked at me like I'd sprouted a third eyeball, or taken up cannibalism. "Are you out of your mind?"

"I want to solve the murder," I said. "Hal didn't do it, Alyssa. He's too nice a guy, and besides, how could he be dumb enough to make himself look so guilty?"

"Ask around, Kojak. Most criminals are dumber than you'd think—and I don't recall anyone accusing Hal of being a candidate for Mensa."

"Still, I've got a feeling about him." I paused, frowning at Alyssa, and suddenly realized what was different about her: there wasn't a cat in her lap. "Hey, where's Fauntleroy? I thought you two were inseparable."

"I don't know," she said, with genuine concern. "He must have run off after the murder. I haven't seen him since."

I checked my watch. Ninety minutes had gone by since Greg's last bow; nobody had gone home, because we were all on salary and Trumbull refused to wrap for the day. He and studio management were holed up in a conference room, searching (rumor had it) for some way to salvage the fatal episode. Perhaps they could capitalize on Greg's mishap, work it into the advertising.

In the meantime, the cops were taking statements, which was stupid because nobody was around when Greg got shot, they'd all been sent away. Not that it mattered; the murder was *on film*, for God's sake. Once that footage got out, anyone watching CNN would become an eyewitness.

But where was Fauntleroy?

"You don't suppose," I said, putting it gently, "that who-ever killed Greg, *really* killed him, did something to that cat?"

"Why?" she snapped. "To keep him from testifying?"

Dumb idea, I thought, recoiling from her gaze. But I couldn't shake the feeling that Greg's shooting had some-thing to do with Fauntleroy's unexcused absence.

"Right here," said Carmine Bella, the sound engineer for *Creepy Tales,* a shy but brilliant man who worked his con-trol board like a pianist tickling the ivories. "Here, this is the moment when the shooting occurs."

Alyssa and I were plugged into auxiliary headsets, listen-ing to the playback from Carmine's reel-to-reel. We heard the cameraman say, "Rolling," Carmine's voice adding, "Speed," then Trumbull's fateful order: "Action!"

Instantly there was a gunburst, painfully loud. But it wasn't a sharp, clean sound; it had a broken, stuttering quality, as if the noise level had crested and fallen more than once.

"That's the answer!" I blurted. "Did you hear it, there was another gunshot—from a gun besides Davies's."

"Fired from a grassy knoll, I suppose." Alyssa ripped off her headset and tossed it to Carmine. "Doesn't prove a thing, Felix. Of course there were two gunshots, from the .38 and the squib rifle. They tried to synchronize shots, but nobody's perfect."

I sighed, realizing she was right. As a detective I made a good stand-in; the first and only lead I'd thought of only seemed to confirm the house verdict. I thanked Carmine and sauntered away, wondering what to try next.

That's when Alyssa surprised me.

"My turn," she said, snagging my elbow. "If we can't prove Hal's innocent, maybe we can show he's guilty. What do you say we search his trailer?"

"And you think *I'm* crazy," I protested. "The cops won't let us near it, and it's probably locked up anyway."

"Not to worry," she said, producing a ring of keys.

"Rheingold's troops are busy interviewing nonwitnesses, and why should they care about the trailer anyway? They've already got their smoking gun—literally!—so they don't need any more physical evidence. Anything we find will be a pleasant surprise."

Odd choice of words, I thought, but I followed her through the carny props and canvas chairs, past nervous technicians and fitfully dozing extras, to Hal's trailer in a quiet corner of the soundstage. Nobody was watching as Alyssa chose the proper key and unpadlocked the trailer's rollup gate.

We opened it and slipped inside.

Don't ever think you've seen everything—at least, not until you peek into a trailer like Hal's. There were torches, hatchets, double-bladed axes, headsman's cowls and suits of chain mail, severed limbs alphabetically sorted (EYEBALLS, FINGERS, TOES), monocles, eyepatches, tricorn caps, army/navy/air force insignia, skulls and thighbones, vampire dentures, tommy guns and gold doubloons. Any time or place in history, Hal could open a drawer and put you there.

"Where does he *get* this stuff?" I wondered, but Alyssa wasn't listening.

"Look at this," she said.

She was holding an eight-by-ten glossy of Greg Newbury, pulled from a folder in a cardboard box. Someone had put cartoon Xs over Greg's eyes, and (in case that was too subtle) drawn an arrow pointing to his head, embellished with a skull and crossbones.

"What were you saying," she asked, "about Hal being such a nice guy?"

"Go figure," I said.

Alyssa ran off to confer with the police, looking intolerably pleased with herself, and I sat down on an apple box to pout about it. Alyssa's devotion to detail made her an ace crimestopper, but it wasn't the outcome I'd been hoping for. Trying to help Hal, it seemed, had only tightened Rheingold's noose.

I was still brooding when I happened to glance under the trailer, where I found a clue overlooked by everyone: a pair of green, opalescent eyes, watching me intently. I said, "Here, kitty," and Fauntleroy sidled out, eyeing me with suspicion. After a moment he deigned (reluctantly) to sniff my fingertip, then he relaxed a bit and rubbed against my ankle. There was a funny marking on his fur.

I felt my own hackles rise.

"You may not be an Oscar-winning feline," I said, stroking his back, "but you've just exposed a murderer."

Alyssa wasn't happy when I called her back to the set, hours later. Trumbull had finally wrapped for the day, sending everyone home; filming would resume tomorrow, mostly inserts and second-unit stuff, since (luckily) most of the crucial scenes were already in the can. After much debate, Rheingold had agreed not to suspend the production, because the murder case was so open-and-shut against Hal Brennan.

At least, until now.

"This better be good," said Alyssa, storming onto the stage with a swirl of her reddish-blonde locks. "I didn't leave a warm bubble bath and a juicy romance novel just to deflate one of your crackpot theories."

"Deflate away," I said. "This one's pretty bulletproof. What stumped me, see, was the motive. Everyone had an obvious reason to kill Newbury, but the real one was a little more subtle."

She sighed. "Well?"

"Greg Newbury was murdered," I announced, "because he smoked those horrible cigars."

Alyssa gaped at me, then burst out laughing. "Really, Felix, you've outdone yourself. That's so bizarre that I'm not even pissed, just curious—who's supposed to have committed this peculiar homicide?"

I gave it a beat before answering. "You did."

She gaped even wider. "*Me?* Why, because of second-hand smoke? Trust me, I've got better things to worry about."

"I know. Like checking continuity for every scene—that's what a script girl does, right?—watching the line readings, the costumes and props and pretty much everything, making sure all the shots match. You're good at it, too. It takes an obsession with details, powers of observation most people don't have."

"Thanks," she said coldly. "But where do the cigars come in?"

"Newbury smoked everywhere," I said, "even on film. Which was a problem, because the scenes were shot out of order. No matter how careful you were with every other detail, you couldn't hide the fact that *his cigar was burning down*, constantly shrinking with every puff. After the editing, when the shots are rearranged, that cigar will seem to grow and shrink like Pinocchio's nose, because none of the shots will match—and everyone will blame the script girl. You."

Her mouth opened and closed, wordlessly.

"Of course," I went on, "it didn't help that Greg meddled with every aspect of the production, insisting on so many last-minute changes that it made your job a living nightmare. You wanted him dead more than anyone, and the list of suspects goes clear around the block."

Alyssa faltered, and for a moment I thought she might confess, then and there. But she just shook her head.

"This is ridiculous," she said. "We *know* how Greg died, from a .38 caliber head wound. The gun was loaded by Hal Brennan and fired by Mel Davies. I wasn't even there."

"Sure you were," I said. "It's true Trumbull chased you off, but that was part of the plan, wasn't it? The set was cleared at your suggestion—I checked—so you could go to a hidden vantage point, get Greg in your sights and shoot him dead at the precise moment when Trumbull yelled 'Action.' That's why Carmine's playback sounded so ragged, because there were *three* shots, not two."

"You really believe all this?"

"I'll tell you what convinced me. It was a little furry friend of yours."

I walked over to Hal's trailer and slid the gate up, revealing a black Persian nestled on a throw pillow. The cat was licking its fur and paid us no attention.

"Fauntleroy!" Alyssa cried. "You found him!"

"He was hiding," I said. "Which struck me as peculiar,

because he must have heard your voice but he didn't go anywhere near you. What would make a cat avoid someone like that, after being so affectionate just minutes earlier?"

"I don't—" she began, but I cut her off.

"Here's what I think happened. When you got in position to perforate Greg's head, Fauntleroy was right there beside you. Maybe you tried to chase him off, but cats are persistent—especially when you don't want them to be. That feline was right beside the gun when it fired, and the noise scared him so badly he stayed in hiding for hours." I scratched his hindquarters. "Poor little guy."

"You can't prove any of this," said Alyssa.

"Sure I can. Five bucks says one of the guns in this trailer's been recently fired. Not Davies's gun, but the one that *really* killed Newbury—the one you stole from this trailer, then replaced, probably while you were planting that glossy photo that you seemed to find so easily.

"But there's more. They can tell if someone's recently fired a gun. It's called a nitrocellulose test, you look for fine particles in the skin, and you're probably thinking that doesn't matter because (with your attention to detail) you were careful to wear gloves during the shooting and discard them afterward. But here's something I'll bet you didn't think of." I picked up Fauntleroy, held him out for inspection, showing the scorched marking on his fur.

"They can do the same test *on this cat*."

I smiled sweetly. Alyssa didn't return it; instead she dove past me, into the trailer, and by the time I disentangled Fauntleroy, I was looking into the barrel of a .38 revolver.

"What can I say, Felix?" she said, a bit sadly. "When you're right, you're right."

And she fired at point-blank range.

I grabbed my chest and tumbled backward, cartwheeling into a lightstand. Alyssa stuck the gun in her purse and bolted for the exit, but she hadn't gone four steps before the spotlights came on and cops exploded from the scenery, on all sides.

"Cut and print," said Taylor Trumbull, appearing from nowhere, as smug as I'd ever seen him. "You okay, kid?"

"Sure thing," I said, getting to my feet again. I turned to Alyssa, now in the grasp of two big cops. "I was afraid you'd figure it out—that we'd found the real murder weapon and reloaded it with blanks. But I was hoping you'd act impulsively and do something dumb." I grinned. "Boy, was I right."

"I'll say," said Trumbull, moving a gelatin filter to reveal the still-whirling camera behind it. "An on-screen confession will be tough to beat in court."

Alyssa growled something too low for me to hear, which was probably just as well. Then Julia Rheingold hustled her offstage, headed for the prison cell they'd been reserving for Hal Brennan—who now stepped from the shadows, a free man.

"Thanks, Felix," he said, taking my hand in both of his. "If it wasn't for you, I'd be facing a murder conviction."

"Maybe not," I told him. "Ballistics would show that the gun you loaded wasn't the murder weapon—though you might have had trouble when they found the gun that was. The hard part was pinning it on Alyssa. My deductions were very neat, but it was all circumstantial; we didn't have a case until she panicked and betrayed herself."

"One thing still puzzles me," said Trumbull, stooping to scratch Fauntleroy's neck. "When she shot you, Felix, you fell backward and looked deader than Greg was. She'd already confessed by then, why continue the charade?"

I took a deep breath and thought, *Here goes*. "It was kind of an audition," I explained. "When word of all this hits the trades, *Creepy Tales* is going to be the hottest series going. You're going to have lots of parts to fill, and I want to do more than just stand around while the acting's done by someone else."

Trumbull raised an eyebrow, but he didn't say no. "It *was* a good death," he admitted. "Maybe we can find you something." And he walked away, actually seeming to consider it—which is all any actor-in-waiting expects. I'll be ready when he is.

When it comes to dying for dollars, hey, I'm your man.

The Magician's Palace

•

Edward D. Hoch

It all began on the morning Dante the cat went missing,
seeming to disappear as completely as he did during the
various magic performances in which he was a sometimes
unwilling partner. Jenny Stowe had come in to help clean
the place at 8:00 A.M., just as she did most mornings when
she wasn't working as an extra on one of the television
films shooting around town. Being part of the crew that
cleaned the Magician's Palace wasn't exactly her idea of
Hollywood glamour, but at least it brought in a needed pay-
check each week while she was waiting to break into the
movies.

Jenny had been waiting for thirteen years to be discovered, and occasionally now, in her mid-thirties, she wondered if her time was past, if she'd spend the rest of her life
cleaning places like the Magician's Palace while she
worked occasional jobs as a film extra. At first the work as
an extra had been worth a letter home, alerting the family
that she was in the opening scene of this new blockbuster
film. Sometimes she even had a line or two of dialogue in
a movie, though in the last year or so her work had mainly
been confined to crowd scenes in TV films. She'd stopped
writing home some time back.

But she wasn't thinking about that right now. She was
thinking about Dante the cat and where he might be hiding
in the vast labyrinth of rooms that made up the Magician's
Palace. Not yet as elaborate as the Magic Castle about a

15

mile away, the Palace was strictly a supper club with magic performances scheduled throughout the evening on the main stage and in two small additional rooms catering to close-up performers. Dante, a fittingly black cat of indeterminate age, usually perched on the counter by the hostess's station, greeting all comers with a benign indifference. Occasionally he performed in one of the magic acts when there was need of a black feline for a proper occult atmosphere.

Jenny had taken to feeding the cat when she came in to clean each morning, getting out the bag of cat food or unwrapping some special treats she'd brought from home. Dante always appeared within minutes of her arrival, purring softly and rubbing against her leg in the only brief show of affection he ever allowed himself. But this morning there was no purring, no rubbing, no Dante!

"Where's the cat?" Jenny asked Alf Frazier after she'd been searching for ten minutes. Alf was the manager of the Magician's Palace, an old-timer who'd made a living doing card tricks in Vegas lounges until he welshed on a gambling debt and got his fingers broken.

"How the hell should I know?" Frazier groused. "Maybe he got ate up by a dog. Serve him right."

"Alf!" She knew most of Frazier's attitude was an act, but she was in no mood for it this morning. "Come on, help me look."

"Can't, babe." Everyone under fifty was a babe to Alf. "I'm waiting for a phone call."

Jenny sighed and went off to continue her search. She'd already covered all the main floor rooms including the kitchen, where Dante was forbidden to prowl, so she headed for the basement stairs. The other members of the cleaning crew were already at work, their vacuums snoring, as she flipped on the basement light and went down among the discarded props and forgotten relics of a dozen past shows. There were concealed trap-doors in the first-floor stages, for use when needed, and she knew Dante sometimes prowled this area down below. Perhaps he dreamed of an unlucky mouse dropping through a trap some night.

"Dante! Here, Dante!" she called, alert to any movement in the shadows.

Then suddenly he came bounding toward her on his padded paws. "Dante—bad cat! Where have you been, you bad cat? You're all dirty." She ran her hand across its fur and looked at her moist, sticky fingers. It almost looked like half-dried blood on the fur, but Dante showed no sign of a wound. "Where have you been?" she asked the cat. "Show me where you've been."

Jenny was not surprised when the black cat turned and ran toward the cushioned area beneath one of the trapdoors. As she followed the cat, she flipped on another light switch for this area of the basement and saw the sprawled figure of a man. She gasped and took a step back, seeing the handle of the knife protruding from his side. She had never been a screamer and she didn't scream now. Instead, she calmly walked up the stairs and told Alf Frazier, "There's a dead man in your basement. He's wearing a silk cape, so I suppose he's one of your magicians."

The dead man went by the name of Carlo the Great, and even Alf wasn't too certain of his real name. "He was booked by the owner. I met him once in Vegas but I never knew him as anything but Carlo the Great."

That wasn't good enough for the detective sergeant in charge of the case. He was a bulky, balding man with a black mustache and tiny eyes. Sgt. Amos Paige. Jenny knew him well. Five years ago he'd threatened to arrest her for prostitution when she refused to cooperate on a narcotics sting operation. She'd never been a prostitute but she'd gone with a cable television producer once in hopes of landing a part in a film. She was disgusted with herself and never did it again. That was why she particularly disliked Sgt. Amos Paige and his insinuating glances in her direction.

"You find the body?" he asked.

"I found the body. I'm on the cleaning crew here. I was looking for Dante the cat."

"You're Jenny Stowe," he said, dredging up her name from the depths of his memory. "We had some dealings once before."

"I remember."

He said no more to her just then, turning his attention instead to Alf Frazier. "So Carlo the Great performed last night?"

Alf nodded, chewing nervously on his cigar. "He produced flowers from his wand, rabbits from his cape. Nothing unusual but the crowd liked his patter. He went on after the late dinner when the customers are feeling fat and rested."

"Did he use a knife in his act?"

Alf thought about that. "I don't— Wait a minute! Yes, he used a long sharp knife to slice through a grapefruit for one trick. Kept it concealed in his cape till he needed it."

"And the trap-door?"

"He didn't use that at all. In fact, that particular one wasn't even—"

Dante had been sitting on Jenny's lap, quietly purring during the inquisition. Now he suddenly leapt to the floor, running to greet a tall blonde woman who had just entered. "Alf, what are all the police cars doing out front?"

"There's been a killing," Sergeant Paige told her before Alf could open his mouth. "Who are you, Miss?"

"Monica Hayes. I'm one of the owners. What do you mean, there's been a killing?"

"A performer who went by the name of Carlo the Great was stabbed to death overnight. One of your cleaning people found the body." Paige was looking her over as he answered. Monica was worth the look.

"Is that true, Alf?" she asked.

"That's what they're saying. He's dead, all right. They need his real name."

"It was Carlos Costa, I believe. At least that's the name on his contract."

"Had he ever played the Magician's Palace before?" Paige asked.

"Not here. We have a place up in Santa Barbara that I booked him into a couple of times. What was it, a robbery?"

"We don't know yet. He was found in the basement, under one of the stage trap-doors."

"I always worry about those traps." She turned to her manager. "Alf, could it have been an accident?"

Frazier rubbed his fingers. "Maybe. He might have fallen through the trap after he finished his act and the audience left. He still had his knife from the grapefruit trick and when he landed, it could have gone into his side."

"How does the trap-door open?" the detective asked. They had finished their work in the basement and were bringing up the body in a black plastic bag. Jenny Stowe averted her eyes.

"There's a lever in the basement that controls it. We installed this particular trap a few years back for a magician who had an illusion in which he seemed to walk through a brick wall. A large rug was unrolled on stage and a solid brick wall was set in place over it. Members of the audience were invited to examine the wall and make sure it was solid. Then the magician drew a curtain while the audience members stood at both ends of the wall to make certain he didn't walk around it. We had someone in the basement to throw the lever and open the trap-door. The magician couldn't go through it but the rug sagged into the hole just enough to allow him to squeeze beneath the wall. When the curtain was opened, he appeared to have walked through the bricks."

"The lever is in the basement," Sergeant Paige repeated. "There's no lever on stage to activate the trap-door?"

"No."

"That would seem to rule out an accident. Even if someone in the basement accidentally pushed the lever, they would have seen Carlo fall and gone to his aid. If the trap-door was deliberately released while he was standing on it, that indicates a premeditated crime." He made a few notes. "Was he having trouble with any of your employees?"

"Not that I know of," Alf replied.

"What about that bartender of yours?" Monica Hayes asked. "When I first booked Carlo the Great, you told me there might be trouble with someone who'd known him in Vegas."

"Yeah. Brian Korol said he had a fight with him once."

"Was this Korol working last night?"

"Sure. He should be coming in pretty soon now, if you want to talk with him."

Sergeant Paige asked to use the phone and was directed to Alf's little office beside the bar. When he'd finished, he asked Jenny to join him in the office. "I remember you," he said. "Jenny Stowe. You weren't so cooperative the last time."

"You wanted me to help frame someone for a crime. I don't do that."

"Still in the movies, Jenny?"

"I get a part now and then. Extra work, mostly."

"Behaving yourself? Staying off the street?"

That only fueled her growing resentment. "Listen, Sergeant, I was never a prostitute and you know it! When I called your bluff, you dropped those charges."

"What do you know about Carlo the Great?"

"Nothing. I never met the man. We come in the morning to clean the place up. He only works at night."

Paige walked over to the wall to study a large planning calendar where Alf had written in the names of the performers in the various rooms. He had CARLOS penciled in for one of the smaller rooms, while someone named MAGICO was scheduled for the big room. "Isn't that trapdoor under the main stage?"

"I guess so, yes."

"So Carlo the Great wasn't even performing there! What in hell was he doing on the big stage?"

"Don't ask me, Sergeant. I was home watching TV."

"Yeah, I'll bet!" He walked to the office door. "Mr. Frazier, please come in here."

Alf came in, looking worried. "My bartender, Brian, is here now."

"I'll see him in a minute. Look, according to this schedule Carlo the Great was in a small room. How did he happen to be on the big stage when he fell through the trap-door?"

Alf shrugged. "Sometimes after we close, they like to practice in the main room, just to see what it's like. I was in here, going over the receipts. He might have gone anywhere without my knowing it."

"Maybe he never fell through the trap-door at all. Maybe someone stabbed him in the basement and left his body under it just to mislead us."

Jenny knew the bartender, so she strolled out to say hello. "Hi, Brian. Did you hear what happened?"

"Mrs. Hayes was just telling me." Brian Korol was a light-skinned Jamaican who'd come west to work in Las Vegas. Jenny liked him and they often chatted about show business matters after she finished her work for the day.

"Sergeant Paige wants to question you. He heard you had a fight with Carlo once in Vegas."

"That was years ago. He used to think he was a tough guy before he turned to magic."

"How'd you get along this time?"

Korol chuckled. "I don't think he even remembered me."

Paige was coming out of the office, heading their way. Jenny decided it was time to make herself scarce. "See you later," she told the bartender.

It had not been a morning for getting much work done, but it wasn't every morning she discovered a body. Since the police were finished downstairs, she decided to take another look at the basement before heading home. Dante was back purring at her feet, so she scooped the cat up and carried him with her.

The police photographers and the fingerprint people had left every light in the basement burning and, with all this illumination, it didn't seem a frightening place at all. Jenny went immediately to the spot where she'd found the body and started hunting for the lever that would release the trap-

21

door. She found it quickly enough, a knife switch just above a railing. By pulling down on it, she completed the circuit and the doors of the trap fell open, then sprang closed again.

Dante hopped up on the railing and swiped at the switch with his paw. Jenny watched him do it a second time and an idea began to form in her mind.

Ten minutes later she went back upstairs, carrying the black cat in her arms. She found Monica Hayes and told the blonde owner, "I think I know how Carlo the Great died."

Monica eyed her a bit uncertainly. "Look, Jenny," she said at last, "anything you think you know is better kept to yourself. The police don't need a lot of amateur theories and I sure don't want to hear them. You only help with the cleaning here, remember."

Jenny remembered. No one wanted to hear her theories. She stroked Dante's fur and the cat gave a low purr. As she turned to go, she saw Sergeant Paige standing with the bartender and Alf. "If you'll come down to the basement with me, I think I can show you how Carlo died," she told them.

Paige just looked at her for a moment and then gave a laugh. "This your big scene, Jenny? You going to confess, or you going to pull a killer out of the woodwork?"

"Just come down with me and you'll see."

"I'll go," Alf said, and Brian Korol tagged along too. When Paige followed along, Monica Hayes decided she needed to know what was going on.

Once she had them down there, she led the way to the cushioned area beneath the trap-door where Carlo's body had been found. "All right." She stood by the switch for the trap-door. "Now imagine that Carlo the Great is upstairs, after closing, running through his act on the big stage. He's wearing his cape, so the knife he used in his grapefruit trick is hidden in the lining. By chance he's standing on the trap-door, though he doesn't intend to use it in the trick. Meanwhile, most everyone else has gone home. Downstairs here, Dante is on the prowl for mice."

Jenny released the cat and he jumped onto the railing beneath the knife switch. Sergeant Paige took a step forward but Jenny held him back. "Just watch," she whispered.

Dante sniffed around and then boosted himself onto his hind legs. He could barely reach the switch but managed to get his front paws on it. He pulled it down and the circuit was completed. The trap-door above their heads fell open as the bolt was pulled, then sprang back to the closed position. Monica Hayes gasped.

"You see," Jenny told them, feeling like a teacher lecturing her pupils, "Carlo the Great fell through the trap when Dante pulled that switch. I was down here with him earlier and saw him do it, and realized exactly how it happened. Carlo fell on his knife and bled to death. Nobody killed him, unless it was Dante here."

Sergeant Paige was a bit reluctant to accept Jenny's solution, or to admit that anything she came up with might be important to his investigation. But after the scene in the basement, his men packed up their equipment and departed. "I'll want to talk to your employees," he told Alf Frazier, "especially those on duty last night. If I can't find anyone with a motive for killing Carlo, maybe we'll consider this cat business." He glanced distastefully in Jenny's direction. "I suppose stranger things have happened."

Jenny Stowe finished up her work and went into Alf's little office. Monica Hayes had finally departed and Korol was busy behind the bar getting ready for opening time. "It's been a busy day," she told Alf.

"That it has been," he agreed. "I hope the publicity doesn't hurt business."

"It'll probably help. The idea of having dinner at a murder scene will intrigue people."

"I hope so. Monica will blame me if business falls off."

"Alf?"

"Yeah."

"Why'd you kill him?"

"What—?" He started to protest but then his face relaxed

into a grin. "I should have known I couldn't fool you, babe. But you just showed Paige how the cat did it."

"That was an act. I'm an actress, remember. Not a very successful one, but an actress still. I put a little of Dante's catnip on that switch and he went for it, pulled it right down. I tried it earlier to make sure he'd do it, then invited Sergeant Paige down for the big show. I certainly didn't owe him anything else!"

"Catnip! I'll be damned."

"You said you never knew him by any name other than Carlo the Great, but on this schedule here you've written in *Carlos*. You knew he was Carlos Costa. You knew him in Vegas and you knew his real name. Brian Korol told me he used to think he was a tough guy before he turned to magic. Is that when you knew him, Alf?"

He was rubbing his fingers again, as he often did. "Yeah. He's the fella who broke these fingers when I had a little trouble over that bad debt. It was bad enough I couldn't do close-up magic any more, but then the bastard started doing magic himself! That was more than I could stomach. As long as he was in Vegas and I was in LA, I could put it out of my mind. But when he had the nerve to get booked into the Magician's Palace, that was too much. I acted friendly and last night after we closed, I told him he could run through his act on the big stage. I even showed him the best place to stand, right over the trap-door. I pulled the switch in the basement and, when he fell through, I was on him. I grabbed the knife from his cape and put him away." There was nothing more to be said.

Dante came through the office door at that moment carrying a dead mouse. He dropped it on the floor at Alf's feet. "See?" Jenny told him. "I always knew he was a killer."

Cat in the Act

·

Rochelle Majer Krich

Any minute now, the goose liver pâté would begin to sour.

Laney Tolbert stopped in mid-stride and leaned over the platter she'd wrapped more than an hour ago. The iridescent cellophane, clouded with beads of moisture, veiled the platter's contents. She sniffed.

No suspicious odor yet, but it was hot as hell on this August afternoon, and if she didn't get inside an air-conditioned building soon, she might as well dump the pâté (fifteen dollars a pound at Gelson's, but Laney had found it for twelve), the smoked salmon and herring salad, the soft cheeses, and the cream puffs and assorted pastries Douglas Brindell had ordered as a thank-you for Felicity, star of *When the Cat's Away*, now that the show had earned the highest ratings nine weeks in a row, surpassing *Roseanne* and *Seinfeld*.

"Mr. Brindell wants the best," the production assistant had told Laney after he'd given her an itemized list. "I'd like you to arrange the food on a platter. Waterford would be nice. You *do* have Waterford?"

"We have a large selection of all types of crystal and porcelain giftware." Little snot.

"Did I mention the jam? Felicity *loves* raspberry jam."

He'd mentioned the jam three times. And the pâté and fish salad twice. She'd begun to tire of the production assistant and his muffled, nasal whining but reminded herself

25

that making Douglas Brindell a satisfied customer might lead to other customers in "the industry." Which was, after all, why she and her best friend and partner Kate had decided to do gift baskets—to expand their business.

Laney had jotted down the rest of the production assistant's instructions, thanked him sweetly for placing the order, assured him with clenched teeth that, yes, it would be delivered at 3:30 P.M. to Felicity's trailer and, no, she wouldn't forget the raspberry jam; she wondered what Felicity, feline star of Hollywood's small screen, would do with an expensive crystal platter after she licked it clean of its last morsel of food. Her owner would probably keep it for her, along with her other trophies. (Do cats keep their trophies on a mantel?) Or her manager would. Or her agent. Or maybe each one would get ten percent of the platter.

Turning right off Pico Boulevard onto the studio property, Laney had admitted to herself that she *was* a teensy bit excited—although she'd lived in Los Angeles all of her thirty-seven years, she'd never been on a studio lot. Her ten-year-old son Ned and six-year-old daughter Kimberley had begged to come along but had settled for Laney's promise to get an autograph. Macaulay Culkin was their first choice, but they would be happy with lesser gods. Abigail, thirteen and practicing the art of being blasé, had said, "Big deal. Mom's going to see a cat." But under her breath she'd muttered, "If you see Luke Perry or Christian Slater . . . ?" and blushed when Laney smiled.

The guard at the studio gate had surpassed Abigail in being blasé and hadn't been impressed that Laney was bringing haute cuisine goodies for La Felicity. He'd run his short, stubby finger along a list in his log, thumbed through a stack of papers, then finally handed Laney the drive-on pass Douglas Brindell had arranged for her.

"Soundstage twelve," he told Laney. "The visitor lot's to the right. Don't park where it says RESERVED." He was scowling at her as if he read in her brown eyes that she planned to leave her Volvo in the slot belonging to the studio's CEO.

"I wouldn't think of it." She smiled. "Thanks so much."
Driving away, she caught his smirk in her rearview mirror.

Now, twenty-five minutes later, she knew why the smirk:
he'd undoubtedly known that she'd have a long hike from
the lot to the soundstage—had undoubtedly known, too,
that she wouldn't find it on her first try. Or her second. The
straps on her new sandals were chafing her toes. The Waterford platter was growing heavier with every step. And so
far, she hadn't seen one damn star.

At last she found it—Soundstage Twelve. There was no
one within yoo-hooing distance to open the door for her.
She anchored the platter in the crook of her left elbow and
held it against her rib cage, gripping the edge with fingers
slippery from perspiration, and prayed that the pâté *et al.*
wouldn't slide off the platter onto the ground as she opened
the door with her right hand. At this point she didn't much
care about the crystal.

The refrigerated air inside the high-ceilinged building
was wonderfully inviting, even if no one else was. She
glanced around, straining at first in the semidarkness near
the door, and discerned a multitude of people and equipment—video cameras, ceiling lights, stage rigging and
boom mikes and their operators. Many of the people were
holding walkie-talkies. The floor was a serpentine tangle of
electrical cables.

Laney stepped farther into the room. To her right were
two-tiered bleachers filled with men, women and children.
The audience. To her left were two black canvas director's
chairs, both vacant. At the center of the room toward the
front, two actors—one male, one female—were allowing
the crew to mark their positions on the stage floor with fluorescent tape in the shape of a capital T: green tape for the
woman, yellow for the man. A slight, blond-haired man in
jeans was running a tape measure from one of the cameras
to the female actor.

Also having her position blocked—with pink fluorescent
tape—was Felicity, a stately, beautiful snow-white cat.
From a distance Laney couldn't see the color of her eyes,
but she knew from having watched the show with Kimber-

ley and from having seen the cat's face reproduced on Felicity T-shirts, Felicity stuffed cats, Felicity board games, Felicity jigsaw puzzles, and Felicity lunch boxes (the matching thermos had ears and a spigot in the center of her dainty, whiskered mouth) that they were emerald green. The cat, a consummate professional, stood with imperial nonchalance, motionless except for her elegant tail. Laney admired her patience and decided Ned could never be an actor.

A tall, emaciated woman wearing earphones on top of her long, straight black hair was standing near the stage area. She was writing notes on a clipboard and looked as if she would know where to find Douglas Brindell. Laney picked her way across the cables and approached her.

"This is for Felicity," Laney told her. "I was told to leave this in her trailer." Do I say, "Miss Felicity?" she wondered. "Felicity the Cat?" Then again, Charo was Charo, Madonna was Madonna.

The woman turned and eyed Laney, then the platter. Laney thought, but wasn't sure, that she sniffed the air; she forced herself not to bend down and smell the goose liver.

"Douglas Brindell ordered this. Where can I find him?"

"I have no idea. Maybe with Felicity, in her trailer." She saw Laney glance at the cat on the stage. "That's her stand-in, Georgette. Felicity's trailer's to the right, around the back of the building. Her name's on it."

"It's three twenty-six, Gloria," announced a woman behind Laney. "Cast call is three-thirty. Why am I the only one here?"

The woman with the clipboard turned. Laney turned, too, and recognized Andrea Parsons, the tall, slender, blonde-haired human star of the show.

"I'm sure everyone will be here any minute, Andrea."

"The cat, too? *That* would be a first. Simon always has her make a grand entrance." She glanced at the platter Laney was holding. "Goodies! Can we share?"

"This is for Felicity," Gloria said. She sounded uncomfortable.

"How nice. I hope Simon leaves her at least *one* morsel."
The actress smiled at Laney and walked away.

"Is the trailer air-conditioned?" Laney asked Gloria.
"The food is perishable," she added, seeing the quizzical
look on the woman's face.

"I guess." She turned toward the stage and resumed
scribbling on the pages attached to her clipboard.

Andrea Parsons, Laney noted, had seated herself in one
of the director's chairs. While the cat's away? A tall, large-
framed man with curly light brown hair approached the actress and said something to her. Andrea smiled and shook
her head.

Georgette meowed. The brown-haired man walked to the
stage and stroked the cat's back.

Dreading leaving the cool sanctuary and facing the heat,
Laney made her way across the cables to the exit. Again,
no one was there to open the door for her. Securing the
platter against her body, she decided its cut-crystal edge
would probably leave a permanent ridge on her skin. A
souvenir of her trip to a studio lot. Hardly one she could
share with Ned or Kimberley.

Felicity's name was printed in hot pink letters on a white
plate affixed to a pink trailer. Laney was about to climb the
trailer steps when the door opened and out stepped a short,
overweight, middle-aged balding man who looked vaguely
familiar. He seemed startled to see Laney.

"Mr. Brindell?"

"Nope." The man checked his watch, bolted down the
steps as if he'd just remembered an appointment with Michael Eisner at Disney, and hurried away.

"Do you know where—" Laney called after him, but he
had disappeared around the back of the trailer. She walked
up the steps and knocked. When no one answered, she
opened the door and poked her head inside.

"Hello?" She stepped inside the trailer. Felicity stared at
her from a multitude of posters on the walls. Laney set the
platter on a Formica table and opened the small refrigerator.
It was crammed with food, and she wasn't about to empty
it to make room for the platter. Let Douglas Brindell or his

p.a. do that. She found the thermostat, set it to sixty-five degrees, then left the trailer, pulling the door shut behind her.

Back at the soundstage, she found Gloria the clipboard woman. Actors and cat were still in their positions.

"Felicity wasn't in her trailer, but I left the platter there," Laney said.

"*That's* Felicity, with her manager." The woman pointed to the director's chair where Andrea Parsons had been sitting five minutes ago. "She arrived just after you left."

Laney glanced at the cat on the stage, then at the celebrated feline lying on the lap of a rotund bearded man wearing a bow tie. The likeness between Felicity and her stand-in was remarkable. Sitting in the other chair was a pony-tailed man with impossibly long legs that ended in boots. The director?

Laney turned back to Gloria. "I'll need a check."

The woman frowned. "I can't authorize a check."

"Could you locate Mr. Brindell? I'd like to get going."

"We're really busy right now." Her tone was aggrieved. Laney smiled pleasantly.

Gloria sighed and pushed a curtain of black hair behind a multi-studded ear. "I'll be right back." She walked across the room and exited through a doorway.

While Laney waited, she glanced around the room. There were signs of restlessness among the children in the audience. The director was standing, talking with Andrea. Felicity was occupying his chair; her manager was still in the other one. So this is Hollywood, Laney thought, and looked at the stage. The stand-ins looked as bored as she felt.

It was ten minutes before Gloria returned. "Mr. Brindell is in conference," she told Laney. "He knows nothing about a platter for Felicity."

"His production assistant ordered it. Robert Farrady."

The woman frowned again. "Who?"

Laney repeated the name slowly.

A third frown. "I don't know anyone by that name."

Laney wanted to tell her that frequent frowning would

30

create premature wrinkles in her twenty-something-year-old face. "He's Mr. Brindell's assistant."

The woman shook her head. "There is no Robert Farrady."

"Places!" another person echoed.

Felicity leaped off her manager's lap, arched her beautiful back, and padded regally toward the stage area. Her manager followed. The man and woman stand-ins strolled off the stage.

Andrea took her position near the cat. Felicity hissed. The actress frowned and turned her back on her costar. Georgette stared uncertainly at Felicity. Felicity bared her teeth. Georgette quivered, then skipped off the stage area and into the arms of the large-framed, brown-haired manager/owner. Man and cat left the building.

The short, overweight man Laney had seen coming out of Felicity's trailer waddled past the two women, wiping his mouth with the back of his hand on his way to the stage. She recognized him now as Eric Morgan, Andrea Parson's klutzy landlord on the show. Kimberley, and sometimes Ned, enjoyed his pratfalls.

"Sorry I'm late, everyone," he said. "Last minute visit to the john. Hey, Andrea. How's it going? Hey, Felicity."

"Now that Eric's finally here, can we get started, please, Jason?" Felicity's manager called to the red-haired director.

"In a minute," Jason replied calmly, peering through the lens of a camera.

From her purse, Laney withdrew an itemized bill and extended it to the clipboard woman. "Robert Farrady, Mr. Douglas Brindell's production assistant, ordered goose liver pâté, smoked salmon and herring salad, cream puffs, assorted pastries, cheeses. And raspberry jam." She smiled thinly. "He also specified an *expensive* crystal serving dish. The total, including tax and delivery, is $376.42."

"Felicity doesn't like raspberry jam." The woman ignored the offered bill. "Obviously, there's been some mistake. There *is* no Robert Farrady. Mr. Brindell won't authorize payment."

"I won't have Felicity standing here indefinitely!" the

manager warned in a rising falsetto. "Jason, we've talked about this before."

"Yes, we have, Simon," came the nonplussed reply.

"Well, what good is talk when—"

"Oh, for God's sake!" Andrea Parsons snapped. "She's a goddamn cat, not a queen."

"She's the *star* of this show!" he squeaked. "She's the reason *you're* not collecting unemployment."

"I was fine before you and Miss Kitty Litter arrived, Simon. I'll survive without her, don't you worry."

"Oh, really? I'm not sure Douglas would agree with you. You're not irreplaceable, Andrea."

"Let's calm down, okay?" Eric said, chewing on a granola bar. "Okay, Simon? Andrea?"

"*No* one is irreplaceable, darling. Felicity was a sweet thing, but you're turning her into a monster. And you're not doing her any favors by behaving like a certain difficult stage father we all know. *His* son, by the way, just lost out on a plum role because—"

"I am *not* difficult! I'm protecting Felicity's rights."

"Meow, meow."

Too bad the microphones weren't picking this up for the audience, Laney thought. She faced Gloria again. "I'd like to speak to Mr. Brindell myself."

"I'm sorry, but this isn't our problem. We didn't place the order. You'll have to take the platter back."

"I can restock the crystal, but the food is a loss. I'll be out more than a hundred dollars." And she had no autographs.

"Look, I wish I could—"

"You're deliberately blocking Felicity!" the manager screeched. "You moved out of your T. Gloria, I want you to come here and see what Andrea is doing!"

"Picture is next!" someone yelled.

"Picture's up!"

Gloria shrugged at Laney and walked toward the stage. Laney started to follow her, then turned and marched toward the exit, stubbing her exposed toe on the cables and tripping. So much for a dignified exit, she thought, but no one had noticed.

The trailer was frigid. Bending down to lift the platter, Laney noticed that the cellophane had been unwrapped, several cream puffs had disappeared, and someone had dug trenches into what had been a perfectly rounded mount of pâté.

Cursing Robert Farrady, whoever he was, and the person who had pillaged the platter, Laney grabbed the Waterford and returned to the soundstage. She maneuvered the door open again, slammed it shut as forcefully as she could with her free hand, and worked her way back to the stage area and Gloria.

"Listen," Laney said, her voice fueled with anger.

The woman whirled and, holding an admonishing finger to her mouth, glared at Laney.

"Roll camera!"

"Rolling, rolling!"

"Rolling!"

"Quiet, please!"

"Aaaand *action!*" announced the director.

Eric Morgan knocked on the door to the set.

Andrea scooped up the cat. "Well, I wonder who that can be." She crossed to the door and opened it. "Oh, hello, Mr. Kirkmeister," she cooed. "Felicity, look who's come to see us."

A throaty purr was amplified through the booms.

Instant best friends, Laney thought, wondering who was the better actor—Andrea or Felicity. The platter was heavy; Laney's feet ached. She wished she could sit until the damn shoot was over, but aside from the director's chairs, both still occupied, she didn't see any other seats. She put the platter on the floor, and for what seemed like an eternity, half listened to inane chitchat about the "landlord's" surprise party for his wife.

". . . have some bicarbonate?" Eric Morgan/Mr. Kirkmeister finally asked. "My stomach's killing me." He burped loudly.

Andrea and Felicity looked at each other, their eyebrows raised.

The audience laughed.

Felicity scampered offstage. A moment later she returned to the landlord, a familiar yellow box secured in her mouth. The audience applauded. Laney felt like groaning.

"Thanks, my dear." Eric Morgan bent down, removed the baking soda box from the cat's mouth, and patted her head. As he was straightening up, he staggered, then caught his balance by grabbing onto the arm of a sofa.

A child in the audience squealed with delight.

"See you at the party," he said. "Remember, mum's the word."

"Don't worry, Mr. Kirkmeister, Felicity and I know how to keep a secret. While the cat's away, right, sweet'ums?"

An assenting purr from Felicity.

Morgan turned to leave. He staggered again and crashed into the couch. Andrea and Felicity exchanged glances.

More laughter from the audience.

Morgan rose, then clutched his stomach and sank to his knees. A second later his head dropped onto the floor.

The cat froze. The hairs on her body rose stiffly.

For a sitcom, Laney thought, this wasn't very funny.

"Cut!"

"That's a cut!"

Morgan was convulsing.

Andrea screamed.

Felicity hissed and bared her teeth.

"Oh, my God," Laney moaned. "The liver!"

She finally met Douglas Brindell. He arrived just after the paramedics had strapped Eric Morgan onto a stretcher and carried him out of the soundstage.

"Will he be okay?" Brindell's face was almost as ashen as the unconscious actor's. His eyes were on the stretcher being slid into the paramedics' white van.

"Hard to say," the paramedic said. "Blood pressure's extremely low, and his skin is cold and clammy. Could be cardiac involvement. We don't know what it is yet."

It's the liver, Laney mouthed. She felt sick. Why had she bought the less expensive pâté? Why hadn't she refrigerated it? And why had Eric Morgan sneaked inside Felicity's trailer and stuffed his mouth with other people's food?

She hesitated, then stepped forward and cleared her throat. "Excuse me," she said to the paramedic. She explained quickly about the food platter and the fact that Eric Morgan had probably sampled its contents. "He was clutching his stomach," she added.

Douglas Brindell was staring at her. "Who would order a platter in my name?"

"Where's this platter?" the paramedic asked Laney. "They may want to run some tests for botulism."

"In the soundstage."

"We're just about ready to leave. If you can get it stat, fine. If not, bring it to Cedars-Sinai, the emergency room."

"I'll get it," Brindell offered. To Laney, he said, "Where did you leave it?"

"I was standing near Gloria, but I can't describe exactly where. I'll find it."

She raced toward the building. Inside, she made her way across the cables to where she'd been standing when Eric Morgan had collapsed. Someone was there now, crouching. At Laney's approach, the person stood. Georgette's manager. Minutes before, Laney had noticed him near the paramedic van, along with the other cast and crew. He was holding the platter.

"That's mine," Laney told him. "The paramedics need it."

He handed it to her. "I was wondering who left it here. Did they take Eric away, yet?"

"They're leaving right now."

Laney hurried back to the paramedic and gave him the platter. She stood with Douglas Brindell and Gloria and the others and watched the van drive away, its siren blaring.

"Poor Eric!" Andrea Parsons sighed.

"Think he'll be all right?" Gloria asked quietly.

"God, I hope so!" Brindell exclaimed. He ran his hands through his thick, graying black hair. "What on earth was he doing in Felicity's trailer?"

"You realize it's only sheer luck that Felicity didn't eat that tainted food." Simon frowned accusingly at Laney, then hugged the cat, which was nesting in his arms. "Someone's watching out for us, sweetheart." He smoothed her white fur.

Felicity's purr was appropriately subdued.

"You don't know Robert Farrady, Mr. Brindell?" Laney asked.

He shook his head.

Now was not the time to press the issue of who was responsible for the food. In fact, she might as well kiss the $376.42 goodbye. Her partner Kate would not be pleased. Neither would her husband Brian.

"I guess I'll be going, then," she said.

"I'm sorry about all this," Brindell said. "At least you can get the Waterford back. So it won't be a total loss."

Laney was dusting ceramic figurines when two men entered the shop two days later and identified themselves as LAPD detectives.

"Mrs. Tolbert, we got your name from the studio," said the older of the two. "We're here about the food you delivered."

She blanched. "Eric Morgan isn't—?"

"He's going to be okay."

Relief coursed through her. But she was still responsible. "It was botulism, wasn't it?"

"Arsenic."

"Arsenic!" She gaped at the two men. "*Arsenic* in the *liver*?"

"In the raspberry jam," said the younger detective. "Luckily not enough to kill a person. We'll need to know where you bought everything."

She nodded and thought, *Arsenic!*, then took out her notebook and dictated the information they needed.

"Who placed the order?" asked the older detective.

"Good question." Laney repeated everything from the time "Robert Farrady" had phoned until Eric Morgan had collapsed.

"When and how long was the platter out of your sight?"

She considered, then said, "I took it to the cat's trailer at three-thirty. I came back to the soundstage and stayed there for at least ten minutes. Then I returned to the trailer and picked up the platter. Someone had eaten from it."

"Did you see any suspicious behavior?"

She'd witnessed bickering and friction but nothing she could label suspicious. She shook her head. "Sorry."

He handed her a card. "Call if you remember anything."

"What about my Waterford platter? Does the hospital still have it?"

He shook his head. "Evidence."

After the police left, in between dusting figurines and helping customers, Laney wondered about "Robert Farrady." He'd spoken with a nasal, whiny voice. A *muffled* nasal, whiny voice, she remembered. Had the voice been disguised?

The arsenic was obviously for Felicity.

Who wanted her gone?

Someone who hated celebrity animals? People hated Barney the Dinosaur. There was an I HATE BARNEY newsletter. Maybe there was an I HATE FELICITY club.

Or maybe the competition wanted to bump off the famous feline and knock the show out of its number one spot. Hollywood was a rough town, Laney knew. She'd seen *The Player*.

Andrea Parsons probably wouldn't cry if Felicity were gone. Laney had witnessed hostility between the actress and the cat. Maybe Andrea was jealous of her costar's popularity. And Simon had implied he could have Andrea taken off the show. Andrea was an actress; she could easily have disguised her voice.

But Andrea, Laney recalled, had been in the soundstage the entire time Laney had been there. She couldn't have laced the raspberry jam.

Laney put down a figurine and picked up another. Georgette's owner could have done it, she thought. Georgette was a perfect stand-in for Felicity, and almost identical double. Her owner had had opportunity to add the arsenic to the jam. And he'd been holding the platter when Laney returned to the sound stage after Eric Morgan's collapse—had he been planning on disposing of the evidence now that a person had been poisoned instead of a cat?

Felicity probably earned a terrific salary for Simon. That could pay for a hell of a lot of raspberry jam.

And a few Waterford platters and a set of stemware, too. Which reminded her—she'd have to call the detectives and find out when she could get her Waterford back.

Something niggled at her memory. She frowned, trying to concentrate.

How did—?

She put down her dust cloth and thought for a few minutes, reconstructing what she'd heard, then nodded.

"Thanks for seeing me, Mr. Brindell."

"You said it was urgent. How can I help you?"

Laney opened her purse, took out the bill, and handed it to the producer. "I'd like a check right now, please."

Brindell frowned. "I'd hardly call this 'urgent.' And I have no intention of paying this. I never authorized the order."

"Yes, you did." Laney smiled and leaned back in her chair. "In fact you ordered it yourself. *You* were Robert Farrady."

"Really? And why would I do that?" His smile was icy.

"To deflect suspicion from yourself." She crossed her legs. "How'd you know the platter was Waterford?"

"What?" He stared at her and blinked rapidly.

"Just before I left the studio lot that day, you told me I could get the Waterford back from the paramedics."

"I just assumed . . . This is ridiculous! I'm going to have to ask you to leave. Clearly, this episode has unhinged you."

"You mentioned the raspberry jam three times. You said Felicity loves raspberry jam, but Gloria told me she doesn't."

"I'll call security if I have to, Mrs. Tolbert."

"*Simon*, on the other hand, loves raspberry jam. I phoned Gloria. She verified that fact. And Andrea implied Simon would devour everything on the platter." She paused. "You wanted to poison Simon, not Felicity. That's why you were shocked when you found out Eric was poisoned instead. You're lucky he didn't die."

Douglas Brindell was silent for a moment. Finally, he sighed. "You know, I'm relieved this is over. I was sick about what happened to Eric. Sick."

"Arsenic can kill people."

"I didn't use enough to kill anyone. I just wanted Simon off the set for a few days. And I wanted to scare him, too. I admit it." He leaned forward, his hands clasped. "Do you have any idea the misery that man creates just by being around? The demands? The delays? The cost overruns?"

He sank back against his seat. "I don't even care about the show anymore. It's number one, but every day is hell around here because of him. I hate him! *Everybody* hates him!" He paused, then said, "Did you tell the police?"

In the movies, this is where the about-to-be-killed heroine lies and tells the bad guy she left a tell-all letter for the cops. In the movies, the bad guy never believes her anyway. "Not yet. It'll look better if you go to them. But if you don't—right now—I will."

He nodded.

She picked up the phone receiver on his desk and dialed the number the detective had given her. When someone answered, she asked for Detective Hernandez and handed Brindell the receiver.

He hesitated, then grasped it firmly. "Detective Hernandez? Douglas Brindell. There's something I have to tell you ..."

The producer was pale when he hung up a few minutes later. "I'm meeting him at the station in an hour," he told Laney. "He didn't make any promises. I'd better call my lawyer."

"Good luck."

"Thanks." He studied her. "Weren't you afraid to come

here? How'd you know I wouldn't kill you to stop you from talking?"

"According to my husband, I have nine lives. And your secretary's in the next room. I'm a good screamer." She smiled. "I didn't think you'd planned to kill anyone." She paused, then said, "There *is* one more thing, Mr. Brindell."

His shoulders tensed.

"About the $376.42 ... ?"

The Ten Lives
of Talbert

•

Barbara Collins

At 8:00 A.M. on Rodeo Drive, the immaculate street was
devoid of its native Jaguars, Rolls-Royces and Ferraris. The
only vehicles, prowling or parked, were of the dreary domestic variety—Ford, Chevrolet, Dodge—but for the occasional Japanese, which were only a marginal step up.

The sidewalks, too, were deserted, except for a few
shoppers hovering near the fashionable storefronts, waiting
for the doors to open.

Tourists.

Charles watched them from inside the locked glass door
of his exclusive boutique, Chez Charles. He could tell they
were tourists, no matter how well they dressed, because the
real people of Beverly Hills simply never came out until
the sun burned the haze out of the air.

He hated them. The *touristes*. Clopping into his shop in
their *vulgaire* shoes and *prêt-à-porter* clothing, carrying
bourgeois bags, smelling of cheap *eau de toilette* . . . Why,
they couldn't even afford a simple bauble, let alone a cre-
ation from his chic spring *haute couture*!

So when the *racaille*—the riff-raff—came in, he would
raise his eyebrows in surprise and look down his nose at
them disdainfully and say, *"Oui?"*, drawing the word out as
if it were three. That was enough to make most flee.

But every once in a while some stupid woman would
pretend she was actually interested in purchasing a ten
thousand dollar, hand-beaded gown. When that happened,

41

Charles would gaze at her appraisingly, then state condescendingly that his creations did not come in *grande* sizes.

Charles made a disgusted sound with his lips as he stood waiting by the front glass door; just the thought of some ... *paysan* ... trying on one of his magnificent gowns made his skin crawl. His designs were only for the rich and famous!

A sleek white limousine pulled up.

Instantly excited, Charles unlocked the door with a trembling hand and stepped out into the pleasant spring morning.

Even now, he couldn't believe his luck! When the call had come in a month ago, he thought it a hoax: a woman claiming to be the great Simone Vedette, enduring icon of the silver screen of the thirties. He nearly slammed the phone receiver down. Because, except for some fleeting tabloid snapshots taken of the actress on a beach somewhere, and a trashy unauthorized biography written by the woman's adopted daughter, the reclusive star had avoided contact with the public for over forty years!

But as Charles listened to the woman's low, sensual voice, laced with aristocratic breeding, the more he believed the call was authentic.

She told him she was being honored at the Academy Awards, and had, after much coaxing, agreed to personally accept the Oscar for Lifetime Achievement. She needed a gown—a beautiful dress—like the ones she had recently spotted in his store window. Could she see him some morning before hours?

And now, the aged immortal star—really the only legend left alive since the deaths of Dietrich and Garbo—was about to exit the limo, its windows darkened for privacy, to purchase a gown from him! From Chez Charles! Elusive fame would at last be his. Once he leaked the news to the tabloids, that is.

The chauffeur, a middle-aged man with graying temples, smartly dressed in uniform and cap, opened the car's back door.

Charles wiped his sweating palms on the sides of his tailored trousers. Moved closer to the curb.

But instead of the living legend, out of the back of the limo climbed a plain-faced woman of Mexican descent who could have been thirty, or forty or fifty years old, wearing a cotton print housedress, horned-rimmed glasses and oversized headscarf.

This was not Simone Vedette!

Perhaps under different circumstances, Charles would have laughed at the ludicrousness of such a common woman getting out of a limousine; but instead, he stood frozen in disappointment and confusion.

But then the pleasant woman turned and bent slightly and extended a hand into the car.

A long, slender gold-braceleted arm appeared, taking that hand, then a shapely black-nyloned leg extended outward toward the curb, as the great Simone Vedette was helped from the limo.

Charles sighed with relief, then grinned with pleasure. The grande dame of the cinema was still quite beautiful!

She was small, perhaps five foot three, not the five foot seven or eight he had imagined. She wore a simple black dress (too short) and a large, wide-brimmed black hat (too big). A gold necklace (too heavy) graced her surprisingly firm and unwrinkled neck. In one hand she carried a red quilted Chanel bag (too overpowering); the other arm held a white cat (too furry).

Charles moved closer to the great movie star, catching the scent of her perfume (too floral), and bowed as if to royalty. *"Bonjour, madame,"* he gushed.

"Good morning," she responded in a voice that was low and warm. But her face was cold, chiseled: thin, arched eyebrows, large deepset eyes, high hollow cheekbones, long straight nose, narrow bowed lips. She did, however, look like a woman in her fifties, instead of someone in her eighties. Her plastic surgeon must be *fantastique*!

"This is my housekeeper, Lucinda Lopez," the actress said, introducing the peasant woman who stood quietly nearby. "And my cat Talbert." She scratched the animal's

43

neck, and it undulated in her arms. "Both go everywhere with me."

Charles gave the housekeeper a cursory look, then smiled at the cat as genuinely as he could, for a man who abhorred such creatures.

"Entrer?" he said with a flourish of a gesture.

Charles opened the glass door, and Simone Vedette went in, the housekeeper in tow. He followed, shutting and locking the door behind them.

"Elle est là-bas," he instructed, as the two women hesitated just inside; he pointed toward the back of the shop.

The movie star and the Mexican woman headed that way, through the outer room which was just for the general public.

Charles had spent hours arranging this outer room, knowing Simone would pass through it, displaying his creations just so . . . but the actress took no notice as she made her way along.

The housekeeper, however, ooohed and aaahed at this and that, which only caused him great irritation.

They went through a thick red-velvet curtain, tied back to one side.

"Asseyez-vous à la chaise, s'il vous plaît," Charles smiled.

Simone Vedette looked at him blankly. "I don't speak French, young man," she said. "And I wish you'd stop."

Charles blinked. "But, I thought . . . I mean, your name . . ."

"I was born in Brooklyn," she said simply.

Charles stood dumbfounded, then recovered and gestured grandly to a gilded satin-covered French Empire chair. "Won't you please sit down," he said.

The great star sat, the cat curled on her lap.

He didn't bother to offer the housekeeper a chair; she found herself a place next to a rack of clothes.

Charles stood before the actress, bending slightly toward her, pressing his hands together, prayerlike.

"I have designed for you the most incredibly exquisite gown!" he exclaimed, then paused for effect. "And after

44

you wear it at the Academy Awards, the media will dispense with their traditional fashion dissection—what did Cher wear? Who designed Geena Davis's gown? Who cares? *No one*, not once you have been seen wearing ..."

"Yes, yes," the actress interrupted impatiently, but her curiosity was clearly piqued. "Please, bring it out!"

The white, fluffy cat on her lap looked up at him with bored blue eyes.

Eagerly Charles disappeared behind a large dressing screen, where the gown was hidden, displayed on a platformed mannequin. He gazed at the dress, his eyes gleaming like the six thousand sequins and pearls he had sewed by hand onto the sheer beige silk soufflé.

The gown was worth twenty thousand; he would charge her forty.

Carefully, tenderly, Charles covered up the mannequin with a large gold lamé cloth. Then he rolled the platform out from behind the screen, positioning the statue in front of the actress.

With a smile, he slowly pulled on one end of the gold material, teasingly, exposing the bottom of the drop-dead gorgeous gown, and then, with a *snap*, yanked it completely off.

Simone Vedette gasped.

Charles beamed, looking at the dress. It truly was his finest work. A masterpiece that would soon make his name synonymous with the likes of Dior, Valentino and Gaultier!

His eyes went back to the actress, who was still gasping, leaning forward, but now clutching her chest. The cat on her lap rose to its feet, struggling to keep from falling.

"Madame!" Charles cried out, alarmed. Something was wrong with the woman!

From behind him, the housekeeper shrieked, further terrifying the cat, which leapt from his mistress' lap onto the mannequin, claws bared, clinging, ripping as it slid down the delicate material, sequins and pearls popping and dropping onto the floor, where the last of the legends now lay— but no longer living.

Charles stared in shock and disbelief at the dead woman

at his feet. Had he been foiled by his own brilliance? Had he finally done it?

Created a dress to die for?

Brenda Vedette sat in a leather chair in a posh office on Wilshire Boulevard in Beverly Hills.

The woman, in her mid-thirties, attractive, with straight, shoulder-length blonde hair, was dressed in a dark gray suit, an inexpensive copy of a Paris original. Across from her, behind a massive mahogany desk, was Mitchell Levin, a slender, bespectacled man in his sixties, who was her late mother's lawyer.

Brenda pulled a pack of cigarettes from her purse. "Mind if I smoke?" she asked.

By way of an answer, the lawyer pushed a glass ashtray toward her on the desk.

She lit the cigarette, took a puff, and blew the smoke out the side of her mouth. Then she asked, "So, am I cut out of the will, or what?"

Mitchell Levin looked down at the document before him. "No," he said cautiously, "you aren't. However, there are a few provisions . . ."

Brenda laughed hoarsely. "Like what? I find a job, get married, quit smoking?"

The corners of the laywer's mouth turned up slightly, but more from disgust, Brenda thought, than amusement.

"These provisions," he explained, "have to do with your mother's cat, Talbert, and housekeeper, Lucinda Lopez."

A sickening feeling spread slowly through Brenda's body. *That crazy old broad hadn't left the bulk of everything to them, had she?*

Brenda took another puff of the cigarette and said as blandly as she could, "Go on."

Mitchell studied the papers in his hands. "It was your mother's wish that Talbert remain at her home in Malibu in the comfort he has been used to, and under the care of Lucinda, until his death, at which time the estate will go to you."

Brenda sat numbly and said nothing.

Mitchell said, "Now, you can *try* to contest the will, but I'm warning you ..."

"Mr. Levin!" Brenda snapped, working indignation into those two words, and the ones that followed. "I have no intention of going against my mother's wishes!"

Most likely prepared for a fight, the lawyer looked a little stunned.

Brenda leaned forward and forcefully stubbed out her cigarette in the ashtray. "My mother and I may not have seen eye to eye, but she certainly has the right to do whatever she wants with her money."

Brenda sat back in her chair, lowered her voice. "And she was correct in being concerned about Talbert ... I wouldn't have wanted him. And I'd have sold the house. It holds nothing but painful memories for me." Her voice cracked at the end.

There was an awkward silence. Tears sprang to her eyes.

"Do you think it was *easy* being raised in the shadow of the great Simone Vedette?" Brenda blurted. "She *never* should have adopted me ... she just didn't have the right temperament! And she was *too old*."

Brenda looked down at her hands in her lap and shook her head slowly. "My mother expected so much from me, yet gave so little in return. I guess that was why I wrote the book ... Any attention I could get from her, no matter how negative, was better than nothing."

"It hurt her deeply," the lawyer said.

"Well, *she* hurt *me!*"

Brenda sobbed into her hands.

Mitchell Levin reached into his coat pocket and pulled out a handkerchief. "Here," he said softly, giving it to her. "Use this."

Brenda dabbed at her eyes with the cloth. Composed herself. Looked at the lawyer. "I just want you to know, I did love my mother, and I'm sorry that book was ever published. And I'll certainly comply with any of her last wishes."

Mitchell gave Brenda a little smile; it seemed genuine.

"Your mother would have been proud to hear you say that," he told her.

Brenda nodded. Then, as an afterthought, she asked, "Oh . . . my monthly stipend . . . will it continue?"

"The same as usual."

The young woman stood. "Then if there's nothing else . . ."

Mitchell rose from behind his desk. "Goodbye, Brenda," he said, extending one hand. "I'll be in touch. Take care of yourself."

"Thank you," she returned warmly, and shook his hand.

Out on the street, Brenda got into her five-year-old Ford Escort convertible, which was parked at the curb. She plucked any old cassette from the many tapes scattered on the seat next to her, and inserted it into the dash. Then with dated disco music throbbing, pulled out into the traffic.

She looked at herself in the visor mirror.

Her mother wasn't the *only* Vedette who could give an Academy Award performance . . .

So she wouldn't get her inheritance until the cat was dead? Fine. How long could a cat live, anyway?

After all, accidents did happen.

A dark-haired woman in sunglasses, T-shirt, backpack and jeans walked her dog along the beach in Malibu, where expensive oceanfront homes crowded so close together they almost touched, with barely enough room between them for the fences that separated these patches of precious, puny real estate.

It was early afternoon, and anyone who might notice the young lady would not give her a second thought—even though the dog on the leash was a vicious pit bull—because the woman was carrying two socially and ecologically correct items: a pooper-scooper and a sack.

The dog seemed well behaved, stopping occasionally to sniff at this and that. The man the woman had bought the pit bull from had said the animal liked people . . . it was just *cats* the dogs hated.

Bewigged Brenda let the dog lead her down a narrow passageway between the tall wooden fences of two homes.

She stopped by the fence belonging to the house on the right. Quietly she pulled back a board she had loosened late the night before.

She peeked through.

Talbert—that fat, lazy puss—was having his usual afternoon nap on the patio. He lay on his side, in the shade of a tall potted plant, legs stretched out, dead to the world—as he soon would be. The housekeeper was nowhere in sight.

Brenda unleashed the pit bull and gently pushed its head toward the opening in the fence.

The dog resisted at first, but then suddenly it caught sight of the sleeping cat, and with powerful legs propelled itself through the opening, splintering the wood, leaving an outline of its massive body on the remaining boards, moving like a freight train into the yard.

Brenda wanted to watch, but didn't dare. She stayed only long enough, hidden behind the wooden fence, to hear the snarls of the dog, and yowls of the cat, and then screams of the housekeeper, who must have come running out of the house . . .

Brenda hurried along the passageway between the fences, putting on a red nylon jacket. The pooper-scooper and leash, along with the black wig, she stowed in the backpack.

Quickly she moved down the beach—just a pretty, blonde power-walker out for some exercise. Half a mile away, off Pacific Coast Highway, was her parked convertible.

Throwing the backpack in the back seat, she got in and started the car. She grabbed a tape from off the passenger seat and stuck it in the player.

Think I'll go over to Cartier and get that diamond tennis bracelet I've always wanted, she mused to herself.

"After all," she said aloud, smiled, driving off, the music of the Bee Gees blaring, "I can afford it now."

* * *

Later that night, under a sky bedecked with a million dazzling stars (though not as dazzling as the diamonds on her wrist), Brenda pulled the convertible into the driveway of her late mother's house.

She got out and pressed a buzzer on the gate of the wooden fence.

After a moment an intercom speaker crackled and Lucinda's voice said, "Yes? Who is it?"

The housekeeper sounded weary.

"It's Brenda. I've come to get a book."

There was a long pause. Then, "Okay. I let you in."

Brenda waited for the buzzer and pushed open the gate.

She walked slowly by the patio, which was awash in outside lighting. Everything appeared normal. No disturbed deck furniture or overturned potted plants. Even the fence had been repaired. It was as if nothing had ever happened.

But as Brenda approached the back door of the beach house, she noticed a dark stain on the patio cement.

Blood, perhaps?

She repressed a smile as the housekeeper opened the door for her.

"Hello, Lucinda," Brenda said, as she entered the house. She was standing in a comfortable, tastefully decorated TV room. It was where her mother had spent most of her time.

"I need to find a book a friend loaned me," Brenda explained. "She wants it back, and I think I gave it to my mother."

The housekeeper stared at her with large, liquid eyes behind her old-fashioned glasses.

"Is something wrong?" Brenda asked, feigning concern. "You don't look well."

"This . . . this afternoon," the woman began haltingly, "a terrible thing happened."

"What?"

"A big dog got through the fence and attacked little Talbert!"

"No!" Brenda said, aghast. "How awful!"

"I called the police, and they had to *shoot* the dog."

"How horrible!" Brenda shook her head slowly, then

50

looked down at the floor. "That poor, poor cat . . . What a cruel way for it to die."

"Oh, Talbert's not dead," the housekeeper said.

"Not dead?"

Lucinda pointed to the other side of the room, where Brenda now saw the cat, sleeping on a pet-bed on the floor next to a chair. Several of his paws were bandaged.

"He got away from that bad dog," Lucinda explained, "and climbed the . . . what do you call it? On the side of the house?"

"Challis," Brenda said flatly.

"*Si.* The challis. We're lucky it was there."

"Yes," Brenda replied slowly. "Lucky."

The room fell silent.

"You don't have to worry about Talbert, Miss Brenda," Lucinda said firmly. "From now on, I'm not letting him out of my sight."

Brenda smiled weakly.

The housekeeper smiled back. "Now, what was the name of that book you wanted?"

It was hot in the tiny, dingy apartment on Alameda Street, but the air conditioner in the window wasn't plugged in.

Brenda stood by the dirt-streaked window looking down on the filthy street below. She had rented the third floor room, directly over the building's entrance, three weeks ago, under an assumed name.

She stepped back a little from the window as a limousine pulled up at the curb.

The chauffeur got out and went around to the side of the car, where he helped Lucinda out of the back seat. She was wearing her usual cotton housedress and headscarf and was carrying a sack of groceries, which she brought every Saturday morning to her elderly mother, who lived below, on the first floor. Looped around one arm was a green leash, and at the end of the leash, was Talbert.

The housekeeper made her way leisurely up the sidewalk of the apartment building.

She climbed the short flight of steps, bag in both arms, the leashed Talbert trailing behind.

Brenda, her head pressed against the dirty window pane, watched until the moment Lucinda disappeared from view into the building, Talbert bringing up the rear; then Brenda opened the window further and shoved the massive air conditioner out.

It crashed on the steps below, making a terrible, metallic racket, the leash winding out from under it like a green tail.

Brenda shut the window, gently.

In the late afternoon, as the sun descended on Malibu, shimmering on the ocean like tinsel on a tree, Brenda wheeled her convertible into the driveway of her mother's house.

She got out, carrying a small basket, and rang the buzzer.

She had a present for Talbert, Brenda told the house-keeper, and could she come in?

Inside the TV room, Brenda's eyes darted to the little cat bed on the floor by the chair, but it was empty.

"The pet store around the corner from me is going out of business," Brenda said to Lucinda, "and everything was half-price." She paused and held up the basket in her hand. "I thought Talbert might like these treats and catnip and stuff."

Lucinda looked at her sadly.

Brenda let her mouth fall open. "Don't tell me something *else* has happened to Talbert!" she said incredulously.

The housekeeper nodded.

"What?"

"An air conditioner fell down on him."

"An *air conditioner*?"

Lucinda told her what had happened.

"That is so incredible!" Brenda said, then added sadly, "I'm going to miss that sweet little animal . . ."

"Oh, he's all right," the housekeeper said.

"All right?"

"Because the air conditioner fell on the steps," Lucinda

explained, "there was a little space for him. It did hurt his tail, though."

Perhaps hearing his name, the white Persian entered the room from the kitchen. His front paws were still bandaged, and now so was his tail.

Brenda glared at the cat.

Lucinda bent down, gently picked up the animal, and kissed his diffident face.

"It must be true what they say," the housekeeper said, speaking more to the animal than Brenda. "A cat does have nine lives."

In her convertible, Brenda ejected the cassette out of the player, snatched another off the passenger seat, and shoved it inside.

"That mangy beast doesn't have nine lives," she fumed, "he has *ten!*"

She tore out of the driveway, tires squealing, music cranked.

Maybe she needed something so lethal it would snuff out every last life fat Talbert had left. It was time to stop playing Wile E. Coyote to his Road Runner.

Time for something a little more high tech . . .

Brenda bought a modem and hooked it up to her home computer. Then she joined Internet and, going through an anonymous server known as a double-blind to protect her identity, posted this message: LOOKING FOR WAY TO KILL NEIGHBOR'S EVIL, ANNOYING CAT. WILL PAY $1,000. SIGNED, SLEEPLESS IN LA.

Within hours, her computer began to beep as hundreds of responses poured in from all over the world; evidently, a lot of cat haters traveled the information highway in cyberspace.

She heard from a terrorist group in Tangier who wanted the money for guns, and a Russian physicist suggesting she use red mercury—the latest in modern warfare, and some nut from New York who offered to do the job for free . . .

But the message that intrigued her the most read: ACME

ELECTRONICS, 555 ACME RD., CUPERTINO (SILICON VALLEY).
COME AFTER HOURS. BRING TAPE OF THE CAT'S MEOWING.

This person seemed serious.

"But it's a mouse!" Brenda said disappointedly, looking at the small brown rodent on the workbench in the cluttered back room of the electronic store.

"A *robot* mouse," corrected the middle-aged man who had introduced himself as Steve. He was about average height and weight, with sandy hair and a close-cropped beard; not the skinny, nerdy type with glasses Brenda had expected.

Brenda's eyes widened. "*That's* a robot?"

The man nodded. "You've heard of robot bugs?" he asked.

Brenda shook her head, no.

"They're miniature robots used mostly for espionage, but they don't really look like bugs." He paused and affectionately caressed the mouse's back. "This is my genius. It can squeeze under doors, scurry around in the heat ducts, hide under the furniture—just like a real mouse—only there's one little difference . . . this one explodes."

"Cool," Brenda said.

He looked at her sharply, eyes as brown as the mouse. "Did you bring the cassette?" he asked.

She nodded and dug into her purse and handed him the tape she had made of the cat meowing; she had recorded it the day before when she went over to sunbathe on the patio.

"Oh, and I have the money," Brenda added. She reached in her jacket pocket and pulled out ten one-hundred-dollar bills and put them on the workbench.

He smiled, but the smile was lopsided. "That's good," he said, "but it won't be enough . . . Brenda."

A chill went up her back. She hadn't given him her real name. And her identity on her computer message was supposed to have been kept secret!

"I cracked your anonymous ID," he shrugged. "Anyone

who hides behind a double-blind has something to hide, I always say. Next time protect yourself with a password."

Brenda felt her face grow hot. She didn't know what to say.

"I also accessed your home computer files," he continued.

"*Which* files?" she demanded.

" 'Dear Monica, I won't get my inheritance until the cat is dead . . .' "

Brenda grabbed the money off the workbench and bolted for the door. But the man beat her to it, blocking the exit.

"Get out of my way, or I'll scream!" she shouted.

He put both hands up in the air. "Whoa! I'm not going to touch you . . . I just want a little money, that's all."

She backed away from him. Narrowed her eyes. "How *much* more?"

He lowered his hands. "Ten thousand."

"Ten thousand!" she said, almost choking on the words. "I haven't got that kind of money!"

"But you *will* have," he said slyly. "That and a lot more . . ."

She stared at him.

"Look," he explained, his voice softer, "that robot is worth five grand, easy. I'll need to replace it. And then I want to build another."

She considered that, vacillating. The robot mouse *was* a neat gizmo, she thought, and would certainly do the trick.

But then she had a few more thoughts. Blowing the cat to kingdom come wouldn't exactly look like an accidental death. She would certainly be suspected . . .

Brenda looked at Steve, who was grinning at her smugly.

But the authorities could only get to her through him . . . and he *already* knew too much.

"Okay," she agreed, "I'll pay you ten thousand. But not until I get *my* money. Then you'll get *yours*."

That would give her enough time to figure out how to kill him.

She made a mental note to remember to ask for the tape of the cat back . . . wouldn't want any evidence left behind.

"Deal." He smiled and held out his hand for her to shake, which she did. "Now, let me show you how this cute little mouse works."

A tiny sliver of moon hung high in the sky, like the slit of a sleeping cat's eye, as Brenda drove her convertible slowly along the highway in front of her mother's house.

She parked the car in the mouth of the driveway and got out.

In the stillness of the night, she crept along the garage. She bent to the ground and carefully removed the mouse from her jacket pocket and placed the small robot on the cement, underneath the fence, between the boards and the ground.

There the mouse would stay, tucked away, for however long it took, until the cat meowed. The robot would then identify that particular sound, and with the guidance of a heat-seeking device, zero in on the animal and blow it to smithereens.

She smiled at the irony of a mouse chasing a cat—and killing it.

Brenda walked back to her car and slid in behind the wheel. She stuck a tape in the player, started the car.

"MEOW!" said the speakers.

Brenda froze, realizing what she had done. She looked over quickly to the space under the fence where she had put the mouse.

Even in the darkness she could see the small rodent move out of its hiding place and cut a path right toward her.

Brenda floored the car's accelerator, and with tires squealing and rubber smoking, backed out of the driveway and sped off.

She could outrun it, she thought. *After all, how fast could a little mouse go?*

Brenda flew down the highway, then suddenly she slammed on her brakes and made a U-turn, her tires squealing, as she bumped up on the curb, nearly running over a derelict who was sifting through a garbage can.

That should throw the little vermin off, she thought.

Furtively, she glanced over her shoulder. Under the bright street lights, she saw the small brown mouse make a tiny U-turn of its own, still tracking her, closing in.

Brenda went faster, her car careening, taking Malibu Canyon Road at a dangerous speed, the vehicle twisting and turning as it slid sideways into a pole.

The impact knocked Brenda nearly unconscious. But she did manage to say, "Oh, shit."

And there wasn't time for another word, before her world flashed white, then red, then black . . .

"Mas vino, madre?" Lucinda asked, a wine decanter in her hand.

"Por favor," her mother answered. The woman, slender, with short, silver-gray hair, leaned forward in her lounge chair on the patio and held out a crystal goblet toward her daughter.

Lucinda filled the glass with Château Latour, and as she did, her mother told her in Spanish how beautiful Lucinda looked in the dress that she was wearing.

Lucinda smiled. She *did* feel like a movie star in the beige gown with sequins and pearls! If Talbert hadn't ripped it, she never would have owned the dress. So upset was Mr. Charles that he just *gave* it to her! And the rips that she herself had sewed shut hardly even showed, much.

Whenever she wore the dress—usually with one of her colorful headscarfs and sandals—she proudly told whoever would listen that the gown was designed by Chez Charles on Rodeo Drive. It was the least she could do for that nice man!

Lucinda looked over at the sleeping white cat, stretched out on the patio. Held in its paws was the little pouch of catnip that Brenda had given him.

Poor Brenda, thought the housekeeper, *whatever had the girl been up to the night she died in that fiery crash just a few miles away?*

The police said there had been a witness. A poor man without a home saw the whole thing. He claimed Brenda was killed by a mouse that chased her down the highway! But, of course, that was silly.

A portable phone on the patio table rang and Lucinda picked it up.

"Hello?" she said.

"Miss Lopez?" a male voice asked.

"Yes?"

"This is Harold Davis, from Harold's Pet Emporium," he said. "Got a male white Persian for you."

"*Gracias,* Mr. Davis," Lucinda replied, "but I won't be needing the cat now." She paused, then added, "However, if I *should* want another in the future, can you get me one as fast as you got me the other two?"

Spacecat

•

Barbara Paul

The very dead man had invaded McCat's space, cramming himself into the nice hollow made by the oblique juncture of two mock computer banks. What's more, the very dead man was leaking blood all over the place. Someone was going to have to do some serious housecleaning before McCat would use *that* space again.

He leaped to the Captain's chair and switched his tail at the two strangers to show his annoyance at the present revolting state of affairs. Like most humans, they didn't notice.

His humans weren't paying any attention to him either. They clustered around the two strangers, quiet in a way McCat had never heard them be quiet before. Finally Male Stranger looked around and said, "What's this supposed to be? The bridge of a spaceship?"

"That's right, Detective," Boss Human said nervously. "We're shooting a flash-and-dazzle space adventure called *CyberTime*." He stared glumly at the dead man. "We *were* shooting it."

"You'll have to cancel?"

Boss Human grunted. "Nathan was in eighty percent of the scenes we've got in the can. I don't know if we can get the financing."

"To start over?"

"To start over."

Female Stranger spoke. "And this happened right after

he'd shot a scene? How long from the end of that to the time he was found?"

"About fifteen minutes," Boss told her. "Twenty at the most. We'd just stopped to make a minor adjustment on the set . . . a prop was missing. We weren't shooting here—we were over on the engineering deck."

None of this was solving McCat's problem. He wanted his space back, but all these humans were doing was talking. He let out a low growl to remind them of his displeasure.

"What was that?" Female Stranger asked.

"Just the studio cat," Boss said. *Just?* "Why was Nathan's body stuffed in there? Crammed into that little nook like that? He's not really hidden."

"You weren't shooting here, you said. Then the lights were off?"

"That's right, Detective."

"Then most likely this was only a temporary hiding place. You weren't using the set—it was convenient. Maybe the killer meant to move the body later."

"Yeah," Male Stranger added. "And that makes it sound spur of the moment. Which of you found the body?"

"I did," said Tinyvoice Human.

Female Stranger walked over to her. "What were you doing on this set . . . when everybody else was on a different one?"

"I was looking for the missing prop," the other woman said so softly as almost to be inaudible. "It wasn't in the prop room, and this was the last place it was used."

"You're in charge of props?"

She murmured something.

"I can't hear you."

Tinyvoice raised her volume to a whisper. "Not in charge," apologetically. "I'm on the properties crew."

"Did you find the missing prop?"

"Yes . . . oh! I think I dropped it when . . . when I saw Nathan." Tinyvoice started looking around.

"Here it is," said Groomer Human, picking up a plastic gizmo from the floor. "It doesn't do a damned thing—but oh, it does flash pretty lights and it looks high-tech as all get-out." He held the prop out to the two strangers. "No blood on it, if that's what you're wondering."

Male Stranger took the gizmo and weighed it lightly in his hand. "He was hit with something heavier than this. Then the killer pushed the body into this cranny and hid the weapon. All in fifteen to twenty minutes."

"Impossible," Boss said flatly.

"Your time schedule," Male Stranger reminded him. "Are you sure it couldn't have been more than fifteen or twenty minutes?"

"Positive."

"Less, I'd say," Groomer added.

The two strangers exchanged a look. "Reenactment?" Female asked.

Male sighed and nodded. "All right, everybody. I want you all to go stand exactly where you were standing when you finished the last scene."

"On the, er, engineering-deck set," Female added. "Let's do it now. Come on, folks."

With a minimum of murmuring, McCat's humans turned and started walking away. The two strangers, both of them named Detective, followed.

"Come here, Mackie," Tinyvoice whispered and swept him up into an embrace. "I need a hug." It was McCat who got the hug, but he endured it because Tinyvoice was a good sort.

He also allowed her to carry him to where the others were going, as it was obvious he wasn't going to get his space back anytime soon. On the other set, his humans were standing around looking uncomfortable ... all but Groomer, who was patting his hair and smoothing down his clothes.

McCat wriggled free of Tinyvoice's light grasp and headed toward a machine that sometimes purred and gave off warmth. But the machine was cold and quiet; not a good space today. McCat leapt to the top of a semicircular railing that was part of the set and walked daintily along the narrow top, looking for exactly the right spot. When he found it, he settled down, tucked in his paws, and did his Sphinx act.

Groomer was inspecting his short claws, undoubtedly hoping they'd grown some since the last time he'd looked. In response to something Female Stranger said, he replied, "I was seated right here during the entire scene." He sat down and checked his reflection in a computer screen.

"I was moving around a lot," a woman's voice said. "I'm sorry . . . this is upsetting. I can't remember my blocking. I'm not sure where I was at the end of the scene." McCat knew that voice; it was Noseburner.

"Continuity!" Boss yelled. "I think you were down by Exit A, but let's check it." The human named Continuity hurried forward with a script.

McCat's eyes closed as the humans went on moving around and talking. It was the same boring thing they did every day. Yak-yak-yak, change space. Change space, yak-yak-yak. He dozed.

Suddenly McCat's sinuses were on fire and his eyes watering. He whipped his head around. Noseburner! She was headed straight toward him! He jumped down from the circular railing and dashed off the set as fast as his legs would carry him.

"That cat hates me," Noseburner said wonderingly. "He's always doing that."

McCat didn't hate her; he just hated her smell. Her smell *hurt*. Noseburner kept her painful smell in a bottle on her dressing table. On days she forgot to open the bottle, McCat liked her well enough.

But right now he felt the need for a little privacy; he'd had enough of the humans for a while. The game room would be empty this time of day.

A long mirror inside the door caught his attention. His reflection showed spanking-clean white fur, big yellow-green eyes. A fine figure of a feline.

McCat had two spaces in the game room. His public space was at the end of a long counter where he could watch what was happening. Every morning some of the humans came in and changed into creatures with scales or tentacles or feathers. They changed to bright yellow or green or purplish blue. Some of them developed forehead diseases. Even their smells changed. Then at the end of the day they'd all change back into humans again. It was a pretty good game.

But McCat had a private space there as well, and that was where he was headed. He'd discovered a cabinet door latch that didn't quite catch, letting him crawl into the dark, warm place and nestle on the freshly laundered make-up towels. It was, if truth be told, his favorite space in the entire universe.

McCat nudged the cabinet door open and started to step inside—but stopped in shock, one paw suspended in midair. The place reeked of the same blood that had ruined his other space, and a big metal thing was taking up his sleeping room.

These humans! Had they no respect whatsoever? Didn't they understand a cat's need for privacy. Did they think they could just go in anywhere they wanted and claim the space for themselves?

McCat threw back his head and *YOWWWWLLLLLLLLED* until someone came to see what the matter was.

More strangers had come, taking up room and interfering with the day's rhythms even further. Most of them had left, eventually, taking the very dead man with them; a few strangers wearing uniforms remained. But no one had cleaned away the dead human's bloodscent; McCat was beginning to think that that good space was gone forever.

But he'd found a new one, temporary in nature but nice nonetheless. He snuggled happily in the lap of Female Stranger, who was absently scratching him between the shoulder blades. McCat purred in contentment; it was the one spot he couldn't scratch for himself.

"They use those pieces of pipe in nearly ever damned set they've built here," Male Stranger was saying. "Then they shoot steam through them to create 'atmosphere'—that's why the murder weapon had holes drilled in it. The killer just picked up one piece of pipe off the pile of spares."

"Which nullifies the spur-of-the-moment theory," Female pointed out. "That death was planned. Someone carried the pipe around until the opportunity came up to use it."

"And that doesn't even rule out the actors. All those flowing robes and big loose sleeves? I thought spacefaring people wore jammies and miniskirts."

Female shifted her position slightly in her canvas deck chair, causing McCat to open one eye at her. "What was Nathan doing on that other set? The props woman was there looking for their missing gizmo. But why the star of the picture?"

Male thought a minute. "Someone asked to meet him there?"

"But why there? Why not a dressing room or the make-up room or someplace private?"

"Could be Nathan insisted on someplace out in the open?"

Female nodded slowly. "That's good. He knew there might be danger to himself. So he'd agree to meet only in an exposed area . . . except that it turned out to be not quite exposed enough. I think we'd better talk to the director again." She turned her head and said something to one of the Uniform Humans.

"Guy from the ME's office guesses epidermal hematoma," Male said. "The blow opened an artery, looks like. And before you ask . . . he said a pipe that heavy would do the job by itself. He didn't have to be hit especially hard."

"So we can't rule out the women. Reenacting where everybody was standing at the end of the last scene eliminated exactly three people from this mob we've got here. You know, I don't think we're going to nail this one through external evidence."

Male didn't look happy. "Motive. Personalities. All that messy stuff."

Uniform Human came back with Boss, who approached them with a look of horror on his face. "You're sitting in my chair!" he said accusingly to Male.

Male looked around at all the empty deck chairs nearby and raised an eyebrow. "Sorry?"

"You're in my chair!" Boss went on in an outraged voice. "You don't sit in the director's chair, not ever. You sit in *God*'s chair . . . but *never* in the director's chair!"

Male raised both hands. "All right, all right." He got up and pulled over another chair while Boss reclaimed his own. McCat approved; one had to be on constant guard against space-usurpers.

Female said, "Tell me about this Nathan. I never heard of him. He was the star of the movie?"

"Costar," Boss answered. "Or rather co-costar. Buddy picture plus female. A Hope and Crosby road picture."

"A comedy?"

"Not intentionally." Bitterly.

Male and Female exchanged a look. Male asked, "Not going well?"

"Three stars, three acting styles. And not one of them willing to give an inch." Boss glowered. "Not exactly what you'd call ensemble acting."

"So who was Nathan?"

"Oh, he was another of those Shakespearean Brits who've learned there are big bucks to be made doing American science-fiction flicks. This was his first Hollywood movie, but he'd made a name for himself in European cinema. Did a couple of plays on Broadway."

"Then he didn't know many people here?"

"Yeah, he did. Show people move around a lot. He'd worked with some of our people before."

"With you?"

"Not with me. But we'd met, a couple of times."

"What kind of man was he?"

Boss shrugged. "Smug. Looked down his nose at the colonials. It may have been a defense mechanism, though. I think he might have been nervous doing this kind of picture. His last role was Richard III."

Female leaned forward, crowding McCat a bit. "What made you think he was nervous?"

"Oh, he just acted edgy all the time. As if he was walking on eggs. So careful of everything he said and did."

"As if he knew he was in danger?"

Boss stared at her. "That never occurred to me, but considering what happened to him—yeah, maybe so. But he didn't really act afraid, you know. Just sort of . . . wary."

They questioned him further, but Boss didn't know much about Nathan's personal life. The English actor had been married and divorced several times, but was currently unattached. Boss wasn't even sure where he lived.

After telling the director he could leave, Male looked at his partner and said, "Not much there in specifics, but it does look as if Nathan was involved with someone he knew was dangerous."

"Blackmail?"

"With Nathan as the blackmailer? Could be." He sighed. "A Hope and Crosby picture, the man said. *The Road to Saturn.* So, what next?"

"Let's go talk to Dorothy Lamour," Female said.

McCat fussed a little when she gently pushed him off to the floor. He trotted along behind as they headed toward one of the trailers used as dressing rooms, wishing Female would perch somewhere and make a lap again. Then abruptly he stopped: it was Noseburner's trailer door they were knocking on.

The woman herself opened the door with one hand while holding a towel in the other. "I just got out of the shower," she said, "but come on in."

McCat sniffed the air cautiously. No burning sensation in his nose or eyes; was it safe? At the last minute he slipped into the trailer just before Male closed the door behind him.

"Well!" Noseburner exclaimed when she saw McCat. "You've decided to honor me with your presence?"

"You don't like cats?" Female asked.

"I like them well enough, but *that* cat doesn't like me. He's always running away from me." She sat down at her dressing table and toweled her still-damp hair briskly, looking a question at the two detectives.

Male asked, "How well did you know Nathan?"

A sigh. "Nathan claimed he had a role in *Coming Up for Air.*" At the detectives' blank looks, she added, "That's a movie I made in Rome years ago. You didn't see it? But if

Nathan was in it, I don't remember him. It must have been a very small role."

"I thought Nathan was a big star in Europe," Female interposed.

Noseburner smiled at her condescendingly. "He is now. He wasn't then." She tossed her towel aside, a gesture that generated a flash of light from her left hand.

Female gaped. "Is that an engagement ring?"

The leading lady gazed approvingly at the huge stone she was wearing. "I am going to marry Sam Steinmetz. As soon as this picture is finished."

The detectives nodded; everyone in Hollywood knew who Sam Steinmetz was. In Hollywood, there were big producers, Big Producers, and BIG PRODUCERS. Sam Steinmetz belonged to the last group.

Female smiled. "Well . . . best wishes to you both. Is Mr. Steinmetz producing this picture?"

"Oh, yes," Noseburner replied airily. "I told him I'd never done a sci-fi movie, so he bought several properties and told me to choose one."

"But as far as you're concerned," Male said, determined to bring them back to the subject, "you didn't know Nathan at all before *CyberLine* started shooting?"

"*CyberTime*," Noseburner corrected. "As far as I was concerned, Nathan was a total stranger. Afraid I can't help you there, Detective."

McCat was fastidiously exploring every corner of the trailer, checking for traces of the hurtful smell that might have escaped from the bottle on Noseburner's dressing table. He thought he caught a whiff of it once or twice, but it was gone before his eyes could start watering. Once he'd assured himself this space was safe, he settled down to take a bath, tongue-washing his already clean white fur.

Noseburner was talking to the two detectives about the movie's director. "Did he tell you that he almost directed Nathan once before? A television adaptation of a play Nathan had done in New York. It was for PBS—no money to speak of but a good showcase."

"What happened?"

"Nathan preferred a more . . . prestigious director. A bigger name. And since he was the star of the show—what Nathan wanted, Nathan got."

Both detectives' eyes gleamed; it was the first hint of a motive they'd come across. "So the director bore a grudge against the actor?" Female asked.

A throaty laugh. "Not enough to *kill* him, Detective! But yes, there was tension between them." Casually she pulled a bottle toward her and removed the stopper.

There it was: fire in the sinus, in the nostrils, behind the eyeballs. A growl started low in McCat's throat and rose to a high whine. He hissssssed—and felt the fur on his back stand on end. He started dashing back and forth, looking for an escape route. Closed doors! Closed windows!

"What on earth?" said Noseburner.

McCat sneezed rapidly eleven times in succession and then started scratching frantically at the door, meowing piteously. *Can't you see I'm dying here?*

"It's your perfume," Male said.

Wonderingly, Noseburner looked at the stopper in her hand and then replaced it in the bottle. "The damned cat doesn't like my perfume?"

Male picked McCat up and stroked him soothingly. "That looks like an allergy to me. All that sneezing?"

"Wait a minute," Female said. "I'm wearing perfume. He sat in my lap okay. No reaction."

Male nodded his head toward the dressing table, his arms full of cat. "Then it's just *that* perfume. Cats can be allergic to only one brand."

McCat gradually calmed down as the hurtful smell dissipated to a tolerable level. The three humans forgot about him, although Male kept stroking him automatically. Female said, "Back to Nathan. Even though you don't remember him from before, did you get friendly with him later?"

Noseburner laughed her throaty laugh. "My, there's a loaded qustion if ever I heard one. We were neither friendly nor unfriendly. He did invite me to lunch one day but I didn't go."

"Why not?"

"He wanted to have food sent in to his trailer. That's not my idea of a luncheon date. And his trailer is smaller than this one." She gestured vaguely. "At least, it looks smaller from the outside."

"You've never been inside his trailer?"

"No reason to go. If he'd wanted to visit, he could have come here."

"But he didn't."

"That's right, Detective. He didn't. Nathan wasn't one for casual chat. Too reserved. He didn't really fit in here, on an American movie set."

"Reserved, hm? Did he seem edgy, nervous? Uh ... wary?"

She shrugged. "I didn't notice."

Again, the detectives learned nothing about Nathan's personal life in spite of their additional questions. Evidently the man just didn't open up about himself. They thanked Noseburner for her cooperation and left, Male still carrying McCat.

"What about the other star of the picture?" Female asked. "Want to talk to him?"

"Might as well," Male answered. "If he can stop primping long enough."

Groomer's trailer was on the other side of the huge set, as if he and Noseburner were putting as much distance between them as possible.

In answer to their knock, the star himself sang out, "Come in! Come in!" They opened the door to see the man they were looking for sitting at his dressing table, combing his hair. When he saw their reflections in his mirror, he said, "Ah, the *gendarmerie*! And you brought Mackie with you. Come here, Mackie, you sweet thing." Without rising from his chair, he reached up and took McCat out of Male's arms and arranged the cat artfully across his crossed legs, holding him in place with both hands and making as handsome a picture as he could. McCat's tail began to switch back and forth; he didn't like being used as a prop.

The two detectives found places to sit and asked their

usual questions about the dead man. Unlike the others, Groomer had a lot to say about Nathan. Unfortunately, it was all gossip.

"They say," Groomer purred insinuatingly, "that Nathan keeps a pimp on retainer. Different woman every night. They say Nathan almost broke the pimp's arm when the poor shmuck forgot and sent a hooker who'd been there once before." He giggled. "Nathan *really* worked at maintaining a macho image."

Male was scowling. "A nervous, reserved, macho actor," he muttered. "I wonder if any of you were seeing the same man."

"Oh, my dears, we saw only what Nathan wanted us to see. The man was acting *all* the time. So affected! Always giving a performance."

Both detectives managed to keep a straight face; Female asked, "I suppose you didn't know Nathan either before this picture started filming?"

"What do you mean, 'either'? Almost all of us had crossed paths with Nathan at one time or another."

"Your leading lady didn't. Or at least she says she doesn't remember meeting him."

"Is that what she told you?" He laughed a descending-scale musical laugh. "Oh, that woman—she is *incorrigible*!" He got to laughing so hard the he ignored the animal in his lap and carelessly stuck a finger into McCat's ear. McCat bit his hand and jumped down to head for a hiding space he'd spotted.

Groomer cradled his not-really-injured hand and growled unpleasantries at the white cat. Male interrupted by asking, "What was so funny? Wasn't she telling the truth about not knowing Nathan?"

The actor immediately forgot about McCat at this golden opportunity to spread a little dirt. "Oh, they knew each other all right! Did they *ever*. She and Nathan were in a movie together once, a dreadful piece of tripe called *Coming Up for Air*. But the way I hear it, they were hot and heavy for each other from Day One. Couldn't keep their hands off each other. She was the star and he had some minor role ... Lady Chatterley going for a roll in the hay with the groundskeeper, don't you know. Steamed up the lenses of the cameras, they did—and they weren't even playing love scenes!"

"But why would she pretend not to know him?"

"Why, because of Sam, of course!"

"Sam Steinmetz?"

"It makes perfect sense, my dears. If you were engaged to marry Mr. Samuel VIP Steinmetz, would you want him to know you were working closely every day with a former lover? Sam doesn't tolerate opposition of any kind. I mean, he doesn't *tolerate* it!"

Female looked at him skeptically. "How sure are you about this?"

"It's common knowledge. Ask anyone."

"Then why doesn't Sam Steinmetz know about it?"

If the question caught him off guard, he didn't show it. "I have no idea. But I hope you're not going to give the game away by asking him! Why spoil the fun, Detective?" He laughed again. "For thirty years Sam Steinmetz has been the most notorious skirt-chaser in this town—but he's always preferred nubile young things with long legs and hollow skulls. And yet when he's finally pinned to the matrimonial wall, it's by an aging movie queen who has always demanded selfless adoration from all around her. Ah, well. She's been around the block a few times herself. They're a good match."

Male was disgusted. "This is a murder investigation, not a parlor game. You knew Nathan before? From where?"

Unperturbed by the detective's tone, Groomer said: "Oh, we first met in a shabby little production of *Hamlet*—that was back before either of us was established. This was in Ireland, of all places. But I barely knew Nathan to speak to. We were never in any scenes together."

"Which one of you played Hamlet?"

Groomer scowled at the question. "Neither of us. I was Osric and Nathan was one of the guards who open the play."

"Osric?"

"You don't know the play, Detective? Well, you see, it's about this courtier named Osric—"

"Save that for later," Female cut him off. "Where else did you know Nathan from?"

Groomer went on to detail a number of brief meetings widely separated from one another over a period of years; it was the kind of relationship any two professionals might develop during the course of their work. No, they had never become friends, Groomer said; there never was enough time for that, even if they had been so inclined—which they weren't. "I've spent more time with Nathan filming this cornball space opera than I spent all those other times put together."

By then both detectives were thoroughly tired of the sound of Groomer's voice, so they thanked him for his co-operation and got up to leave.

"Take that nasty beast with you," the actor instructed. McCat knew when he wasn't wanted; as soon as the trailer door was opened, he scooted out.

The two detectives followed more sedately. "Want to check out Nathan's trailer next?" Female asked. "Do you know where it is?"

Male didn't know. "Look—there's the director. Let's ask him."

Boss was hurrying along with a worried look on his face when the two detectives stopped him. "Will this take long? I have a meeting with the producer. We have some decisions to make." He was fidgeting, having trouble standing still. "We have to see if there's a way to complete the picture without Nathan."

McCat bumped his head against Boss's leg, recognizing the human's need for comfort and reassurance. Female asked where Nathan's trailer was, and when Boss told her, asked one more question. Was the story true that Groomer had told them about the hot affair between Nathan and Noseburner?

Boss looked startled, and then laughed shortly. "Don't believe a word that man tells you. He's the most vicious gossip in town—he always spreads rumors about the people he's acting with as a matter of course. Once he even started a rumor that Elizabeth Taylor was going to get a sex-change operation. But he and our eminent leading lady have never gotten along well, and he had a special reason for wanting to smear Nathan."

"What special reason?" both detectives asked in unison.

The director took a deep breath, which failed to stop his fidgeting. "Well, when we were in preproduction, this wasn't a buddy picture at all. There were only two leads, male and female. But then the chance to sign Nathan came up—and the single male lead was divided into two different roles. You see? He lost half his lines once Nathan came on board." He saw the expressions on the detectives' faces and hastily added, "Forget that. He does all his attacking verbally. You don't want to arrest him. Don't take my one remaining male lead away from me!"

"Will he get his lines back if you decide to complete the picture?" Male asked.

"That's one of the possibilities we're going to consider." Boss sighed. "Look, I really do have to go." And without another word he was gone.

The two detectives looked at each other a moment. Finally Male said, "I don't think we can believe a word *any* of them tells us."

Female was inclined to agree. "Let's go check Nathan's trailer," she said.

McCat followed along, having nothing better to do; his ears perked up when he saw they were going into a trailer he'd never had the opportunity to explore before. The very dead man who had nested in that space didn't like cats, the poor benighted human. McCat slipped between Male's legs and was the first inside.

Male and Female started looking in drawers and opening boxes, sometimes breaking locks to do so. Noseburner had been right; this trailer was smaller than hers . . . and smaller than Groomer's as well. It still made a roomy enough dressing room; but if there was some sort of status attached to the size of the trailer an actor was given, Nathan had definitely been low man on the three-star totem pole.

"This is all fan mail," Female said, shuffling through a pile of letters. "No address book—probably at his home. If we—" She broke off.

McCat was sneezing. Six quick sneezes. Pause. Two more.

The two detectives looked at each other. "Perfume? She said she'd never been in this trailer," Female said. "She lied to us?"

"How long does a scent like that linger?" Male asked. "She had to have been in here recently."

"*After* Nathan was murdered? Why?"

"Looking for something is my guess."

"Wait a minute, wait a minute, we're jumping the gun here. The cat could be allergic to something other than her perfume, something in here." She thought a minute. "Let's find out. You hold him and I'll go find stuff to test."

Male picked up McCat and went through his soothe-the-kitty routine once more while Female gathered up everything she could find that might have provoked an allergic reaction. But McCat was equally indifferent to everything she held out for him to sniff, from Nathan's shampoo to his aftershave.

"Then she did lie to us," Female concluded. "If she did come here looking for something, I wonder if she found it."

Male put McCat down and picked up a ring of keys he'd found in one of the locked drawers. "Safety-deposit key here. We'll have to get a court order to open the box."

Female looked at her watch. "But not today. Everything's closed now."

Male sneezed. He pulled out a handkerchief and wiped his nose. "Hey, can you catch an allergy from a cat?"

At noon the next day the two detectives sat in a coffee shop eating lunch. It had taken them all morning to find a judge, get their court order signed, and to examine the contents of Nathan's safety-deposit box.

Male scraped most of the sprouts off his sandwich. "Read the list again."

Female picked up a list of the contents of the safety-deposit box. "Three thousand dollars in twenties. A will leaving everything to his son Philip, currently residing with his mother in London. An old photograph of a man and woman, mid- to late-thirties. Nathan's parents?" She paused to take a swallow of coffee. "A British passport. A certificate of marriage between Nathan ... and an Ethel Shnorhokian." She stumbled over the pronunciation. "God, what a name. Wife Number One? Philip's mother?"

"Maybe. I wonder if he goes by 'Shnorhokian,' since he's living with his mother." Male didn't really wonder; he just wanted to show off pronouncing *Shnorhokian*. "What else?"

"Insurance policies, naming Philip as beneficiary. Copy of a property lease ... evidently Nathan didn't plan to stay in California long enough to buy. Shares in a pharmaceutical company based in LA, not very many. Probably a recent investment." She sighed. "And that's it. No mysterious locket with an inscription in Chinese, no faded newspaper clipping about somebody's early career in porn flicks, no gum wrapper with a coded message printed on the back. None of that helpful stuff they always find in the movies."

"And to round things out, the lab boys say no prints on the murder weapon. A pipe that smooth, it should take prints."

Female shrugged. "Wrap a piece of cloth around one end. What about those pharmaceutical shares? Could there be anything there?"

They couldn't think of anything. Male said, "Maybe Mama Shnorhokian hired a hitter."

She waved a hand dismissively. "Not a professional job. Whoever bashed Nathan's head in was so rattled that he—or she—walked away from the scene still carrying the murder weapon. And then hurriedly stuck it into the towel cabinet once he realized he was holding incriminating evidence in his hand. Or she. No, this is no long-distance killing ... the answer's in that movie studio." She checked the time. "Speaking of."

"Right." They paid their bills and left.

On the drive to the studio, Male said, "We have three

soft motives. All based on hearsay, all full of holes, and not one of them strong enough to convince a jury. The director's career was roadblocked at one point by the dead man. Motive—revenge? The leading lady doesn't want her fiancé to find out that a former lover is on the scene. Motive—self-protection? The leading man's status was reduced when half his lines were handed over to Nathan. Motive—ambition? Can you honestly believe that anyone would commit murder for any of those reasons? And don't tell me old men are killed for the change in their pockets. That's not *these* people. Watch out for that van."

"I see it." She eased the car over a little to the right. "But all those seemingly foolish motives might just be the tip of the iceberg. What if Nathan had blocked the director's career not once but a number of times? Say he was trying to do it again, even agitating to get the director replaced on the picture. Then the director's motive would be more than just some melodramatic desire for vengeance. He'd be fighting for his professional life."

Male snorted. "You could play that game with all of them."

"That's my point! We just don't *know* what else might have been going on."

They drove in silence the rest of the way to the studio. The guard at the gate waved them in; they found a guest parking place near the soundstage where *CyberTime* was being filmed.

Male watched three shaggy-haired actors dressed as cavemen hurrying by. He asked his partner, "Did you ever want to be a movie star?"

"Sure I did, when I was a little girl." She laughed. "Doesn't everybody?"

He grunted. "I wanted to be a cowboy in the movies. Not a cowboy. A cowboy *in the movies*."

Inside the soundstage building, they found a bustle and activity that had been totally lacking the day before. The detectives didn't have to ask to know that filming on *CyberTime* was going to proceed—not as planned, but proceed nevertheless. They tracked down the director.

76

"We're going to give Nathan a posthumous death scene," Boss explained with such exuberance that he was practically dancing in place. "We'll use a double, and distance shots—and we'll send him off with the biggest and flashiest explosion that Effects can come up with!"

Female blinked. "You're going to blow up this set?"

Boss was horrified. "God, no. We'll put him in a shuttle or a dropship or something small like that. Designer's working on it now. But it's going to work out all right!"

Male said, "And Nathan's lines?"

The director grinned crookedly. "Guess who gets those. The good part is we won't have to change much of the script . . . this really is going to work out all right. Look, I've got a zillion things to see to and I—" He left without finishing his sentence.

The crew was setting up to shoot on the engineering-deck set, redoing the scene they'd started filming yesterday . . . but this time without Nathan. On the set, the detectives spotted their companion of the day before, perched atop a mysterious piece of machinery that was humming softly.

"You don't know us today, Mackie?" Female asked.

McCat yawned and ignored her.

Soon the crew was finished and the actors sent for. Tinyvoice, the woman who'd found Nathan's body, finished one final check of the props. When she left the set, Male stopped her. "The cat's still on the set."

"Yes, he's in a number of the shots," Tinyvoice whispered. "Adds a homey touch."

The two actors in the scene arrived, sweeping on to the set like Lords of the Universe. Groomer called for Make-up to come spray an errant lock of hair. Noseburner took her place near a viewscreen, McCat watching her warily all the while.

But as soon as Boss yelled out "Action!"—an overhead light went *Pop!* and showered down sparks on the set. Groans and complaints about safety hazards rose all around; Groomer whined, "I could have been burned! Such carelessness! It's unconscionable!"

"Calm down—no one's hurt," Boss called out. "It's just a lamp replacement. It'll only take a minute."

Female felt something rub up against her leg. She bent down and stroked McCat's white fur. "Decided you didn't like it there after all, did you?"

Male nudged her. "Come on." They made their way over to where Boss was nervously pacing back and forth behind the camera, his head craned back to watch the progress of the light technicians.

Male stepped into his path. "I'm sorry to break in on you at a time like this, but we do have an investigation to conduct."

"Make it fast," Boss snapped.

"We've just learned Nathan had a son who's living with his mother in London. Philip is his heir."

"Yeah, so?"

"So we'll need to notify them," Female said, feeling McCat winding around her ankles. "But we don't know which of Nathan's ex-wives is Philip's mother. Do you know?"

"Oh, hell." Boss frowned in concentration. "I did know. Can't think of the name."

"Was it Ethel Shnorhokian?" Male asked.

Boss's head jerked around in astonishment. Then he laughed. "Man, have you got your facts twisted! Philip's mother in London? Ha! No way. You want to talk to Ethel Shnorhokian? There she is."

He was pointing at Noseburner.

Male sucked in a breath. "That's her real name?"

"Can you see 'Ethel Shnorhokian' on a theater marquee? Yeah, that's her real name."

"Oh, wow." Female looked at her partner. "That's it, then. The rest of the iceberg." She turned to Boss. "We're going to question her *right now*. Your movie will have to wait."

"What?" the director screeched. "That's crazy! You can't hold up production just to ask questions!"

"Yes, we can," Female told him firmly and turned to follow her partner out on to the set. McCat padded along

78

behind her; he could tell from their voices that something out of the ordinary was happening. Boss came too, still making angry noises that no one seemed to be paying any attention to.

Male stopped in front of Noseburner. Police guidelines recommended private interrogation. But not here and now, not with this woman. "Ethel Shnorhokian?"

She glared at him. "That's not my name anymore." Groomer snickered.

"I really must protest, Detective," Boss said loudly. "You can't interfere with our schedule like this! Who do you think you are?"

"Keep quiet." Male turned back to Noseburner. "You lied to us."

She made a sound of annoyance. "Because I didn't tell you the name I was born with?"

Female stepped in. "You lied to us about never going into Nathan's trailer."

"I didn't go in!"

"You were there yesterday. We have a witness." Female was careful not to look down at McCat. "We know you were inside that trailer. Do you understand? We *know* you were there. So don't bother to lie."

Noseburner licked her lips, said nothing.

"And you went in *after* Nathan was killed," Female pushed on. "Why? What were you looking for?"

"Oh, all right, all right! I was looking for a book Nathan had borrowed. I wanted to get it back before the trailer was sealed up or whatever it is you police types do."

"A book?" Male said. "Don't you mean a single piece of paper? One piece of paper proving that you and Nathan were married?"

An astonished silence fell over the set. Then: "You actually *married* him?" Groomer rolled his eyes. "Really, darling, what a stunning lapse in taste."

"No!" she shouted. "This is preposterous. Nathan and I were never married!"

"We have the marriage certificate," Male told her evenly. "It was in Nathan's safety-deposit box."

"But you can't have it! I de—" She clamped her lips shut.

"You destroyed it?" Male finished for her. "And it didn't occur to you that he might have more than one copy?"

Groomer was openly laughing. "Oh, SuperSam the Metz of Stein is not going to be happy with you, darling! How in the world are you going to explain away an ex-husband that you just somehow forgot to mention?"

She whirled on him. "You shut up!" Boss, who'd had so much to say earlier, was standing there with his mouth hanging open.

"Was he?" Female asked. "An *ex*-husband? Did you and Nathan ever get a divorce?"

"Well, of course we were divorced!" Noseburner cried.

"Then we'll need to see your divorce papers."

"Divorce papers? I don't know where any divorce papers are! Do you expect me to keep track of everything?" Her voice rose so high and shrill that McCat hissed.

"Then tell us where and when you were divorced. We'll check with the authorities there."

Everyone waited for her response; this time even Groomer kept quiet. Noseburner said, "I don't have to tell you anything!"

"The truth is," Male said, "that you and Nathan never were divorced. He was holding that over your head, threatening to queer your marriage to Sam Steinmetz. Is that how Nathan got a costarring role in this picture after it was already set for only two leading roles? You talked Sam into signing him . . . in exchange for Nathan's silence?"

Noseburner didn't respond.

"He was blackmailing you," Male went on, "but not for cash. You were to be his pipeline to one of the most important men in Hollywood. That was to be your arrangement. *And it would never end.*" He sighed resignedly. "So you killed him."

After a moment of dead silence, Female said, "You know we're going to arrest you for murder, don't you? You can prevent that by telling us where you were divorced. If you were divorced, there's no blackmail. One more chance before we take you in. Where and when were you divorced?"

Noseburner raised her head. "I want my lawyer."

"Right." Female turned to her partner. "Care to do the honors?"

"Why don't they ever confess, the way they do in the movies?" Male pulled out a pair of handcuffs and read Noseburner her rights.

"What are you doing?" Boss screamed. "You can't arrest her! Are you trying to destroy me?"

"Take it easy," Female said.

"But she can't be replaced! Steinmetz will cancel the picture! You *can't* arrest her!"

Female raised an eyebrow. "Are you seriously suggesting we let a murderer go free so you can make a movie?"

"Y-y-you can arrest her after the picture's done!" Boss stammered. "Keep her under guard—twenty-four hours a day! We'll pick up the tab!"

Female just smiled and shook her head. Boss sank down to the floor of the set with a groan and sat there with his legs stretched out in front of him, holding his aching head with both hands.

And just like that, it was over. The last McCat saw of the two interesting strangers, they were leading Noseburner away. From this space. Forever.

McCat could live with that.

Cap'n Bob and Gus

·

Bill Crider

I think it was S. J. Perelman who said that Hollywood was a dismal industrial town controlled by wealthy hoodlums, or something like that. Maybe he was right. But it seems to me there are just as many rich lunatics as there are rich hoodlums. In fact, the guy who was bellowing at me on the phone was probably both.

I was trying to calm him down. "Mr. Gober, I can't understand a word you're saying. Maybe if you'd stop yelling."

"Goddammit, Ferrel, I'm not yelling! You want yelling? I'll give you yelling!"

He turned things up a notch or two. He sounded like a buffalo with a bullhorn. I decided there was no need trying to make sense out of things until he ran down.

It took about five minutes by my watch. When I was sure he was finished, I said, "Go over the part about the parrot again."

"Goddammit, Ferrel, have you been listening to a word I've said?"

"Yelled. A word you *yelled*."

That set him off again. He pays me pretty well, so I guess he's got a right to yell if he wants to. He's the head of Gober Studios, and in 1948 his pictures grossed nearly as much as those of any studio in Hollywood. As best I could tell, Gober was hoping to do even better in '49, but apparently something had happened to the parrot.

I didn't know what a parrot had to do with Gober's box office, and I didn't want to fool with one, but I'm on retainer to the studio. Usually that involves keeping some star's name out of the paper for having gotten boozed up and assaulted a cop or maybe having knocked up someone's underage daughter. I could handle that kind of stuff, but a parrot? I wasn't sure about a parrot.

And then I thought I heard something about a cat.

"Hold on there a minute, Mr. Gober," I said, trying to interrupt his semicoherent soliloquy. "Did you say something about a cat?"

"Goddammit, Ferrel!"

He always seems to start off that way. Sometimes I think I should just go ahead and have my name legally changed to Goddammit Ferrel and let it go at that.

"Goddammit, Ferrel, haven't you been listening to me at all? This is not just a cat we're talking about here. This is *the* cat. This is *Gus*."

"Oh. Gus."

"That's right. Gus. And the parrot is Cap'n Bob. Cap'n Bob and Gus. They made us a hell of a lot of money last year, and now Cap'n Bob is missing!"

Well, it had finally happened. I'd always thought Gober was more stable than most of the studio heads I'd met, but now I knew I'd been wrong. He'd flipped his lid, blown his wig, twirled his toupee.

Cap'n Bob and Gus were cartoon characters. So how the hell could one of them go missing?

As it turned out, it was easy.

The way Gober explained it, Cap'n Bob and Gus were not merely cartoon characters. They were real. Gus was owned by one of the layout men, Lyman Birch, who'd brought him to work one day and showed him off to the other men in the cartoon studio. Not to be outdone, a backgrounder, Herm Voucher, drove home and got his parrot. It seems that kind of behavior wasn't unusual among the cartoon crowd.

Gober said that when the animals got a glimpse of one another, it was hate at first sight. The parrot flew off

Voucher's shoulder and went for the cat like a P-38 after a Messerschmidt. The cat howled and took off through the studio, mostly across the tops of drawing boards and people's heads. There were animation cels, paper, and drawing pens flying everywhere, and one bald guy got severely scratched on the noggin.

The rumpus might have continued for hours if someone hadn't held a drawing board up in front of the parrot when it was coming out of a turn. The bird smacked into the board and hit the floor and Birch grabbed it. Took them another hour to find the cat, who was cowering in a supply room.

Inspired to near genius by that little fracas, the artists and writers created the first Cap'n Bob and Gus cartoon, giving the parrot an eye-patch and a tendency to mutter sayings like "A-r-r-r-rh" and "Avast, ye swabbies." Matters progressed from there, with several Gus and Bob adventures following in rapid succession. *The Berber of Seville*, with the Cap'n as an opera-singing Arab who does Rossini as he's never been done before or since, won an Oscar.

The story about the cat and combative parrot was funny to me but not to Gober, who also couldn't understand his artists' and writers' continuing need for stimulation and motivation. They insisted that they couldn't write, much less draw, if the parrot and the cat weren't on permanent display in the studio. When inspiration flagged, someone would let the animals out of their cages, and things would get lively almost immediately. The artistic result would be something like *Cat-mandu*, with Gus on the trail of the Abominable Snowman, who turned out to be an awful lot like the Cap'n. Or *Cat-O'-Nine-Tales*, in which the cat played Scheherazade to the bird's smarmy King of India.

Gober might not have understood anything else, but he understood the result.

"And that's why you have to find that parrot!" Gober finished up.

What could I say? He was paying me, even if he wasn't paying me very much, so I told him I'd be at the studio in half an hour. Then I hung up the phone and got my hat.

* * *

I pointed my old hoopie, a 1940 model Chevrolet with a smooth vacuum shift, down Wilshire and turned right when I got to Vine. Eventually I got to Cahuenga and turned left. Gober Studios was located not far from Universal, though the layout wasn't as fancy. A guy I knew named Harry was on the gate, and he waved me on through without looking up from his copy of *Unknown Worlds*.

I drove right up to Gober's office. It was the nicest building on the lot, of course, and there were a couple of postwar Buicks, both of them big black Roadmasters, parked right in front. One of the cars belonged to Gober. I didn't know who the other belonged to. Maybe his secretary, who was undoubtedly paid a lot better than I was.

She was also a lot better-looking: blonde, six feet tall and built like the proverbial brick sanitary facility. She also had a voice like Veronica Lake, so I figured she was worth every cent Gober paid her.

She was efficient, too. She ushered me into Gober's office almost before I got my hat hung up. Then she quietly faded away. I stood there ankle deep in carpet and looked at Gober.

Gober got up from his desk, which was polished walnut and about the size of a football field, and by the time the door had closed behind me, he was heading my way.

"Goddammit, Ferrel, what took you so long? Let's get going."

He was about five-three with wide shoulders and hair that was slicked down on his head. If he used Brylcreme, he'd used about a dab and a half. He was wearing a suit that hadn't come from Robert Hall, and there was fire in his beady eyes. I could see that he was ready to get to the bottom of this parrot business.

I didn't move. "Get going where?"

He didn't even slow down. "The cartoon studio." He passed right by me, opened the door, and headed out. He looked back over his shoulder without stopping. "You coming, or not?"

I followed him and grabbed my hat off the rack. He was already down the steps and striding across the street. He didn't even look up at the two elephants that nearly stomped him.

I waited until the elephants passed and stretched my legs to catch up. "What picture are those from?"

"The elephants? Some goddamn jungle epic, one where Rick Torrance gets to run around for seventy-five minutes with his shirt off."

I'd seen one of the Torrance showcases. The guy looked a hell of a lot better with his shirt off than I did.

We went around Studio A, a cavernous aircraft hangar of a building, and I was having to struggle to keep up with Gober. For a guy with legs not much longer than most people's fingers, he could really move. It was a hot day, with plenty of that California sun, and I didn't feel like running. The pace didn't bother Gober, though. He did everything fast.

The cartoon unit was housed in a building in back of Studio A, and frankly, the building didn't look like much. There was a lot of wood, a shingled roof, and a bad paint job. Drop it in the middle of an Army base and it might pass for a barracks except for the sign on the door: HOLLY-WOOD HOME FOR THE CRIMINALLY COMIC.

Gober didn't seem to notice the sign. He bounced up the steps and threw open the door. Before it slammed into the wall, it was caught by a tall guy with thinning hair. After making sure it wouldn't slam, he let it go and put an arm over Gober's shoulders.

"Welcome to the asylum, boss," he said. "It's damn good to see you!"

When he took his arm away, I could see that he'd taped a piece of paper to the back of Gober's sharkskin. KICK ME, it said in big red letters.

"Never mind the glad-handing, Birch," Gober said. "I've got a guy here who's going to find that damn parrot of Voucher's."

Another man came running up to join us. He was round

and red-faced and even shorter than Gober. He would have been perfect for one of the seven dwarfs if Disney ever wanted to do a live-action version.

"Cal Franks," Gober said to me.

"There's no need for anyone to look for the parrot," Franks squeaked, waving his arms. "We've got something better!"

"Get out of my face, Franks," Gober said.

"You might want to listen to him," Birch said. "He might have a point. We're used to having the Cap'n around to stimulate our brains, and now that he's gone, we're not getting much done. We need *something*, even if it's a cockatoo."

"A cockatoo is a much better bird than a parrot," Franks insisted, heartened by the show of support by Birch. "More colorful, more—"

A chorus of voices interrupted him. "No cockatoos! No cockatoos! No cockatoos!"

The voices stretched out the O sound in the first word so that it sounded like "N-o-o-o-o-o."

I looked over Gober's head and past the two men standing in front of him. There were fifteen or so other guys gathered in the room, all of them chanting monotonously. "No cockatoos! No cockatoos!"

"Shut up, you goddamn clowns!" Gober bellowed.

He had a real talent for it. They shut up and stood looking at him expectantly. He grabbed my arm and pulled me forward for the introductions.

"This is Bill Ferrel. He's a private dick, and he's going to find that parrot. I want you all to cooperate with him and do what he says. He's the boss here now."

You could tell by looking that at least half those jokers were just itching to make some kind of half-witty remark that had to do with *dick* and *privates*, but they restrained themselves.

They were a strange-looking bunch, too. One of them was wearing an aviator's cap with the earflaps dangling down. If he was the bald guy who got scratched, maybe he was wearing it for protection. Another beauty was wearing a suit coat over a dirty undershirt. A couple of other swells were smoking cigarettes normally, but one had his stuck in his ear. Every now and then he'd suck in his cheeks and then exhale some smoke. Don't ask me how he did it.

One guy separated himself from the group and came toward us.

"Herm Voucher," Gober said out of the corner of his mouth.

Voucher was so skinny he'd have to be careful not to slip down the straw when he was drinking a malted, but he had an Adam's apple that would keep him from going all the way down. It was big as a softball, and it bobbed up and down when he talked.

"You've got to find Percy," he said. "We can't go on without him."

"Percy?" I said.

"That's the parrot's real name," Gober informed me. "Cap'n Bob is just a stage name."

"I get it," I said. "The bird has an alias."

"So does my cockatoo," Cal Franks said. "His real name's Diogenes, but his stage name's—"

"No cockatoos! No cockatoos! No—"

"Shut up!" Gober bellowed. They shut. Gober turned to me. "Goddammit, Ferrel, you can see what I have to contend with around here. But it's all up to you now. You do what you have to do, and find that goddamn bird."

He turned on his heel and left. The KICK ME sign fluttered as he passed through the doorway, and then he was gone.

The room was suddenly completely silent. No one was looking at me, though no one seemed to be doing any work, either. One guy lounged against the wall reading a racing form. One, who was wearing a sword that looked like it might have belonged to Basil Rathbone at one time, rested his hand on the hilt and stared at the ceiling.

Then, very low, so that I almost couldn't hear it at first, a low murmuring of voices began.

"Sam Spade."

"Philip Marlowe."

"Mike Shayne."

"Sherlock Holmes."

"Boston Blackie."

The voices came from all over the room, and each one was different. I wondered if everyone there had studied ventriloquism.

"All right," I said. "Let's get something straight. You guys may all be geniuses, but I think you're nuts." I opened my coat so they could see the butt of the little .38 I wore in a shoulder holster. "And if anybody puts a 'Kick Me' sign on my back, I'm going to shoot his hand off."

"We wouldn't dream of doing a thing like that," Voucher said. "We want you to find Percy."

"That's what I plan to do," I said, without having a single idea about how I'd accomplish it or even if I could. "Who's in charge here?"

Lyman Birch smiled. "Did you say *charge*?"

The guy with the sword whipped it out of the scabbard and stiff-armed it in front of him at about a forty-five-degree angle.

"Charge!" he screamed, and ran straight at us.

Herm Voucher pulled me aside while Birch opened the door. The swordsman ran right on out and down the steps. I could see him heading in the direction of Studio A as Birch closed the door.

"I still don't see why you have to find that stupid parrot," Franks said. He was standing right beside me. I'd moved around a little, but he was on me like a stick-tight. "Diogenes is much better. He's better trained, he's—"

"No cockatoos! No cockatoos! No—"

"Shut up," I bellowed. I wasn't as good as Gober, but I was good enough. "I've had enough of this crap. Now tell me who's in charge of this menagerie. Is there a producer here?"

From the expressions on their faces, you would have thought I'd asked if Typhoid Mary was in the room. Then there was a lot of histrionic gagging, with people hanging their heads over wastebaskets and out the windows. I knew I must be on the right track. Everybody hates producers.

"You must mean Barry Partin," Birch said.

"He'll do. Where's his office?"

"Back there." Birch pointed to a hallway at the back of the long room where we were standing.

"Good. I'll talk to him first, and then I'll want to talk to some of the rest of you. Don't wander off."

I didn't wait for an answer. I crossed the room, avoiding the drawing tables and the men who didn't move out of the way, which was all of them. Hard to believe that I'd thought Gober was a lunatic. He couldn't hold a candle to these guys.

It was only when I neared the doorway that I noticed the cage on the floor. It was a wire cube about four feet on a side. A gray tabby cat slept on a mat inside. He was huge. Curled up like that, he looked like a black basketball. There was something greenish peeping out from under one of his paws, but I couldn't tell for sure what it was.

On the left side of the door, there was another cage. This one was on a stand, and there was a cockatoo in it. The cage was very clean except for a few dark splotches that had landed on the newspaper covering the bottom.

"Is this Diogenes?" I asked no one in particular.

"Yes," Cal Franks said. He'd followed me across the room, though I hadn't noticed him. I couldn't shake him. "He's quite a handsome bird, don't you think?"

"No cockatoos! No cockatoos! No—"

I wheeled around, digging under my coat for the pistol, but no one was even looking in my direction. In fact, everyone was bent over his drawing board, working busily. Those guys were good.

I turned back, but I didn't comment on the handsomeness of Diogenes. I left Franks there, or hoped I did, and went through the door to look for Partin.

I walked down a short hall, past a couple of rooms that were devoted to storyboards featuring rough drawings of Cap'n Bob and Gus, and down to an office that had a closed door. The nameplate on the door read BARRY PARTIN.

I knocked, and a man's unhappy voice told me to come in. I opened the door and saw a sad little man in a baggy coat sitting behind a desk that was a mere shadow of the one in Gober's office. The carpet matched the desk; it was mashed flat and almost worn through in spots. The only things I liked in the office were the two pictures on the wall. One was of Gus and Cap'n Bob decked out as Holmes and Watson in *Catch as Cat's Can*. The other showed Gus, his eyes bugged out and his hair ridged down his back as he confronted Cap'n Bob in *Who Ghost There?*

I looked away from the pictures to the man at the desk. "Mr. Partin?" I said.

His face was as baggy as his coat. "Yes," he said. "Who are you?"

"I'm Bill Ferrel. Mr. Gober wants me to look into the disappearance of the parrot."

"Thank God," Partin said. There was a look of genuine relief on his face. "I thought maybe you were a new animator."

I didn't blame him for looking relieved. If I'd been in charge of that passel of bozos, I wouldn't have wanted another one dumped on me, either.

"No," I said. "I'm not an animator. I'm just a detective."

Partin smiled and some of the bags in his face disappeared. He asked me to have a seat. "You think you can find that bird?"

I folded myself into an uncomfortable chair by his desk and told him that I didn't have any idea. "I don't even know what's going on. When did the parrot disappear? Who would have wanted him? Have you gotten a ransom note or a call?"

I'd left the door open when I entered the office; Partin got up and walked over to close it. He stuck his head out, looked down the hall, and then swung the door shut.

"Surely you can see it," he said, as he crossed the frayed carpet back to his desk.

I couldn't. I didn't even know what he was talking about. "See what?"

91

He looked at me as if he thought I was a pretty poor example of a detective. "It was Cal Franks," he said.

"Oh. The cockatoo."

"That's right. He's been trying to get me to hire that cockatoo for the past year. He says he's not insisting on a leading role for it, not yet. A supporting role would be fine to start, he says."

"But you don't believe him."

"Of course not. But what *I* believe doesn't matter. The whole crew's against him. They don't like him, and they don't like his bird."

The part about the bird I knew already. "Are they really that serious about Cap'n Bob and the cat?" I asked. "I didn't know cartoonists used models."

Partin sighed. The bags came back into his face. "They don't, not usually. But you saw those people. They're all crazy. One of them actually put a 'Kick Me' sign on my back just yesterday."

I wasn't exactly shocked. I said, "You're kidding."

"No." He shook his head sadly. "Someone actually did it. I would never have known except that Rick Torrance kicked the hell out of me in the commissary. He thought it was a riot."

I almost hated to change the subject, but I did. I said, "Tell me what happened on the day the bird disappeared. What were the circumstances?"

"I don't really know. When we left on Monday afternoon, the parrot was in his cage. When we got here yesterday, he was gone."

Today was Wednesday, which meant that Gober had waited a day to call me. Maybe everyone had thought the parrot would come back on his own.

"What about the cockatoo?"

"Franks brought him in this morning. He said they needed a replacement for Cap'n Bob and they needed it now. They're supposed to be working on a new cartoon. *The Maltese Parrot.* Gus as Bogart, Cap'n Bob as Sidney Greenstreet. Maybe you saw the storyboards."

I had, but I hadn't noticed the subject matter. "I guess *The Maltese Cockatoo* just wouldn't work."

Partin shook his head. "It would work fine. I think. But I don't know for sure what's funny and what's not anymore, not after being around this place. I'd rather work with Rick Torrance and the elephants than those maniacs out there."

"Who was the last person to leave the building on Monday? It wouldn't have been Franks, by any chance?"

"I don't know. I went home early. I had a headache. I seem to be having a lot of them lately."

He looked like he might be having another one, not that I blamed him. I felt like having one myself.

"I want to talk to Voucher and Birch. Franks, too. Is there someplace private?"

He waved a hand to indicate his shabby office. "Nowhere but here."

"Would you mind stepping out while I talked to them?"

There was a look akin to fear on his face. "Go out there with . . . them?"

"Maybe you could walk over to the commissary, get a cup of coffee. Take an aspirin."

"Aspirin. Yes. A fine idea." He practically jumped out of his chair. "I'll just go out the back way. You can call in whoever you want."

He was out the door and gone before I had a chance to say anything else.

I went out and called Lyman Birch. When he got there, I was behind the desk, so he had to sit in the chair. He ran nervous fingers through his thin brown hair and asked me what I wanted.

"Just a little background. How much does the studio pay you for the use of your cat?"

His mouth tightened. "Are you trying to insult me?"

"Nope. Just asking."

"All right." He attempted a smile and just missed. "I was just checking. They don't pay me a thing. I'm just glad Gus is able to help out."

"And Voucher feels the same way about his bird?"

"Naturally."

Birch tried to relax, but it was impossible in that chair. He ran his fingers through his hair again. When he did, I saw something that looked like scratches just above his wrist. He saw me looking and put his hand down.

"What about Cal Franks?" I asked.

"I wouldn't want to say anything about Cal."

"Sure you would. I hear that no one likes him."

"Cal's all right. Not a bad guy at all if you get to know him."

"And he's been trying to get his bird a job here. Why is that, if there's no pay?"

"Cal just needs attention. He's always hanging around, or hadn't you noticed that?"

I'd noticed. "So he thinks if his bird got famous, he'd get plenty of attention?"

Birch shrugged. "Seems that way to me."

"How far would he go? Would he do a birdnapping?"

"Birdnapping? That's a pretty good one."

I could almost see Birch's mind working on a cartoon script. Gus stealing Cap'n Bob off the perch and holding him for ransom, maybe. I tried to bring Birch back to the subject. I said, "Would he?"

"Huh? Oh, maybe. You saw the things that go on out there. Anything could happen."

Birch was right, and that was the trouble. How could anyone tell what that bunch might do?

"Who was the last one to leave the building on Monday?" I asked.

"What?" Birch snapped to attention. "Why do you want to know?"

"I want to know who might have been alone with the bird, especially if it was Franks."

"It wasn't Franks." There was a long pause, and then Birch said, "It was me."

Well, that gave things a different slant.

"I always hang around to spend a little time with Gus," Birch explained. "He lives here now, and I like to let him out of that cage every day for a while. He needs the exercise."

That was true. If Gus were any bigger, they could use him as a stand-in for one of the tigers in Rich Torrance's next picture.

"But there's a back door that goes to the parking lot," Birch went on. "It's supposed to be locked by whoever leaves last, but I may have forgotten on Monday. The watchman usually takes care of it later if we forget, but someone could probably have come in that way after I left. And I think one of the windows might have been open. It gets stuffy in here if you close all of them."

Partin had mentioned the door but not the window. I wondered for a second or two how much *he* liked Cap'n Bob. Then I remembered that Partin was a producer. He liked anyone, or anything, that made money at the box office.

"Was there anyone else who might have wanted to get rid of the parrot?" I asked.

"No one," Birch said. "We all loved that bird. He was a gold mine."

He didn't sound exactly sincere. "The bird didn't like Gus, though," I pointed out. "I hear that when the crew needed inspiration, all they had to do was open the doors to the cages."

Birch nodded. "Gus was terrified of that bird. But he always calmed down after being attacked."

We talked a while longer, but I didn't learn any more than I'd known before. The building was easy to get into, everyone loved Cap'n Bob, and Cal Franks had ambitions for his cockatoo. I sent Birch out and asked him to invite Herm Voucher in to see me.

While I was waiting for Voucher, I telephoned Gober's secretary and told her to have the watchman get in touch with me. She complained that she'd have to wake him, but I told her it was an emergency.

Then Voucher showed up. He practically had to duck to get through the doorway. He was even more uncomfortable in the chair than Birch had been. His eyes teared up when we talked about Cap'n Bob. Or Percy, as Voucher insisted on calling him.

Voucher had thought at first that the parrot might have gotten out accidentally. "One of the windows was open. He could have gotten out of the building, but he would have come back when he was hungry."

"But he didn't," I pointed out.

"No," Voucher said. "And he was such a gentle bird, a real treasure. There was never another one like him. And to think that idiot Cal Franks thinks Percy can be replaced by a cockatoo!"

"No cockatoos!" reverberated in my head, but the ringing of the phone cleared them out. I talked to the watchman, thanked him for his time, and turned back to Voucher.

"Do you think Franks had something to do with Cap'n, uh, Percy's disappearance?" I asked.

"I wouldn't want to say anything bad about Cal," Voucher confided, "but the truth is that he's just like a lot of stage mothers I've seen. He knows *he'll* never be famous, so he wants to make his bird famous instead."

"And what about Lyman Birch?"

"What about him?"

"He loved Cap'n, uh, Percy just like everyone else?"

"Why, of course he did." Voucher's Adam's apple bobbed. "How could he not?"

Good question. I dismissed Voucher and asked him to send in Cal Franks.

Franks sat in the chair, and his toes dangled a few inches above the threadbare carpet. I'd been thinking about things, and I already knew what I was going to ask him.

"How did you know the parrot wasn't coming back?"

He was so startled that he almost fell out of the chair.

"What?" His face grew even redder than was usual with him. "What do you mean? I didn't ... I mean, how *could* I have known? I don't know what you're talking about!"

He did, though, and I told him so.

"Sure you knew. Otherwise, you wouldn't have moved that cockatoo into the cage so soon. Gober waited a day to call me about getting the parrot back, so he must have thought there was still a chance of that happening. Voucher thought so, too. But not you. You moved your bird right on in."

"I ... I knew I could move him back out if Cap'n Bob came back."

"But you aren't planning to move him, are you? You might as well tell me about it, Franks. I think I know what happened. What did you do, come in by the back way to pick up something you'd left behind and see the whole thing?"

Franks's shoulders slumped, and he leaned back in the chair. His toes were farther from the carpet than ever.

"Yes," he said. "That's what happened. How did you know?"

"Never mind that. Just tell me your side of it."

He didn't want to, but he was going to. He couldn't hold it back any longer.

"You're right," he said. "Cap'n Bob won't be back. I saw it all. My car was parked around back on Monday. When I got in, I remembered that I'd left a book at my desk. I came back to get it, and that's when it happened."

"Birch killed the bird?"

"What? No, of course not. He wouldn't do that."

"Wait a minute," I said.

Obviously I didn't have it figured quite as well as I'd thought. I'd seen something green—a feather?—in the cat's cage. There weren't any other feathers around anywhere, so it wasn't molting season. Birch, by his own admission, was the last one to leave the building, and according to the watchman, the door had been locked. Nobody else could have come in.

So I figured that Birch had finally gotten tired of the humiliation dealt out to his cat and decided to do away with the humiliator. The scratches on his arm would have come from the parrot's claws. Maybe Birch had even let the cat play with the carcass a little after it was all over. Birch was also the only one supporting Franks's plea to let the cockatoo take the parrot's place, and since no one liked Franks, I inferred that Franks had something on Birch.

It seemed that I was right about the last part, but not about the first.

"The cat killed the bird?" I said.

Franks dug around inside his jacket and came out with a handkerchief. He wiped his face, but it stayed red. He wadded the hanky and replaced it.

"That wasn't the way it happened at all," he said.

Well, nobody's right all the time. But I was doing even worse than usual.

"Why don't you tell me what happened, then." I was tired of guessing.

"Like I said, I came back inside. I guess Birch didn't hear me. He was down on the floor, playing with his cat. I must have scared him, and he jumped back and hit Cap'n Bob's cage. The cage fell over, and—"

He stopped and went for the hanky again, but I thought I could get the rest of it.

"The parrot got out," I said. "And flew out the window."

"He got out, all right," Franks told me after he'd rubbed his face. "But he didn't go for the window."

Damn. I was going to have to turn in my PI license if I didn't improve.

"Where did he go, then?"

Franks put the hanky away. "He went for Gus."

"So?"

Franks shuddered. "So Gus jumped him."

"I thought the cat was scared to death of him."

"He was. But Cap'n Bob was a little addled. The fall, I guess. He miscalculated and went by Gus and hit the cage, got a claw hooked in the wire and couldn't get loose. It was what Gus had been waiting for."

"But he didn't kill him?"

"No. But it was awful. Cap'n Bob was squawking, and Gus was yowling and scratching. The feathers were flying, and the fur, too, let me tell you. Lyman was trying to get them apart, but he couldn't."

So that's where the scratches came from.

"Something must have separated them," I said.

Franks nodded. "Finally the Cap'n got loose somehow, and started flying around the room. It didn't take him long to find the window. And then he was gone."

"Didn't you go after him?"

"Sure we went after him. He flew over the fence and landed on a palm tree."

"Did you try to get him down?"

"The tree was on a delivery truck with two or three others. It was gone before we could do a thing. God knows where it is now."

"But nobody killed the bird."

"No. But we couldn't very well tell anyone what had happened. They would have blamed us. Gober might even have fired us. So we decided just not to say a thing."

"And you brought in your cockatoo. Whose idea was that?"

Franks gave me an indignant look. "Well, it wasn't mine. Lyman thought maybe we could get by with it, substitute one for the other, but you saw how they were acting out there."

No cockatoos! I thought.

And then I thought, *But why not?* This bunch was just goofy enough to go for it.

The whole maniacal assembly was looking at me expectantly as I stood in the doorway between the cages of Gus and General Joe, which was the cockatoo's stage name.

"I've cracked the case," I said.

No one looked more surprised than Birch. "You have?"

"That's right."

"Where's my parrot, then?" Voucher asked.

"Right there," I said, pointing to the cockatoo.

"Huh?" I think all of them said it at once. And then someone said, "No cocka—"

"Hold it!" They held it. "This is *not* a cockatoo. This is Cap'n Bob in *disguise*."

"Huh?"

Birch caught on fast. "I *thought* that bird looked familiar," he said.

"Are you sure?" Voucher asked.

"Let the cat out," I said. "And we'll see."

Birch had to wake Gus first, but he finally managed to drag him out of the cage. There was a feather in there, all right. Birch and Franks had cleaned up, but they hadn't gotten that one.

Gus stretched out his front legs and spread his toes while his rear end went up high. He swished his tail a time or two.

"Now, Cal," I said, and Franks let the cockatoo out.

It was hate at first sight this time, too, and General Joe shot off the perch like a V-2. Gus sprang to a drawing board and then to the head of the guy wearing the aviator's cap. He hit a hanging light fixture as he jumped to another guy's head, and then he was back on the floor, scuttling under tables and upsetting everything while General Joe patrolled the airspace and waited for a chance to dive bomb him.

By that time people were cheering and whistling and clapping, and even Voucher believed that his parrot was back.

In disguise, of course.

When Gus cleared the tables and the cockatoo dived, I snatched up a drawing board and got it in his way just in time. He thudded into it and dropped to the floor. Franks grabbed him and stuck him in the cage. I didn't see where Gus had gone. Probably to the supply room.

Birch saw me to the door amid a general atmosphere of hilarity and relief. *The Maltese Parrot* would be finished on schedule, Franks's cockatoo would be a star (in disguise, since he'd be drawn as Cap'n Bob), Voucher had his bird back (also in disguise), and all was right with the world.

Birch thanked me and clapped me on the back as he wished me well.

When I got to the Chevy, I took the "Kick Me" sign off and threw it in the back seat before I went to tell Gober the good news.

A Crazy Business

·

John Lutz

Megan steered her Volkswagen Beetle to the curb and sat looking at the curlicued black iron gates to the Freevogel estate. Then she glanced again at the white three-by-five card with its scrawled message: "Actress wanted, to play very special role in ongoing project."

She'd noticed the card pinned to the bulletin board of the quick-stop market where she and a number of other young actresses and actors living in the nearby low-rent (for California) apartments did their shopping. Instead of merely copying the phone number, she'd taken down the card and slipped it in her purse. She had no way of knowing how long it had been pinned to the cork bulletin board, and there was no sense in letting even more people see it. Megan was in a competitive business.

After calling the phone number on the card, she hadn't been very enthusiastic. A man named Edwin had first asked for her description and credits. The description—mid-twenties, brunette, young Myrna Loy type—was fine, and quite accurate. The credits amounted only to summer stock in Wisconsin, a few television commercials in New York, then a walk-on and work as an extra in crowd scenes during the three months she'd been in California.

Then Edwin had gone all conspiratorial and told her that the job required complete confidentiality, the ability to drop out of sight for the rest of the summer, and might result in a substantial movie role. She'd told him that was a fairly conventional line, and he'd laughed and agreed, but assured her he was serious and his was a business-only proposition. And when he told her the address she was to come to for her interview, she'd agreed immediately. Why not? One thing she'd learned was that acting was a crazy business, and breaks came in strange ways. And there was something about this Edwin; he sounded like an older man, but even if he wasn't, he didn't seem at all the type who would demand that she sleep with him as part of the job.

Of course, Megan had been fooled before.

But not often enough to prevent her from taking another chance.

Now here she was, in Beverly Hills, above the smog level, sitting in the sunshine across the street from what she was sure was a fabulous mansion somewhere on the other side of the gate and beyond the fence and trees. Maybe this was a waste of time, or maybe when that gate opened it would provide access to success beyond her dreams. The diamond-bright, diamond-hard possibility of that success was always present. People broke themselves on it. Others knew they would probably break, but still they kept trying, compromising, changing, laying their hearts and hopes out to be kicked and torn. It was almost unbearably sad when she let herself think about it. Showbiz.

Megan crammed the gearshift lever into first and gunned the rattling little engine, steering the ancient VW up to the gate. She cranked down the window and pressed the red button on the intercom box. The voice she'd heard earlier on the phone—Edwin's voice—asked who was there.

"Megan Clark," she said, louder than was necessary. "I have a one-o'clock appointment."

The small metal speaker box emitted static for a moment, then became silent. Megan sat and watched some bees droning around thick honeysuckle up near the fence. One bounced off the windshield, and she hastily rolled up the window to within an inch of closing, so none of them would find their way into the car.

"Come in, please," said a voice from the intercom, and

she looked up to see the wide iron gates slowly swinging inward to admit her.

The house wasn't a disappointment. It sat at the end of the curving driveway like the realization of a dream. At its entrance was a stone portico, and on each side of the main house—which was a stone and stucco structure with a marvelous peaked tile roof—stretched many-windowed, obviously newer wings. The end of a swimming pool was visible beyond one of the wings, the California sun sparking silver off its blue water. Off to Megan's left was a stone carriage house of the sort that sheltered several vehicles below and provided living quarters for a chauffeur above. It had a steeply peaked, red tile roof like the house, and lush ivy covered one of its walls. The nearest of the three overhead doors was open, and the gleaming black trunk of a very large car was visible.

Feeling inadequate in her tiny, dusty Volkswagen, Megan parked it beneath the portico and climbed out. Its air conditioner barely worked, and perspiration caused her dress to stick to her back and thighs. She pinched the thin blue material and pulled it out away from her body, feeling cool air move beneath it. Then she bent down and peered in the car's outside mirror to make sure her hair and makeup were okay, slipped into her coolest persona, and approached the tall door and pressed the doorbell button. Westminster chimes were barely audible from deep inside the house.

She'd worn her simple but flattering navy blue dress with matching high heels and knew she looked demure but with sensual possibilities. It was cool and pleasant in the shade of the portico roof, and her confidence swelled. She'd followed Edwin's telephone instructions and hadn't told anyone about where she was going. Not even Bette Bennett, her roommate, had been taken into her confidence. Bette was a struggling actress, too, and had recently lost her part as Blanche when a local theatrical company had gone bankrupt and been forced to close *A Streetcar Named Desire*. Bette had been a perfect Blanche, but had only managed six performances. Usually the two women shared their secrets, but Megan had figured Bette wouldn't want to hear about anyone else's stroke of luck while she was still in mourning for Blanche.

The tall door opened without a sound, and there stood Edwin.

At least she presumed it was Edwin.

He proffered his hand and confirmed his identity, then ushered her into a vast foyer decorated with a red and black Oriental rug and Chinese prints. As she'd suspected, he was an older man, at least in his late forties. His face was long and somber, with gentle, watery brown eyes. He was tall, with thin arms and legs and a fleshy roundness to his torso, like a spider. The fact that he was dressed in a black pull-over shirt and white walking shorts that revealed his hairy legs added to the impression.

"We can talk in the den where we'll be comfortable, Megan. Would you like something to drink? I've a fresh pitcher of lemonade."

"That sounds wonderful," she said, and walked behind him through a hall and into a spacious room furnished in dark woods and black leather. The carpet was red, as were the floor-to-ceiling drapes. One wall was made up of shelves containing hundreds of leather-bound books, no doubt valuable collectors' items.

Megan sat down on—or rather in—a huge leather wing chair and watched Edwin pour two tall, slender glasses of lemonade from a silver and glass pitcher sitting on a tray on a polished wood credenza.

It was then that something rubbed against her right ankle and she drew in a sharp breath as her body jerked in surprise.

Then she saw that it was a large, tiger-striped orange cat, and she smiled and leaned over to pet it. The cat purred sensuously and eased its arched back and tail through the tunnel of her hand, then lay curled at her feet.

"You've passed the first test," Edwin said approaching with a glass in each hand. "Whiffy likes you."

"Whiffy?"

"Yes. He's really what this is about." He handed her one of the glasses, then gazed down at her with somber brown orbs and said earnestly, "Whiffy's a lucky cat, and he brings luck."

Megan didn't know quite what to say, so she sipped her lemonade and found it delicious. "Everyone could use a lucky cat," she finally said, realizing immediately the words were inane.

"Let's hope he's brought you luck," Edwin said with a smile. His face was lined, with bags beneath his eyes. And he had wide, full lips arcing downward even when he smiled and emphasizing rather loose jowls, as if some force beneath him more powerful than gravity were tugging hard at his features. Yet when he smiled he appeared ten years younger and was really very charming.

"This must be about more than the cat," Megan said, also smiling, beaming her own considerable charm his way.

Edwin sat down on the black leather sofa and said, "Yes, it's about Laura Weston."

That threw Megan. Laura Weston, one of the major female leads of the sixties and seventies, had committed suicide three years ago, making her movies all the more popular on cable TV and leading to something of a revival of her star status.

"Your expression suggests I've surprised you," Edwin said. "You see, though this house's owner of record is one Wayne Freevogel, it is actually owned by the Weston estate. Laura was ... well, let's say, unnaturally fond of Whiffy, and she left a great deal of money in trust to be used only for his care. Her dying wish, recorded quite poignantly on videotape, was that Whiffy's remaining life be carefree and comfortable."

"I don't see what this can possibly have to—"

Edwin smiled again and held up a hand to interrupt her. "Since Laura Weston has become quite a valuable actress since her death, the estate wishes to preserve her memory, the public's perception of her as the feisty and practical fireball beauty who first gained fame in *Border Woman* thirty years ago."

"I'm beginning to understand," Megan said. "The estate has to fulfill the requirements of the trust, but it doesn't want the public to learn that Laura Weston was the sort of woman who'd leave a fortune to her cat."

"Ah! Exactly, Megan. So Whiffy needs constant and loving care, as defined in the trust. But beyond that, the estate feels that in Laura Weston's memory it should help struggling young actresses, women such as she was before she was blessed with fame. Young women such as yourself."

Laura stared out the window, where a jay was nattering and flapping in an oleander tree. She noticed that Whiffy was staring at the bird too. "Let me see if I get this," Megan said. "You want to hire me to stay in this house secretly and take care of Whiffy?"

Whiffy contorted his body and stared up at her, smiling insofar as a cat can smile.

"More than that, Megan. I told you Whiffy was a lucky cat who brought luck, and I meant it. The estate also owns controlling interest in Blackmere Studios, as you know, one of the most successful independent producers in the business. A Blackmere crew is presently in Mexico, scouting locations and preparing to construct sets for *Low Sierra*, an epic love story about an American woman and a Mexican bandit chief who rode with Pancho Villa. The actress who cares for Whiffy through the rest of the summer will be rewarded not only with generous pay, but with a role in the film."

This was getting interesting, Megan thought. In fact, downright spellbinding. Blackmere specialized in high-budget art movies that opened on few screens but ran for months and built an audience through word of mouth and excellent reviews. Last year's production of *India, India* had garnered three Oscar nominations.

Apparently Edwin could see she was excited. "It won't be a starring role, of course," he said almost apologetically. "But you will have lines and your name will be in the credits."

She knew she was beaming. "That sounds . . . fine," she said, not wanting to make a fool of herself by sounding too eager. Fine, nothing—it sounded fabulous!

Edwin shrugged. "It can be a start, if you have the talent

and can deliver the goods. And of course your contract with
Blackmere will include a clause committing you not to
speak of your connection with the Whiffy trust, under pen-
alty of voiding the agreement."

Megan realized that Blackmere had something to gain by
getting her signature on a contract—her silence. Which
made it all the more likely that she'd get the part. At last
she had the necessary edge, the break, that gave her some
advantage over other actresses. It really was a crazy business. "When do I begin? I mean, with Whiffy?" she asked.

"As soon as possible. Tomorrow, if you don't have anything pending. Any commitments."

"Tomorrow is possible," Megan said. "I only need time
to pack."

"What about where you live? Your lease, if you have
one?"

"That won't be a problem for three months."

Edwin stood up and offered his hand again. "I'll have
our standard trust contract regarding care of Whiffy ready
for you to sign tomorrow."

She got up and almost hugged him, but she shook his
hand instead.

"The contract will reiterate," he said with a note of caution, "that due to the sensitive nature of your position, complete secrecy is necessary. Any breach of that secrecy will,
I'm afraid, necessitate legal action. Of course, being an actress, you should understand how much money is involved
in maintaining Laura Weston's public image."

"Of course! And there's something I especially like
about this job. I always thought Laura Weston was terrific!"

Edwin laughed in delight, then showed her out the way
they'd entered. "Complete secrecy," he cautioned her again,
as he shook her hand in parting. He stood in the portico and
watched her as she steered the Volkswagen down the curving drive toward the iron gates. In the rearview mirror, she
saw him slowly raise a long arm and wave to her.

Of course she told Bette.
How could she not?

Bette was the same physical type as Megan, only with red hair instead of brown. Her round and luminous green eyes were even wider than usual as Megan related what had happened at the Beverly Hills estate.

"It sounds crazy," she said, when Megan was finished talking.

Megan shrugged as she continued stuffing clothes into her old leather suitcase. "That's the kind of business we're in."

"Oh, I can't deny that." Bette padded into the kitchen in her house slippers and returned a few minutes later with a can of beer and a glass. She poured half the beer into the glass and handed it to Megan, keeping the can for herself. "I guess if I were you, I'd go for it, too," she admitted, taking a swallow of beer then wiping the back of her hand across her mouth. Nothing like the genteel coffeesipper in her television commercials.

Megan set her glass on the dresser and continued packing. "Wild as it sounds, I believe Edwin about the movie role," she said. "And I believe him when he says the Weston estate needs for the trust Laura Weston set up for her cat to remain secret. I'm counting on you not to say anything, Bette. Swearing you to secrecy."

"You know you can trust me," Bette said.

Megan smiled. "Sure I do. Or I wouldn't have confided in you. It's just that it's maybe the most important thing in my life. My career might depend on it."

Bette walked across the room and touched her shoulder. "You didn't make a mistake in telling me," she said, "and I'm flattered that you know our friendship is that close."

Megan did believe her, though she knew she hadn't confided her secret to Bette because her trust in her was complete. It was simply that she had to tell someone the fantastic thing that had happened to her. The break she needed to begin molding her dream into reality. Sharing news like that was a compulsion, and Bette was the person she trusted most.

While she didn't regret having told Bette about her arrangement with Blackmere Studios, she did have some reservations. After all, how could she know and trust her totally? After all, Bette was an actress. But Bette would surely keep quiet until Megan's star had risen, then nothing could dim its luster. Not a news story, not a lawsuit, nothing. After all, fame fed on controversy.

When Edwin had finished politely helping Megan get settled in an upstairs bedroom with a canopied bed and gold-flocked blue wallpaper, he gave her a handwritten diet for Whiffy that included tuna steaks, sardines, and even caviar. Russian only. Supplies were stored in the wine cellar and in the kitchen's ample refrigerator and freezer. "And by the way," Edwin added almost as an afterthought, "the smaller refrigerator and freezer is stocked with food for you to prepare for yourself."

They went downstairs to the kitchen, and he demonstrated where everything was and made sure Megan was familiar with the wide range of appliances.

"I wish we could supply you with a cook," he said, "but secrecy demands otherwise. For the next two months you're to remain in the house or on the grounds. I'll be traveling back and forth to the location in Mexico, where I'll spend most of the summer. I stay at an apartment owned by Blackmere Studios, but you might see me on the grounds from time to time attending to business here. The cars need to be maintained, even though they stay in the garage most of the time. And I bring a crew in twice a month to do yardwork. You're to stay out of their sight, if at all possible, and keep Whiffy indoors when work is being done. The lawn people use a great deal of equipment with sharp blades. If anything were to happen to Whiffy . . ."

"I understand," Megan assured him. As if appreciating her concern, Whiffy appeared from beneath a marble-topped table and trailed his furry body along her ankle, purring softly.

"He still likes me," Megan said. "That's good."

Edwin didn't smile when he said, "It's absolutely essential."

"Of course."

"Laura Weston was something of an eccentric," Edwin said, "like so many major stars who were not merely actors and actresses, but larger-than-life personalities of their times. Icons the likes of which we won't see again. We might not agree with all their posthumous wishes, but the law is the law, and it's firmly on Whiffy's side."

Megan looked down and smiled at the fat orange tabby. "Lucky Whiffy."

"And he brings luck," Edwin reminded her, smiling this time as brightly as his undertaker's features would allow, a charming man gradually and graciously surrendering to mortality.

The first week went slowly, then the summer arranged itself into a pleasant routine. Megan became fond of Whiffy, a cat who continually demonstrated his affection for her and seldom strayed. He did seem to take his gourmet diet for granted however, and yowled angrily at her one evening when she didn't feel like going down to the wine cellar to replenish his supply of crab meat, and tried to feed him tuna two days in a row. She didn't make that mistake again.

Megan spent most of her days reading, watching television, and eating. Her own diet was almost as tasty as Whiffy's. She began tuning in to an exercise program on TV every morning in an attempt to shed excess pounds. If everything continued to go well, she'd be in front of the cameras at the end of summer. She had no idea how she was going to be used; Mexico was a warm climate, and she might have to appear in shorts or even a scanty swimsuit. The extra flesh on her hips and thighs would have to go.

She saw Edwin only a few times, walking the grounds, entering or leaving the spacious and shadowy garage, or instructing the lawn service crew.

On the third week, she opened the door and found a large padded envelope leaning against it. Inside was the screenplay for *Low Sierra*, along with a note from Edwin instructing her to study it.

Megan fed Whiffy but skipped breakfast herself and sat out by the pool, wearing tinted glasses to protect against the reflected sunlight while she began reading the script.

She soon decided it was very good. There were only three speaking parts for women. She concluded that she was probably expected to play Hortensia, the daughter of a Mexican woman and an Irish physician who'd once saved Pancho Villa's life. Hortensia loved a doomed bandit, and pursued that love despite the admonishments of her traditional and fearful mother. Hortensia had some terrific scenes, especially one where she and the bandit made desperate love in a runaway buckboard, and she killed herself near the end of the film after learning of her lover's death at the hands of *gringo* bounty hunters. Perfect!

Megan found herself roaming around the mansion working to polish her Spanish accent, and once when she was preparing for bed she surprised herself by breaking into an impromptu flamenco dance in front of the bedroom's full-length mirror. Unable to decide if she looked sexy or simply foolish, she stopped dancing after a minute or two, but she continued to grin.

Her wanderings revealed little about the mansion. It had an oddly unlived-in feel, which wasn't surprising. Apparently no one actually did live here on a permanent basis other than Whiffy, though the pretense was maintained, even to the point of keeping several cars in the garage. In one wing was an office with a large desk and oak file cabinets, all locked. Outside of the den, kitchen, and Megan's bedroom, much of the furniture was draped in white throw covers and appeared spooky even by daylight, so she didn't go far in the rambling house after her initial exploration. She found herself spending much of her time in or by the swimming pool. It helped to pass the time, lent her supple young body a deep, even tan that made her look almost Latin, and provided the exercise needed to complement her morning calisthenics.

She thought about calling Bette and assuring her that everything was going. . . . well, swimmingly, but discovered that the phones were disconnected. And why shouldn't they be? She'd pledged her secrecy to Edwin and Blackmere Studios. A small price to pay.

It was having no one to talk to that bothered her most. In the second month she began talking to Whiffy. After all, it was better than talking to herself. He seemed to listen intently to everything she said, cocking his head to the side and occasionally switching his tail. She even began bouncing Hortensia's lines off him. He purred and arched his back sensuously, seeming to approve of her Spanish accent. She decided that only if he began reciting the doomed *bandito*'s lines would she stop talking to him.

In the first week of August, Edwin confirmed her conclusion and left instructions for her to begin studying the part of Hortensia. He also left a Spanish-language tape and a video cassette describing the Guadalajara area where most of *Low Sierra* was to be filmed.

Megan's heartbeat quickened as she studied the contents of Edwin's package, and that night she stayed up late, working on her part.

The third Saturday in August, Edwin himself appeared at the door and asked if she could be ready to leave for Mexico within the hour. He had made temporary arrangements for Whiffy, and he would drive the cat to be looked after by one of the Weston trustees, then return for Megan. He reminded her to bring her script; she might find it useful, especially if she'd made any notations on it.

After surprising herself by saying a tearful goodbye to Whiffy, the lucky cat who had indeed brought her luck, she stood in the portico and watched Edwin drive away in a black Cadillac stretch limo that he backed from the garage and maneuvered down the curved driveway. Whiffy was seated in the back of the limo, along with a supply of gourmet delectables and the rubber mouse that was one of his favorite toys, but Megan couldn't see him through the tinted windows. Had they made eye contact, she was sure he would have responded. He might see himself as a star, but he was a friendly cat.

An hour later Edwin returned and helped Megan load her suitcases into the same limo.

"It's finally time for you to relax and enjoy the trust's part of the bargain," he said with a wink, then he opened the limo's door for her.

While Edwin drove south, she sat back in the rich upholstery, sipping bottled water and watching the Mexico tape on the limo's color TV. As perfectly as everything had turned out, and bright and large as her future loomed, she still felt a remote dissatisfaction. Then she smiled as she realized the source of her vague discontent.

She missed Whiffy.

Edwin stood where Megan had stood a week earlier in the shade of the portico and watched the taxi make its way along the driveway toward the house.

The cab parked within a few feet of him, and he helped the very old man and woman from it while the driver unloaded their bags from the trunk.

"Mr. and Mrs. Freevogel," Edwin said. "You didn't have to take a cab from the airport. I would have been pleased to pick you up."

The old man, who was bent and thin and walked with a cane, waved a gnarled hand in dismissal. "No need for that, Edwin. We had no idea what time our flight would arrive, and we didn't want to phone you from London."

Edwin knew the real reason they hadn't called him was that Mr. and Mrs. Freevogel had become senile and were intimidated by the prospect of making a long-distance call.

"Have you prepared the upper floor?" Mrs. Freevogel asked. She was a short woman, thin like her husband. Though she walked without the aid of a cane, her movements were slow and arthritic.

"Everything's prepared, ma'am," Edwin said. The Freevogels spent virtually all of their time on the upper floor of the mansion, where their bedroom was located and where Edwin had the dialysis machine moved back in for Mr. Freevogel. They were both too frail to go outside often, and it was Edwin, the Freevogels' long-time factotum, who would be extremely busy the rest of the year, buying and preparing food, taking care of various other household chores, and waiting on the Freevogels.

"Ah, there's Whiffy," Mr. Freevogel said. "I thought that blasted cat would have run away by now."

"He knows when he has it good," Mrs. Freevogel said. "Edwin spoils him when we're away, don't you Edwin?"

"Yes, indeed, ma'am." He reached down and stroked Whiffy's arched, furry back.

"Lucky kitty," Mrs. Freevogel said with a dry, seamed smile. "And now, Edwin, do help us upstairs so we can rest. Summer in Switzerland is getting more tiring every year."

After getting the Freevogels settled, Edwin retired to his living quarters above the garage. His room was modest but comfortable, with furniture from the main house and a large-screen TV with a built-in video player. On almost every flat surface and on the walls and tucked in the frame of the tall dresser mirror were photographs of the late Laura Weston, whose screen image Edwin had loved passionately since his youth and *Border Woman*, when she'd been widely publicized as the new Myrna Loy.

He lifted the lid of a small cherrywood box in his dresser's top drawer, drew from it one of several locks of hair, and pressed the feathery lock to his cheek for a moment before returning it. Then he stripped down to his underwear, brushed his teeth, and went to the closet and got down the box of video cassettes that had been used most of the summer in camcorders concealed throughout the main house. He fed into the player's slot the top cassette, shot with the automatic camcorder in the guest bedroom. He pressed the "Play" button, and by the time he'd stretched out on the bed with his head propped on his pillow, his fingers laced behind his neck, Megan Clark was on the screen preparing for bed. She was smiling, obviously immensely happy.

Soon, he knew, she would do a flamenco dance.

It was late September, and Edwin had cleaned the pool and was touching up the driveway's iron gates with black enamel, when a tiny gray sports car parked across the street. A striking redheaded woman in her twenties climbed out with a great show of leg, struck a pose as she glanced around, then strode toward him. When she got closer, he saw that she had startlingly bright green eyes. Quite a beautiful woman.

She smiled dazzlingly, aiming her charm at him like a gun. "Would you be Edwin?"

He rested his paintbrush across the top of the can and straightened up.

"My name's Bette Bennett," the young woman said. "I'm a friend of Megan's."

Edwin said nothing. His blood was racing, but he kept his composure.

"You know," Bette Bennett said, "Megan Clark."

"Ah! Of course," Edwin replied. He was smiling now, thinking furiously, his mind grasping like a hand searching for something to grip. He'd been in dangerous situations before and always kept his head. His resourcefulness was a point of pride with him.

"Megan didn't tell me anything about the deal she had with you," Bette Bennett lied admirably, "but I'm afraid I snooped and found out about it. We're roommates, you know."

"Yes, Megan mentioned you. She spoke warmly of you." He'd show her how to lie.

"I'm an actress, too," she said.

He believed that one. "And a beautiful actress."

She lit up at the compliment. "It's . . . uh, been such a long time since I've seen Megan. I mean, I know she's on location in Mexico, but I got worried. I thought I'd better come here and make sure she's okay."

"Okay?" Edwin smiled. "Why, she's fine. Working out wonderfully." As he spoke, he decided he could get the rest of the week off if he told the Freevogels there was a family emergency with his mother in San Francisco. He'd done that before, hiring temporary help to stand in for him in his absence. The Freevogels believed fervently in the institution of family and didn't know Edwin's mother was long dead.

"In fact," he said, "Megan's part has been expanded. And she has a sister now. Casting's in the process of trying to find the right actress for the role. That's why the shoot's been somewhat delayed and Megan hasn't returned."

He let her get the idea. Watched her eyes really light up. They were luminous. She was truly beautiful. Even more so than Megan.

"It's been said that Megan and I are the same type," she told him, almost but not quite winking at him.

He smiled slowly. "Well, I don't know. Casting isn't part of my job. In fact, I know very little about actual moviemaking."

"Megan and I have lived together for months, almost like real sisters," Bette pointed out. Like most young actresses, she was a woman who knew how to clutch in different ways at the brass ring. And she was naive. They all were, in their fashion. It was because they believed in the dream that Hollywood offered. And why shouldn't they believe? The dream had come true for Laura Weston and many others.

"Megan did stress the confidentiality of her arrangement with Blackmere, didn't she?" Edwin asked.

Bette stood up straight as a Girl Scout. "Oh, absolutely! We both understand that. I told you, we're like sisters."

Edwin still had Megan's address up in his room. "I know this is short notice, but this is a crazy business. If I picked you up outside your apartment with the company limo early tomorrow, could you be ready to leave and spend a week on location in Mexico?"

"Oh, my God, yes!"

"I can't promise you an entire week," Edwin cautioned. "It all depends on the results of your audition. I'll give you a *Low Sierra* screenplay to study as we drive to Guadalajara."

"I'll be ready," Bette told him. "You can count on it."

Edwin smiled like a kind uncle. "Well, even if you don't land the part, at this stage of your career, it should be a profound experience for you."

"And I'll be with Megan."

A Crazy Business

"Yes," Edwin said, "I can promise you that."

"Oh, look!" Bette cried. "That must be Whiffy!"

She bent low to stroke Whiffy, who had squeezed between the iron bars of the gate and had a streak of black enamel on his tail. He purred instantly at her touch. "He's a beautiful cat."

Still smiling, gazing benignly down at Bette, Edwin said, "He's a very lucky cat, and he brings luck."

Lizzie and the Wonder Boys: A Bit of Sun Before Midnight

•

Tracy Knight

Percy Parkhoffer lay quietly in his nursing home bed, gently stroking the back of the petite calico cat that stood on his chest, kneading Percy lovingly with its claws, mesmerizing him with its half-open golden eyes. It was as if Fate or Providence, having taken note of Percy's encroaching sense of hopelessness, had gifted him with the feline, a stray adopted last week by the Hollywood Film Actors Retirement Ranch and allowed to roam the halls at will, a fluffy bundle of meandering therapy for the residents to enjoy. Percy could not have been happier or prouder that the cat had chosen to spend most of its time in his room.

He gazed at Lizzie—that's the name Percy had given her, after his favorite female foil on the vaudeville stage—and examined her closely. She was so perfectly formed. The left side of her face was pure black, the right side a sandy yellow brown. She had a snow-white vest and paws. The remainder of her body was adorned with long flowing fur, a flawless blending of her three colors. Much of the time she held her tail vertically, like a flag, as if she recognized the depth of her beauty and was unafraid to celebrate it.

"My life is so much better with you here," Percy said, patting Lizzie's tiny head over and over. She narrowed her eyes with comfort, and it almost looked like she was smiling.

Since Edgar Tillerman—Percy's partner in the comedy-psychic act, the Wonder Boys—had suffered a stroke, little sunshine seemed to warm the halls and rooms of the Film Actors Retirement Ranch. Emulating Percy's mood, the past few days had delivered an unusually persistent pattern of gray skies and winter rains.

"You're a good kitty kitty kitty," Percy crooned, voice still trembly from his own stroke six months ago. Lizzie responded by tapping him with her small paw, first on the chin, then pressing the paw against his nose and carefully drawing it down slowly across his mouth and chin, just like he'd trained her. She performed the movement in a serious, workmanlike manner, as if she'd stumbled upon a perfectly mystical genuflection to her great god Parkhoffer.

From the doorway, a harsh voice barreled in like a thunderstorm's first crash. "Time to get those lights out!" The cawing directive from the nurses' aide—her name was Cindy, according to her tag, she'd never introduced herself—provoked Lizzie to turn around, arch her back, and expel a quick *pffft* toward the invading human.

Percy sighed. "Won't be long," he said, returning his attention to Lizzie, who now closed her eyes and began purring. "Sammy Califf gave me a call a while ago. He's going to bring Edgar down before bedtime. It's his first trip outside his room since the stroke two weeks ago. One of our old comedies is playing on cable tonight. I thought we'd watch it together for awhile, until Edgar gets sleepy."

The aide walked to Percy's bedside. Her brown hair was pulled back so tightly it drew her arched eyebrows up an extra inch, adding just that much more severity to her appearance. "You know," Cindy said, ice-blue eyes flaring on her thin, angular face, "I get a little sick of you, all of you. You think that because you had some fleeting fame a lifetime ago, you shouldn't have to follow the same rules everyone else does. You know, nobody likes to work with you."

Though he should have been accustomed to her disposition after a month of listening to her, the words still stung.

Percy continued stroking Lizzie's back. After a few moments of uncomfortable silence, he said, "That's what this place is for, young lady. FARR is full of retired actors who fell on hard times. The Guild set this up so we could at least have a little dignity and comfort before we die. Now, c'mon, what's gonna be hurt by Edgar and me watching ourselves on the television?"

She crossed her arms and Percy could hear her impatiently tapping her foot against the floor. "You're losers, you know that? You used to make more money in a day of work than I do in a month . . . and just look at you."

Percy closed his eyes, pushing away the anger he felt creeping up his chest. "Young lady . . . Cindy, why don't you pet my friend Lizzie. You'll be amazed at how much she calms you down."

The aide took two steps backward and frowned in disgust, as if Percy had just exposed himself. "You keep that damned thing away from me!" she said. "I never touch cats. I hate them!"

"Hate cats? For heaven's sake, why?"

Cindy shuddered. "They're creepy, they're dishonest, and when you pick them up you can feel their guts through their skin."

Percy shook his head. He couldn't comprehend such an attitude. "Sorry you feel that way, Cindy."

"And why do you let that cat paw at your face? It's gonna claw you to shreds, and I'm going to be the one that has to clean you up."

"I taught her to do it. Only took a couple of days. She's a quick study, Lizzie is. I read a lot of psychology when I was younger; it's called 'shaping.' At first, I simply petted her every time she accidentally touched my chin and, before you knew it, we'd created our own little communication system. Every time she wants to be petted, she paws at my face—no claws either, so it won't end up being more work for you, I promise."

"Hmm. The whole thing sounds pretty stupid to me." Cindy started out of the room.

"Autumn Sprinkles," Percy called after her.

She turned back toward him, shoes squeaking on the linoleum. "What the hell are you talking about, old man?"

"Autumn Sprinkles. That's your perfume. Am I right?"

"Yes," she said, as if she resented his identification, and yet was just the tiniest bit intrigued. "How'd you know?"

"You forget, young dear, I was a professional psychic. Learned to use my senses to their utmost. You know, you should watch one of Edgar's and my films sometime, see how we performed back in the old days. In fact, you're welcome to join us tonight. Might make you laugh."

"I doubt it," she said, and disappeared into the hallway.

Percy grabbed the universal control clipped to his bedsheet and pressed the blue button until the head of his bed raised enough for proper television viewing. Lizzie meowed, expressing polite distress at her shifting, fleshy bed.

"It's okay, kiddo," Percy said, again stroking her and feeling her rumbling purrs.

He punched the remote control and the TV screen assumed a snowy glow. Then he clicked the channel selector past a panoply of rock music, cartoons and gunfire until the Classic Movie Channel appeared.

"Coming up next," a disembodied voice intoned behind a swirling color logo for the network, "Percy Parkhoffer and Edgar Tillerman—The Wonder Boys—starring in that 1938 classic *Abracadabra Dupes*! Right after these messages . . ."

Hearing the fanfare, a sense of poignant nostalgia swelled in Percy's chest. He thought he might cry. These days, it was hard to believe that the Wonder Boys had once been heralded as the hottest entertainers to grace film and stage. Now they were broken-winged sparrows in the gilded cage of the Film Actors Retirement Ranch.

"Got room for another audience member in here?" It was the FARR security man, Sammy Califf, a lanky, blond twenty-five-year-old who had become perhaps the only new friend Percy had made since his arrival two years ago. Sammy pushed the wheelchair holding Edgar, whose head bobbed to one side with the rhythm of the wheels' rotation. Sammy also managed to guide a rolling IV stand, its long tube taped to Edgar's forearm. Attached to the back of Edgar's wheelchair was a green oxygen tank, its transparent tubing extending over Edgar's shoulders and terminating in two small nodes which were inserted into his nostrils.

As Percy considered his partner's appearance, it was difficult to retain the cheerfulness he'd been committed to showing Edgar. Once jolly and round, Edgar had shrunk into a skeletal caricature of his former self. His shiny scalp was graced with only a few patches of errant white hair.

"Just in time, old buddy," Percy said, sitting up a bit farther in the bed, relegating Lizzie to coil up in his lap. "Our movie's starting in a minute."

Edgar grunted, a sound Percy had never before heard from his friend. Since Edgar's recent stroke, he was unable to speak or move the right side of his body.

Edgar raised his left hand, waving it in the direction of the drowsing Lizzie.

Marshaling the necessary will to push down his own depression, Percy assumed a friendly smile. "Oh, you mean my new girlfriend here? I'd like to introduce you to Lizzie. Edgar, Lizzie; Lizzie, Edgar. She's the finest feline friend a fellow could ask for. You know, she's supposed to roam the halls here, but she spends most all of her time with me. I guess I've still got that animal magnetism, eh?"

Edgar grunted again, then gave a brief snort, likely his attempt at laughter since the left side of his mouth curved upward, even while the right side sagged.

Sammy pushed Edgar's wheelchair and IV stand to the bedside, then rolled them backward until Edgar was sitting abreast with Percy.

"There you go, buddy," Sammy said. "Say, you guys mind if I watch a bit of the show with you?"

"Not at all."

Edgar cleared his throat, then pointed toward a pad of paper lying on Percy's bedside table.

"You want paper and pencil?" asked Sammy. He found a cushioned lap desk in a cabinet and placed it across Edgar's lap. As he handed the pad and pencil to Edgar, Sammy said, "With him having trouble talking, Edgar's spending a lot of time writing notes. Even some dirty notes to the nurses, right?"

Edgar grunted again as he scribbled on the paper. Finishing, he tapped the pad with a palsied finger, then pointed toward Percy. Sammy tore off the sheet and handed it over.

Percy read the first line. *Did you know that Marco died last night?*

"Marco," Percy said, absently rubbing Lizzie's back. "My, my. I saw him in the dining room just yesterday. He looked okay to me. That's terrible. Such a nice man. A fine singer, too. He'll be missed."

The next line read, *That's four of us in the past week.*

"Yeah," Percy said, managing a weak laugh. "We're dropping like flies, old friend. Guess we might as well expect it when we're in our eighties."

The third line stopped Percy cold. *Someone is killing us.*

He turned to Edgar, reached over and squeezed his shoulder. " 'Someone is killing us'? Mean ol' Father Time, maybe. Let's face it, partner, we're not spring chickens anymore. Hell, we're barely *winter* chickens."

Edgar looked down into his lap, seemingly disappointed at Percy's response.

"It's okay, boys," Sammy said. "No need to worry about anything. I'll look after you." Then, from behind Edgar's back, Sammy pointed to the old comedian, flattened his hand, and jiggled it back and forth, pantomiming what Percy interpreted as, "Edgar's mental faculties are shaky since the stroke."

Percy's attention was drawn to the television. "Here we go, gents, a true film classic is upon us." He punched the volume knob on the remote as the screen jumped to black-and-white life with the title credits.

The three men lapsed into easy silence as they watched the movie's opening scene, which found Percy and Edgar performing their comedy psychic act at a place called the Blue Mouse Club. Edgar was in the audience, receiving objects from audience members, the identities of which a blindfolded Percy would bumblingly, yet correctly, discern, to the audience's delight. The next scene featured the two engaged in a backstage debate, Percy arguing the necessity of continuing their act, Edgar vehemently asserting that they should hunt for a lost treasure he'd read about, punctuating his remarks by periodically bopping Percy on the forehead with a practiced aplomb only Moe Howard could equal.

The Wonder Boys had been the only performers—the *only* ones—to successfully combine a psychic act with good old slapstick.

As the singularly winding, almost incoherent plot unfolded—something about the Wonder Boys searching for a prince's lost gem from the Isle of Tantrum—Sammy laughed aloud several times. Each laugh begot a great wave of emotion within Percy. It was hard to remember, sometimes, that he and Edgar had been adored by the public; they couldn't walk down any American street without being recognized and asked for their autographs. Now they were forgotten ghosts, whiling away their final days with their fellow wraiths in this warm tomb called FARR.

Abracadabra Dupes hurtled on to its hilarious conclusion—a slapstick sequence featuring a large group of starched dilettantes, marked by Edgar's numerous hurlings of "Aztec mud pies," and Percy yanking long hatpins from his sleeve and dispatching the wide-eyed rich people, two at a time, with *boinks* to their backsides.

At the end, having chased off everyone, only Edgar and Percy remained on screen, holding the lost Gem of Tantrum to the light. The "gem" began to melt and, as it dawned on the Wonder Boys that they were now the proud owners of a fancy ice cube, they collapsed to the floor, wailing and honking dramatically as they hugged one another. Then, rising slowly, they sang the closing song in perfect harmony:

> *Though the fog is thick and gray*
> *And your friends have gone away.*
> *Though your fortunes took their flight*
> *Buddy, life's still at its height.*
> *Ohhh, ain't it a wonder, boy?*
> *Wuhhhhn—derrrr Boys.*

The end credits rolled.

God, how much like us that movie is, Percy thought. We

assumed we had created a gem of a life, but when it finally was held to the light, it melted away.

Percy was only mildly surprised to find tears rolling down his cheeks. He looked over and saw that Edgar was similarly stricken.

"Those were good times, weren't they, partner?" He reached over and rubbed the back of Edgar's neck. "Now look, you've got to work on getting better. Within a month, I expect a nice bonk on the forehead, you understand? A full bonk—no sissy stuff. Just look at me. Three months ago, I couldn't get out of bed. I'm using a walker now. Not bad, right?"

Edgar grunted, and winked with his good left eye.

As Sammy wheeled Edgar and his IV out of the room, Percy said, "I didn't know Hai Karate was still being manufactured."

Sammy turned around, puzzled. Then a smile spread across his face. "That's right, that's what I'm wearing, chief. You've still got the power." He gave the thumbs-up sign before he and Edgar departed.

Percy lowered the head on his bed. Lizzie took advantage, immediately moving up to his chest and lying down, her head underneath his chin.

"Know something, Lizzie?" Percy whispered. "I always heard that you critters sucked the breath out of babies. I'm not much use to anyone anymore, so why don't you spare a baby and take my breath instead? Would you? Would you do that for an old friend?"

Lizzie ignored him, purring her way into a sound sleep.

Midnight the next evening found Percy pressing the call button and cursing into the darkness.

Sammy stuck his head in through the doorway. "Watcha want, Percy?"

"Lizzie," he said, almost embarrassed by his need. "I haven't seen that cat all day. Where is she?"

Sammy stepped into the room. He left the lights off and pulled up a chair to Percy's bedside. "I haven't seen your cat. But I need to talk to you. The reason no one's an-

swered your call button is because something's happened."
He laid his hand on Percy's forearm. Percy knew something
was wrong, terribly wrong, just from the tone of Sammy's
voice. "I just came from Edgar's room," Sammy said.
"There are several nurses in there. The doctor's been
called."

"Is he . . . is he . . . ?"

Sammy shook his head. "I don't know, buddy. I just
don't know."

Percy raised his hands and pressed his palms against his
eyes. "Oh, Jesus. I don't know what I'll do."

Sammy gently patted Percy's arm. "Let's pray he makes
it through."

At that very moment, Cindy the aide stomped into the
room. Without so much as a rude greeting, she said, "I
hope you're happy, Mr. Pergoffer."

"Parkhoffer."

"Whatever," she spat. "You can consider yourself responsible for your friend's condition. Congratulations."

"What . . . ?"

She stomped closer, baring her teeth so much they were
visible in the near darkness; it almost looked like a smile.
"So you thought you were so smart, training that dirty cat
to tap you on the face, huh? Well, she went into Edgar's
room and managed to pull out his nasal cannula doing that
little trick you taught her. The oxygen tube slid over to one
side of his face and we didn't notice when we looked in
and checked on him. Luckily, I found the cat in there. Everybody saw me chase her out but she got away from us,
the little wench."

Percy felt life and hope exiting through the soles of his
feet. "Is Edgar dead?"

"No, but he's damned lucky just to be in a coma." Then
she turned to Sammy. "Get your lazy butt out there and
find that cat. I want it taken to the shelter and gassed or
shot or strangled or something, the sooner the better!"

"No, don't," Percy said. "Lizzie wouldn't hurt anyone."

"Do it!" Cindy shouted.

Sammy got up and scuffed one shoe against the floor. Then he shrugged and followed Cindy out of the room.

Percy closed his eyes, hoping sleep would capture him or, better yet, death. The irony of him having a role in his best friend's, his partner's, coma was beyond the ken of human tolerance.

After spending fifteen minutes unsuccessfully courting slumber, he felt something at the foot of his bed, the unmistakable deft steps of Lizzie as she began walking up the length of his body.

"Lizzie. Come here, my friend."

Arriving on his chest, Lizzie nuzzled his chin, wiping the side of her face against it. He caressed her little body and smiled weakly to himself. As he rubbed his own face against hers, requiting her love, he was struck with a sudden insight, a lightning bolt which, at first, he couldn't believe. Anger began roiling in his stomach.

Just then, every light in the room was turned on. "There it is!" yelled Cindy. "Go get that thing and take it to the shelter! And keep it away from me!"

After Percy's eye adjusted to the flood of light, he saw Sammy, shoulders slumped, standing next to the nurses' aide at the doorway. Sallow regret on his face, Sammy walked to Percy's bedside and gently wrapped his fingers around Lizzie's frame. As if she knew what was coming, the cat deployed its claws, gripping Percy with every bit of strength she owned. As Sammy pulled her off, Lizzie cried out, ripping several small holes in Percy's pajama top as she lost her hold.

Sammy did his best to cradle the cat but she was inconsolable, yowling repeatedly, flailing her limbs, sad golden eyes focused directly on Percy: *Won't you help me? I'm your friend.*

Holding the struggling Lizzie close to his body, Sammy leaned down next to Percy's ear and whispered, "Between you and me, I'm just going to put her outside. She'll have a chance that way. There are plenty of mice around. I won't take her to the shelter. I promise, okay?"

Percy managed to nod.

"If you're done with your goodbyes," Cindy said, "it's off to the gas chamber with the little murderess." She turned on her heel. Over her shoulder she said, "Consider yourself lucky if Edgar doesn't die, Parkhoffer. If he does, I'll be nominating you as an accessory to a murder."

She flicked off his lights, leaving Percy enveloped by the darkness, the grief. And the anger. Somehow—call if psychic, call it instinct, call it paying attention—he knew what had happened to his partner, and perhaps to all of their deceased friends during recent days.

But Percy was just an obsolete old man sitting on the bench, waiting to be called into death's final game. Nothing more. No one would listen.

Percy wouldn't touch food the next day, wouldn't even leave his room. He lay silently in bed, staring out the window, watching the sheets of rain pummeling the glass.

At dinnertime, Sammy appeared with a tray of food.

"You gotta eat something, friend," he said, placing the tray on the bedside table. "You can't help Edgar by starving yourself."

"How is he?"

"Still in a coma, but he's hanging in there. Now do us all a favor and eat something." Sammy began walking out of the room but then turned back, worming his bony fingers down into his front pocket. He pulled out a crumpled piece of paper, smoothed it out and laid it on Percy's chest. "Almost forgot. I found this on the floor next to Edgar's bed. Thought you'd want to have it since it's addressed to you. Doesn't seem to make any sense, though. I imagine Edgar was still having a hard time thinking."

Percy immediately raised the head of his bed, then held the note at arm's length so he could see it clearly.

Percy, my first and only friend,
Comedy is not dead, you know. In laughter lies eternal duty.

Modestly,
Edgar.

Percy looked up to Sammy's eyes.

"What do you think?" Sammy asked. "A strange good-bye note? I told you, it doesn't make any sense."

"It makes all the sense in the world. Sammy, you're the only one around here who seems to appreciate Edgar and me. So—if it's not asking too much—would you do me, do *us*, a favor, even if it sounds silly?"

"You know I would."

"I want you to keep your eyes on Cindy, that nurses' aide. She's murdering us."

"Percy . . . what are you saying? I mean, she's a crank and everything, but . . ."

"Just do it. Please. Remember—I'm the psychic."

"Okay, if you say so."

"I do. And make it stealthy, too. Don't let her know you're watching."

Eyebrows angled downward with concern, Sammy nodded and slowly backed out of the room.

Percy interlocked his fingers over his chest and sighed through his smile. For the first time in at least a decade, he felt genuinely valuable. In fact, suddenly it seemed that his life had a chance of becoming complete. If only Edgar would awaken, if only little Lizzie would return to his bosom.

Was that asking so much?

Wailing sounds pierced the dead of night and, at first, Percy thought a flock of screaming angels had come for him at last.

Sirens.

Sammy opened the door, spilling a wedge of hallway light across Percy's body. "How did you know?" Sammy asked, panting. "How did you know?"

"Why? What's happened?"

"I caught her! I caught Cindy! She was in Edgar's room, fiddling around with his IV. I saw her take out a syringe. She was going to inject something into his IV! I knew an aide wasn't supposed to be doing anything like that, so I ran in and grabbed it from her and called the nurse supervisor. She took a look at the syringe and said it was filled with insulin. Edgar isn't diabetic! It would've killed him and no one would have ever known. Cindy finally confessed that she injected him with insulin last night. *That's* what threw him into the coma; it didn't have anything to do with him losing his oxygen. That was just a cover. And she disconnected his call button so he couldn't get any help, the poor guy. Now the supervisor thinks that Cindy's done this to some of the other residents. So you see? She injected him with insulin last night, then pulled his oxygen—and blamed your cat—so people would think that that was what caused his death. But Edgar didn't die, so she was going to try and finish him off with another dose of insulin tonight." Sammy stopped for a moment and took a deep breath. Then he said, "The police have come for her. It's over. So answer me, Percy: How did you know?"

Warm tears spilled down Percy's cheeks. He smiled. "Like I said, Sammy boy, I'm a psychic. That was my life."

"Well, you're sure as hell a good one," Sammy said, moving back into the hall and joining the din of voices there.

Funny, Percy thought as he lay there in the darkness, how well the partnership worked, even though we're just two old washed-up entertainers.

Actually, he corrected himself, *two* partnerships. Edgar and me, sure, just like always. But Lizzie and me, too.

When Lizzie had slinked into his room the night Edgar slipped into his coma, when she'd rubbed her cheeks against his, Percy had immediately known something was wrong. Lizzie smelled of Autumn Sprinkles, Cindy's perfume. And, as she angrily proclaimed to anyone who'd listen, Cindy would never touch a cat. Never!

Not unless she wanted Lizzie in the room while she cast poor Edgar into oblivion. That way, she could pin Edgar's troubles on a mute, four-legged patsy. After hearing of the trick Percy had taught the cat, what better way to mask a murder?

But at the time, Percy knew that the odor of perfume on a cat's fur was flimsy evidence of anything, which is why

130

the note Edgar scribbled in his last conscious moments had proven so important.

> *Percy, my first and only friend,*
> *Comedy is not dead, you know. In laughter lies eternal*
> *duty.*
>
> > *Modestly,*
> > *Edgar.*

Of all of their methods for secretly conveying information during their comedy psychic act, it was without a doubt the most elementary. When Edgar had written "My first and only friend," he was telling his partner to pay attention only to the first letter in each word of the subsequent message.

CINDY KILLED ME

With consciousness slipping away, perhaps Edgar could think of no other way to let Percy know what Cindy had done. And perhaps Edgar trusted no one else with the truth but his oldest, dearest friend.

Fotunately, while Edgar had provided Percy with the evidence he sought, the message was literally wrong, Edgar lived, at least. Edgar lived.

Long after the sirens had retreated into the rainy Hollywood night, Percy still lay staring at his ceiling, wide-awake. It wasn't that anything was bothering him; it was just the excitement of the night, the fact that he'd shown himself, shown the world, in a tiny way no one would appreciate but him, that the Wonder Boys lived.

He was surprised to find his brain shimmering with a curious hope, and with life.

Percy heard a scratching at the window. Without looking twice, he pulled his walker to his side, eased himself out of bed, and took himself to the window as fast as his weak legs would permit.

On the sill outside, Lizzie marched back and forth, back

and forth, tail held proudly high as she gazed longingly into
the room with her golden eyes. She was sopping wet.

He pushed up the window, then the screen, and his feline
friend bounded into the room, running directly to the bed.
By the time Percy made his way back, Lizzie had taken up
residence on the pillow, making a nice wet spot there.

"Make way for a grateful old man," Percy said, sliding
under the covers. Lizzie made a little chirping sound—a
meow without opening her mouth—and politely moved to
one side. As soon as Percy laid his head on the pillow and
pulled the covers up to his neck, Lizzie leapt onto his chest
and began her slow, rhythmic trampling dance.

Within seconds, her dance slowed and she lowered herself, lying down, pushing her wet face beneath Percy's chin
and nuzzling him with affection.

"You're a good kitty kitty kitty," he cooed. "Lizzie, remind me sometime and I'll tell you all about that mean person Cindy. It'll be hard for you to believe that anyone could
hate life so much."

Lizzie turned onto her back and became blessedly tran-
quil as Percy massaged her damp belly.

"Oh . . . and thank you for remembering me. Lizzie, my
best friend Edgar—you met Edgar, of course—well, he's
sick right now, you see. I hope he wakes up. If he does,
we'll have a nice celebration, all of us. I'll spring for some
tuna fish, my friend."

Lizzie chirped in response.

Softly, Percy began to sing the song like a lullaby:
"Ohhh, ain't it a wonder, boy?"

Lizzie opened her golden eyes and meowed.

"Sorry. Ohhh, ain't it a wonder, *girl*?"

Lizzie purred and Percy hummed. Soon, together, they
drifted off into warm, untroubled sleep.

Credit the Cat

·

Jon L. Breen

Charlie—that's my grandson—always reads the credits. There he'll sit, as all the other moviegoers file out in front of him, craning his neck to see the names of the key grip, best boy, location caterer, star's personal trainer, and producer's assistant.

In my day, the credits all came at the beginning of the picture, and you only got your name in them if your work showed on the screen—and sometimes not even then. I never got and never expected screen credit in any of my various capacities: publicist, studio troubleshooter, unofficial script doctor, even less official detective. Maybe today I would. Maybe today it would say "Problem Solving Consultant—Sebastian Grady," right between Car Chase Choreographer and Wound Design Intern.

Charlie was the same way as a teenager, back in the seventies (mine and the century's) when we first got to know each other and go to the movies together. He was a funny kid, an adult in some ways and the most insecure kind of adolescent in others. He already fancied himself a movie historian, conversant with obscure names of old actors and directors his classmates never heard of—Lowell Sherman, Jack Mulhall, Glenda Farrell, Edgar G. Ulmer—and since I was a part of that history, he enjoyed my company in a way his mother for some reason thought was unhealthy. No good reason for that, except that she didn't like me because of my unavoidable association with my son, her ex-husband. I don't think my company was bad for Charlie. I wasn't a child molester or a dope peddler after all. A dream peddler, at worst.

I remember the day in the bicentennial year of 1976 we went to see a matinee of *The Pink Panther Strikes Again* in Westwood. We both loved the *Panther* series, not only for the supreme comedic ability of Peter Sellers as Inspector Clouseau but for those inspired cartoon opening credits with the Panther himself kidding and dodging. In the credits for the first movie, he'd been a sad sack victim, but after that, he always won with his pantherlike *savoir faire*, while the cartoon version of Clouseau took all the lumps.

When the picture was over, Charlie and I came out into the sunshine, squinting as we joined the surging crowds of UCLA students and other Westwood pedestrians. I proposed a postmovie hamburger, and Charlie of course agreed. I suggested a coffee shop about four blocks away, and Charlie wanted to get the car. He hated exercise in those days—still hates it, I think, but now at least he does it. I pointed out it would not be all that easy to find another place to park in Westwood at that hour of the day, and he finally agreed with my reasoning.

I still walk at a brisk pace today, and as a young man in my seventies, I was even quicker. I had to shame Charlie into keeping up with me. When we were seated looking at our menus, my grandson, apparently with a sense of wonder at my rapid pace, said, "Just how old are you anyway, grandpa?"

"Old as the century," I said.

He looked at me kind of skeptically, wondering if I was putting him on. "What does that mean?"

"Just what I said. I was born the very first day of the twentieth century. That made it my century. I own it."

"Right," he said with a smirk. "Nice of you to let the rest of us use it."

"Don't mention it."

I was never sure what else was running through his adolescent brain. If he was a normal teenager, he was entertaining lustful thoughts about Lesley-Anne Down, the female lead in the movie—I sure was. But sex was a subject I wouldn't bring up unless he did. Old movie trivia was always our common ground. Even then, he figured he knew it all, so after we'd ordered our burgers and milk shakes, I asked him how many movie references he'd spotted in the picture's opening and closing cartoon sequences.

"Aw, they're too easy," he said.

"Some of them are easy, but a couple of them are pretty hard."

"Well, let's see, I'll do the easy ones first. There was *Jaws* right at the end, and at the beginning, the Panther walked into the Alfred Hitchcock profile, and he turned into Batman and King Kong." He reeled those off nonchalantly. Even his high school classmates would have recognized those. "Then there was the dance hall come-on bit from *Sweet Charity*, and Lon Chaney getting unmasked in *The Phantom of the Opera*." He was still nonchalant, but I could tell he was proud of his lightly worn erudition. Not many high school kids would know Chaney or *The Phantom*. I don't need to remind you, this was years before the Andrew Lloyd Webber stage version.

Then our hamburgers came, and my voracious grandson consumed half of his in one bite. The refueling seemed to make Charlie cast off his sophisticated veneer and sound more like a kid when he said, "My favorite bit was when the Panther was splashing along like Gene Kelly in *Singin' in the Rain*. And how about him running across the hill like Julie Andrews in *The Sound of Music*? I'll never be able to see that again without laughing."

I agreed. "And she's the wife of the director, Blake Edwards, too. Must have some sense of humor. So, is that it? You got all of them?"

"I think so. Didn't I?"

"I believe I spotted one other."

"Oh, yeah," he said ruefully, as if hoping I wouldn't remember. "You must mean that bit where the cartoon Clouseau gets caught in a windstorm and the whole front of a house falls on his head."

"Yeah?"

"And the Panther's there, too, but it misses him because he's standing right where the open window lands." Charlie scowled, frustrated because he couldn't peg the reference. "Is that from some other cartoon, a Bugs Bunny or Road Runner or something?"

"Why do you think so?"

"Well, it's hard to imagine doing a gag like that with real people. You could use some kind of trick photography, but it'd look phony."

"It happened. And without trick photography."

"Okay, I give up," Charlie finally said after a few minutes of agonizing. "What movie is that from?"

"*Steamboat Bill, Jr.* with Buster Keaton."

"Keaton!" Charlie slapped his forehead in disgust. "You hardly ever get to see the old silents. Why is that?"

"Only a few of us still want to watch them, I guess."

"Did you know Keaton?"

I nodded casually. I have to admit I liked feeding the illusion that I knew everybody who was ever in the picture business. "Sure, I knew Buster all right. Nice fellow. Very talented. He'd started on stage with his father and mother in an act called the Three Keatons. It was known as the most violent turn in vaudeville. The whole point of the humor was that his father would throw him around and abuse him, turn him into a human mop, among other things. But of course Buster learned early to take a fall, so he'd never get hurt. The secret was never to land on the back of your head, your elbows or knees, or your tailbone. He developed that poker-faced expression as a kid, because it just made the roughhouse comedy all the funnier if he never reacted other than to look miserable. He and his father never did the act the same way twice. They'd try to surprise each other by introducing new moves into the act."

"Sort of like Inspector Clouseau and Cato," Charlie suggested.

"Right. When Keaton got into movies, around World War I, it was considered beneath the dignity of a 'legitimate' vaudeville performer. At one point, William Randolph Hearst had offered the Three Keatons a chance to do a movie series based on the *Bringing Up Father* comic strip, with Joe Keaton, Buster's father, as Jiggs. But they turned it down. Thought pictures were a passing fad, I guess. Buster left the act and broke into silents with Fatty Arbuckle. Then he moved out here with the Joe Schenck company, and after a while he was making a lot of money and using his father as a bit player in his movies. He wanted to get into making features ahead of Lloyd and Chaplin, but Schenck vetoed the idea."

I'm sure Charlie took all this information into his memory banks, but he wanted to get back to the falling house gag.

"You say they did that gag live without trick photography?"

"Sure."

"Do you know how?"

I nodded. "Buster told me about it himself. Matter of fact, he came to my office the very day after he got back from Sacramento, where they filmed the movie."

"Why did he come to see you?"

"Somebody'd tried to kill him on that shoot," I said casually.

Charlie looked suspicious. He sometimes seemed to think I was making up the stuff I told him. The fact was, I never told him anything but the truth. Didn't even embellish it much. Didn't have to.

"Okay, grandpa," he said finally. "This I got to hear."

"You'd probably like another hamburger to go with the story, huh?" I signaled the waitress and ordered him one. A second was more than I could manage, but I remembered that two hamburgers was the normal ration for a teenage metabolism.

"To begin with," I said, drawing the account out for all it was worth, "they were originally going to have a flood as the climax of the movie, which made sense because the story was all about riverboats. But Schenck vetoed it because so many people were killed in floods every year, somebody in the publicity department thought it would be in bad taste. So they decided to do a cyclone instead. Now

Buster knew very well more people were killed in cyclones and hurricanes than in floods, but he went ahead and made the change. I'm glad he did. I don't know how they could have got any footage about a flood as impressive as what they got out of their cyclone.

"The falling house gag was one Buster had thought about for years. They went about constructing the gag very carefully, as you can imagine. They started by building the framework of the house. They laid it all out on the ground, making sure the hinges were nice and strong, and built the upper-story window around Buster. The window, which would be high in the V-shaped roof, about eighteen feet from the ground. When the front of the house fell, the window would come right where Buster would be standing, allowing for a three-inch clearance all the way around."

"Three inches?" Charlie stopped in mid-gobble to consider the implications of that.

I nodded. "Three inches from each shoulder, three inches from the top of his head, three inches from his heels at the bottom."

"I think I would have allowed a little more than that."

"I think I wouldn't have tried such a fool stunt at all. But the smaller the clearance, the greater the impact of the gag would be. They marked the placed in the ground where Buster's heels would be with big nails. They had to make the false front very heavy. It weighed two tons."

"Oh, sure. If it misses, it might as well crush you completely, right?"

"There was a reason. During the sequence, they had the wind machines going to simulate the storm, and they had to be sure the phony wind wouldn't change the course of the falling wall, make it bend or twist. So it had to be heavy, and they had to be careful about the angle of the wind machines, too. They did the shot in one take, with the director hiding in his tent and the cameraman looking the other way."

"Well, I guess it worked, if Buster was there to tell you about it."

"Right. But Buster discovered just before they were go-

ing to film the gag that someone had moved the nails marking the place where he was supposed to stand."

Charlie cringed as he considered the implications.

"If he hadn't discovered it and redone the measurements,
the house would have killed him."

"Did he have any idea who did it?" Charlie asked.

"Oh, he had a suspect all picked out, and I have to admit
the guy was crazy enough to have pulled a stunt like that.
He was Hugo Formby, the cat trainer."

"A cat trainer?? You mean lions and tigers?"

"No. He trained domestic cats. He'd had an act in vaudeville for years: Formby's Cats. He claimed he could train
cats to do anything dogs could do. I never saw his act, but
those who did told me the cats did virtually nothing. He
created the illusion they were doing amazing things with
his line of patter. Well, he felt the pull of the movie business, like a lot of other people in the twenties, but his particular *shtick* didn't really lend itself to cashing in on the
movies, since his cats would be on their own without benefit of his descriptive commentary. And you can't train a
domestic cat to do all that much. Actors don't like to work
with animals anyway, and they especially don't like to
work with unreliable cats. Formby hung around the studios
for years, trying to convince people to use his cats in their
pictures, but he mostly failed."

"Come to think of it," Charlie said, "you don't see cats
that much in movies. Except cartoon cats like Sylvester or
Tom or the Pink Panther."

"Sure, because it's so hard to train them. Some say it's
because they're dumber than dogs."

"It's because they're too independent," Charlie said
fiercely. The boy always favored cats.

I nodded judiciously. "That's what others say. I don't
take sides. But I do know you can't train a cat to do tricks
like you can a dog. There's never been a cat Rin Tin Tin,
and there never will be. But try to tell Hugo Formby that.
He always claimed his cats could do anything on film a
dog could do, and he made himself a real nuisance in those
days. Everybody in town knew him, and when they saw

him coming, they'd walk in the other direction, or cross the street to avoid him. Eventually, he got real bitter about it."

Charlie was thinking back. "That old Busby Berkeley musical you took me to last week had a cat in it."

I nodded. "*Footlight Parade.* The cat Jimmy Cagney gives Frank McHugh to help him plot out a dance number."

"That cat just let people carry him around, didn't scratch or anything. I figured he was drugged."

I shrugged. "Not necessarily. Some cats are that docile. That wasn't one of Formby's cats, I don't think. He didn't sell them as docile. He sold them as doing things. His pitch was so unbelievable, I don't know if anybody even bothered to look at his cats. Come to think of it, he was long gone from Hollywood by that time anyway."

"Why did Buster Keaton think Formby would try to kill him?"

"Well, Buster refused to suspect any of the people around him, the director Chuck Reisner or the people he worked with on all his pictures, Clyde Bruckman, Fred Gabouri, and the rest. He trusted them too much. He had to blame it on an outsider, and he spotted Formby hanging around the set the morning they shot the stunt. If Formby had come up and given him his usual use-my-cats-in-your-picture pitch, Buster wouldn't have been suspicious. But Formby didn't come to make his pitch, didn't make himself known to Buster at all. So what was he doing in Sacramento that day anyhow?"

"Did you find out?"

"Sure, I went to see Formby. It was hard to find out where he lived. Nobody at the studios knew or cared. Finally, I located him in a cheap boarding house in Hollywood. He'd fallen on evil days, and I think his cats were eating better than he was. As soon as I mentioned the name Buster Keaton, he went on a tirade. He really hated Buster, and I think he had to be a little bit nuts to feel so strongly about such a decent guy. It seemed the Three Keatons had once aced him out of a spot on a bill in vaudeville that would have sent his career soaring, or at least that's the way he saw it. Then when he came to Hollywood, he expected to get some help from an old theatrical colleague, but Buster wouldn't use his cats or recommend him to anybody else. I asked Formby what he'd been doing in Sacramento while the *Steamboat Bill, Jr.* company was on location there."

"And what did he say?"

"He'd come to the end of his rope trying to sell his trained cats to moviemakers and finally decided he might have to give up movies and go back on the stage, but he'd burned his bridges with the American vaudeville circuits. He'd heard there was a representative of an Australian circuit staying in Sacramento, so he'd gone up there to give the guy his pitch. Apparently he did a good job, because the guy had offered him and his cats a Down Under tour. Formby knew Buster was in town, and as soon as he left the Australian, he'd come to Buster's movie set with the idea of gloating. 'You tried to ruin me, you acrobatic stone-faced bastard, but I have the last laugh.' At the last minute, though, he decided there wouldn't be any pleasure in a meeting with Buster: it would just give Buster a sense of relief. So Formby left without talking to anybody.

"I didn't buy his story. It sounded pretty lame to me. At the same time, I couldn't believe he would have been allowed to get anywhere near the setup for the house gag. It must have been an inside job of some sort. Trying to figure it out, kind of thinking out loud the way I do, I gave Formby most of the details: how the nails in the ground had been moved and almost nailed Buster. Formby started to get this sly look in his eye. As I talked, he was almost clapping his hands with glee, as if he couldn't wait to get out what he wanted to say next. A lot of people in Hollywood thought Formby had a screw loose, and at that moment, I could believe it.

" 'All right!' he said, a wild look in his eye. 'I confess. I did it. I tried to kill Keaton, and I'm only sorry I failed.'

"I was still skeptical. I asked him how he'd done it. He said, 'Well, of course, I had help.' He reached for a marmalade cat at the foot of his worn sofa, pulled the malleable animal up to show him to me, and said, 'It was Gladstone here who did it, really. But I taught him. I showed him how to move those nails, claw 'em out of the dirt, move 'em a few inches. You'll never take us alive.'

"I looked at Gladstone in amazement, stroked his belly admiringly, and said, "Mr. Formby, you have quite a cat here. That is truly amazing.'

" 'I agree,' Form said, 'and yet Hollywood never appreciated us and what we can do.'

" 'But this is a serious matter,' I pointed out. 'You and Gladstone are guilty of attempted murder. I really ought to tell Buster Keaton what you did. And notify the Sacramento police, of course. But I understand what drove you to it, I truly do.' I pondered for a few moments, like a judge on the bench. Finally, I said, 'I'll make you a deal. You and your cats leave Hollywood, take that Australian tour deal, and never come back here again. Do that, and I'll forget what you've told me today.'

"I could see the pride in Formby's eyes. He shook my hand and agreed to the deal. As far as I know, he never did come back to Hollywood. I never saw the guy again."

My grandson was looking skeptical. "Wait a minute, grandpa. I love cats, and I know they're really smart, but I don't see how a cat could do that. Get the nails out of the ground, maybe, but put them back in?"

"I know. I felt the same way. Formby was just a harmless crank. But why not make the poor guy feel good and rid the studios of a pest at the same time?"

"But if Formby hadn't really tried to kill Buster Keaton . . ."

"Somebody else did. Formby was doing his cat act on a stage in Melbourne or someplace by the time the second attempt on Buster's life came."

"Second attempt? There was a a second attempt?"

I nodded. "And a third."

Charlie's face was a map of exasperation. "Well, who did it?"

I looked at my watch and said blandly. "I'll have to tell you the whole story some time, but now that you've finished your hamburgers, your mom will be mad if I don't get you home in time for dinner."

My grandson Charlie's made a great career for himself. I still hear from him every once in a while, usually with a reference to our mutual love for movies. Not long ago, he was at New York University for some kind of seminar and happened into a restaurant called the Olive Tree Cafe that was showing Charlie Chaplin's *A Woman of Paris* on a big-screen TV. He wrote to reassure me the silents aren't dead. I knew that.

The Catnap

·

Les Roberts

As movie sex symbols go, Eric Winslow was pretty short, about five feet eight in his ostrich-skin boots. He insisted that they cast the supporting players in his films by their height, too, so he wouldn't look Lilliputian among them, and always made sure the cameraman kept the angle low to make him appear taller. He had blond, stringy hair and a sullen, pouty mouth, and although I thought he was far too pretty to be truly sexy, there were legions of women who disagreed with me, because he commanded about ten million bucks per picture, and his projects almost always made money.

Ten mil for eight weeks of work, and he was only twenty-seven years old.

On this particular Monday morning he was wearing tight, carefully faded jeans and a plaid western shirt to match the Southwestern decor of the house, but he didn't look much like a cowboy as he wandered the Great Plains of the living room of his hacienda-in-the-hills, sucking on a mug of coffee with his own picture on it. He'd had the house built a few years before, when earth colors accented with pastels, the "Southwestern look," had been the Los Angeles trend for about fifteen minutes, up near the top of Coldwater Canyon above Beverly Hills, not too far from the estates of Marlon Brando and Jack Nicholson. I guess he thought he ought to live up there near the two movie legends because, like them, he was a star.

144

The Catnap

Not in your wildest dreams, Bunky.

Winslow's attorney and personal manager, Alexander Halliday, was watching him stare out the window at the greenish brown foliage of summer and the brownish yellow smog that hovers over the Los Angeles basin year-round, and I was watching Halliday, one of Hollywood's most prominent power brokers, who'd called and asked me to "take a meeting" because, in addition to holding a private investigator's license, I also carry a little card that says I'm a member of the Screen Actors Guild, and he thought I'd understand his client's "need for confidentiality."

But so far Winslow had offered no confidences—not much more than a mumbled hello and a dead-mackerel handshake. He hadn't offered anything, actually, and I was coveting his morning coffee. He seemed vague and distracted. For the first few minutes I thought he was on something—downers, perhaps—until I realized he was simply a space cadet.

He was even spacey on the screen. They threw him into every big-budget picture that came along, whether he was right for the part or not. He'd walked through one of the big-money revisionist westerns like Wyatt Earp on 'ludes, he'd played a hotshot young lawyer as if he'd watched too many old reruns of *The Defenders*, and he'd even done a latter-day costume movie for which he'd learned to fence. No one was going to forget Errol Flynn because of Eric, but there was no denying the camera loved him and so, apparently, did moviegoing America.

After I'd watched him pace for a while, I raised an eyebrow at Halliday, who simply shook his head at me as an indication that I should be patient. So I waited, counting the moments of my life as they ticked by. Maybe they thought just observing America's number one box office attraction look out the window was an unrivaled treat for me.

They were wrong.

"What seems to be the problem?" I finally said.

Eric Winslow stopped walking and looked at me as if I'd belched in church. He ran the fingers of both hands through his too-long hair, then patted at it to make sure he hadn't spoiled the effect.

"The little bitch stole Tennis Shoes," he said.

I'd figured when Halliday called to ask me to meet with Eric Winslow that it had something to do with his highly publicized separation from his wife of three years, Megan Evans, who was not quite as big a star as he was but was on her way. He'd divorced his first wife when he and Megan had done a picture together in Spain, and since that time they'd been Hollywood's golden couple, the darlings of the tabloids and of *Hard Copy*, their comings and goings and dinings and dancings breathlessly reported as if civilization as we knew it revolved around where they ate lunch.

For my money they were no Tracy and Hepburn, no Bogart and Bacall, not even Dick Powell and June Allyson, and it's a sad commentary on the world we live in that people give that much of a damn about two pretty and untalented people. But when their press agents had announced they were Splitsville and that Megan was going to move in with another young, hot actor, Skyler Layne, whom she'd met on her latest film the ensuing media blitz had even knocked O.J. and Burt and Loni and Joey Buttafuoco off the front pages. Megan Evans was obviously a dangerous lady on location.

The various demands and countersuits for property division and support payments had kept America breathlessly engaged for the past two weeks, and I'd imagined that whatever investigating Winslow wanted me to do would save him a bundle. I didn't think, however, that purloined athletic footwear was important enough to hire a private detective. "Your wife stole your tennis shoes?" I said.

Winslow gave me the kind of contemptuous look usually reserved for people who say "him and me" at a Mensa meeting.

"Tennis Shoes is Eric's cat," Halliday explained.

Let me state up front that I don't dislike cats. I just don't own one because something in their dander makes me sneeze violently, but I have been known to admire them, especially in their kitten stage, and even pet one on occasion. I did break up a relationship once because the woman in question insisted on little Merlin spending the night snuggled between us and purring loudly enough to keep the neighbors awake, and for my money three in a bed is one too many, sneezes or no.

But on the whole I find cats engaging little creatures. I had my doubts, however, whether any cat was worth three hundred dollars a day for a PI's time. Plus expenses.

"I've had him for five years," Winslow elaborated in that slurry whine that set adolescent ganglia aquiver. "Even before I met her. He's no community property, damn it, he belongs to me. And when I came home last night he wasn't here. I want him back."

He gave his head a toss so that his hair shook out around his shoulders, a gesture I'd always associated with Veronica Lake. "Megan thinks she's so damn smart, but this is going to wreck her in the business." I didn't know if he meant leaving him was going to destroy her career, or stealing his cat, but either way he intoned it like a prophecy of Nostradamus.

"Is it possible that he got out of the house by accident and is wandering around somewhere?" I hoped not; the hills and canyons of Los Angeles are full of coyotes whose ecosystem had been displaced by the building of luxury homes, and wandering domestic pets didn't usually survive the night.

Winslow shook his head resolutely. "He never went out by himself. Not once in his whole life. He was a house kitty."

I sighed and took out my notebook. In my wildest imaginings I'd never believed that I would speak the next sentence in relation to a cat. "Can you describe him?" I said.

He moved across the room to a grand piano I'd bet the farm had never been played and took a framed photograph from its polished surface. "Here," he said.

Tennis Shoes, posed regally in the photo on a satin sofa cushion I recognized as the one on which I was currently sitting, was your basic garden-variety black cat with a white muzzle and four dainty white feet. Thus the name, I surmised. You can't put one over on me; that's why I get the big bucks.

"This isn't much to go on," I said. "There must be fifty thousand cats in Los Angeles that look like this."

Winslow snapped his head around to glare at me. "That's a pretty lousy thing to say."

"Take it easy, Eric," Halliday soothed.

"He'd damn well better remember who he's working for."

"At the moment I'm not working for anybody," I reminded him. "And I can live with that."

"I don't like this guy much, Alex."

"At least that levels the playing field," I said. I stood up and started for the front door, or at least where I thought the front door was. The house was so enormous, I really couldn't remember.

Alexander Halliday jumped to his feet. "Wait a minute, Mr. Saxon. I'm hiring you, not Eric. Let's not get into personalities, here. That's not the issue."

"What is the issue?"

"Getting Tennis Shoes back," Eric Winslow said. All of a sudden he sounded on the verge of tears, his eyes shiny and his little chin quivering. I guess he really was upset about Tennis Shoes, because he sure wasn't a good enough actor to make anyone think so if he wasn't.

"What about getting your wife back? Is that a possibility you'd ever consider?"

He thought about it for a while. "Sure," he said. He was easy to get along with. "If she returns my cat."

The tabloids were saying that Megan Evans had "gone into seclusion," so I figured my best starting point was with Skyler Layne. A few quick phone calls told me he was renting a house in the hills in Malibu, so I drove up there that afternoon. The traffic on the Pacific Coast Highway was as dense as it always is, and the beach homes on the ocean side of the road were built so close together that the best anyone in a moving car could hope for was a fleeting glance at the water.

As I turned up into the hills, I noted that most of the natural vegetation and been burned away by the horrendous fires of 1993, as well as several of the houses. It always amazes me that people choose to live up there; it burns out an average of once every six years or so.

Layne, at twenty-four, was pretty much in demand as an actor at the moment—in Hollywood we call guys like him "the flavor of the month"—but he was nowhere in the vicinity of Eric Winslow's money category, so I wasn't surprised to find that his rented house was an ordinary-looking ranch-style home with a small front lawn and a pool and sundeck around the side, the type of home you'd find in a middle-income housing tract in one of the dreary bedroom communities that sprawled for miles east of Los Angeles. Anywhere else the place would have gone for a hundred and twenty thousand, tops, but the breathtaking view it commanded of the Pacific Ocean probably upped its selling price to somewhere in the vicinity of three million bucks.

There was no sign of Megan Evans. Or of Tennis Shoes either, but then I remembered he was a house kitty.

They were all wannabes, these young actors with sullen good looks and no talent who blew in from the Midwest or from San Diego with visions of elbowing aside the true movie greats of the past and present for their little piece of fame pie, and although I vaguely remembered seeing Skyler Layne in a film recently, I couldn't quite remember what he looked like. I wouldn't have recognized him if he'd walked up and bitten me on the ankle.

I parked in front of the house on a crushed oyster-shell driveway, got out of the car and rang the front doorbell. I didn't hear a bing-bong from inside, so I rang again, waited, shifted my feet, glanced over my shoulder at the three-million-dollar view and tried hard to be impressed, but smog has never really been my thing.

I wasn't sure the doorbell was working, so I rapped on the thick panel with my knuckles. To my surprise the door swung open. I didn't much like the idea of that.

I stuck my head inside. "Hello? Mr. Layne?"

The only answer I got was the low hum of the air conditioner. I stepped into the tiled entry hall and took inventory.

The living room was broad and wide with a big expanse of picture window so vast that it seemed to bring indoors the well-tended half-acre of garden landscaped with exotic palms, bottlebrush and jacaranda, and some expensive statuary depicting what looked like Greek gods and goddesses in the anatomically correct nude. Inside, the carpets were green, the woodwork all blond and modern-looking, the upholstery flowery. I felt as if I'd stumbled onto the set of *The Secret Garden*.

"Skyler Layne?" I called out again.

The skin on the backs of my wrists prickled, not a good sign. I wasn't carrying a weapon—I don't usually, only when I think I might need it—but there was something in the air making me wish I was. I turned right and walked down the long hallway.

The first door I got to was the master bedroom. The bed had been slept in but not yet made. The covers on the left side were turned down, the sheets wrinkled, and several pillows were piled up, the top one bearing the imprint of a head. If Skyler Layne had slept here last night, he'd done so alone. I took a few steps into the room until I could see into the open door of the bathroom. Except for a pair of red silk hip briefs on the floor by the shower stall, it was empty.

Under my feet something crunched—it seemed to be coarse grains of sand or stone. Skyler Layne was either a pretty good housekeeper or knew where to hire one, but whoever was responsible for clean-up hadn't done a very thorough job on the kitchen floor.

I checked the guest room farther down the hall, but it hadn't been used recently. At the end of the corridor was a study, inexpensively paneled with a built-in entertainment center featuring a TV set about as big as the movie screen at the old Sepulveda Drive-In. The thought of Beavis and Butthead cavorting fifty-two inches across was enough to give anyone pause.

I went back down the hall, through the entryway and into

the kitchen. In the sink was a mug with the MGM lion's picture on it and the dregs of coffee in the bottom, and a used cereal bowl and spoon. On the counter beside the sink was a light dusting of instant coffee crystals and an opened box of Honey Nut Cheerios. Compared to most bachelor pads inhabited by young men, this one was as sterile as an operating room.

I went back out into the living room, pulled open the sliding glass door, and went out onto the patio, the wind from the nearby coast ruffling my hair.

The breeze brought with it the faint sound of music, or at least of an insistent rhythm, and I followed the noise around the side of the house, through a wrought-iron gate to the back. The pool shimmered aquamarine despite the perennial Malibu overcast, and I could see a padded lounge chair and a redwood table that matched the deck, on which a Diet Pepsi was drawing flies and a boom box the size of a freight car was pumping out noisy and irritating gangsta rap from Snoop Doggy Dogg.

Skyler Layne, it seemed, had already achieved a small measure of immortality, to take his place beside William Holden in *Sunset Boulevard* and Alan Ladd in *The Great Gatsby*. Like those legendary actors in their best roles, he floated face down in the pool, his body a ghastly grayish white and the blood from a fatal gunshot wound in his temple staining the water pink.

But there was no director around this time to yell "Cut!"

The sun had finally pounded its way through the morning haze and was drumming down on my head and neck. I'd taken off my jacket, but there was still a damp spot on my shirt at the small of my back.

"A cat?" Los Angeles sheriff's deputy John Anger, from the Malibu substation, shook his head in deep disgust. "You mean somebody's paying you big bucks to find their cat?"

"It beats holding up convenience stores," I said, tucking the photostat of my PI license back into my wallet.

"Barely. So you came up here looking for the cat, it that what you're saying?"

"I had reason to believe it might be here, yes."

"And you're not going to tell me whose cat it is?"

"Client confidentiality. Sorry."

"You're not a lawyer," he said, "you can't claim privileged information."

"No, but I'm working for a lawyer, Alexander Halliday, and that's just as good."

"We'll check that, of course."

I shrugged. "Knock yourself out."

He squeezed out a sour little smile, but a smile nonetheless. Anger was evidently not one of those cops who thought all private investigators should be banished to an island off the coast of Madagascar. We were on the pool deck behind Layne's house watching the technicians and police photographers finish up. The solitary swimmer had been fished out of the water and taken down the hill in a body bag; all that remained was an ugly pink tinge. The pool would have to be drained.

"I don't want this turning into a media circus," Anger said. "We're trying to keep the press out of this as long as we can. So you didn't know Skyler Layne?"

"I know who he is," I said. "Or was. But I'd never met him. He was renting this place, wasn't he?"

"Yeah, but don't get the idea that he was killed by mistake. The house belongs to an elderly widow who's been staying with her children in Fort Lauderdale for the last three months." He pushed his cap back on his head, revealing a startling tan line. "She lives within five hundred yards of the Pacific Ocean and she takes a vacation in Florida. Go figure."

"Any idea when he was killed?"

"We won't know until after the P.M., but from the look of him he'd only been in the water a few hours."

"If I were you, I'd try to find Megan Evans. They were engaged."

He put his fists on his hips. "I read the papers, too. But gee, thanks. You ever think about giving lectures on criminology?"

"Too busy. Right now I've got to go find a cat."

He grinned. "You're a regular one-man pussy posse, aren't you, Saxon?"

"It's a living," I said.

I drove down the hill slowly, took PCH south until I got to Santa Monica Boulevard, then turned eastward toward the towers of Venture City shimmering in the sunlight like a bad set in a science-fiction movie. Artists International Agency—AIA—had their lavish and overstated offices there, and they represented Megan Evans in all her film and television dealings.

Specifically, Barbara Milkis represented Megan Evans. Revered and even feared in certain circles, Milkis had closed some of the biggest movie deals of the sixties and seventies. She retired for five years while she got out of her system a marriage to an oil tycoon who was a minority owner of a professional football team, then came roaring back in 1991, fifty pounds heavier and wrangling a new stable of viable young clients like Megan, and proceeded to rewrite her own legend.

She never missed a premiere or a SHARE benefit, was obnoxiously active in her own favorite charities like Actors and Others for Animals and AIDS research, and with the exception of her former husband, who, for all anyone knew, she hadn't been intimate with either, she'd never been linked romantically to anyone, in or out of the movie business.

Her office, on the fortieth floor of one of the Venture City towers, was arranged so that visitors had to sit very near the floor-to-ceiling window, from which they could see the ocean and Catalina Island on the rare clear day in Los Angeles, and otherwise could nervously grip the arms of their chair, as I did, hoping their incipient vertigo wouldn't kick in and make them agree to damn near anything just so they could get out of there.

And she wasn't glad to see me.

She inspected my license and then handed it back as though it had accidentally fallen into the john. "I'd never submit you for the part of a private eye," she said in a lumberjack's voice that had been carefully cultivated by twenty-five years of Marlboros and five-to-one vodka martinis at Spago. "You don't have the psychological weight."

"Don't blame me," I said, "blame Jenny Craig."

"A smart ass, huh. Well, I'm busy as hell today, so let's not mess with each other's heads, all right? I'm not going to tell you where Megan is, and I'm not going to tell the newspaper ghouls, or the police either, should they ask. The poor kid's been through hell these last few weeks. First the break-up, and now this Skyler Layne thing."

"You heard about that already?"

"Jungle drums," she said. "Nobody in this town goes to pee without my knowing about it."

"I'll bear that in mind next time I drink a six-pack. Was Skyler Layne a client of yours, too?"

"Be real!" she said, scorn dripping from her tongue like maple sap in April. "He was nothing but a glorified dayplayer. He only wanted to marry Megan because he thought it'd make him a star—but I've got a big oil painting of *that*! In two more years his career would be dead in the . . ." She stopped, but couldn't suppress her smile. "Bad choice of words, huh?"

I had to agree with her there.

"And a bad career move for Megan, too. I hope that now she comes to her senses and patches things up with Eric."

"Eric won't care that she'd been sleeping with someone else?"

"Are you kidding? Are you kidding me? Eric Winslow has jumped every loose chickie in this town—before, during and after he married Megan, so I don't think that kind of middle-class, polyester thinking is going to enter into it. The man's got more notches on his gun than Billy the Kid."

"I never heard he had that kind of reputation."

She rolled her eyes. "Being a cocksman is politically incorrect these days, or hadn't you heard? His people always keep it pretty hush-hush."

I sighed. His "people." Nowadays, a star's entourage is almost as famous as the celebrity. You hear the whispered, awestruck buzz in the trendy restaurants of Beverly Hills and Malibu: "There's Tom Cruise's people," the fringe crowd will say. Or: "He's one of Cher's people."

"No wonder Megan left him," I said.

She glared at me through oversized, pink-tinted spectacles that went out of style in 1972. "What are you, some religious fanatic? You just don't divorce America's favorite stud-muffin and run off with fag-bait like Skyler Layne."

"He didn't have psychological weight either?"

She took a sip of chilled Evian water from a crystal goblet on her desk and relaxed her considerable bulk into the high-backed glove-leather throne on which she conducted her business. "What's your angle in this? Why do you want Megan Evans so bad?"

"I don't. I want Eric Winslow's cat."

She started to laugh. Her whole body shook with mirth, and there was enough of it to make me worry about being up here on the fortieth floor so close to the San Andreas Fault.

Finally she caught her breath and reached under her glasses with her fingers to wipe her eyes. "Oh, dear," she said, and fanned her face with her hand. "You mean to tell me Eric is actually paying a private detective to retrieve his cat? Is that what this is all about?"

"I'm not at liberty to say."

"Then you can pound sand," she said, and made a shooing motion with both hands. I felt like a chicken in the roadway.

I stood up, fighting off the rush of dizziness I always experience when I'm up high and trying not to look down forty stories, and put one of my business cards on her desk. "When you do talk to Megan, will you have her get in touch with me? Or," I added—a little archly, I admit— "have one of her people do it for her?"

Her eyes narrowed. "I certainly will," Barbara Milkis said, and with great and grave ceremony ripped the card into little pieces and tossed it into the wastebasket.

Nobody quite knows how Jackie Hatch makes his living. He lives well, in an upscale apartment just off the western

FELINE AND FAMOUS

edge of the Sunset Strip, and he's the confidante of everyone in town who matters, from Kevin Costner and Michael Ovitz to Jessica Tandy and Julia Roberts. He was a regular at the Bel Air Hotel for breakfast, Le Dome for lunch, and wherever there was a Beautiful People Party in the evening, and I don't think anyone in Hollywood has ever seen him pay for anything besides valet parking.

It's generally assumed that he's a homosexual because his walk, speech and gestures are effeminate, but no one has ever seen him *with* anybody, male or female. Appearing gay certainly got him in places he might not be allowed otherwise in Hollywood, because the female stars can relax with him as a male companion who isn't going to try and jump their bones, and the male stars can assume he's no threat to embarrass them publicly by taking women away from them. But for all I know, Jackie spends his spare time sitting in country-western bars in a muscle shirt, drinking Bud, arm wrestling, and spiriting a different woman into bed every night by telling them little harmless gossipy secrets about Denzel Washington or Demi Moore.

I found him at his usual cocktail-hour hangout, the Polo Lounge at the Beverly Hills Hotel. Trendy film-industry watering holes have come and gone over the last thirty years, but the Polo Lounge is forever. Jackie was sitting at a banquette near the door, so anyone entering couldn't possibly miss him, and he couldn't miss them, either. There was a white telephone on his table, right next to his champagne cocktail.

"Well, if it isn't the shamus-to-the-stars," he called out when he saw me, waving a languid hand in greeting. "Are you here to buy me a drink?"

I slid into the banquette beside him. "I'm here to trade you a drink."

His eyebrows arched. "For what?"

"Some information."

He idly fingered the ascot he was wearing in lieu of a necktie. "Information costs more than a drink in this town," he said. It's funny how people who live here always refer to Los Angeles, or at least to the nongeographic but spe-

The Catnap

cific psychological boundaries of Hollywood, as "this town." Often there's a rude modifier just after "this."

"Doesn't that depend on the information?"

He glanced at his Rolex. "I wouldn't tell you what time it is for less than a hundred."

"Maybe I have some information I can trade you, then."

He laughed. "I doubt that."

The cocktail waitress came over. She was gorgeous, much prettier than most beauty contest winners, and about twenty times as sensual. I ordered my favorite Scotch, Laphroaig. It's a single malt with a smoky, peaty taste that they only serve in the best places. Like the Polo Lounge.

"On the rocks?" she said. Well, maybe they don't serve that much of it.

"Neat, please—in a snifter."

Jackie pointed to his own drink and nodded, and the young woman went away to fill our order and to dream of the day when she'd have made it, when she'd be drinking a Polo Lounge champagne cocktail instead of serving them.

"What I have for you is primo, Jackie."

He leaned back in the banquette and crossed his arms across his chest, a sardonic smile twisting up one corner of his mouth. "Skyler Layne was found floating in his pool with a gunshot wound to his head at about noon, and you were the one who discovered the body," he recited.

I was a little taken aback. "I'm impressed," I said. "How did you find out?"

"I knew it three minutes after you called the authorities in Malibu. Was that your primo bombshell?"

" 'Fraid so."

He snickered, savoring his little triumph.

"You're a hard man, Jackie," I said. I took a wad of money out of my pocket—I always carry it loosely in there rather than in a wallet or money clip—and counted out five twenties and pushed them toward him. What the hell, I was on expenses; it was Eric Winslow's money anyway, and a hundred dollars to him is like a nickel to everyone else. Less, even.

Jackie didn't touch the money. "What's this for?"

"The whereabouts of Megan Evans."

He looked at me with some amusement.

"She walked out on Eric Winslow and no one has seen her since. Everybody's got to be somewhere, Jackie."

He flicked at the bills with a polished fingernail. "Divorcing the biggest star in Hollywood to marry a guy who was snuffed less than eight hours ago, this wouldn't buy you a wad of her used Kleenex."

"Suit yourself," I said. I raked the money toward me and stuffed it into my shirt pocket, and I couldn't miss the sudden flicker of panic in his eyes. He started to say something when Miss Gorgeous arrived with the drinks on a tray, bending over a trifle more than absolutely necessary when she put them on the table; for all she knew, I was an important producer or agent.

Jackie took his and swallowed half of it. "You won't find out anywhere else," he warned.

"Sure I will. I'm a detective, remember?"

"Yes, but my sources are impeccable. You know that."

"I'll find your sources, then, whoever they are, and save myself a few bucks—eliminate the middle man."

He ran his fingers up and down the stem of his glass in a gesture that can only be described as masturbatory. "Well," he said, licking his lips, "since we're old friends . . ."

I took the money out of my pocket and he snatched it away, his hand as quick as the strike of a rattlesnake.

"London," he said.

"Megan is in London?"

"At a little inn just outside, actually."

"How long has she been there?"

"Since she walked out on Eric. She's there under another name, and probably wearing a dark wig. She wants to lay low from the press until the tumult of the separation dies down." He shook his head sadly. "Bad move. It's going to hurt her with the great unwashed moviegoing public, mark my word."

"Are you sure she's in London?"

"Be serious," he said scornfully. "My source is unimpeachable."

"Who's your source?"

"If I told you that," he said, "you might give the next hundred to him." He took another sip of champagne, a smaller one now that he wasn't agitated any more. "Now you can tell me something."

"It'll cost you a hundred bucks."

He laughed. "Oh, it's not worth nearly that. Just my idle curiosity, that's all. Why do you want to find Megan Evans?"

"I don't," I said. "I'm looking for her cat."

The laughter evaporated like morning dew on an August afternoon and his expression turned pettish. "Fine, don't tell me," he snapped. He slid out from beneath the table, stepped down from the little banquette and stood looking at me, hands on top of his butt, fingers pointing toward the floor. He'd been taller sitting down.

"You're a queer duck, Saxon," he said.

"Look who's talking."

After he left I finished my drink at my leisure; Laphroaig is too good—and too expensive—to chugalug, even if you're in a hurry.

Miss Gorgeous came by with the bill, giving me another scenic view of her cleavage along with a dazzling smile. If she'd known I was an out-of-work actor and a part-time private investigator, she probably would have made a paper airplane out of it and flown it over from the bar.

The amount of the check surprised me, so I ran my finger down the items listed there. They included three champagne cocktails from before I'd arrived, as well as the drinks Jackie and I had together. I wondered who would have picked up the tab if I hadn't come in.

Somebody would have. That's just the way it works, even at the Beverly Hills Hotel.

I ransomed my car from the valet. It took a while because it was a Chevy Corsica, and they only park the Rolls-Royces and Mercedeses and Ferrari Testarossas up front where anyone can see them. I drove east on Sunset, winding past the mansions whose annual tax assessments would feed a family of four for ten years, then hit the Strip, and finally wound up in Hollywood proper, heading toward my office on Ivar Avenue just a block and a half from Hollywood and Vine, a corner fabled in folklore but now, in the nineties, about as glamorous as the boys' locker room in a junior high school.

The office was dark save for the desk lamp in my inner sanctum. My assistant, Jo Zeidler, had gone home already, but she'd left my phone messages in the middle of my blotter along with a typed note:

ALEX HALLIDAY PHONED FOUR TIMES BETWEEN 1 O'CLOCK AND 5. HE'S HYSTERICAL. CALL HIM BACK SOONEST!

J.

XOXOXOX

Jo was as fond of capital letters for emphasis as she was of kisses and hugs, although she saved the real ones for her husband Marshall, a waiter in a Westwood restaurant and screenwriter manqué.

I have my own bottle of Laphroaig stashed in a standing metal supplies cabinet—sorry, the bottom drawer of the desk is full of my pictures and resumés. I poured a stiff shot into a cardboard coffee cup, but it didn't taste as good as the one in the Polo Lounge snifter. Then I sat down and called Halliday.

"Jesus Christ, where've you been?" he said, and on the last word his voice soared up into that rarified altitude where only dogs can hear.

"Looking for your cat," I said.

"Who gives a damn about the cat anymore?" he said. "The police were at Eric's house all afternoon. They had a search warrant and everything. Don't you realize he's looking at a murder rap?"

"Did he do it?"

There was a pause, and I could hear him breathing. He sounded a little wounded. "What an absurd idea!"

"Wronged husband, crime of passion, grieving cat lover. No jury would convict him. Don't worry—he'll skate."

"You aren't funny."

That hurt. I always thought I was.

"You've got to find out who killed Skyler Layne."

"I don't investigate murders, Mr. Halliday. The police do that, and they take a dim view of private investigators getting under their feet. I could lose my license."

"Eric could lose his career."

A man had been shot in the head and left floating in his swimming pool like a fallen eucalyptus leaf—but trust a Hollywood power player like Alexander Halliday to keep his priorities straight.

"You find Layne's killer and get Eric Winslow off the hook, I'll pay you anything you want," he said.

"You still want me to look for the cat, too?" I said, but for an answer I got a dead telephone line.

I hung up and took a pull on my single-malt. After the third sip I didn't even notice the taste of the cardboard.

Megan Evans had been in London for the past two weeks, Jackie Hatch had said, and if so, her passport would verify that. So she wasn't on my short list of Skyler Layne's probable slayers. Besides, as far as I knew, she didn't have a motive. She loved the guy. Enough to walk out on a ten-million-dollar-per-picture meal ticket.

Eric Winslow, on the other hand, had a great reason for wanting his competition dead. In addition to the normal anger over loss of consort that a jilted husband might feel, there was his ego to consider. With movie actors you always have to factor in the ego. Here he is, the biggest box office star in the world, and his gorgeous young wife walks out on him for a nobody. He was probably brooding up there in his *faux* hacienda that everyone would think he was lousy in the sack—and for a sex symbol that's pretty much the kiss of death.

And movie stars like Winslow, who are accustomed to having tough guys fall at their feet with one punch, often tend to confuse the characters they play with reality.

I was liking him for the killing and feeling good about it for about fifteen minutes until it started bothering me that he'd hired me to chase down his missing cat. Not something one is likely to do on the same morning he'd taken a human life. And I'd been with Winslow at ten o'clock, and watched enviously as he drank his coffee and didn't offer me any. It was possible he'd been out at the crack of dawn to do some killing, but not likely.

My next thoughts were of Alexander Halliday. But although he might be angry with Skyler Layne for stealing Megan away from his client, killing him seemed a trifle extreme. And he'd been there at Winslow's house that morning, too.

Of course, any one of the three of them might have hired it done—but I didn't think so.

By the time I finished my drink, it was seven o'clock and I'd done a good bit of thinking. I put the bottle away, made a few phone calls, and then headed back west. The sun was a huge orange ball burning a permanent image onto my eyeballs.

The house was on the flatland just south of Sunset, the so-called low rent district in Beverly Hills, even though the homes there sold for around eight hundred thousand, six hundred of which was just so you could boast of a Beverly Hills address. On such fine points of social status was Hollywood run. I parked at the curb and walked up the flagstone path to ring the doorbell. The chimes inside sounded like Big Ben, and from around the side of the house I heard the throaty bark of a large dog, at least as big as a golden retriever.

Barbara Milkis answered the door with a martini glass in one hand and a leather-bound script under her arm. She'd switched from her office power suit to a voluminous flowing garment that used to be called a muumuu when it was popular thirty years ago. She was surprised to see me. Stunned, even.

"What the hell do you want?" she said.

"Tennis Shoes."

She cocked an eyebrow. "Are you collecting for the Good Will now?"

"That's very amusing, Ms. Milkis. But we both know that Tennis Shoes is Eric Winslow's cat."

"I don't have him."

"Are you going to invite me in?"

"No, I'm not, since I don't have the cat. Or did you come for something else, too?"

"You never know," I told her, and squeezed past her, not an easy task, since her bulk just about filled up the doorway.

Her entry hall was atrium-style, with a skylight and about twenty huge potted palms and tropical plants. I kept looking around for Stewart Granger to step out of the bush in his safari suit.

"You have a lot of balls forcing your way in here."

"See? I have more psychological weight than you thought."

"You also have one minute to state your business and get out of here."

"For starters, I'll take the cat. And if you don't hand him over, Eric Winslow will swear out an arrest warrant. For— catnapping, I guess."

She put the martini glass and the script down on a marble table and leaned against the jamb of the open door. "Megan took the cat when she moved out. It's with her— wherever she is."

"I don't think so," I said. "Megan is in London, and it so happens that England has a six-month quarantine on pets. She'd hardly have taken the animal with her."

Her eyes turned down at the corners when I mentioned London. "Pretty good, Saxon. All right, so I have the cat. Megan dropped him off here on her way to the airport. If it's important enough for you to barge into my home, I'll give him to you." She pushed herself off the door and started for the sweeping staircase. "Satisfied?"

"Not entirely. Because Megan didn't leave the cat with you, she left it with Skyler Layne."

She posed at the bottom of the staircase, head thrown back. The kind of thing Joan Crawford might have done—if Crawford had weighed two hundred and fifty pounds.

"Stefan!" she called loudly, and after a few seconds I

heard a door open toward the back of the house. Then a tall, muscular blond man came out of the kitchen in white shirt sleeves, a plain black tie and dark pants. An iron-pumper, from the look of him. I figured he was her driver—they never call them chauffeurs in Hollywood any more unless they wear livery and drive a limousine. He was about thirty, and had ice-blue eyes and one of those tight mouths you just know is going to speak with some sort of accent.

"Stefan," Milkis said, "would you show Mr. Saxon out, please?" Since I was standing about ten feet from the door, even Stefan couldn't have missed her meaning.

The blue eyes turned on me, even more icy than before, and he took a step toward me. I thought I could probably take him, but I didn't feel like trying.

"I wouldn't, Stefan," I said. I didn't give him a reason, but something in the way I said it made him think about it a little. He stopped halfway between me and his employer.

"All right, so I got the cat from Layne's," Milkis snapped. "After I talked to you I figured the poor little thing was scared to death up there, and there was nobody to feed him, so I went up and got him and brought him home here. Is that a crime or something?"

"As a matter of fact, it is—crossing a police line and violating a crime scene. But that's not what happened."

"No?"

"No. Because I walked through Layne's house before I found his body, and there was no Tennis Shoes anywhere."

"He was probably hiding under a bed."

"Did he take his litter box with him?"

"What?"

"I went into Layne's bathroom. There were little grains of sand and gravel on the floor, just like cat litter—but there was no box."

She pushed a strand of hair out of her face and looked over at Stefan.

"I think you killed Skyler Layne," I said. "You knew that if Megan left Eric Winslow for Skyler, her career would be ruined. I heard that all over town—including from you.

And you just couldn't stand the thought of all that potential money slipping through the cracks—or the scandal, which might taint your other clients. So you figured with Layne out of the way, you could make Megan come to her senses and go back to Eric, who's a much bigger star and could do her some good."

"You ought to be writing screenplays," she murmured.

"But your grand passion is animal rights, isn't it, Barbara? And you couldn't stand the thought of that poor little cat starving to death up there with no one to feed it—so you brought it home with you, and the litter box, too."

She motioned to Stefan, and suddenly there was a little .22 handgun in his meaty paw. It glistened silver in the light.

"I guess I had one detail wrong," I said, raising my hands away from my body so Stefan wouldn't get itchy. "You had your driver do it all for you." I pointed. "You'd think he'd have been smart enough to get rid of the murder weapon."

"But you won't be around to tell anybody," she said. "Stefan, take him somewhere and get rid of him."

Through the open door we all watched as three cars pulled up. One was a sheriff's vehicle, and the other two were from the Beverly Hills Police Department. Contrary to popular belief, the BHPD does not drive Lamborghinis.

"I took the liberty of telling someone already," I said, indicating the cars. "And Stefan, I'd put that thing away if I were you. If they walk in and see you with a gun in your hand, they'll just surely blow you away."

It was Deputy Anger who finally found Tennis Shoes, cowering under a bed in one of the upstairs guest rooms. He was one of those limp, hanging cats that simply relaxed every muscle when picked up, as sullen and detached as his owner, Eric Winslow.

He seemed to like me all right, though. He curled up on my lap and purred contentedly in the car, while I sneezed violently all the way up the hill into Coldwater Canyon.

The Krystal Caper

•

Jill M. Morgan

Xandra, short for Alexandra (Defender of Mankind) Adair, was known in Hollywood as the Psychic to the Stars. Her clients included some of Movieland's top celebrities, the very wealthy and the very superstitious.

A flamboyantly dressed, exotic looking woman, Xandra's dark eyes reminded the trusting who stared into them, during expensive psychic sessions, of wet obsidian. "Dark as passageways into the Otherworld," she often claimed, commenting on her extraordinary eyes. Tinted contact lenses helped that impression, as did eye drops to keep them glistening, as if her feelings were so close to the surface, she was always about to cry.

She lounged comfortably in her Bel Air home overlooking the Hollywood Hills, satisfied that her street address represented her current status. Potential clients knew by her zip code that she was one of them, not someone who might reveal their hopes and fears to the latest scandal sheet, or discuss their personal lives on talk shows. She had a reputation of being discreet and sincere. All of which cost money, lots of it.

Life hadn't always been so comfortable. She'd begun her career in Hollywood as a third-rate actress with distinctive eyes, a memorable figure, but little talent. After two lean and mean lackluster films to her credit, the outlook for a promising future in the industry looked bleak.

That's when Curtis Adair discovered her and made

The Krystal Caper

Xandra his protégé. Curtis was known in the industry as a producer's producer. He could bring in a film well under budget, and had access to some of Hollywood's most prestigious names as cast members for productions of the famous Adair Entertainment Corporation.

Like so many others, Adair had been smitten by Xandra's appearance and her image of sincerity. It was a rare combination in a community that prided itself on success and acquisitions. Willingly, he fell into the beautiful dark passageways of her eyes, so deeply, he eventually married her.

The marriage lasted a few years, long enough for Adair to realize his wife was a merchant, as was everyone else in Tinseltown. She simply sold her wares in a more exotic fashion than did most of her peers. The divorce was quiet. Xandra got the Bel Air estate, a sizable bank account that permitted her to remain in the status neighborhood, and a name she could market to the best of her abilities.

Acting was no longer an option—at least, not the sort done in films. What she'd observed in the years as Curtis Adair's wife, was the insecurity of so many of Hollywood's wealthiest actors and actresses. Everyone was only as good as their last part. Age wrinkles affected actresses; receding hairlines terrified actors. Performers were a commodity who sooner or later suffered the consequences of growing old in the public eye. Insecurity was a market Xandra knew how to promote to its best advantage.

Aware of the extremely thin boundaries of security for those in the film community, she stepped out of the film spotlight and into the cozier world of psychic channeling. She had a ready network of acquaintances whose unlisted telephone numbers were a gold mine in the making. Each number was a dollar sign, if not for that particular actor, actress or scriptwriter—writers often being the most superstitious of all—then for their friends and associates.

The cat came into the situation strictly by chance. Or fate. That sounded better for a woman who now earned her living delving into the mystic revelations of the Otherworld.

Krystal, a luxurious white Turkish Angora, had been the

gift of Octavio, one of Xandra's former romantic involvements. As a lover, Octavio had been in the triple-A league: attentive, attractive and assertive in the manner Xandra liked her men to be assertive—about loving her, about lavishing her with nice gifts, and about satisfying her every need.

Eventually, Xandra had grown bored by him, and Octavio had drifted away to pursue other interests. His hopes that the ex-wife of Curtis Adair might introduce him to the right director turned out to be disappointing for the aspiring actor. The cat, however, proved to be a well-chosen gift, one for which Xandra was extremely grateful.

The cat was the image of elegance and luxury. She was a flawless perception of feline loveliness, small boned, a thick coat of ultrasoft Angora white, pink nose and pink shells of tiny pointed ears, and the most gorgeous gold-rimmed green eyes Xandra had ever seen.

Xandra knew a good thing when she saw it. In this very special cat, she saw the future, and it was in dollar signs. She named the cat Krystal, bought herself the prerequisite crystal ball and a few other psychic phenomena accoutrements, and hung out her clairvoyant shingle.

It didn't take long to spread the word about Xandra's new talent. Friends speculated on this sudden and hitherto unknown ability.

"How is it that you've never told us before about this psychic aptitude?" asked the favorite leading lady present in a room full of beautiful people.

"That's simple," said Xandra. "Before the cat became my channeler, I didn't realize I had psychic awareness. Krystal is my familiar, my spirit guide."

The term drew some impolite laughter, until Xandra demonstrated how Krystal had advised Melanie Parks to accept the role of Audra Winston in *Green Hills of Home*. The Oscar on Melanie's mantle was a subtle, but telling, tribute to Krystal and Xandra's bankability, something the entire roomful of celebrities and movie moguls understood.

Interest in Xandra and the cat grew from that night. By nine o'clock the next morning, twelve of Hollywood's finest had phoned to schedule their own session with the Psychic to the Stars. This fact was doubly astounding, since it was generally unheard of for filmland's nobles to lift a bleary eyelid before noon.

Xandra told a worried Melanie Parks that now they were even on the debt that Melanie owed her confidante for suppressing an unpleasant little rumor about an altered identity due to felony charges still pending against a young woman from Iowa named Mary Parker. Xandra wouldn't turn in Melanie, and the Academy Award-winning actress wouldn't retract her statement about Xandra's psychic ability.

It all worked out very profitably. A month later, Xandra had more clients than she knew how to advise. She got their psychic charts mixed up, fumbled their predictions, conducted more one-sided conversations with the dead than a mortician, and raked in the money with expertly manicured nails.

It was about as perfect an acting role as Xandra could have asked for. Krystal performed superbly as the empathic medium, a channeler of the future. All that was required of the cat was to sit in a state of relaxed stillness, as though concentrating on the store of knowledge flowing through her. Xandra did the rest.

Krystal seemed to enjoy the attention devoted to her, the palm-warming strokes of her meticulously groomed white coat, living her feline life in the virtual lap of luxury. Her costume, one that showed her importance, was a diamond-studded gold collar.

Xandra flaunted her own gold and diamond jewelry at every opportunity. She was known for the golden ankh she wore from a beautifully detailed necklace. It was her trademark piece, competing with the rich display of diamonds and other elaborately set stones. The cat's diamonds were inferior quality gemstones, but genuine.

Krystal was never allowed out of the house, unless accompanied by Xandra for the taping of her weekly network TV show. It never occurred to Xandra that anyone would stoop so low as to catnap a star for its diamond collar. If it had occurred to her, she would have tied a satin bow around the cat's neck, instead.

She came home from a taping—the infomercial selling ankhs, personalized psychic charts, and publicizing her 800 number for channeling—to find her bedroom window broken, the house robbed, and Krystal stolen.

The only crime Xandra reported was the missing cat.

Losing Krystal devastated Xandra. She couldn't eat, couldn't sleep, couldn't read charts or advise her clients on anything. How could a clairvoyant see without her channeler? Everyone knew she had only gained second sight through her contact with the cat. Now, her soothseeing, moneymaking eyes had been stolen. Without Krystal, Xandra's days as Psychic to the Stars were over.

Krystal wasn't just any cat. She was a known presence, and couldn't be replaced. Even a cat that looked exactly like Krystal wouldn't work. Too many clients had stared into Krystal's mystical gold-rimmed green eyes. They knew this cat as they knew nothing else. She had bonded with them, and they would absolutely be able to tell the difference with a substitute.

Xandra was fortune-teller enough to read this future as bankruptcy and tribulation.

Never one to sink quietly into defeat, Xandra set out to gain back her cat, launching a campaign never before witnessed in the history of television. It was carried on every nightly news station, and likened by jaded broadcasters to an announcement of the Second Coming.

"Krystal, Cat Channeler to the Stars, has been stolen."

Photos of Krystal the Clairvoyant Cat were featured on the front page of every newspaper, large or small. There was no distinction. It was a story for the masses. On some level, everyone related, from karma-headed New Age-ers, to cat-wielding D.C. politicians.

Cat lovers of the United States and the world united.

It was bigger than sightings of Elvis, bigger than the sordid love life of princes, bigger than any scandal Hollywood could invent. This was *real* theater, human pathos, and the public ate it up.

The Krystal Caper

In a flurry of intense publicity, billboards, bumper stickers, even skywriting jets, advertised for the return of Krystal. The cost was exorbitant. A flood of letters poured in, sympathizing with Xandra for the loss of her beloved partner. It was wonderful publicity, the stuff of magic, but no one came forward with the missing cat.

Xandra upped the odds.

Calling forth her innermost resources as an actress, Xandra took the worldwide stage, the news media, and declared a war with the catnapper. She dressed the part, dark, loose flowing layers of a mysterious, robelike costume, the prominent display of her trademark ankh, enough diamonds and jewels to fry the receptors of half the cameras transmitting her image, and a definite air of menace toward the keeper of her cat.

Scriptwriters all over Hollywood took notes. This was a movie of the week in the making. When Xandra opened her mouth to speak, the world held its breath and listened.

"I have tried to be patient," she said. "I have waited for you, the abductor of an innocent pet, to return my beloved Krystal to her rightful place beside me. Her gentle spirit cries out to me, and I can no longer be silent."

She took a deep breath, focused her dark eyes on the cameras, and issued her threat. "Until Krystal is returned safely to me, whoever holds my cat must face the consequences. Ill luck will follow anyone who stands in the way of psychic channeling, and of the return of Krystal to her rightful home. Misfortune will grow worse and worse, the longer the innocent is kept against her will."

She stepped closer to the cameras. "I am speaking directly to you, thief." Her eyes glittered with undisguised fury. "Your future will hold nothing but misery, until you return Krystal to me. For your own sake, I warn you, restore the channeler to her soul mate, or prepare to meet your fate."

It was stirring, emotionally packed drama. Every network and cable channel carried the declaration. Xandra had drawn the line in the sand.

It took every penny she had to publicize Krystal's abduction. She mortgaged the Bel Air estate, hocked all her jewels, borrowing the ones she wore for the broadcast, and took a heavy advance against her psychic television salary—all to finance the publicity she was generating now. Without the cat, she didn't have a future in this town. It was all, or nothing.

"I want her back," said Xandra. Her eyes filled with tears, real ones. It wasn't until that moment that she realized how much she missed the cat. It wasn't about publicity anymore, or her career, or anything but the bond of . . . was it love?

When she turned away from the cameras, her eyes overflowing with genuine, heartfelt tears, the switchboard at the studio lit up with callers offering their support.

"I understand," an elderly man said. "I lost my Shasta last year."

"Don't give up," said a young woman, sounding as if she'd been crying.

The public gave her their support and sympathy. She received bundles of mail, with letters describing cats found by people trying to claim the reported reward. Some included photos. Each time Xandra stared into a photograph, she hoped, but none of them were pictures of Krystal.

Heartbroken, and having tried everything she could think to do, Xandra went home, drew the drapes and closed the door to both friends and clients, and waited.

Octavio watched the broadcast in his West Hollywood apartment. He turned up the volume, trying to drown out the noise from the crowd lined up to get into the Snake's Club across the street. Normally, he would have watched the noisy, lively youth file into the club. They were more interesting than anything on television, but not this night.

He stared at Xandra's image on the screen. The emotion seemed genuine, the tears squeezed from her eyes at exactly the right moment for maximum impact on the audience. The pathos, the human connection, even the threat of dire consequences, as if she were leveling some sort of gypsy curse. What a performance!

The Krystal Caper

The cat's claws kneaded Octavio's leg through the material of his best suit pants. Try as he might to keep the shedding creature off his lap, the cat found her way there at every opportunity. It was a lap cat, only content if she were being petted and cosseted. Xandra had spoiled the animal by constant attention. Grimacing, Octavio tried to ignore the pinpricks to his thighs.

The plan had been merely to get back at Xandra for not loving him anymore, and for giving him terrible advice on his career. He had set out to do this by taking from her what she cared about most. He'd never thought it through as far as what he would do with the cat when he got her. Now, that was becoming a problem.

He stood, dumping Krystal unceremoniously off his lap. The cat's claws dug into the fabric of his suit pants and dragged all the way to the floor. Ragged threads spiked the expensive cloth like inventive seams, ruining the only good pair of slacks Octavio owned. Worse, the sharp little claws had gone straight through to his skin. He bore red tracks on his legs.

He hopped around the room until the stinging eased. This entire plan was not working. Xandra had public sympathy on her side. No one considered him. Logic made him admit that no one knew about him, but that didn't matter. His feelings remained hurt over the way the public had surged to her in their support.

The cat found Octavio's supper on the small wooden table that served as a dining room, and lapped condescendingly at the grilled chicken breast. Krystal was used to better.

It was the only food in the house. Octavio might have snatched it back and eaten it himself—he was that hungry—but Krystal had positioned the chicken filet between two pilfering paws, and glared at Octavio with an attitude of usurper's rights. Besides, the chicken had white cat hair on it, now.

The whole apartment was covered in long, luxurious Angora cat hair, the carpet, the couch, the single chair, and especially Octavio's bed. Krystal preferred the side nearest the window.

Octavio decided, seeing the chicken disappear in tiny mouthfuls; he had to do something.

Xandra's threats didn't worry him too much. He hadn't put much faith in her psychic abilities since the disaster she'd made of his acting career. Her advice had landed him out of a steady role on a daytime soap, and into an unending turnover of casting calls for deodorant commercials, waving a feathered wing from a stuffed chicken suit outside a fast-food restaurant, and being the example of *before* for a hair replacement spot.

She had succeeded as Psychic to the Stars. He had plummeted to smelly, balding guy with the chicken feather.

He was so broke, he would have gladly sprung the cat's diamond-studded collar from its pearly neck and sold it to the highest bidder, but with all the publicity surrounding the abduction, he was sure that whoever bought it would turn him in for the sizable reward.

The cat had become more than a nuisance. She ate his food, left hair balls in his bed, and raked her way through every piece of clothing in Octavio's minimal wardrobe. He looked like something dragged through a cactus and covered in so much fur, his clothes needed shearing. He could knit his own angora sweater from the hairs that fell off when he walked.

He didn't take a single breath that didn't reek of cat. The bed smelled, the apartment smelled, he smelled. Krystal needed a bath.

Octavio didn't volunteer.

Instead, he called his sometime girlfriend, Mona. A waitress/actress, Mona went out with Octavio when she was too broke to buy food on her own. She was calculating, moneygrubbing, unintelligent, a little vicious, and beautiful. It was the beautiful part that kept Octavio showing up at her door. She didn't like him, he didn't really like her, but they provided each other with occasional comfort.

He decided he might provide Mona with a cat.

It wouldn't be a good idea to leave the collar on Krystal.

Mona would have that diamond choker off the cat and onto her wrist before Octavio was out the door. Or she'd try to sell the stones. That would put him in the place where he didn't want to be—jail.

Carefully, he removed the collar from Krystal's neck, slipping the gold chain into the pocket of his pants. He wondered how he would smuggle the cat out of the apartment without attracting unwanted attention.

A gagging sound came from behind him. Turning, Octavio saw Krystal sitting on his side of the bed, coughing up a hair ball onto his pillow.

He grabbed the cat, tossed her into a laundry bag, and slung the squirming bundle over his shoulder. Out the apartment door and down the building's steps, he ran. Nobody stopped him, but the cat's claws dug through the canvas bag and into his back.

A parking violation ticket stuck out from under the windshield wiper of his car. Handicap zone. He couldn't believe it. Furious, he bent down to check for a handicap symbol. He'd pulled into this space right after some other guy, and he'd never seen any—

The blue wheelchair motif was clearly painted on the surface of the parking space.

It had nothing to do with the clairvoyant's curse on him, absolutely nothing. Nor did the flat tire, running out of gas, or that funny sound the car's engine started making. Xandra didn't have any power over him. She was a fake.

"A cat, how cute," cooed Mona.

She was in an insecurity-induced friendly frame of mind. Her last three auditions had been washouts. Her demoralization worked for Octavio. He took advantage of her deflated ego to dump the cat, finagle a free dinner, and pursue an evening of romance with the lovely Mona.

So much for dire warnings.

"Octavio, you wonderful man."

He liked the way she said his name, rolling the vowels over her tongue as if caressing them. They kissed a lingering goodbye at the door. She gave him a bottle of wine. He went home relaxed, well fed, and feeling better about himself than he had in a very long time.

The phone's ringing jarred him awake at two in the morning. His heart did a chug or two, reminding him that he was mortal.

"What?" he asked, croaky-voiced and wits dulled by sleep deprivation.

"Get over here," came the harsh, austere, uncharitable voice of Mona the lovely. "Now!" she added, not sounding so lovely anymore.

"Mona, is something wrong?" Octavio inquired.

"Your cat, that's what's wrong," she yelled. "It's shredded my furniture, used my silk robe for a litter box, and has given me the worst sneezing fit I've ever had in my life."

"You're allergic to cats?" he asked solicitously.

"Allergic?" she wheezed into the phone. "I'm broken out in hives!"

Octavio tried to think clearly. He wasn't about to bring the cat back to his place. What could he tell her?

"Sweetheart," he said, "you'll have to keep it until morning. I have an audition first thing tomorrow. I'll swing by your house after that and we'll talk."

She sneezed into the receiver. "I'm not going to live until—"

"In the morning," Octavio said, "I promise."

He hung up, waited ten seconds for her to slam down the receiver and start to redial, then took his phone off the hook. He could imagine Mona's expression, face puffy with hives, nose red from sneezing, eyes runny as leaky faucets, and rage boiling over in the quick kettle of her brain.

Of course, he would *not* drop by in the morning, or any other time in the near future. His relationship with Mona had become awkward. Cumbersome. The truth was, he was scared of her.

He opened the bottle of wine she'd given him, drank two glasses, and went back to bed.

He woke at 9:45, the noise of a very large, dying insect droning in his ears. One cautiously raised eyelid peeked at the blur of light. The image cleared simultaneously in mind and eye; morning, very bright light, alarm clock ringing . . .

Octavio bolted out of bed, clutching his now thudding heart. His audition! How had he slept through the alarm? It was ringing its metallic little guts out, *b-r-r-ringing* away to a frenzy.

He slammed his palm onto the shut-off button. Silence struck his reeling mind with the heavy thought: *You missed your audition.* No audition, no job, no chance.

A few minutes of loud yelling produced nothing but a sore throat. Pulling at his hair only hurt his scalp. Jumping up and down brought pain to his poorly supported arches. He couldn't hurt himself enough to feel better.

He stared in unforgiving hate at the offending alarm clock, as if it had betrayed him by not ringing loud enough to shake him from his sleep, shake him out of bed. He stopped glaring at it only when he realized he was grinding his teeth down to nubs.

The perfect audition, the wonderful job . . . gone.

There was a single chance. He steeled himself to call his agent. Maybe something could be done.

"Lawrence, good morning," he sang out, seemingly full of good spirits. It was the best acting he'd done in years. "I've had a minor problem," he began, hoping to make Mount Vesuvius sound like a pimple.

"Where have you been?" Lawrence always prided himself on his mellow tone of voice, but for Octavio, it was flat with an icy edge. "The audition," his agent said meaningfully, "remember?"

"I-I'm trying to explain that, Larry. It's silly, really. My alarm—"

"I've been trying to phone you for an hour and got nothing but a busy signal."

Octavio knew why. Mona, the cat, sneezing and hives. He couldn't rid his mind of the picture of him taking the phone off the hook. Oh, he didn't feel good. It was not a nice day, It was as if . . . *Ill luck will follow anyone who stands in the way of psychic channeling, and the return of Krystal to her rightful home. Your future will hold nothing*

*but misery. For your own sake, I warn you. Prepare to meet
your fate.*

It was Xandra's fault. She had put a curse on him like a
bulldog sinking its teeth into the bone. She wouldn't give
up. It would only get worse.

"Come on, buddy," Octavio tried a little male bonding
persuasion, "it can't be that bad."

"You're finished in this town," said Lawrence, in a
voice that sounded as though he'd put on an expensive
suit with too tight a collar. "This was your last chance,
and you blew it."

Octavio had a few choice words for Larry, but the agent
hung up. For the next hour, Octavio stared into the dim re-
cesses of his room, dwelling on the fact that the final job
of his career had been in a chicken suit.

Morosely, his hands slipped into his pockets like ships
sinking into the sea, and touched the cat's collar. *Misfortune
will grow worse and worse, the longer the innocent is kept
against her will.*

How could anything get worse? What was he going to
do next, break out in boils? That was it. He had to return
the cat to Xandra. He was cursed, and her curse was going
to stick until he brought back the cat.

"Oh, God," he groaned, realizing he had to face Mona.

If he'd had a suit of armor, he'd have worn it. As it was,
he put on the clothes he'd meant to wear to the audition, a
nicely tailored shirt that showed off his chest, and his only
good pair of dress pants, the ones with claw tracks scored
down the legs.

He arrived at Mona's door with the half-empty bottle of
wine in one hand, and a bouquet of stolen flowers in the
other. He barely recognized the swollen-faced creature who
opened the door.

"Mona?"

Her eyes were nearly swelled shut. Her nose bulbed red
and porcine, looking sore and painful.

He thrust the flowers toward her. She sneezed.

"I'm here to take the cat," he said.

Her laugh was unlovely. "I booted it out hours ago." She

slammed the door in his face, reopened it, grabbed the wine, and slammed the door again.

Octavio stood on the porch, flowers in his hand, no cat. The thought surfaced to his brain, like the last air bubbles of a drowning man—No cat, no end of the curse.

The alarm clock still rang in his head, *b-r-r-ring*. He had to find that cat.

"Here, kitty," he called, staggering down the steps. "Here, Krystal."

He looked behind bushes, in alleys, on rooftops, and in fenced backyards. He met beetle-browed husbands with no sense of humor, and snarling dogs. He looked under cars, behind trash bins, around swimming pools. His knees were filthy from crawling on the ground, his hands smelled of days' old trash, and his feet were wet. And still, he had no cat.

Hair hung lankly in Octavio's eyes. He didn't want to touch his face with his fingers, they were too grimy. The sensible thing would be to go home, to give up, break out in boils or a plague of frogs . . . whatever Xandra had in store for him.

Defeated, he stumbled toward his car, when . . . a tiny *meow* rang like crystal on the air. Octavio turned, his eyes searching. No cat.

"Kitty? Here, kitty."

The *meow* rang out again, clear and sweet. It came from somewhere above him. Shading his eyes from the glare of the sun, he looked up. The cat, looking frightened and forlorn, clung unsteadily to the top branch of a tree.

It was a very tall tree.

"Come down, kitty." Octavio pressed his hands against the tree trunk, staring up. "Come on, Krystal. Here, kitty, kitty."

The cat didn't move.

The branch looked too thin to support the animal for long. A shift of weight and the limb would crack—sending Krystal, and all hope of Octavio's chance of ever breaking the curse, plummeting to the concrete sidewalk below.

"Please, please come down," he begged.

The cat didn't move.

Resigned to his fate, Octavio dropped the filched flowers and began to climb. He was at the third branch when he noticed he had gained an audience. A few kids and a couple of old guys stood at the base of the tree, watching his progress.

"Stand back in case he falls," warned one man.

Octavio felt his legs begin to quiver. He hated heights. He didn't like planes or hotel rooms in skyscrapers, and he wasn't too fond of mountains, either. He was not a climber.

That's why he had failed at his career, he thought miserably. He hadn't climbed that ladder of success. He carefully pulled himself up by the next branch and hugged the tree.

Don't look down, he thought, but couldn't help it. A real crowd had gathered. He heard their hushed silence, as if they were waiting for him to vault from the tree trunk and land broken at their feet.

"I am *not* going to fall," he muttered to himself, trying not to plead. Whining was so unattractive.

Up he climbed, valiantly working at keeping his wandering attention riveted on the cat. *Don't look.* It was a long, long way down.

The thing was, what did it matter if he fell? What did he have left? An apartment with no food, an agent who despised him, an acting career that had slid irrevocably toward a job as an orange-haired clown at kids' birthday parties.

He climbed the last two feet without breathing. Breath was too heavy. It weighed more than the thin branches could hold. In one desperate grab, Octavio snatched the cat by its fluffy middle, tucked it under one arm, and started down the tree.

The branch cracked. It gave way beneath him.

"Whoa," he yelled, as his legs skidded along the rough bark of the tree trunk, his free hand scraping uselessly at the air. The cat squirmed in his grasp, hissing and digging her tiny claws into the soft flesh of his hand.

"Oh. Ow. Oh!" he shouted. Down the tree they slid, branches breaking as they fell. A gasp rose from the crowd gathered below. He glimpsed a video camera and someone filming.

A sturdy branch caught Octavio like a horseshoe on a stake, stopping his downward plunge. He rocked sickeningly, wobbling side to side, until the stars he'd seen when he hit the branch cleared from his head. He reached out to grab the tree. The world slowly stopped spinning.

"Are you all right?" asked the man with the video camera. His jacket said something about cable TV. "Would you like some help?"

Octavio judged the remaining distance. Less than four feet. He gathered what remained of his splintered pride and descended in a little jump, grunting pathetically when he hit the ground.

The crowd surrounded him. "It's Krystal, Cat Channeler to the Stars!" someone shouted. "He saved Krystal." The film crew recorded the momentous event.

Before Octavio knew what hit him, he was bundled into the back of a news van and driven at the head of a growing parade of horn-honking vehicles to the streets of Bel Air. The sophisticated inhabitants of Bel Air did not come outside to gawk, but could be seen to peer from behind sheer drapes at the entourage.

Octavio slipped the diamond-studded collar from his pocket while in the closed quarters of the van, and fastened it around Krystal's fluffy neck. The camera crew filmed him carrying the cat to Xandra Adair's door. The nation waited. The world was poised. Octavio held the now docile cat in one hand, and knocked with the other.

The door opened a narrow crack. Xandra squinted into unaccustomed daylight. "Krystal?" She gasped. "Krystal, you've come home!"

The crowd cheered. Xandra flung the door open wide and hugged the cat. She danced into the mass of onlookers, holding her cat close to her and smiling for the camera. The story made every television station in the country, and most worldwide.

KRYSTAL, CAT CHANNELER TO THE STARS, IS RETURNED,

the national headlines read. PSYCHIC XANDRA ADAIR AND CHANNELING CAT, KRYSTAL, ARE REUNITED.

The publicity generated a renewal of interest in Xandra, and in Krystal. Soon, there was far too much work for Xandra to handle by herself. She called upon Octavio to help her, declaring him a second psychic whom Krystal had graced through her gratitude and channeling.

Octavio, for his part, didn't mind the costumes of his new life as a psychic. He had no objection to the gold and jewelry he must wear for his part, nor for the fine clothes Xandra bought him. He quickly resumed his relationship as lover to Xandra, and became known as the stalwart protector of Krystal, beloved Cat Channeler to the Stars. Like Krystal, he had come home.

He was enough of a professional not to mind third billing.

Just an Alley Cat

•

Jan Grape

Damon Dunlap got me into this mess, thought Robbie. Well, to be fair, it wasn't all Damon; their daughter Kristen had a hand in it, too. They had twisted her arm and convinced her that she and Kris should enter a big mother/daughter bowling tournament, out in Hollywood, California, not far from where Kristen and her family lived.

The Dunlaps lived in Frontier City, Texas—the county seat of Adobe County, and although it was only forty miles from Austin, it was small enough and remote enough not to have a whole lot of crime. It was a good place for a retired Austin policeman to live and be a county sheriff, which Damon was.

California, thought Robbie—movie stars, sunshine, palm trees, lush vegetation like bougainvillea, oleander, daffodils, nasturtiums, climbing roses. She knew the state had mountains and the Pacific Ocean with beaches, but unfortunately she hadn't had a chance to see many sights. The murky, smoggy air obscured the May sunshine, the mountains and the ocean. And movie stars don't usually hang out in bowling establishments, she thought. She had enjoyed the palm trees, the blooming flowers and shrubs, the few she managed to see enroute to and from Kristen's house and the bowling center. There simply wasn't time to take sightseeing excursions.

Fairways Bowl on Hollywood Boulevard was an older facility, in a rather seedy part of Hollywood, and had sus-

183

tained some damage in the recent earthquake. But the inside had been totally renovated, redecorated and new synthetic lanes had been installed. The center, Kristen explained, hoped to establish some strong regional games and eventually host a state tournament.

The outside of the building looked shabby, but the inside shone like a newly minted coin. The walls, down the length of each side, from the lane approaches to the pit areas, were decorated with carpet in shades of black, teal blue and lavender.

The same color theme had been carried out in the furniture and the carpeted floor areas. The bright, cheerful interior did nothing to quell the queasiness Robbie felt in her abdomen. Even her surprise at seeing a white kitten stroll past the snack bar didn't help. Robbie could feel her breakfast lying like a lump inside her stomach. "It's just like when I had to recite a poem or give a book report in high school—I'm petrified:" Robbie put her bowling bag on the floor and sat at the table where Kristen indicated they would sit.

"Mom, it's no big deal," said Kristen. She lifted her bag off her shoulder and placed it under the table. "It's just bowling as usual. You came out to visit and we decided to come over and roll a few games." Kristen, at thirty-four, was a little over five months pregnant and wearing the pregnancy well—her dark hair and eyes shone with vitality.

A moment later, when the kitten pounced on a tiny bit of paper on the floor, Robbie laughed. The kitten had two black dots over one eye and looked to be about three months old. It quickly tired of batting at the paper and ambled down the hallway towards the kitchen, probably for a handout, thought Robbie.

"Right. And we're going to have *fun* and maybe win enough money to cover our entry fee," Robbie said. She didn't believe it for a second. She wished she and Damon were back home in Texas. She wished she were anywhere except here at Fairways Bowl.

Robbie bowled two mornings a week at home in Frontier City. It was good exercise and got her away from her computer terminal and out among people—a plus for a writer. She'd never entered a bowling tournament before and was as nervous as that kitten would be in a room full of rocking chairs. A few minutes later she realized the kitten's antics had helped her nerves settle down.

"Kris?" Robbie asked. "Did you see a kitten stroll by a little while ago? She—well, I think she looks like a she—is so cute and funny I'm feeling much better."

"The kitten is the center's mascot. The story around here is that the cat's mother, known as City Kitty, lived in back where the pin setting machinery is located," said Kris.

"Unbelievable. With all that noise?" Robbie asked. Most cats she'd ever known hated loud noises.

"City Kitty was deaf and it didn't bother her. She'd lived here for years. The new owner's daughter wanted to take City Kitty home, but her father wouldn't let her.

"When City Kitty got pregnant, the owner's wife told her daughter that she could keep one of the kittens but later, for whatever reason, the mother said no. Homes were found for all except the runt, that little white one," said Kris. "City Kitty was killed about a month ago. I think she drank some antifreeze or something."

"How awful." Robbie shuddered. "But it's weird to see a cat in here. I've heard of businesses like bookstores and antique shops having cats, but never a bowling center."

"I guess it's just an alley cat," said Kris.

Robbie groaned at her daughter's pun and wondered what the kitten's name was—if she were mine, I'd call her Domino, because of those two spots, she thought. She liked cats, although they hadn't had one since the three Dunlap children grew up and left home.

Talking about the cats gave Robbie's mind a respite from worrying about the tournament, but she kept trying to think of other things and not her bowling.

Count your blessings, she thought, otherwise we wouldn't be having this wonderful visit with Kris, son-in-law Steve, and our precious grandson, Cason. When Steve Wolfe took a new job with a big recording label that had necessitated the move from Austin—where the Wolfes had lived—Robbie and Damon had promised to visit Glendale. At least once a year, they'd said.

Originally the plan was for a late August trip when Kristen's baby was due, a little boy the Wolfe family planned to name Riley.

"As long as we can be there when our new grandson arrives," Robbie said. "I was in the delivery room when Cason was born and am not about to miss Riley's birth."

She'd been working hard on her second mystery novel until she'd fallen into a pit called writer's block. Everyone told her the sophomore slump was perfectly normal on a second book and that she just needed a break. Damon even mentioned how she could have one of her characters hail from California and the trip considered research.

So, here she sat at Fairways Bowl getting ready to let her daughter down. Kristen was quite optimistic, but Robbie knew Kris was also very competitive. A trait her daughter was probably born with, and knowing this had added to Robbie's discomfort.

Their opponents for the first game were Denise Quayle (not related to the former vice-president) and her daughter, Linda Louise.

"That's the owner's family," said Kris. "They've only been here three or four months. I think they came from the Midwest someplace."

Denise was a tall, large-boned woman in her fifties with iron gray hair cut short as a man's and wore thick-lensed glasses, which made her blue eyes seem twice as large as they actually were.

Linda Louise was a pimply faced, overweight girl with lank, mousy-brown hair. She was a quiet seventeen-year-old who didn't smile and spoke barely above a whisper.

Robbie thought something might be wrong with the child, but she couldn't put her finger on exactly what it was.

Denise's husband, Charlie, was short, weighed about one hundred and thirty pounds sopping wet, had a fringe of white hair around an otherwise bald head, and eyes the color of a charcoal briquette. He darted from lane to lane, talking loudly as he made sure everyone had signed in and was ready to begin. When he stopped at their lanes—eleven and twelve—he barely acknowledged Robbie and Kristen.

"Aren't you ready yet, Denise?" Charlie whined. "It's time to turn the lanes on for practice."

Denise Quayle was tying her bowling shoes.

Charlie's voice became harsh as he added, "I want to see the Quayle name in the win column, Denise."

The five-minute practice was quickly over and the three-game series began. Kristen and Robbie won the first game by a good margin and after being behind in the second game, managed to squeak out a win in the last frame. Denise couldn't seem to find a strike line, but Linda Louise bowled like a robot—making numerous strikes. Her biggest problem was that when she left a ten pin, and she left it regularly, she could never pick it up—which can wreck a good game.

Eventually Robbie noticed that Linda Louise wore hearing aids in both ears; they'd been hidden by her hair. She wondered briefly if she had been born with a hearing problem. That would explain the girl not talking much and her seeming to be unfriendly.

While Robbie and Kris got ready for the final game, Charlie Quayle came over and said something to Linda Louise. Robbie didn't hear what he said, but when he walked away his daughter looked ready to cry.

Kristen started the first frame of the third game, left two pins standing, but picked them up for a spare.

When it was Robbie's turn, she almost wrenched a muscle in her leg because her left foot stuck at the line just as she threw the ball and the ball went into the channel for a zero. She called the control desk and asked to have the approach on lane twelve cleaned.

The owner was talking with a big man dressed in a three-piece tan suit, who looked like a banker, and Quayle took his own sweet time answering the intercom.

Robbie threw her second ball and only knocked down five pins because her foot stuck again.

"I don't see nothing, lady," Charlie Quayle said when he

finally came over and heard the problem. "Alls I can say is check your shoe. You probably stepped in water or something."

Robbie couldn't figure Quayle out. Was his attitude because of his wife and daughter's losses, his stress level from the tournament or what?

"We'd like to have the approach cleaned anyway," said Kristen. "If it isn't too much trouble. Since I'm pregnant, I don't want to take any chances out there."

Robbie saw the set of her daughter's jaw and knew Kristen was trying to keep her temper.

Charlie glared for a moment, then whipped a towel from his back pocket, gave the area an exaggerated swipe and stomped away.

Robbie walked disgustedly back to her chair and checked her left foot once more. "It's not my shoe. There's something on that approach."

She saw Quayle return to his conversation with the man at the control desk. The man looked angry about something and he poked his finger into Charlie Quayle's chest twice—mouthing something she couldn't hear—before turning and walking out the front door.

Maybe that *guy* has something to do with Quayle being so ill-tempered, she decided.

Linda Louise and Denise Quayle acted oblivious to the sticking problems Robbie was having. After they both got strikes on lane eleven and gave each other high fives, they moved over to lane twelve.

Linda Louise stepped on the approach to lane twelve with no hesitation. After positioning her feet, she pushed off and swung her bowling ball, moving forward to the line. Her foot stuck, then slipped and when she tried to stop, she fell flat on her face—smashing her nose and skidding part way into the conditioning oil which is put on the lanes. The foul light went on and a buzzer sounded indicating the line had been crossed; its raucous noise was heard above the falling pins in the adjoining lanes.

"Oooh, my baby," said Denise, rushing to her daughter.

"My baby's hurt." She yelled out to the control desk. "Somebody call an ambulance."

Robbie and Kristen and two other bowlers who had seen what happened hurried over to help Denise get Linda Louise up, but the young woman was out cold.

Denise sat down and reached out to cradle Linda Louise's head.

"Wait." Robbie placed her hand on Denise's shoulder. "I don't think you should move her," she said. "She might have a neck injury, too. Wait until medical help gets here."

Denise looked up directly at Robbie and whispered, "He tried to kill her."

"Who?"

Denise glanced towards the control desk.

Robbie followed the woman's gaze and saw Charlie Quayle talking on the phone—supposedly calling 911.

Denise positioned her face away from the counter and whispered, "Charlie."

Robbie was surprised by the hatred in the woman's eyes and it seemed magnified by her thick glasses. "Her father tried to kill her?"

"Yes. But he's not her father, he's her stepfather."

"Why would he try to kill your daughter?"

By then, Charlie had hung up the phone at the control desk and was making his way towards lanes eleven and twelve and the knot of people clustered around the still unconscious girl.

"She's out like a light," said Robbie as Quayle elbowed his way to the front of the group.

Charlie Quayle ignored her and stood over his wife and stepdaughter. "Can't the bitch ever do anything right?"

Robbie gasped at his cruelty.

Charlie must have suddenly realized how ugly his words sounded and turned around. Before he walked away, he muttered, "Help's coming."

It took nearly a half-hour for Linda Louise to be revived and loaded into the ambulance. The paramedics said she'd be okay, the girl only had a mild concussion, but would have to spend the night at a nearby hospital. The police came because the accident had been reported first as an assault. Denise rode in the ambulance with her daughter and thirty minutes after they'd gone, the tournament continued.

Robbie and Kristen were declared the winners by default. Since they'd already won the first two, it meant they'd swept that series.

Robbie was glad their games were scheduled later that evening. She was too upset thinking about the danger to the unborn Riley if Kris fell.

"But I didn't fall, Mom. I promised my little Riley I wouldn't take chances if I bowled."

"What if . . .?"

"It'll be okay," said Kristen. "We'll have time to settle down and when we come back tonight, we'll be ready."

When Robbie and Kristen got back to Kris's house, they put out the deli sandwiches they had picked up on the drive back. "That way we can eat and have time to relax," said Kristen.

Steve had worked that morning, but had returned home already. He and Damon had given Cason an early lunch and the little boy was in the backyard swinging on the new swing his grandpa had installed while Kristen and Robbie had been bowling.

Naturally the lunchtime conversation centered on the accident and Robbie related what Denise had said about Charlie trying to kill Linda Louise.

"Why would she make such an accusation?" asked Steve.

"She was probably just upset," said Kristen. "I don't see how she could think Charlie caused Linda Louise to fall. It looked like an accident to me."

"Unless, maybe he put something on that approach to make sure she'd fall," said Damon. With his many years of experience in law enforcement, he knew that stranger things had happened.

"A totally unreliable method of murder," said Robbie. But she couldn't forget the look in Denise's eyes.

"Theoretically, I suppose it's possible," said Damon.

"After lunch, I think I'll call the police officer who investigated and kick it around with him."

"Damon, the local police might not like a Texas sheriff nosing into their business." But Robbie knew she could have saved her breath. When Damon had questions about anything suspicious, he was like an old hound dog scenting a rabbit. He wouldn't quit until he found all the answers.

That evening Robbie and Kristen bowled well and easily won their second three-game series. Robbie's heart had stayed in her throat every time her daughter got up to the line and Kris had noticed. "I'm being careful, Mom. Relax and we'll win some games."

Denise didn't show up, but was probably staying by her daughter's side at the hospital, thought Robbie. Charlie Quayle was there, however, and was still in a bad humor. Fortunately he ignored Robbie and Kristen completely.

Kristen was elated by their win and was confident they would place in the money brackets. After they'd returned home, she kept saying she thought they had a good chance for the top five.

"Maybe you'd better prepare for losing," said Robbie. "I don't know if I can bowl that well tomorrow."

"Mom," said Kristen. "We've got a good shot here. As long as we keep focused . . ."

"Right now all I want to focus on is bed," said Robbie, yawning. "I'll see you tomorrow."

She and Damon went into the guest bedroom. When she took a good look at her husband's face, she knew Damon had been waiting to talk to her. This was a new facet to their relationship, brought about because she'd helped him with a couple of cases in recent months. Always before, he'd been close-mouthed about police business.

"I talked to that cop," said Damon.

"And . . . ?" Robbie undressed and put on her nightgown.

"They found out Linda Louise recently came into a bunch of money, inherited when her real father died. If something happened to her, Denise Quayle gets it all."

"Money is always a good motive."

"Yes. He also thinks Charlie Quayle *could* have put something on the approach to make it slippery, but he didn't think it was likely. Too much danger the wrong person would fall. The center and the owner would be subject to a lawsuit if someone else fell. He wrote it up as an accident."

"But you think there might be something he overlooked?" Robbie yawned and had a hard time keeping her eyes open as she listened.

"Not exactly. It just strikes me funny that he supposedly cleaned off the approach after you complained, yet immediately after that, Linda Louise fell. I mean, he knew the girl would be bowling next and that does bother me."

Robbie went to the bathroom, cleaned her face, quickly brushed her teeth and climbed into bed. She wanted to listen, but tonight she couldn't think, she was too tired.

Damon said, "Makes you wonder if he added something with that towel. Besides, people have come up with crazier schemes. I just can't figure out how to prove he did anything."

"I'm sorry. Can we discuss this tomorrow? I'm beat." She didn't hear his reply because, as soon as she stretched out, she was asleep.

It was late morning when Damon, Steve and Cason drove to the bowling center with Robbie and Kristen. Cason was all excited because he could watch his Granny and mother bowl. He liked bowling; he was in a kid's bumper league on Saturday mornings.

Charlie Quayle wasn't around when it was time for the opening ceremony. The employees said he hadn't been in all morning. The tournament officials ran around for fifteen minutes wondering where Charlie might be, and someone called the Quayle's house. There was no answer, although the rumor mill said that Linda Louise had left the hospital that morning just after breakfast.

Finally, when someone decided the delay couldn't continue, a brief announcement was made concerning the finals that evening and everyone was wished "Good luck and high scores," which signaled the tournament's start.

Robbie and Kristen were to bowl on lanes nineteen and twenty. Their opponents were a nice lady from Orange County and her forty-year-old daughter from Sacramento. Everyone got busy putting shoes and wrist braces on, checking the tape in their bowling balls and getting ready for practice.

Suddenly, a piercing scream from a girl on lane twelve stopped all action. Other screams followed. Robbie and Kris started towards the commotion and, as they neared, Robbie saw the body of Charlie Quayle lying across the sweeper arm of the pin setting machine—face down. He looked quite dead, and perched on his back with an air of indifference was the white kitten with two black spots above her eye.

"Oh, my stars and nightgown," said Robbie. When she turned to look for Damon, she saw he was already elbowing his way to the far wall at lane one, heading to the back of the pin decks. She looked around for Cason and saw Steve bringing him over to Kris's table. Steve maneuvered the child into a chair facing away from the bowling pins and the body. Kris gave Cason a coloring book and a box of crayons to keep him occupied.

Robbie soon found herself in the role of counselor to the girl who'd been on lane twelve when Charlie Quayle's body came sweeping out. The girl, whose name was Taffy, was nearly hysterical for a few minutes; eventually, though, Robbie got her calmed.

In the midst of helping Taffy, along with a few other bowlers who were obviously upset over seeing a dead body, Robbie noticed the man that Quayle had been talking to the day before. He was dressed exactly as yesterday, except this time his three-piece suit was cream-colored. He walked down to the manager's office, stayed a few minutes, then, after pausing briefly to speak to one of the female lane attendants at the control counter, the man left.

The next few hours were chaotic, as the police and assorted medical examiner's personnel took care of Charlie Quayle's body and investigated the death.

The police talked to the bowling participants without

finding anyone who'd seen anything. Only a few people were regulars at Fairways and even fewer bowlers actually knew Charlie Quayle. No one claimed to know him well.

Damon brought over the homicide detective named Grady Stanning, who wanted to hear Robbie's version of Linda Louise's accident. She told him about the remarks made by Denise about her husband trying to kill her daughter.

"Which gives Mrs. Quayle a motive to kill Mr. Quayle," Stanning said. "The woman may have just been mouthing off, but I intend to question her. Come on, Sheriff, let's see if we can locate the wife. Maybe a surprise visit will loosen her tongue."

Damon followed Stanning to the control desk. Robbie wasn't too surprised at Damon hanging around the police officers. He might be on vacation, but his cop's mind was involved as usual.

Damon returned a few minutes later. "So much for surprise. Some guy who works here called and Denise Quayle was home. He told her Charlie was dead," he said. "She and Linda Louise are supposed to be on their way over."

Damon continued to tell Robbie what he'd learned, talking in a low voice so they wouldn't be overheard. "Several employees said Quayle was in big financial trouble. They saw him talking to a man known to be a loan shark and this man was seen here at the center both yesterday and today."

"That must have been the man I saw arguing with Mr. Quayle, just before Linda Louise fell," said Robbie. "I saw him again today, a few minutes after the body came out on the sweeper rack."

"Did you get a good look?"

Robbie thought it over. "I might could pick out his mug shot," she told him. "But I'm not sure about spotting him in a line-up. I'd hate to have to swear to anything."

"Detective Stanning says only one shot entered Quayle, but they haven't found a gun and there's no estiamte on the time of death yet."

"Poor man," said Robbie. "I didn't particularly like him, but I'm sorry . . . I guess I'm more sorry for his family, although they may be better off now. The way he treated that girl was inexcusable."

When Denise and Linda Louise arrived, the police took them to Quayle's office and talked to them for a long time.

Damon wasn't in on the questioning but talked to Stanning afterward and reported to Robbie, "Stanning seems to think the man you saw, the one who looked like a loan shark, is the killer. He's also suspected of being a hit man, but he's never been convicted of anything."

"So that's it?" asked Robbie.

"As near as I can tell. I have a strange feeling Denise and Linda Louise know more about this than they're telling but . . ."

"Why?"

"Police reports were filed against Quayle for child abuse about six months ago, back in Iowa where the Quayles used to live. And there's a hospital report that Linda Louise went to the emergency room about three months ago with some type of head injury. That may be why she wears hearing aids."

"You think Denise or Linda Louise could have killed him?" asked Robbie.

"It crossed my mind. Either one probably had good motive and perhaps the opportunity," said Damon. "Or they could have hired that guy—that hit man." He looked around the center. "What are they going to do about the tournament?"

"We're not sure yet," said Kristen, who'd just walked up. She and Steve had been with Cason in the game room, playing with the kitten, for nearly an hour.

The tournament officials had a hard time deciding what to do. After they talked to Denise Quayle, who insisted the games continue, it was decided that all the action would move away from lane twelve, and the games reset on lane twenty-five. It would take longer using only half the lanes, but people were willing to wait.

A few bowlers dropped out, maybe from nerves rather than respect, but most continued with their bowling and tried not to think about the murder or the victim.

Robbie and Kris were scheduled for late in the evening and went home for a couple of hours. The smog cleared out and Robbie finally got to see the mountains before the sunset.

That night she and Kristen bowled well and finished the tournament with the fourth highest total pins. They won enough money to recoup their entry fee and part of Robbie's expenses of the trip to California.

The night before they left for home, Damon talked to Det. Grady Stanning. When he got off the phone, he said the man suspected of murdering Quayle had been arrested. "They still haven't found the murder weapon, but they think they have a strong case against him."

Later, as Damon and Robbie lay in bed, her back against his front, spoon-fashion, he said, "Stanning told me an odd fact about the Quayle case. I've been thinking about it, but can't find a connection."

"What's that?" Robbie asked.

"The police noticed a funny slickness on Quayle's hands and a greenish-yellow stain on his shirt. And you know what it was?"

It took a few moments before she answered him, he was rubbing his foot up and down her leg, which always sent chills down her spine. "I can't imagine."

"Antifreeze."

Robbie sat straight up in bed. "That's why she killed him."

"Who?" he asked.

"Linda Louise. She might could have taken the abuse herself, but she must have caught him trying to kill her kitten. So she went berserk and killed Quayle."

"Robbie, you've lost me," he said.

Robbie told him about City Kitty and the kitten she called Domino.

"There's no proof; besides, where did she get a gun?" he asked. "What's more, does she even know how to shoot one?"

"I don't know. But I know she did it, as well as I know my own name." She lay back in bed, snuggling up against her husband of thirty years. "Are you going to tell Stanning?"

"I imagine so, but I'm not sure you can make a case for Linda Louise shooting him. I'm still inclined to think Denise did it. Her child was hurt badly this time and the time before. I could see her trying to protect Linda Louise because eventually he might have succeeded in killing the girl."

"Maybe," Robbie sighed. "I guess either one could be guilty, but take it from me, Linda Louise is the killer."

"I can call Stanning tomorrow before we leave." He began rubbing his foot down her leg again and caressing her shoulder. "Tonight I have more important things on my mind."

Two days after they arrived back in Texas, Damon got a phone call from Detective Stanning out in Hollywood.

"Denise Quayle and Linda Louise have disappeared," he told Robbie after replacing the receiver. "And so has that kitten. They have a five-state alarm out for them."

"All that for just an alley cat," said Robbie, "but Linda Louise loves her." Damon looked puzzled briefly until the light dawned.

"I can't help hoping they get away," she said.

"Robbie, you can't be serious. You want a killer to get away?"

"I don't know. I kind of feel sorry for them." She gave Damon a big hug. "I'm just expressing an opinion, is all."

The Cat That Got Away

•

Ted Fitzgerald

He'd always saunter into the lounge at the start of the last set, leap atop the piano, curl up into a ball and drift off to sleep. After all, it was late, and Megan Moran's voice at this time of night was always like a sensual lullaby whispered into your ears only.

The Curaçao Club was a small place, a glorified closet, really, on the Sunset Strip where established performers could try out new material. Megan had been headlining for a month and I'd taken to stopping by for her last set after late-night shoots at the studio. Club soda and music only, thank you. It wouldn't do for the star of *Police Reporter* (10:30, Friday nights, on most of these CBS stations) to be pulled over by the CHP for DUI. Besides, all the intoxication I needed was right up there on stage; reddish-blonde tresses, long and unruly, that were a sultry eruption down the side of a heart-shaped face, deep evergreen eyes, a robust figure outlined by a tight red sequined gown, a go-ahead-and-try manner and a voice that was pure passion softly poured. You could say that Megan Moran had caught my attention.

So much so that I'd elbowed my way into a group of regulars who'd go out for coffee after closing time and discuss the great issues of the day: Sugar Ray Robinson versus Carmen Basilio, Sherman Adams and whether Elvis Presley would play the lead in the film of *Catcher in the Rye*. Megan would often sit in, the cat napping in her lap. She

198

displayed intelligence and sharp wit, and even smiled when I came up with the occasional wisecrack or half-intelligent comment. But I rarely addressed any comments to her directly. Odd, given my former profession, reporter, and my current reputation as one of Hollywood's more eligible bachelors, but the simple truth was, I felt shy and uncertain around her. There was an older sister matter-of-factness about Megan that discouraged guys from putting the moves on her.

And it didn't help that she focused her most serious attention on the cat, an unremarkable brown and white striped tomcat named Benjamin.

It was Benjamin who started the ball rolling the night I walked into the club and he was *not* atop the piano.

Megan's club sets were usually upbeat. Billy May had arranged her last album and his bounce was evident. But tonight it was Harold Arlen and "The Man That Got Away" and it was painful. Beautiful in a way, but haggard and hurting, like Billie Holiday in life these days. The audience was visibly uncomfortable and Earle "No Relation to Buddy" Greco, the club's dapper, diminutive owner, stared at Megan with a vacant expression I'd seen on shopkeepers watching their stores go up in a three-alarmer.

"What gives with Megan?" I asked. "Dirge city tonight."

"What don't you see up there, big fella?"

"The cat?"

"She gets this way whenever he's on the prowl."

"The prowl?"

"She never had him fixed, all the years she's had him. You'd think he's too old. I could care less, but when she sings this way, no one wants to drink or they want to drink too much. I lose booze sales or furniture, take your pick. This kind of torch stuff may sell records but it's like taking a match to this place."

It was Friday and we'd finished filming for the week, so I decided to live dangerously and order a rye and water. Megan's agent, a Prohibition sharpie, with an Ernie Borgnine build and a Yul Brynner pate, named Nick Capri, waved me over to his table near the stage.

"Still got the hots for Megan?" he asked by way of greeting.

I hadn't thought it showed. "I just appreciate good music, Nick."

"Good lungs you appreciate, sonny. Stick around. Megan's been asking for you. Wants to see you after the set. In her dressing room."

He winked and I ordered another drink.

Megan Moran drank Irish whiskey and held her tears inside. It was quiet now and dark inside the club, patrons and band past tense and the four of us grouped around a ringside table. As she did before a number, she paused to measure her audience then got down to it.

"His name is Benjamin. Not Benny or Ben, Benjy or B.J. It's a grownup's name because he acts more like an adult than any man I've ever known. He's been with me longer than any boyfriend or husband and has treated me with more respect. He's the one male I've always been able to count on."

Neither Capri nor Greco said a word.

"He makes me feel happy," she continued. "When he takes off, I get the blues right down to my bones and it comes out in my singing. I recorded my first two albums when Benjamin was on one of his expeditions."

"I have them both," I told her. "I bought A *Solitary Shadow* right after I finished my Korean obligation. I still play it late at night, usually after a romance has gone bust."

"Really?" Her eyes disagreed. "I thought you boys always put Sinatra on the hi-fi and curled up in a fetal position when a woman dumped you."

"Close. We play Frankie to get the affair started, we play you to figure out what went wrong."

"Another time, Cliff, I'd be flattered. Right now, it's Benjamin who's the topic."

"He's a cat. He'll be back, eh, after."

"This is different. He always leaves from home, not here.

Last night, he didn't come out for the last set. When I went back in the dressing room, his food dish was overturned, there were scratches on the floor—"

"A well-behaved animal," interjected Earle Greco. "No problems of scratching before."

"Why are you telling me all this?" I asked Megan.

"He was taken, Cliff. I want you to find him."

That took a full ten-count and half my highball to digest. I was used to the public mistaking me for Pete Perkins, my TV character who's half Horace Greeley and half Mike Hammer, but not a fellow performer. "Megan, it's true I was a reporter before I got the acting bug, but that was several years ago."

"I saw the *Police Reporter* episode where you tracked down the little blind girl lost in the amusement park with the mad bomber. If you could do that, you can find a lost cat. Didn't you say in *TV Guide* that all your shows are based on your actual experience?"

"Well, Jim Manion, the writer and producer, tends to, uh, elaborate slightly."

"Too bad he couldn't elaborate on your acting skills."

That one stung and I didn't have much for a comeback. "As a reporter, when I would try to find someone—a person, that is—there were usually people I could question, talk to. Megan, I hate to be the one to break this to you, but I don't speak tabby."

"You won't need to. I have a few suspicions."

"What are their names?"

"Among the mistakes in my life was a short but all too long marriage to Jock Montana. The cowboy actor?"

"I've met him. We both tested for a role in *Sayonara*, but it went to some Warner Brothers contract player named Garner. It was a bitter divorce, I take it?"

"More for him than me. Jock had trouble dealing with a wife who had opinions and who worked harder and made more money than he did. He also never understood that I'm a lot like a cat. I need my time alone, and not only for work. And he was jealous of Benjamin and the time I spent with him."

"Hold the Ameche: Jocko was jealous of a *cat*?"

"He's an actor. What do you think?"

"Case closed. We're as bad as singers." Her lips curled for a split second. "Other than bad feelings, any reason to suspect Jocko?"

"He was here during the first set last night. Standing at the back, trying to stare me down. I blew him out the door with an upbeat version of 'Cry Me a River,' of all things. He was steamed and he knew about the back door from when I sang here in our married days."

"But why would he wait 'til now to pull this?"

"The divorce was final a year ago but he has called me several times lately, trying to get back together. Maybe he thinks if Benjamin's gone—"

She paused for a deep breath and for the first time I saw Megan Moran as something other than confident or sassy or sexy. I spoke quickly before her gulp became something more.

"You mentioned a couple of suspicions," I prodded.

"I once roomed with a girl name Connie Boulet. She was an extra and the type of gal who worked overtime at not paying her bills. She pulled a midnight move on me and I had to take her to court. We didn't speak for years. Until she breezed in here last night, decked to the nines and reeking business girl."

"Connie the type to carry a grudge?"

"Always had a temper. We exchanged hisses in my dressing room after the first set. She could have spotted the exit. Benjamin she already knew."

"Talk to either of these charmers today?"

"No. Jock didn't answer his phone and I didn't exchange numbers with Connie."

"Ransom a possibility?" Whoa, Cliffy boy. You're really buying into this crazy mess. "If so, what you need is the cops, or at least a private detective."

"No way in hell!" bellowed Capri. "They'd just alert the newspapers and the gossip columnists. As it is, I don't know how much longer we can keep a lid on this. Word gets out Megan's losing her sense over a house pet and driving away audiences, we'll never be able to work out a deal with Liberty Records. At best, this whole thing'll make you look like a silly—"

"Female, Nick?" Megan cut him off neatly. "Who was it that suggested sounding out Liberty because Consort Records is so cheap?" He muttered a response. "Can you speak up, Nick? I didn't hear you."

"You, babe. Sorry."

Megan turned to me. "Cliff, will you help me? As a friend? Put your brains to work on this for a couple of days?"

What *was* I doing this weekend besides studying next week's script? "There are some people I could talk to, Megan, but they'll ask why I'm looking for your runaway tabby."

"Benjamin," she corrected. "But, Cliff, can't you think of a reason you'd be asking questions about me?"

There was a hint of a smile on her lips, the suggestion of a glint in her eyes. With that, I was a goner. So was Megan, into her dressing room.

Capri and Greco surrounded me, warning, cautioning, concerned about discretion and leaks and business and money. I assured them that they had a diligent, honest, trustworthy and pure cat chaser on their hands. Megan's parting words had put resolve in my spine and a schoolboy's grin on my face. I had something to do this weekend and, if the gods were impossibly benevolent and allowed me to become the hero and find Benjamin, I might have something to do next weekend as well. With his owner.

The next morning was Saturday, but I caught Bud Le-Moye, a flack for Consort Records, at his office. I fed him a story about meeting Megan and being interested in more than her singing and could he send me over a bio.

"Good luck, Lochinvar!" he laughed. "Nice, but distant, our Megan. You should be reading Camus instead of *Variety*, maybe play the bongos. She's more keen on brains than muscle, sport."

"Bud, believe it or not, I once had a conversation with

Steve Allen at a network party. We chatted for a half-hour about Adlai Stevenson, nuclear disarmament and abnormal psychology. And I held my own. I'm not as dumb as I look, you know."

"Convince your agent. Look, I'll messenger over a package, but bone up on your Kerouac is my best advice."

Bud's ribbing irked me. Just as every gorgeous starlet is considered a dim bulb, every strapping, good-looking TV leading man is automatically thought to be unable to add up anything more challenging than the aforementioned starlet's measurements. That's worked to my advantage a few times with the network and my sponsor and, while it's true I don't need to work very hard to round up a date for Ciro's, I like to be appreciated for more than my good looks or physique.

I actually enjoy having conversations with women. Women like Megan Moran. Smart and talented and strong and sexy and nice ... and in love with a damned cat! Thinking about how she'd looked and sounded last night— and the other times I'd seen her—I resolved to find Benjamin and bring him back, for no other reason than the opportunity to have a long private conversation with Megan Moran. About Benjamin, Jonas Salk, the Dead Sea Scrolls, or anything else she'd like to talk about.

Megan's bio was the usual sanitized nonsense, rivaled only by what the network and Butz Beer, my sponsor, had cooked up for me. Megan was a farm girl who'd always harbored dreams of being a singer and actress and who'd appeared in a couple of Republic serials in the late '40s. Her big break had come during a USO tour with Bob Hope in Korea. Consort Records had signed her in '52 and her first albums—*A Solitary Shadow* and *Leave Me Be*—had been big hits; on the more upbeat *C'mon, Get Happy*! the jury was still out. There was no mention of jealous ex-husbands, vengeful former roommates, smitten would-be detectives or AWOL tomcats. Nor was there any sense of her personality, her presence of her throaty laugh, no grasp of the experience or passion which had given her voice its

The Cat That Got Away

sharp, smoky edge and prompted her to declare a cat to be the most important individual in her life. Benjamin was a puzzlement to me, but it was no mystery that someone close enough to Megan to know of his importance had put the snatch on him. And that someone stood to gain something from it. But what?

My immediate difficulty was finding an excuse to check out Jock Montana. Friday's *Hollywood Reporter* solved that problem: It contained a squib announcing that Garner, the Warners' whiz kid who bumped us out of *Sayonara*, was filming a pilot for a Western. I dialed up Jocko to commiserate and see if he wanted to have a few pops and chase a few skirts. He was agreeable, told me to come by about six, he had something to show me.

Midafternoon, I swung by the studio. Jim Manion, writer/producer/director/midwife for *Police Reporter* was doing what he always does on Saturday, working on next week's show. He was simultaneously drinking a bottle of the sponsor's brew, Butz's Utica Best Premium Lager, and working his typewriter at a burp-gun tempo when I walked into our cubbyhole "executive" offices.

"What's up, Cliffy? Got any great story ideas for me?"

"I need something from those mental storage files of yours. Did Pete Perkins ever find a lost cat?"

"I've only written sixty-three *Police Reporter* episodes. Shouldn't take too long." He closed his eyes and nursed his beer and still clattered away at the keyboard. "Let's see: Episode Thirty-one, 'Pound of Peril,' Pete saves the local dog pound from flood waters and a false rabies scare. Episode Forty-three, 'Race Against Death,' Pete exposes a crooked jockey and saves a racehorse from the glue factory." He opened his eyes, stopped typing and reached for a pen and a yellow legal pad. "No, no felines. A terrible oversight on my part. But we do have six shows left to shoot this season and we're only five scripts short. This missing cat thing really happen?"

"Even as we speak."

FELINE AND FAMOUS

I filled Jim in on Megan and Benjamin. I swear a light began to emanate from him.

"Every *Police Reporter* script is based on fact," he said for the three hundredth time since we'd started the series. "Or at least some shred of a true happening. This could be *hot*! Sexy jazz singer in jeopardy. Who among her jaded crew of hangers-on and has-beens hates her enough to kidnap her only child?"

"We're talking about cats, Jim."

"Check the emotional subtext, handsome. Besides, a kid's got more appeal. We'll make her a diabetic." He began scribbling on the pad. "The ex-husband as suspect I really like, but the prostie ex-roomie won't fly with the network or our friends at Butz. Hell, I'll make her a klepto. You seeing any of these people soon?"

"Jock Montana in an hour and a half. Connie Boulet I need your help with."

"No sweat. I'll call my 'technical advisor' over in Central Vice. Meanwhile, you, my best pal, my meal ticket, you watch yourself with Jock North Dakota. I hear he doesn't punch out people just on the big screen. Remember, life isn't like the show."

So Jim was right.

Jocko led with his left and I was obliging enough to lead with my chin. It didn't start out that way, of course. He greeted me at the door of his West Hollywood apartment with hearty good fellowship, a brandy in a snifter as big as his ego and a bound copy of a script.

"Need your advice, Cliff. I'm getting into television, maybe. Like you, only bigger. This is the best pilot script I've ever read. Great deal, too. Revue Productions. Name guest stars. Gil Roland set as my costar. I play a deputy U.S. Marshal in Albuquerque, see? The gimmick is I've got this cat that helps me out. We're looking for a 7:30 timeslot and figure this'll bring in the kids."

I flipped it open and read the title: RAT CATCHER. I grinned and started to make a clever comment when Jock Montana's sucker punch caught me under the chin and sent

206

me ass-over-teakettle across a nearby sofa. Just as my face
was about to become intimately familiar with the floor, I
was pulled back and up onto my feet. Through blurry eyes
I saw a pair of Jock Montanas aim another blast at my face.
Nature then devised a brilliant strategy: my feet went out
from under me. Carried forward by my considerable dead
weight and his own momentum, Jock sailed over me. I
managed to raise my legs and plant both feet in his labanza.
He topped the sofa, slammed face-first into the wall and
slid to the floor like a cartoon character.

Once I was able to stand, I reached into the side pocket
of my sports jacket and extracted a catnip mouse I'd bought
on the way over. Waving the mouse and calling Benjamin's
name, I poked through the house in search of an imprisoned
puss. After twenty minutes and three circuits of the place,
I discovered forty-seven photos of Jock and no sign of Benjamin, or any other animal, save Jock, on the premises.
Which meant that Jock hadn't grabbed Benjamin, had
stashed him someplace else or had done the unthinkable.
When I returned to the living room, Jock was on his feet,
though not by much.

"Where's Benjamin?" I demanded.

"How long you been seeing her, hotshot?" he replied.

"Benjamin's a he, Jock. Your old rival is missing and
your ex-wife, your *very* ex-wife, by the way, thinks he's
been taken. You're the only one mean and stupid enough to
try to hurt her through him. Two questions: You got him?
And where?"

"You didn't answer my question. About my wife."

"I'm not interested in her, Jocko. Just the cat."

"Bad a liar as you are an actor, Vesting. But I know how
it is with Megan. Once a guy gets hooked. And only that
mouser gets to cuddle. If I'd taken dear Benjamin, I
wouldn't have kept him. He woulda had a date with the
freeway."

I headed for the door, turned back and, in my best Pete
Perkins stare-down-the-villain manner, looked Jock Montana straight (as much as possible) in his bloodshot eyes.

"Good luck with the script, Jock. And, Jock? If I find out

you do have Benjamin, or have hurt him at all, I'll be back. And Gil Roland will need a new costar. One who doesn't have to use Polident."

"Really?" He started weaving in my direction.

So, I couldn't leave well enough alone, either.

Life's not like a TV show, I kept telling myself as I pressed an icecube-filled towel against the side of my face where Jock had landed a few dozen lucky shots during our second go-round. I was at the bar of the Club Curaçao waiting for Megan and drinking a highball. I'd substituted the drink for the towel by the time she walked in. Her greeting was impatient.

"I've been out working on your problem."

"Oh?" For a moment there was the hopeful expression of a young girl on her face. Just for moment. "Any news?" she asked. When I didn't respond immediately, her face slid into neutral, though she arched an eyebrow when she spotted my rye-and-water compress. "There a story connected with that?"

"It wasn't exactly Slaughter on Tenth Avenue with your ex, but we did have to mess it up before I got him to admit that he didn't have Benjamin."

I smiled and looked for a small one in return, getting only a dead stare.

"Men are such boys," she said. "I need your brains, not your fists, Cliff. I'm going out there tonight and I'll sound like an old Irish washerwoman lamenting the death of her only son and the audience is going to be in as much pain as I am, and there's nothing I can do about it.

"Contrary to what the fan magazines tell you, Cliff, I've been on my own since I was fourteen and been through a lot. I've sung bluesy tunes because I've lived them, but now I'm tired of them. I'm at the best point of my career now. Maybe a new recording label, a movie role, some other offers even Nick doesn't know about yet. I want to expand my repertoire and my options. And I want to enjoy myself and have Benjamin there with me. Too much to ask for?"

"Megan?" I spoke abruptly, the last mention of Benjamin having torn it for me. "You don't need a cat, you need a man."

She gave me a look which sentenced me to six months' hard labor under a scorching sun and reminded me that not only was I not the great judge of human nature Pete Perkins is, my ability to speak clearly was hampered by the constant presence of my size twelves in my mouth.

"You're looking more like Jocko every minute," Megan told me.

She didn't need to say *that*! I would have apologized anyway. "I do want to help you, Megan. As a friend, knowing there's nothing on the other end but the satisfaction of helping out a pal. I think grabbing Benjamin was a cheap shot and I want you to sing what you want to sing and I've been applying my tiny excuse of a brain to this—"

"Whoa." She touched the side of my face. It stung and I flinched.

"Guess I'll need to tip the makeup gal extra this week."

Megan shocked me by laughing. "Cliff, Cliff. You are the least self-absorbed actor I've ever met. I asked you to help not just because you were a reporter but because you notice and listen to other people. You know how rare that is in this town and that's why I trust you. That and the fact you're the only man with the hots for me who doesn't stare down my dress or try to impress me in some way."

"I also listen to your music."

"Yes, you do." She squeezed my hand for a second. "You're not my usual type, just so you know, but thank you for helping."

With that, Megan went off to her dressing room. The bartender handed me a telephone. Jim Manion was on the line.

"Got an address for Connie," he said. "The Aurora Arms. A rococo apartment house in Beverly Hills much favored by the professionals. There's a doorman but just flash him a smile and tell him you're there to see a friend."

"And it gets into Hedda Hopper's column in no time. Does he just take money to keep quiet?"

"This is a democracy. You can always ask."

"One more thing, James. Next week's script. How about having Pete go undercover as a boxer to expose corruption in the fight game?"

"What are you telling me?"

"Or Pete gets kidnapped and worked over by polio vaccine thieves?"

"Does this have anything to do with your *face*?"

"Democracy, Jim. You can always ask."

The doorman at the Aurora Arms did take cash. And didn't seem to recognize me. Maybe 10:30 on Friday nights is an exceptionally busy time in the doorman business.

Connie Boulet was patriotic: short and ample, with sky-blue eyes, fire-engine-red lips and a mop of Marilynesque white-blonde hair. A woman to stand at attention for.

"Hi, handsome."

"Miss Connie Boulet?"

"So polite! Don't tell me you're with the *Watchtower*?"

"I can guarantee I'm not."

"Then, come in and take a load off. You look familiar. Say, are you the guy from the TV?"

"One of them." I closed the door behind me and, in the spirit of the woman before me, took the direct approach. "I'm here on behalf of a mutual acquaintance. She's lost something and thought you might know where it is."

"What ever you're looking for, it's obviously not a good time."

"It's a cat. A brown and white tom, about eight pounds. Goes by the name of Benjamin."

"Aren't you the slick one? Here I was thinking you stopped by because you heard I was a fun date."

"An expensive fun date, I've heard."

"I ain't in that business anymore."

I gazed around the not-inexpensive apartment. "I just thought—

She smiled. "I got lucky."

Just then I backed into a brick wall about the size and shape of a human hand while my feet left the ground. From somewhere above me came a rumble of thunder that sounded like someone clearing his throat.

Connie said: "Say hello to Lucky."

I said, "Watch the face," just before everything went as black as Nixon's beard.

When I came to, I was on the rug, staring at an enormous pair of alligator shoes. My catnip mouse fell from the sky and bounced. A large paw with serious claws batted it away.

"You are so interested in cats," said a voice from above. "Say hello to Marciano."

Marciano was a big cat, much bigger than Benjamin would ever be, except in Megan's affections. Spotted, lithe, with teeth like bayonets. An ocelot. In an apartment?

"You are no doubt puzzled," rumbled the voice, which had to belong to Connie's Lucky. "Marciano serves to deter any of Connie's former, eh, swains, from pressing their suits anew."

"I am not now, nor have I ever been nor will I ever be—"

"Which leads one to ask what it is you are, Mr. Vesting, and why you are here."

My wallet obeyed the laws of gravity and dropped to the floor. Marciano sniffed at it but refrained from turning it into din-din. Remembering all the old war movies where the stalwart spy holds up under torture and doesn't reveal a thing, I decided to spill my guts. Connie blew her red-white-and-blue top, called Megan names I hadn't even heard in the Navy, informed me that Marciano was the only cat in residence and that Megan didn't need to send her boyfriend to get an answer.

"I'm not exactly her boyfriend," I replied.

"Then my condolences to you," said Lucky. "She is a scintillating woman, a very fine stylist." I was pulled to my feet, my clothes were brushed out, my wallet and mouse returned. "Her decision to expand her songbook to pop standards is a wise one. I only wonder why her record label resists the change.

"No matter. If I encounter your missing cat, I shall effect its return. What you told me about her ex-husband is most disturbing. Any man who mistreats a woman, a child or a small animal is beneath contempt. If I ever observed such behavior, I would be moved to end it expeditiously."

"Maybe," I said, "I can introduce you to Jocko sometime."

Back at the club, Earle Greco handed me a compress without a word.

"Another night of this, Cliff, and it's horror pictures."

"I still look better than Charlie Buchinsky."

"*You* say."

Onstage, Megan was working her way through "Blues in the Night" with the grim determination of a nurse in a frontline combat hospital. I felt for her, as did everyone in the room, but that wasn't stopping people from leaving and me from wondering if she'd make it through the stanza, let alone the song.

Nick Capri brushed by with a scowl and disappeared into the back hallway. From behind me, a new voice ordered a drink. I turned to find Bud LeMoye sitting next to me.

"Supposed to meet Nick here tonight, go over some things," he said after I bought him a Scotch and took some ribbing about my interest in Megan. "But I think I'll sit here and listen to the sound of money being made."

"What do you mean?"

"Sad stuff sells best. The new album isn't taking off the way we hoped. Megan, she wants to be Dinah Shore and sing happy stuff all the time. Got news for her: too many girl singers on the box already. She wants to make the green, she sings the blues."

"Shouldn't she sing what she wants? She's the artist."

"Everyone sings what they want in the shower, Cliff. This skirt doesn't get it, but she will. Sounds like maybe she already has. Jeez, Cliff. You sound like you're taking her side. C'mon, she's only a broad. What's she know?"

That's when I poured my drink into his lap. He jumped up, saw my bruises when I turned my head and surmised, correctly, that if I was still able to walk, I was no hombre to mess with. The sound of a few hands clapping announced the end of the set. Bud shouldered his way past me to the dressing room.

I refused the bartender's offer of a refill and instead pondered what I'd just heard, fitting it in with other comments I'd listened to over the past twenty-four hours. A crazy idea crawled into my brain and howled like a beatnik poet denied his java: an idea no crazier than a recording company wanting one of its singers to be miserable because her singing was somehow more profitable that way.

Out in the parking lot, I slit the catnip mouse and sprinkled the powder on the driver's seat of my quarry's car, then went back to my convertible to wait.

Megan left with the musicians a little while later and my quarry exited about twenty minutes after. I waited until he hit the Strip, then pulled out after him. We ended up at a nondescript office building in a lesser section of downtown. He unlocked a door, entered, and didn't bother to relock it. I waited two minutes, then followed. Inside was an office directory and a bank of pay phones. I dialed Megan's home number.

"I just got in," she said coldly. "Why are you whispering?" She inhaled sharply when I told her I thought I'd found Benjamin. I gave her the address and told her to get a cab straight down to it.

"Why don't you just tell me, Cliff?"

"You have to see for yourself."

With Megan on her way, I slipped off my shoes and took the fire stairs to the third floor. I skulked along in approved Pete Perkins fashion until I came to an illuminated pebbled-glass door. From behind it came two sounds: cursing and meowing. Mostly cursing. Then the sound of furniture being moved, papers dropping, a stumble and a loud crash. I took the cue and threw open the door. Inside was Nick Capri, on his hands and knees, with a hyperactive brown and white tabby who could only be Benjamin the Missing going to town with claws and teeth on Capri's catnip-dusted gluteus maximus.

"Nick," I greeted him. "Hi. And why?"

He gazed up with a look both confused and condescending. "Money. What did you think?"

At that moment, someone else who understood the importance of removing one's shoes in sneaking up on an opponent dropped a bomb on my head, sending me once more into dreamsville.

This time I woke to the sound of a small outboard motor. It took a few seconds for me to realize that the sound was purring and the dampness I felt on my right hand came from a cat's tongue. I moved the hand and stroked fur.

"Hello, Benjamin. Nice to finally meet you."

"Hello and goodbye, hero," said Nick Capri.

I didn't like the sound of that, or the fact I was flat on my back. While Benjamin switched his attention to my jacket pocket, I raised my head. Capri was leaning against a desk while Bud LeMoye stood near the door.

"So, this is about money," I said.

"And control," said Capri.

"Let me guess," I said, probing. "Megan's obligated to Consort for one more album. If it does well, and it should, a renewal will cost you an arm and a leg. But if word gets out that she's behaving erratically and driving away audiences, she'll be vulnerable. Consort rides to the rescue, and signing her to a long-term contract at a bargain price."

"You'd make a better agent than an actor, Cliff," said LeMoye.

"Your kind I understand, Bud, but Nick, why, besides the money?"

"Kid, I discovered a dozen of the biggest talents around. Know how many are with me today? They're nice to me, sure, but they all still leave when the big boys come around waving contracts."

"Megan isn't leaving you."

"She's loyal, more than most, but she wants movies and TV and I don't have the contacts there. It's only a matter of time and I need money, not good wishes and inscribed photos."

"What do we do with him?" asked Bud.

"Offer him a cut. Or offer to cut him. Here's a story for your show, Vesting. An actor's agent, ran with the Purple Gang before he got into show business. In Prohibition we made a lot of tough choices. Life and death, you could say."

"No!"

We all turned to the door. Megan stood there, in a tan trenchcoat, looking for all the world like a distaff Pete Perkins. Benjamin pulled his head out from my pocket, gave out with a loud meow and trotted over to his mistress. She picked him up and fixed her eyes on our hosts.

"No wonder I can only trust Benjamin! Listen to you two!"

"How much did you hear?" demanded Capri.

"Enough to wreck you both!"

"No, no, no," said Capri. "Not after all this, babe!"

She favored him with a look of cool contempt, then tossed Benjamin at LeMoye and followed that up with a solid kick between the legs. LeMoye dropped the cat and dropped on me. I brought up my fist in a haymaker, connected and sent him to Lower Slobovia. I pulled myself to my feet and stopped when I saw Capri holding Benjamin with one hand and a pistol with the other.

"We work something out right now," he screamed. "Or else I'll shoot your boyfriend or throw this furball out the window!"

"I've played this scene fifty times, Nick. The guy in your position never gets away. Too close to the final commercial."

"Cliff, please." Megan faced him. "All right, Nick."

My hand brushed against my jacket and I realized why Benjamin had been so attracted to my pocket. Capri was concentrating on Megan and that gave me enough time to pull the shredded catnip mouse from my pocket and hurl it straight into his face. Catnip dust exploded and so did Benjamin. He leaped onto Capri's face and locked on. Capri screamed, dropped his gun and cartwheeled backwards toward the window. Megan shouted Benjamin's name as Capri fell through the glass, taking the cat with him.

On *Police Reporter*, Capri would've fallen three stories and gasped out a dying confession. Here, he simply lay in the shards and moaned. Megan and I poked our heads through the broken window and watched Benjamin zip down the fire escape to the alley below. Light from a streetlamp illuminated him and threw his long shadow against the alley wall. He stared at us, first at Megan, then at me. Then he nodded and trotted into the darkness.

"I'll go get him," I said.

"No," she said, her voice barely clearing a whisper. "I think he just said goodbye."

"Why?"

"It's time for changes," she said, looking at me. "A lot of them."

She put her hands in mine and I held them while she stared out the window and thought about changes and I thought about what part I might have in them, knowing that, unless Megan wanted different, *this* cat wasn't getting away.

The King of Comedy: or, A Policeman's Lot Is Not a Happy One

•

P. M. Carlson

"Most perfidious and drunken monster!" I quoted, rapping Keystone on his nose. "Get away from my whiskey!" The big tabby-striped tomcat flicked his tail at me disdainfully and scampered up to the balcony that ran over our heads at this end of Murphy's Restaurant.

Well, yes, I reckon you're right, it's foolish for an actress on tour to keep a pet. But Keystone had introduced himself to me in a dank and dreadful Philadelphia dressing room and promptly found and killed a rat that was lurking in the bustle of the dress I'd been about to don. Wouldn't you be grateful? He had a torn ear, a kinky tail, and he amused me because he enjoyed tippling. All in all he rather reminded me of my dear departed papa. Besides, if the divine Sarah Bernhardt could keep cats, dogs, birds, and even lions, shouldn't an American artiste be entitled to a cat?

Murphy's had etched-glass windows and an attractive fretwork railing on the balcony, and passed for a high-class establishment, at least in Northampton. Yes, yes, I know I promised to tell you about Hollywood, and I will. But the story begins in Massachusetts. Besides, in 1898 Hollywood wasn't much more than a few shacks and a pepper tree. Not that Northampton was much better. It didn't even have the pepper tree.

That night, Murphy's was filled with rich and rowdy patrons. In the corner a group of well-dressed men were attempting to sing "A Policeman's Lot Is Not a Happy One," and above us on the balcony a rich fat man and his friends were carousing and beginning to raise angry voices. "I paid you back last week!" said a tall party in stylish peg-top trousers.

"You only paid half, Simon!" The fat man stood and shook a gold-ringed finger at the other.

"Teddy, you're drunk!" said Simon. The fat man turned his back with a stamp of his expensively shod foot.

I was surprised that the stage-door Johnny who was sitting across from me had chosen Murphy's, because he was obviously not as rich as the other patrons. In the ordinary way of things, I would have sent him packing. But Mike Sinnott was so gawky and Irish, and so young, only a year or two older than my dear niece, that I hadn't had the heart to refuse him. Besides, stage-door Johnnies were becoming rarer these days, even though regular use of Cheveu-line kept my hair nearly as red as it had been twenty-five years before, when I first trod the boards.

I soon discovered that young Mike had more on his mind than my red hair, or my splendid performance as Beatrice, or my fashionable Parma-violet traveling suit and my pretty bracelets of gold worked into flowery chains. Mike's concern was quite different. "Miss Mooney," he said earnestly, "please tell me how I too can work on the stage!"

He must have noticed the surprised and skeptical look I cast on his horsy face, his long clumsy arms, his scarred hands. "Oh, I know I look like a gorilla!" He spread out one hand for my inspection. "I've had a job at the iron works. You can see how the molten iron splatters and burns. I must get into a better line of work, perhaps as a singer. I have a fine bass voice. Do you want to hear 'Asleep in the Deep'?"

"I believe you," I said hastily. In fact I had great sympathy for a young man who wished to improve his lot in life, because I too had taken to the stage when I realized that a poor girl from Missouri had few other options. Well, yes, she could marry a poor man, or become a tart, or work for a rich man, which usually amounted to the same thing. In any case she would remain poor. The stage, however, promised riches and fame—though the expenses of dressing properly and of providing for my dear niece had somewhat diminished the rewards it occasionally delivered for me. The theatre would be even more difficult for a youngster as clumsy and unrefined as my young admirer. But I didn't have the heart to tell him so. Youth should have its dreams, don't you think? My dear niece dreamed of a lovely tennis gown trimmed with ombré silk.

I said gently, "The first thing you must do, Mike, is leave Northampton."

Mike nodded glumly. A waiter bustled from the swinging door behind us with the lemon meringue pie Mike had ordered. It was an enormous portion, and I saw that I might have to assist him in finishing it. But before I could make this kind offer, an enormous crash jolted us both from our chairs.

The fat carouser had fallen from the balcony overhead and landed on the next table in a great flurry of silverware, broken china, and splashed soup. The gentleman and lady dining there jumped back, exclaiming.

The fat man lay very still, his knee bent at an odd angle. "Mike! Hurry! Find a doctor!" I exclaimed, pulling out my smelling salts and loosening the fallen gentleman's tight starched collar.

Mike ran for help while a blonde woman who had hastened down the steps from the balcony began to shriek, "Teddy! Darling Teddy! Speak to me! It's your Millicent!" She waded through the wreckage of china and soup toward us, supported by the shorter of the two gentlemen in pegtop trousers who had been arguing with the fat man a moment before. A crowd of waiters and diners began to press around.

"Please, stand back so the poor man can breathe," I said. The unfortunate fellow was in a faint but his pulse was strong, and I yielded my place to the sobbing Millicent and her two friends. All three bent over the fallen Teddy.

Mike soon reappeared at the door, accompanied by a

scrawny police officer and an elegant man in an expensive Chesterfield. "I'm Dr. Dove," he announced, clearing his way through the crowd with his walking stick. He pushed me aside rudely, knelt by the unconscious man, took a gold watch from his pocket to check the pulse, and soon reported that with the prompt application of his patented formula, Dr. Dove's Elixir, to Teddy's cracked skull and broken leg, the plump unfortunate might survive.

The scrawny policeman asked, "Who pushed Mr. O'Brien?"

The taller of the men in peg-top trousers said, "He stumbled, sir."

Millicent looked up tearfully. "That's right! Everyone there is Teddy's friend! Everyone in this restaurant is Teddy's friend! Except—"

All eyes turned to me. "And just who are you, miss?" asked the policeman.

"I'm Bridget Mooney, sir, leading lady of the company now playing the famous French farce *A Flea in Her Ear* and the renowned Shakespearean comedy *Much Ado About Nothing*."

"An actress, eh?" The scrawny officer snorted. "Well, we all know how actors carry on! I wouldn't be surprised if you turned out to be our villain!"

"Why, sir, I was nowhere near the man!"

"It's true, Officer Teheezel, she was down here!" said an old gentleman with a napkin still tucked under his chin and flecks of pea soup in his otherwise snowy walrus mustache.

Teheezel frowned at him. "Well, did you see anyone else push him?"

"But who would push Teddy?" Millicent asked, gesturing at the two fellows in peg-top trousers. "Sam and Simon are our friends! Teddy just stumbled against the rail and fell!"

"Still, you have to watch out for actors," growled Officer Teheezel. But he stopped inspecting me and instead squinted up at the broken balcony rail. I breathed a sigh of relief.

Then Millicent screamed again. "His watch! His beautiful solid-gold hunting watch! It's gone! I gave it to him, and it's gone! It says, 'To dear Teddy O'Brien from your little lambie'!"

Officer Teheezel turned back to me. "Aha!" he cried triumphantly. "There's a gold watch chain up your sleeve!"

"It's a bracelet, sir," I said in exasperation, turning back my lace-trimmed cuff so he could see my golden flowers.

But the scrawny officer didn't pause for logic. "I'll believe my own two eyes, and nothing else!" he cried, fumbling for his billy club as he headed toward me.

Well, now, did you ever hear of anything so unfair? Here I was, an innocent bystander—in fact, a helpful bystander, selflessly furnishing the unhappy victim with my very own smelling salts, a good Samaritan personified, yes indeed! And yet, rather than look for the true villain, this Dogberry of a policeman was about to arrest me! I glanced about for some hero to rescue me. But my young friend Mike had not yet been able to push through the curious crowd and still stood by the front door, and the walrus-mustached fellow was too old and too impressed by Teheezel's billy club to be of much use. "I'm innocent!" I protested again, and before the policeman could raise his stick, I pushed Mike's lemon meringue pie into his face.

There was a burst of laughter from the onlookers, although a few of the more delicate sensibilities among them tried to muffle their mirth out of respect for the law. Officer Teheezel sputtered as he swiped at the meringue that covered his eyes.

I gasped in horror at what I had done. "Oh, lordy, sir, I'm so sorry! Please, allow me to help you! I'll get something to clean it off!" Shouting for a towel, I whisked through the swinging door into the kitchen, past the startled cooks, and out into the night. I found myself in a dark, malodorous alley behind the restaurant.

A scruffy gray-striped bundle flew out before I could close the door. "You're right, Keystone," I told him. "The company in there is not very refined. Let us depart."

We tiptoed toward the street. As we rounded the corner, we were greeted by a booming laugh. A big man was lumbering toward us, silhouetted against the bright front window of the restaurant. Realizing that he'd seen me in the light from the window, I shrank back against the bricks, terrified until he spoke. "Miss Mooney! You are such a . . ."

"Hush!" I hissed, recognizing Mike. "I need a place to hide!" A shout back in the alley added urgency to my plea. "You know this town. Quick, where can I go?"

"Follow me!" My young admirer brought his voice down to a whisper and led me across a moonlit backyard to another dark alley. When we were out of danger he said, "Miss Mooney, you are a delight! I haven't laughed so hard in months!"

"Mike, you must leave this dreary town. Where are we going now?"

"My mother runs a boardinghouse, and there's an empty room."

Mrs. Sinnott was a pleasant Irish woman, obviously fond of her big clumsy son, and somehow divining that I was nearer in age to her than to her boy, she soon installed me in a small second-story room. The furnishings were simple, but the room was quite modern, having been outfitted with an electric lamp invented by my dear friend Mr. Edison. A small window provided a view of a moonlit verbena hedge and a bit of the street. Keystone settled himself on the windowsill as lookout while I gave Mike instructions about fetching the trunk I'd left at my boardinghouse near the theatre. He returned in an hour with my belongings and with news. "As I was loading your trunk into the cart, Officer Teheezel arrived!"

"Did he see you?" I asked in alarm.

"No, no. He was going up to see the landlady."

"But you had already given her the little gift?"

"Yes. She promised me she would say nothing about you. Besides, she has nothing to say! I gave her an address on the other side of town." Mike beamed at his own cleverness.

" 'Sir, your wit ambles well,' as Shakespeare says," I told him. As a reward, I opened my trunk and showed him some of my theatrical souvenirs. He was particularly pleased by a small kinetoscope that dear Mr. Edison had given me.

But I remained worried, and did not have a restful night despite the excellence of Mrs. Sinnott's bed. My dreams were haunted by the specter of the furious Officer Teheezel, wiping meringue from his eyes.

Keystone woke me at first light, demanding breakfast. As I opened the bottle of cream that had come to hand while I hurried out through the Murphy's Restaurant kitchen, I took stock of my unhappy situation. Teheezel, I was certain, would continue to hunt for me, and while he did not appear to be a giant of intellect, he might well learn that I had been with Mike and trace me to this house. Avoiding him during the day would be possible, but in order to earn enough for my niece's tennis gown, I had to play in *A Flea in Her Ear* that night. It is very difficult to hide in full view of hundreds of people. Teheezel struck me as clod enough to arrest a person right on stage, with no regard for the noble, nay, even sacred calling of the theatrical artiste.

I prepared Keystone's breakfast the way he liked it, with a dollop of whiskey, and took the rest of the cream down to Mrs. Sinnott, who served it with our big bowls of Irish oats and then went into the backyard to wash the sheets.

Mike came downstairs, booming out "Asleep in the Deep." "Mike," I said, as much to quiet him as to obtain information, "it seems to me that the best way to escape Teheezel would be to find the missing pocket watch. Who do you think took it?"

In deep thought, Mike had a comical scowl. But he was bright enough. "Most likely one of his friends," he said. "He was arguing with Piggott and Crane."

"The gentlemen in the peg-top trousers, I presume? Do you know them?"

"Not well. Sam Piggot—he's the shorter one—runs a dry-goods store. The tall, thin fellow is Simon Crane. His family has some money, but he's known chiefly as a gambler."

"And gamblers do run up debts," I said, remembering my uncle, who had mortgaged my Aunt Mollie's property and lost it to foreclosure because of gambling debts. "What about Millicent?"

"Millicent is his wife. Why would she take it?"

"Perhaps Dr. Dove took it."

"A doctor wouldn't take a patient's watch!"

"He takes their money for Dove's Elixir."

"No, it must be Crane!" Mike insisted. "But—but how can we prove it?"

"Especially to a policeman who believes his own two eyes and nothing else," I said sadly. "Simon Crane may have pawned the watch already. Do you know where these people live?"

"The doctor's office is only two doors from Murphy's Restaurant. The others all live on Prospect, in the best part of town. Say, we can ask at the pawnshops too," Mike said eagerly.

"Yes. Let's go! I'll fetch my walking cape," I responded, and ran up the stairs.

I took the precaution of donning a dark wig and a veiled hat as well, and soon we were walking through the town. We passed two pawnshops. Mike inquired about hunting watches, but the only ones there were not engraved with messages to Teddy O'Brien. As he emerged from the second shop, crestfallen, I pointed across the street. Simon Crane, in a fresh pair of peg-top trousers, was in deep conversation with a dapper, cigar-smoking man. It was difficult to hear, but Simon appeared to be pleading for something. The other man shrugged and spread his hands in a placating manner, but was clearly shaking his head. Simon Crane turned away despondently.

"Who is the man with the cigar?" I whispered.

"He's the president of the new bank," Mike replied.

"Mr. Crane does not appear to be happy with what the president was telling him," I said, watching as the banker hailed a carriage.

"I bet Crane heads for the pawnshop!" Mike exclaimed. But to his disappointment, the man disappeared into a restaurant.

"Well, let's give him time," I suggested, and we walked

on to Prospect Street, which boasted large Queen Anne houses painted in cheerful colors. Teddy O'Brien's house was a tasteful mustard yellow trimmed with Indian red and forest green. Two elegant carriages waited before it. As Mike and I strolled slowly by across the street, three people emerged from the tall front door: Dr. Dove, hat in hand and with a sad expression; Sam Piggott the dry-goods man, equally serious; and Millicent, weeping once again. The doctor said his adieus and departed in one of the carriages. Piggott murmured to Millicent for a few moments. I had time to reflect that, although I had only seen her in distress and therefore thought of her as puffy-faced and red-nosed, Millicent had the type of ample but small-waisted figure that our new hourglass fashions enhance and that gentlemen tend to appreciate. Certainly Mr. Piggott appeared to enjoy the task of comforting her.

"It does not seem to be the ideal time to accost them about the whereabouts of Teddy's watch," I said to Mike.

"Yes, she is upset."

"Perhaps Dr. Dove's Elixir is not helping Teddy."

We returned to Mike's boardinghouse still puzzling over the situation. I ascended to my room and removed the black wig, which was hot and scratchy, for all its effectiveness. Keystone, on his windowsill, had pricked up his raggedy ears at something below. I glanced out too, and was horrified to see Teheezel striding toward the boardinghouse. The policeman was smarter than I'd expected, or angrier. He looked up, spotted me in the window, and began to jump about, waving his billy club and shouting, "Murderer!"

Clearly, the fellow was berserk. I locked the bedroom door. For good measure I pushed the bed against it, inadvertently knocking over the whiskey bottle in the process. But there was no time to clean it up. I began to jerk the sheets from the bed.

In a moment there was a furious pounding on the door and the key fell out. "Open in the name of the law, you murderer!" cried Teheezel. "Dr. Dove says that poor Mr. O'Brien has expired from the effects of his fall! I know you're in there! I can see you through the keyhole!"

Well, I reckon I'd never seen a fellow as rude as this officer! I was sorry to hear of Teddy O'Brien's sad fate, but I had no desire to discuss it with Teheezel. I looked out the window. It was a long way down, three bedsheets high at least. Young Mike came into view by the verbena hedge, looking scared. Hastily, I knotted the corners of my sheets and blankets together and anchored them to a steam pipe. But when I opened the window to make my escape, Mike shook his head violently pointing at the wall below me. I realized that the knocking at the door behind me had stopped. When I leaned out to look down, a ladder almost hit me in the eye.

Officer Teheezel was determined indeed.

"Sir," I called down to him politely, "you don't want to come up here. I'm nursing a sick cat!" I pointed at Keystone.

Teheezel was halfway up. "What's a sick cat got to do with it?"

"He has hydrophobia," I improvised.

That made him pause. "Hydrophobia?"

Unfortunately Keystone chose that moment to trot across the windowsill and jump back into the room. "Doesn't look like hydrophobia to me," Teheezel declared, and climbed higher.

Well, what's a poor girl to do, when beset by such barbarians? I grabbed the top rung of the ladder and pushed. Slowly, it swayed back, gathering speed as it fell. Teheezel gave a holler and tried to jump off, but landed in the verbena shrubbery on his back, like a great blue beetle, arms and legs flailing about to the tune of Mike's laughter. I ran back across the room, shoved the bed away from the door, and sprinted down the back stairs and out into the yard. Mrs. Sinnott, elbow-deep in lather over the wooden washtub, asked, "What in the world is going on?"

"We have had a visit from a rather unrefined representative of the law," I informed her, and ducked behind a garden shed that sat in the back corner of the yard.

Teheezel, now bedecked with bits of verbena, was on his feet again. The officer may have been slow of wit, but he was quick of eye and spotted me. He ran around the shed to meet me. But I am good at such games too, having practiced them with a variety of shopkeepers in my youth in St. Louis, and by dodging from corner to corner of the little structure in a lively fashion, I succeeded in keeping the shed between me and the uniformed enemy of art. Unfortunately the back fence was forbiddingly tall, and I found no loose planks or other means of escape as I ran back and forth. I began to despair for my future. Then I glimpsed Keystone out in the yard peering into Mrs. Sinnott's washtub. He toppled back with surprising clumsiness. Teheezel gasped and uttered an oath as my little tomcat stood up, swaying, suds all over his face and whiskers, and began staggering toward the policeman.

"Hydrophobia!" yelped Teheezel, believing his own two eyes.

Mike jumped onto the porch, and Mrs. Sinnott gave a little scream too and ran to her son. The officer backed away from the tiny agent of death, his billy club extended toward him, shouting. "Stop in the name of the law!" Of course the cat didn't stop. Teheezel took another step back, tripped, and sat down suddenly in the washtub.

From the safety of the porch, Mike was laughing uncontrollably.

"I'll be back!" swore Teheezel, and raced away, soggy and leaving a trail of flying soapsuds.

I hurried to my dear little rescuer and cleaned his face. "You clever little tom! You deserve a monument!"

Mike stopped laughing. "Miss Mooney! Beware! Perhaps he does have hydrophobia!"

"It's only soapsuds," I informed him.

"But he was stumbling along, like a sick animal!"

"True," I said. "I fear little Keystone imbibed more whiskey than was good for him this morning?"

"Whiskey? You mean he's drunk?"

"He's quite a toper, this one."

Mike began to chuckle again. "Whiskey and soapsuds! And did you ever see anything funnier than that policeman?"

"Now, Mike," his mother reminded him sharply, "the officer says he's coming back. Why don't you two go to the police and straighten this out? And take the cat!"

"The police aren't very reasonable," Mike said.

"Quite right," I agreed. "The trouble is that he has too much faith in his own two eyes."

Mike said slowly, "I can think of a way to destroy that faith."

"Mike, if you can do that, I'll say a good word on your behalf to a New York theatre manager I know. Come tell me your idea." I led the way back into the house and up to the room while he explained, and began to think that the clumsy young fellow might have a bright future after all. Mike's idea was excellent, and worked so well with my own plans that I showed him some particularly rare photographs from my collection.

Twenty minutes later I was crouching under the front porch, and just in time, for Teheezel had returned posthaste. He was accompanied by four other policemen, two of them on bicycles, and by a mean-looking fellow with a huge net, probably the dogcatcher. I was glad that Keystone was under the porch with me, concealed in a basket while he slept off his overindulgence. Mike invited the uniformed visitors in. Two minutes later I followed and tiptoed up the stairs.

They were clustered around my locked door. Teheezel was bent over, his eye to the keyhole. "Open the door!" he shouted. "I can see you're in there! I can see—oh, lordy!" He turned a shocked face to his friends.

"What's wrong, Teheezel?"

"Oh, my, how that infernal woman carries on! She has a jumprope, and no—um—"

"No what, Officer Teheezel?" I asked sweetly from the stairs.

Teheezel whirled to look at me and his jaw dropped. "But—but—" He looked through the keyhole again. "But you're in there, jumping rope!"

The officer was indeed a Dogberry, don't you think? I

muttered, " 'This learned constable is too cunning to be understood.' "

Teheezel, furious, kicked in the door with a great crash, and stared amazed at a completely empty room.

"Teheezel, don't be a looney! She's right there!" cried a more intelligent man, perhaps the dogcatcher. They all started for me. I slid down the banister and raced out the front door, pausing only to knock over a porch chair so that the policemen all stumbled over it as they poured from the door. Thankful that I was wearing my best lace-trimmed bloomers, I hitched up my skirts, leaped onto the better-looking of the two police bicycles, and lit out in the direction of Murphy's Restaurant. The police followed close behind. It was a terrifying few moments, not only because the officers of the law were so near, but because Northampton's streets were largely ruts and holes, and the bicycle bumped and bucked like an unruly mule. But I reached my haven a few yards ahead of my pursuers, dropped the bicycle, and ran up the steps into Dr. Dove's oak-paneled offices. "Help! Where's the doctor?" I cried to the woman in a stylish shirtwaist who sat at a desk before a display of Dr. Dove's Elixir.

"Would you care to state your business?" she asked, quite properly. But I'd seen her eyes shift to one of the doors when I asked for Dove, and I wrenched it open to see the good doctor, watch in hand, taking the pulse of a young man in shirtsleeves sitting on a table.

"Dr. Dove! Help me, please!" I exclaimed, flinging myself onto the carpet at his feet.

Dr. Dove returned his watch to its pocket, peered down his nose at me, and frowned. "Madam, I don't believe I've had the pleasure," he said stiffly, then looked up in surprise. Four policemen, a dog-catcher, the woman in the shirtwaist, and my young admirer Mike were all trying to squeeze through the door at once.

I sprang to my feet and embraced the doctor. "Please, please help me, Dr. Dove!" I begged.

I know, I know, a proper lady would never embrace a gentleman without first being correctly introduced. But I was in particularly desperate circumstances, don't you agree? And hang it, being proper hadn't yet helped much with Officer Teheezel.

Dr. Dove, I regret to say, was not the heroic type of gentleman. He pulled my hands from his waist and said in a frosty voice, "My dear madam, do not make a spectacle of yourself!"

"But, sir, the officer believes I knocked poor Teddy O'Brien from the balcony, and then pilfered his watch! And of course I didn't. You did!"

Teheezel was staring at the doctor's watch pocket. Dr. Dove laughed. "I fear you are deluded, madam. This watch is my own, of course. I've had it for years."

"May I see it, sir, if you don't mind?" asked Teheezel.

"Of course." Dr. Dove handed over the watch with a condescending smirk at me.

Teheezel inspected it carefully and cleared his throat. "Dr. Dove, sir, is your watch engraved?"

"Yes, with my initials, C.P.D."

"Sir—well, maybe someone else should look too, because I'm having trouble believing my own two eyes today—but sir, this watch is engraved 'To dear Teddy O'Brien from your little lambie!"

The other officers, the dogcatcher, and even the woman in the shirtwaist confirmed that it was indeed Teddy O'Brien's watch.

Dr. Dove began to sputter. His patient sprang from the table crying, "I knew I should have gone to Dr. Simpson!"

Teheezel drew himself up to his full scrawny height. "Sir, Mr. O'Brien died under your care! This is indeed a dark deed!"

I nudged young Mike in the ribs and led him from the office. "We've done it! I think Teheezel will leave us in peace now."

"Miss Mooney, I thought it was Simon Crane! How did you know Dr. Dove was the one who stole the watch?"

"I saw him fumbling at Teddy O'Brien's watch pocket while he was checking his pulse," I said.

I know, I know, it was a fib. But let's suppose for a mo-

ment that I had taken Teddy's watch, and suppose I'd then
exchanged it for the one in the doctor's pocket as I begged
him for help. In such a case you wouldn't want me to tell
an impressionable young man like Mike, now would you?
If we destroy the idealism of our youth our nation will
founder, indeed it will. And while Dr. Dove had grown
wealthy from selling his elixir, he was otherwise not a great
ornament to the medical profession. With a better doctor,
poor Teddy might have survived.

Besides, I had to think of my niece's tennis gown. I've
noticed that a watch with initials is worth more in a pawnshop than a watch with a message from someone's little
lambie.

I thought it would be best to introduce a new topic of
conversation. "Mike, it was a splendid idea to show Mr.
Edison's motion pictures!" I said. He had fitted the peep-
hole of the little Edison kinetoscope to the keyhole of the
bedroom door.

"It's magical!" Mike exclaimed. "I've seen Edison motion pictures at the kinetoscope parlors, of course. But I
didn't know there were programs with young ladies jumping rope, without—um—"

"Mike, Mr. Edison was conducting a scientific investigation, and clothing would have obstructed the observations,"
I informed him sternly. "Do you remember Mr. Muy-
bridge's famous photographs of Leland Stanford's horse
galloping? Well, Mr. Edison is continuing those studies of
animal locomotion. In fact, Keystone's locomotion is featured in some of the motion pictures. They dropped him
upside down to record how he lands on his feet every time.
Except when he's drunk, of course."

"Well, this one is a capital motion picture!" Mike said
with an admiring glance. "I can hardly wait to become an
actor too!"

"Dear boy, you mustn't expect too much too soon," I
warned him. "But I'll do what I can."

What I could do was limited by Mike's gawky appearance, but when the young man arrived in New York, I
directed him to a friend who launched Mike's splendid ca-

reer by giving him his first role on stage. Well, yes, it was only a vaudeville show. And yes, Mike had to play a horse. Well, half a horse. The rear half. But it was a beginning. And when we met for a whiskey after his first show to celebrate, he was full of plans. "Miss Mooney, apart from the low pay, this life is splendid!" he exclaimed. "I don't want to be an opera singer now. It's much more fun to make people laugh. You know, I've been wondering if I could make people laugh with Mr. Edison's clever motion pictures!"

Fifteen years later, that's exactly what he was doing. I next encountered him in California, where I was touring as the proper Lady Bracknell and the not-so-proper Lady Macbeth. I wanted to see one of the fabled motion-picture studios of Hollywood, so one morning I hired an automobile to transport me to the Edendale area. Parasol in hand, I strolled along the length of a strange building with translucent sides and roof. They called this studio the Fun Factory; and in fact, there was laughter mixed with the shouts and curses that issued from within. Suddenly I heard a familiar voice behind me. "Miss Mooney!" boomed a man in a handsome summer suit. "Would you like to hear me sing 'Asleep in the Deep'?"

"Mike! You look splendid!" I exclaimed. He did indeed, with his expensive suit and glowing, suntanned complexion. Only the white scars on his hands bore witness to lowlier days in an eastern iron foundry. "Though I should call you Mack now."

"Ah, you know I've changed my name."

I smiled. "I've kept myself informed. They also call you the King of Comedy, and you run this studio, and you've recently become dreadfully rich."

"And here you are, right on cue!" Mack beamed at me amiably. "Miss Mooney, it would be capital if you would take a role in one of my comedies! We're doing a dozen a month, sometimes more. And we always need funny—um, funny mature ladies!"

"Why, thank you, Mack. When my tour ends I'll come speak to you."

"But tell me! There's something I've been wondering for fifteen years."

"What's that?"

"I don't understand—if Dr. Dove wanted to steal that watch—how did he cause Teddy O'Brien to fall? He wasn't even in the restaurant!"

"Why, Mack, I thought you too had seen, and were helping protect the true culprit from the clutches of the constabulary!" I exclaimed. "It was the late Keystone, of course. Teddy O'Brien was standing on the balcony pouting, his back to his friends and his glass in his hand for comfort. He jumped onto Teddy's shirtfront, and startled the man so much he stepped through the railing. The cat, of course, landed on his feet."

"But you said 'late.' Do you mean Keystone is no more?"

"Alas, 'tis true. He grew old, and slow, but he died happy, I believe, attempting to imbibe a magnum of champagne."

Mack removed his hat, looking truly stricken. "Dear old tomcat! I'll never forget how he frightened away that police officer! You and he taught me the key to my success: deflating authority is funny."

"Yes, indeed. We did rather deflate that policeman, didn't we? I noticed that your comic police chief is named Teheezel, in his honor. But Mack, do I hear correctly that you named your studio after the insignia of the Pennsylvania Railroad?"

"So they say." Mack smiled at me. "But we know the truth, don't we, Miss Mooney?"

I looked up at the big sign and smiled too. Mack Sennett's Keystone Studios, home of Fatty Arbuckle, Mabel Normand, Syd and Charlie Chaplin, and the amazing, incompetent Keystone Kops.

Few cats, or humans, achieve such delightful memorials.

Defrauding the Cat

.

Catherine Dain

"Tell me again. What were you doing with twenty-five thousand dollars in your checking account?" Faith started to lean on the round white table, which rocked just enough to slosh cappuccino into her saucer. She stuck her napkin under the cup and crossed her arms instead.

Sitting in the open area at Farmer's Market always sounded better than it seemed once she got there, particularly in June, when the low cloud cover that marked the beginning of summer in Los Angeles cast a pale gray light on what would otherwise be stalls of brightly colored fruits and vegetables. The tables next to the food stands were surprisingly full, considering the lack of sun. Fluorescent T-shirts saying I SURVIVED THE 6.8 marked the tourists. The native Southern Californians all wore multiple earrings and looked hung over.

"Elizabeth's contract. For the commercial. The money was only supposed to be in the checking account temporarily."

"Right."

"And it wasn't taken—the bank was worried about the amount of the check, so when the commodities firm called them to make certain it was good, they called to make sure I had written it, which of course I hadn't. So they didn't pay it. The money is still there." Michael had been holding his cup until he was certain the table was through rocking. He placed it carefully in the pristine saucer.

"Does it ever bother you to live off Elizabeth like this? You've let your practice go to hell."

"My practice hasn't gone to hell. My clients were all cured. The two I still have only see me once a week out of habit, because they like to talk to me. I'd end the dependency, but they're both so entertaining that I'd miss them. And of course it doesn't bother me to live off Elizabeth. After all, I paid six hundred dollars for her. She wasn't even two months old, and I knew she was going to be a star."

"Michael, she was a kitten. How could you know she was going to grow up with an attitude?"

"Because she was *my* kitten, Fay. She was therefore going to damn well have my attitude."

"Faith. How many times do I have to tell you—I don't want to be called Fay anymore." She started to lean on the table again, but remembered in time. "I want to be called Faith. It's not such a great leap, from Fay to Faith. It's not as if I wanted to be called Hope or Charity or anything like that."

"Hope would have made more sense. Hope is what you need, not Faith," Michael said cheerfully, impervious to the glare he got in response. "I've been calling you Fay for too many years now. I'm sorry. And I don't understand why you have this sudden need to change your name."

"Because I'm claiming my own identity. People should be named what they want to be named, not stuck with whatever name their parents happened to stick them with. If you wanted to change your name, I would change what I called you."

"Michaelmas, perhaps? Michelangelo? I rather like that."

"Michelangelo it is, then. Anyway, start again from the beginning. I don't understand how this happened."

"Really, I don't either," Michael sighed. "But someone who knew how much money I had in my checking account called the bank, told whoever answered that I had moved, that I needed new checks sent to my new address, and the bank actually sent them. Sent new checks, ordered in the proper number sequence, to the new address. The recipient then wrote a check to Max Strother Commodities for twenty-five thousand dollars, to open a trading account. Then the bank called to make certain that I was opening an account at Max Strother Commodities—and astoundingly, inefficiently, called my real telephone number, not the new one the thief had given them, which was the only thing that tripped up whoever wanted to pull this thing off."

"How much did the thief have to know about you?"

"My social security number, my mother's maiden name, and the date and amount of my last deposit." Michael paused to watch the pigeons descend on a half-eaten croissant that a young man two tables away had tossed to the concrete. "I really, truly want it to be an inside job, someone with access to the bank computer. Because if it isn't, the only other people who had that information are my mother, Elizabeth's agent, and Jason."

"Jason? I didn't know you'd seen him."

"He happened to stop by the day the check arrived, and so he rode with me to the bank. That's all."

"Oh, Michael. Do you really believe Jason would steal from you? Is he that desperate?"

"He's not employed, and he didn't look well. He might decide he was stealing from Elizabeth, not from me. Jason could rationalize it that way. And he was always so jealous of her."

Michael was still watching the pigeons. Faith turned away from the table to watch them with him.

"Better Jason than your mother," she said.

Michael didn't say anything, and Faith began to wish that she hadn't either.

"Is the bank keeping you informed about their investigation?" she finally asked.

"I don't think they're doing much—as far as they're concerned, nobody lost anything. I talked to somebody at the West Hollywood police station, and he said that Hollywood had jurisdiction, because Max Strother Commodities and the alleged new address are both in Hollywood. He added that it would be a low priority with them, too, because all I could file a complaint for would be stealing checks and

attempted forgery. Even if the person is caught, he or she—
and I'm talking about Barbara, Elizabeth's agent, not my
mother—even with all our problems, I really don't think it
was my mother—would plead it down to a misdemeanor."

"Then let's investigate it ourselves."

"What?" Michael turned back to Faith.

"I love the way you can express so much disdain for an
idea in a single word," she said, uncowed. "Let's check the
address and the phone number, at least. We might be able
to eliminate both Barbara and Jason, even if we can't do
anything more."

"I'd ask if you have a life, but I know you don't. Why
do you want to seize my life? Did you make the mistake of
calling Brian?"

"No. I heard, though. He and Frances are getting married
Sunday. Ten years younger than I am, and she finished her
dissertation. She officially gets her Ph.D. Saturday, the day
before the wedding. Not that I feel bad anymore about
never having finished mine, you know I worked that out.
It's been too long since I dropped out of the program, and
the family counseling license brings me all the clients I can
handle."

Michael nodded and smiled his professional therapist
smile. "Well, I suppose neither of us can feel any more in-
ept than we do now, no matter what our next failure is.
How do we start our investigation?"

"By calling the phone number, of course. And then driving to the address. Do you have them?"

"The bank gave them to me, to make certain that they
weren't mine. They're at my apartment, sitting on my desk.
Do we finish our cappuccino first or start our Nick and
Nora caper at once?"

"I was thinking more Lord Peter Wimsey and Harriet
Vine. Down the cappuccino and let's go." Faith stirred the
cinnamon-topped foam into the brew and drank it in two
gulps. She didn't like Farmer's Market cappuccino very
much anyway.

"I don't suppose there was a couple who didn't sleep together." Michael finished his cappuccino and stood, fishing his car keys from his fanny pack.

"Nancy Drew and Ned Nickerson, but you'll have to wear a football jersey and let me drive."

"Separate cars as far as my place, then we flip a coin. I'll think about the football jersey."

They threaded their way around tables to the aisle between the falafel stand and the gift shop. That led them to the parking lot, where they parted company.

Faith never liked the hunt for a parking space that she had to endure when she visited Michael's Kings Road condo, so she grabbed the first one she spotted, just north of Santa Monica Boulevard. She walked the block and a half, past buildings that all looked alike—four stories over an underground garage, evenly spaced balconies with views of other balconies, white stucco with greenery around the front doors. Michael was waiting on the sidewalk.

"You might as well have walked from Farmer's Market," he said, unlocking the security door. "There were at least three spaces closer."

"If I owned a Yugo, I could have parked in two of them. The third couldn't accommodate anything bigger than a tricycle."

"Suit yourself, but I could have slid the Honda into all three."

"Then we don't need to flip a coin. When we leave to investigate, you drive, you park."

"Investigate. My God, that is absurd."

They took the elevator to the third floor. Michael unlocked the deadbolt, and Faith followed him in.

"My God, indeed," Faith said, having held her tongue during the short trip. "It smells like a cattery in here. You ought to show your meal ticket more respect. When did you last change the cat box?"

"Elizabeth doesn't mind the smell. She was born in a cattery after all. But the cat box is probably still clean. She doesn't like to put her feet in it, so she sort of backs up to it, and sometimes she misses it entirely. Wait here, I'll check."

Defrauding the Cat

The cat in question, looking like a blue pearl with darker blue eyes, was stretched out on a pink velvet chair, staring at Faith with what was undeniably attitude.

Michael returned almost immediately, spritzing the air with a pseudo pine scent.

"At least she hit the paper," he said. "I flushed it down, and the smell will be gone in a minute."

"That cat is lucky she's both smart and beautiful, and you don't want to work for a living. It seems to me, though, that if you can teach the cat to give you high fives on camera, you ought to be able to teach her to use the litter, not the paper."

"The difference is, she likes to give high fives on camera."

"The address and phone number. Quickly. The cat shit smell is not dissipating, and the air freshener is disgusting."

Michael's desk was a rectangle of distressed oak in a corner of the living room. He sat in the bentwood rocker and began sifting through small pieces of paper.

"It can't be too far down. I saw it yesterday."

"Why don't you ever file anything?"

"Here it is." He handed Faith an envelope with an address and phone number scribbled on the back. "If I filed, I'd have to clean out the files. I don't have room for files. What I want is on my desk. Everything else I throw out."

"Let's call the phone number."

Michael pointed to the phone. Faith picked it up and punched in the number.

"Four nine two seven," a woman's voice said.

"Michael Haver," Faith responded.

"I can take a message."

"Is that what this is? A service?"

"That's right. What message do you want to leave?"

"Never mind." Faith replaced the phone. "Let's check the address."

"You know it's going to be a mail drop."

"Yes, but somebody had to establish it. And somebody had to open the trading account, so if we don't find anything out at the mail drop, we talk to Max Strother Commodities."

Elizabeth watched them leave. With attitude.

The La Brea address was indeed a minimall mail drop. Michael parked the Honda right in front.

"It's so simple when you pray to the parking gods," he said.

Faith slammed the car door in answer and marched ahead of him into the narrow store. No one was near the front counter. Both side walls and a center stretch of shelves held boxes, envelopes, tape, and other mailing paraphernalia, carefully arranged to make the selection look larger than it actually was.

"Hello!" Faith called.

A young Asian woman, not more than twenty, emerged from the back.

"Can I help you?" she asked.

"I'm trying to get in touch with Michael Haver—he left this as an address, and I need to talk to him."

"If you leave a message," the young woman said, staring at Faith through large dark eyes.

"But I don't want to leave a message here. I want to find him."

"You leave a message," the woman repeated.

"This is silly, Fay-ththth," Michael said. "All these places offer confidentiality. That's the appeal."

"Look," Faith said. "This is the real Michael Haver. The Michael Haver who gets mail here is a fake."

"This is Michael Haver? You found him?"

"I know this Michael Haver," Faith said patiently. "I want to find the other one, the one who calls himself Michael Haver but isn't."

"I don't know," the woman answered. "You leave a message, I put it in his box. Michael Haver box."

"Do you know when he will be in to pick it up?"

"No. Whenever."

"Let's go," Michael said. "Unless you want to leave a message."

"Thank you for your help," Faith said to the woman.

Defrauding the Cat

Michael was starting the car before Faith slid into the passenger seat.

"Just one more stop," she pleaded. "Max Strother Commodities. If they can't help, we give up."

"I'm surprised you aren't suggesting a stakeout of the mail drop."

"I thought about it, but there are only the two of us, and I couldn't really count on your cooperation."

"You're right. Max Strother Commodities, and that's it. Where is it?"

"Haven't you ever noticed the sign? It's on the woefully tacky part of Hollywood Boulevard, near Western."

"Dear Lord and Baby Jesus protect us." Michael glared at her briefly, but he turned north on La Brea and east on Hollywood. The neighborhood quickly deteriorated from office buildings to souvenir shops to thrift shops to bars.

Michael parked in a space almost directly in front of the Max Strother Commodities sign, which was on the second story of an Art Deco building too small and probably too deteriorated to make the preservationists' lists. Graffiti almost obliterated the sign warning them of a two-hour parking limit.

"I may wait in the car," Michael said.

"Put the Club on the steering wheel, turn on the alarm, and pray to the antitheft gods," Faith replied.

He caught up with her in the lobby.

The elevator door had an OUT OF ORDER sign. They climbed the stairs, not to the second floor, but to the fourth.

"And you complained about the cat," Michael said as they traversed a landing that smelled of old vomit.

Faith didn't bother to answer.

Max Strother Commodities was at the back of the building, behind a frosted glass topped door that jangled as they opened it.

"I'll handle this one," Michael added.

The large office was illuminated only by the gray haze from the windows on the back wall. Five foot partitions had been strategically placed so that visitors couldn't tell how many of the cubicles were actually staffed.

241

Michael and Faith waited until a short man with a burgundy toupee, wearing a white shirt rolled to the elbows, paisley tie loosened, came to greet them.

"Yeah?" he said.

"I'm Michael Haver." Michael automatically held out his hand.

"The guy who gave us the bum check? No, you aren't."

Michael retracted his hand. "I didn't give you a bum check."

"That's what I said. You aren't the guy."

"Can you describe him?" Faith interjected.

"Who are you?"

"Faith Cassidy. Michael's friend."

"Which Michael? This one or the guy who gave us the bum check?"

"This one. We're trying to find the person who forged Michael's name on the check."

The short man appraised the two of them.

"Got ID?" he asked.

Michael pulled out his wallet and displayed his driver's license.

"The other guy was shorter than you are. Almost bald. Fringe of white hair. Wire-rimmed glasses. Nervous. That's why I remember him. I wasn't surprised when I called the bank and they wouldn't okay the check. Or when the telephone number he gave was a service."

"Oh, hell," Michael whispered.

"You know who it is?" Faith asked.

"Thank you for your time," Michael said.

"No problem."

Faith smiled at the little man, then hurried after Michael.

"Who is it?" she asked again as they started back down the stairs.

"I can't be positive, of course, but the description sounds like Barbara's husband." Michael didn't pause or look back at her.

"Then we have to go see Barbara."

"No. You said Max Strother Commodities would be the end of it. And I want to think before I go any further."

Defrauding the Cat

"You have to talk to Barbara—you've known her too long to file a complaint without talking to her—and it seems to me that I ought to be along. A third party."

Michael was moving so quickly that Faith stopped talking. She needed the breath to keep up with him.

A thin young man in a torn T-shirt and jeans was eyeing the Honda when they got to the street. Michael glared fiercely. The young man shrugged and moved away.

"How can I go in and accuse Barbara of stealing from a client?" Michael asked once they were settled, the Club removed from the steering wheel, the engine going.

"You don't accuse her of stealing. You ask her how she's been doing. We approach this as an intervention—we're both licensed therapists, we ought to know how to do to this."

"I hope you're right."

Michael took Hollywood Boulevard back to Fairfax, then dropped down to Melrose. He parked in front of an art gallery two blocks west.

"Barbara's office is upstairs," he said as he hit the security buzzer three times in brief succession. An answering buzz allowed them to open the heavy wood door.

The steps were Spanish tile, the railing wrought iron. The spacious landing had a large fern in front of a window. Another buzzer let them through a second heavy wood door.

"Be right out—I'm on the phone," a voice called.

What should have been a receptionist's office held a mahogany desk cluttered with mail and photographs and a leather couch with more of the same. A signed Frank Romero poster was on the wall.

"Michael darling, what can I do for you?" Barbara swept into the room, a heavy woman in a purple caftan and fringed scarf. "I wish you had called first—I don't have more than a moment."

She presented her cheek to be kissed, and Michael smacked the air next to it.

"Barbara dear, I'm so sorry. This is my friend Faith."

"Oh yes, Fay." Barbara held out her hand. "Michael told me you used to be an actress. So wise of you to change careers—there are so few parts for women your age, and fading ingenues get them all."

Faith smiled. She would have corrected the name, but it didn't feel like the best way to start an intervention.

"I'm just here to listen while you and Michael talk," she said.

"That's fine, I'm sure."

Barbara cleared space for the two of them on the low couch. She perched on the edge of the desk. Faith and Michael looked at each other, then up at Barbara.

"How are you doing?" Michael asked.

"I'm fine, dear, and I don't have time to chat. What is it? Nothing wrong with Elizabeth, is there?"

"Well—not exactly. Almost. Someone tried to steal the bonus from the cat food contract."

"Oh, no. I'm so sorry. Tell me what happened."

Barbara's face wrinkled with concern. Michael and Faith again looked at each other, then up at Barbara.

"Have you ever heard of Max Strother Commodities?" Faith asked, forgetting that she had promised to listen.

"No. Why?"

Michael grabbed Faith's shoulder to keep her from answering.

"Someone forged my signature on a check for twenty-five thousand dollars and tried to open a trading account there. The description sounded a lot like Howard."

"Oh, God. Oh, God." The concern on Barbara's face turned to pain. "Oh, God, don't tell me he did that."

"You knew he had problems?" Faith brushed Michael's hand off.

"Of course I knew. I'm married to him. But I didn't know he'd try to steal from a cat to pay for them." Barbara looked from one to the other. "Howard is a compulsive gambler. He needs help. Would the two of you come with me to talk to him? You're both licensed therapists, you know how to handle this kind of thing."

"We'll do whatever we can to help," Faith cooed.

"Come over for dinner. Seven o'clock. And please, no police."

"You have my word," Michael said, arising from the couch so that he could look Barbara in the eye. "As long as Howard agrees to join a twelve-step program. If he won't go, I file a complaint."

"I'm so grateful." Barbara enveloped Michael in a hug. "This will all work, you'll see."

Faith held out her hand. "Seven o'clock."

She waited until they reached the sidewalk before she said anything more.

"Barbara's lying. She's in it with him."

"How do you know?"

"It was what she said about stealing from the cat. You remember your comment about Jason rationalizing? That's what Barbara did—she wasn't stealing from you, she was stealing from the cat."

Michael considered her words.

"All right. Then she has to join the twelve-step program."

"That's all?"

"And you pay the parking ticket." He plucked it from the windshield and handed it to her.

"I didn't park in the red zone. But I'll pay if it'll make you feel better."

"Nothing will make me feel better. Not until we've explained to Barbara that attempting to defraud a client is going to cost her the agency franchise. To the Screen Actors Guild, Elizabeth is not just a cat—she's a dues-paying member."

"Michael? Would you rather we hadn't done this?"

"Are you kidding? It's the most effective I've felt since I hit a Little League home run when I was eleven." He kissed her on the cheek. "Now let's go back to my place and plan this intervention. But one stop on the way."

"What?"

"I need to buy a football jersey. And next time, you drive."

Second Nature

•

Livia Washburn and James Reasoner

Beth Hallam took a deep breath and tried to ignore the fear in her belly. Then she stepped out into empty space, fighting off the impulse to close her eyes against the terrifying nothingness beneath her. She had to keep her eyes open so she could see where she was falling. Otherwise, she might miss the net stretched out beneath her.

The wind of her fall tugged at the cap secured tightly on her head. The cap had to be tight, or it would have come off and let her long red hair stream up and out around her head. Since she was doubling for a twelve-year-old actor—a boy—having her hair come loose would have ruined the gag. In the ragged shirt and baggy pants she wore, the curves of her body were well hidden, and she and the kid were within an inch of each other in height. Beth had doubled for him in his last picture, too.

The net was hidden in a cluster of large boulders at the foot of the bluff, where the cameras couldn't see it. Beth hit it cleanly, perfectly, knowing that the director would be shouting, "Cut!" right about now. The net gave under her, then sprang back up, tossing her into the air. A wave of exhilaration swept through her, as it always did at moments like this. In all of her twenty years, she had never experienced anything like the feeling of a dangerous gag that had gone just as planned.

She bounced up and down a few times in the net, then rolled to the edge and swung down from it. The second-unit director, an old-timer who had spent a quarter of a century staging stunts like this since coming to Hollywood in the early twenties, hurried over to her and clapped a hand on her shoulder.

"Great job, Beth," he told her. "I never saw your daddy do any better."

Beth tugged the cap off, letting her hair spill free. There wouldn't be any second takes. She looked up at the rim of the bluff, which was a good three stories above her. "Lucas never jumped off a cliff like that," she said with a laugh. "Not even with a horse under him."

"Well, that's true. Not for the camera, anyway. I don't know what he might've done back when he was just a young buck. I'll have to ask him about it someday."

"Don't get him started," Beth said and laughed again. "Not unless you've got plenty of time to listen to his stories."

"Speak of the devil." The second-unit director pointed toward the road that wound along the canyons of this rugged area that, for all its seeming isolation, was only a few miles from the intersection of Hollywood and Vine.

Beth looked where he was pointing and recognized the car bouncing along the road. Her father had driven a black flivver for years, and he was still of the opinion that all cars ought to be painted black, even in this modern day and age. And Lucas Hallam was nothing if not stubborn, as Beth knew from long experience.

"You need me for anything else, Yak?" she asked the second-unit director.

"No, you go on ahead. Say hello to your dad for me."

Beth waved at him and moved off through the hustle and bustle of a movie company on location. There were quite a few trucks and cars parked around the area, and trailers had been set up for the stars to use as dressing rooms. The army of flunkies that went hand in hand with moviemaking hurried here and there, seemingly aimlessly. Beth knew it all made sense if you knew what you were looking at. She had no desire to get that well acquainted with the process. She knew stunt work, and that was enough. It was second nature to her, something that was in her blood. And she came by it honestly, since her father was Lucas Hallam, who had performed gags and worked as a riding extra all through the twenties and well up into the thirties.

As Hallam stepped out of the roadster that he had parked by some of the equipment trucks, he looked like he could still swing up into a saddle and gallop off with a make-believe posse after a gang of celluloid owlhoots. He was a big man, his frame shrunken a little by age but still power-ful. His leathery face had been craggy and lined as far back as Beth could remember, and as the years passed, the lines just seemed to get deeper. The mustache drooping over his wide mouth was iron gray, as was the rumpled thatch of hair under the broad-brimmed brown hat. He leaned against the fender of the roadster and crossed his arms as he watched his daughter come toward him.

"Elizabeth, you look like some sort o' hobo," he greeted her.

She glanced down at the ragged outfit she was wearing. "I'm supposed to. The kid's playing a tramp in this picture. Of course, he's really the heir to a fortune and doesn't know it, or some such claptrap." Beth jerked a thumb to-ward the bluff behind her. "I just jumped off that cliff for him."

"Yeah, I remember you tellin' me about the gag you had lined up. How's he supposed to get out of it?"

Beth shook her head. "He doesn't. He's already done his death scene. They showed me the rushes of it before I did the stunt." She grinned. "It's a corker. There won't be a dry eye in the house."

"Any problems with the gag?"

"No, it went fine." Beth frowned a little. "What are you doing out here, Lucas? I thought you were going to be in the office all day."

Ever since his bones had finally gotten too brittle to do stunt work or stand up to the constant pounding of long days in the saddle, Hallam had concentrated on the one-man private detective agency he had built up over the years. He thumbed his hat to the back of his head and said,

"I got a call from a feller over in Palm Springs who wants to see me about a case. He's promised me a thousand bucks just for hearin' him out, so I reckon I'll drive over there and see what he's got to say. Just wanted to let you know where I was goin' and make sure it won't be a problem."

"You could have left me a note," Beth said.

Hallam shrugged his wide shoulders. "Yeah, I reckon."

Beth smiled slightly to herself. Her father wasn't the most demonstrative man in the world. But she knew him well enough to realize he had come out here to the location so that he could say goodbye in person.

Beth had never known her mother. Lucas had raised her from an infant, somehow juggling the responsibilities of parenthood with his busy career. And Beth loved him dearly. She stepped over to him, came up on her toes, and brushed a kiss across his cheek. "You go on to Palm Springs," she told him. "I'll be fine."

"All right," Hallam said. "I'll give you a call and let you know how things are goin' and when I expect to be back. You got a ride back into town?"

"Sure. I came out on one of the trucks."

"Well, I'll see you in a day or two, more'n likely."

Beth watched him get back in the roadster and drive away. As fathers went, he was a mite . . . unusual, maybe—but that was all right with Beth. She liked to think she was a mite unusual herself.

She got back to the apartment she shared with her father on Fountain Avenue in West Hollywood not long after dark. The telephone was ringing as she unlocked the door, and Beth muttered to herself as she hurried across the living room to answer it. She scooped up the receiver and said, "Hello?" as she tossed her purse into a chair.

A woman's voice said, "I need to speak to Lucas Hallam, please." The words had a brisk, businesslike tone.

"I'm afraid he's not available right now," Beth said. "Could I take a message?"

"Well, hell. I really wanted to talk to the old coot."

Beth blinked in surprise. She'd had the caller pegged as a potential client. "I beg your pardon?"

"Oh, don't mind me, dearie. I knew Lucas back in the old days. My name is Delores Banning. I called his office and his service gave me this number. I need to see him right away."

"I'm sorry, but—"

"It's a matter of life and death."

Beth wanted to stare at the phone. She had never actually heard anybody say that before—except in the movies. She wondered if Delores Banning was an actress.

If so, she was probably a good one, because there was a definite note of urgency and sincerity in her voice. Beth hesitated only a moment, then gave in to an impulse she had felt before.

She said, "I'm Mr. Hallam's associate. Perhaps I can help you."

Well, why not? she thought. She had been around while Lucas was working on some of his biggest cases. It wasn't like she didn't know *anything* about the detective business.

"You're a gumshoe, too, sweetie?" Delores Banning said.

"That's right," Beth said. She felt a little nervous about lying like that, but Lucas was out of town and Delores Banning sounded *really* troubled about something . . .

"Well, come on out to the house. It's on DeMille Drive, over in Los Feliz." Delores Banning gave Beth the number and told her how to find the place. "Make it quick, before something else happens to Chester."

"Chester?"

"That's right. Somebody's trying to murder him."

That made Beth's eyes widen. Delores Banning hadn't been kidding about it being a matter of life and death.

"Maybe what you'd better do is call the police."

"I tried that, honey. They don't care." For the first time, Beth heard something besides brassy self-assuredness in the woman's voice. "Nobody cares about Chester but me."

What would Lucas do in this situation? Beth couldn't remember him ever turning his back on anybody who was really in trouble. In the Old West that Lucas Hallam came from, a man just didn't do that.

She was nothing if not her father's daughter, Beth thought. She took a deep breath and said, "I'll come right out there."

"Thank you, sweetie," Delores Banning said. "By the way, what's your name?"

"Elizabeth."

"Well, you hurry on out, Liz. I'll be looking for you."

Beth hung up and looked at the phone for a long moment. *Liz.* That was what Lucas had called her mother, although he hardly ever talked about her. He had never called his daughter by that name, however. To him, she had always been either Elizabeth or Beth.

Well, there would be time enough to set Delores Banning straight once she got there, Beth thought. For now there were more important considerations.

Like murder and somebody named Chester.

DeMille Drive was a narrow, winding street named after the director, whose mansion was located in the hills of Los Feliz, until recently one of the most exclusive residential areas in Los Angeles. Lately many of the stars who lived in the neighborhood had been moving southwest to Beverly Hills, but there were still quite a few celebrity mansions in Los Feliz. Delores Banning's was one of them. It was a sprawling pile of stone and white stucco perched atop one of the hills and surrounded by acres of lawn. Now, as night was settling down over the city, it was brightly lit. Beth wheeled her cream-colored Ford through an arched stone gate in the fence and started up the hill on a curving drive that led her to the house.

As the car's headlights swept over the lawn, she saw that it could use cutting. The flower beds dotting the lawn were unkempt and full of weeds. Beth frowned. Delores Banning wasn't keeping the place up very well. Not only that, but the wrought-iron gate had been wide open, and the intercom set into one of the stone pillars at the entrance hadn't seemed to be working at all. Beth hadn't been able to get a squawk out of it.

She brought the Ford to a stop in front of the house, and the double doors had opened before Beth could get out of the car. A tall, rawboned woman with obviously dyed black hair swept out of the house and came toward the car carrying a cat in her arms. The woman wore an expensive silk gown that was as rumpled as if she'd slept in it for a week. She said, "That you, Liz?"

"My friends call me Beth, Mrs. Banning. Or is it Miss Banning?"

"Oh, it's Mrs., dearie. I was married to Hubert Banning for thirty-five years."

Beth recalled Hubert Banning's name. He had been an executive at one of the studios, and her father had mentioned him several times over the years. Banning had died several years earlier, Beth seemed to remember.

"Come on in, Beth," Delores Banning said. "I don't like standing out here in the light like this. You never know when somebody's spying on you."

"Wait a minute," Beth said, uncertain whether she wanted to go inside with this woman or not. "You said on the phone that someone named Chester was in danger?"

"Well, of course he is. That's why I want to get back inside the house. The poor dear's already been bushwhacked once." Delores Banning held up the cat. "See?"

There was a bandage on the shoulder of the animal's left front leg.

Chester was a big orange tomcat, nothing fancy about him. He sat in Delores Banning's lap and licked the woman's hand almost constantly, the rough tongue making a faint rasping sound against her skin. Beth thought that licking would have driven her crazy in a matter of minutes.

"He got sick from the poison," Delores said, "but the vet was able to save him. Then he came home with his hind leg all scratched up and Dr. Hubbell said it looked like somebody tried to catch him in a trap. And then there was the gunshot wound." Delores shook her head, her strong but attractive features set in a mixture of sadness and anger. "Someone is definitely trying to kill Chester. And I can't imagine why anyone would want to hurt him!"

Beth sat in an overstuffed armchair with a lace doily over its back. The whole room was furnished like that, chintz and foofaraws everywhere you looked—except for the walls, which were covered with red velvet. Beth could almost imagine what her father's reaction would have been to this place. He would have said it looked like a cross between a preacher's parlor and a Kansas City whorehouse. Obviously, Delores Banning had rather eccentric tastes.

Beth already regretted giving in to the impulse that had made her tell this woman she was a detective. She figured Delores Banning was a little off in the head.

"Are you sure you're a private eye, honey? You look awfully young to be doing work like that."

"I'm older than I look," Beth said.

"I was just the opposite. Looked older than I really was. The boys liked that just fine, though. I was playing supporting roles as grown women when I was barely seventeen. That's how I met your boss; he was working on a Tom Mix picture I was in, back around '28." Delores shook her head. "A long time ago."

Beth nodded. She hadn't told the woman that Lucas was her father, and it might be best to keep it that way. She said, "Let's get back to Chester."

"I want you to find out who's trying to kill him. Whatever your agency's regular fee is, I'll pay it. Money is no object."

That was another saying Beth had never heard anyone use in real life. But Delores had been an actress, and she was probably used to saying things like that in scripts. Beth glanced around at the room with its air of genteel poverty, and Delores went on, "Oh, don't worry about how the place looks. I know it's getting a little rundown. But I can pay you. I promise you that. I can give you cash—"

"No, that's all right," Beth said. "A check made out to Mr. Hallam will be fine. Now, do you have any idea at all who might want to hurt your cat?"

"Told you I didn't. It doesn't make sense. I—"

The front door opened, and there was a quick patter of footsteps in the hallway. A woman's voice called, "Aunt Delores! Are you here?"

A blonde woman appeared in the doorway of the room where Beth and Delores Banning had been talking. She was in her early twenties, well dressed, and undeniably beautiful. She said, "Oh, there you are. I was worried about you." Blue eyes flicked over to Beth. "And who is this?"

The coolness in her tone betrayed dislike, and Beth figured she could learn to return the feeling pretty easily. Delores said, "She's a detective, dear. She's going to find out who's been trying to hurt Chester."

The blonde looked away from Beth, already dismissing her in her mind. "I told you nobody's trying to murder your cat, Aunt Delores. You've been imagining things, just like always."

Delores Banning flinched a little, as if somebody had struck her. Beth felt a quick surge of anger, and she said, "That gunshot wound isn't a figment of anyone's imagination. And I want to know who *you* are."

Delores said, "This is my niece, Nicolette Banning. Nicky, please try to be polite to Elizabeth."

All of the aging actress's previous self-assurance seemed to have drained away in the presence of the younger woman. Nicolette Banning gave Beth a haughty look and said icily, "How do you do."

"Pretty good most of the time," Beth said, her own tone cool. "What do you know about the attempts on Chester's life, Miss Banning?"

Nicolette frowned. She was wearing an expensive gown and a fur stole, despite the warmth of the evening. She said, "I don't like the sound of that. You don't think I had anything to do with bothering the cat, do you?"

The animal in question was curled up in Delores's lap, purring and sleeping soundly, his claws working slightly back and forth. Delores said to Beth, "Nicky wouldn't hurt Chester, Liz. She's the only relative I have left. She takes care of me."

"I try," Nicolette said, her self-appointed martyrdom apparent in her voice. "I called earlier and didn't get any answer. That's why I came over."

"I was up in the screening room, watching one of my old pictures. You know there's no phone up there, sweetie. Hubert never wanted to be disturbed when he was watching a picture."

Nicolette slipped off her stole and tossed it carelessly over the back of a sofa. "You could hire a servant to answer the phone when you're busy. You could certainly afford that."

"I know. It just seems like there are so many better ways to spend my money."

The younger woman's lips pressed together until her mouth was a thin line. Beth saw the reaction and figured she knew what Nicolette Banning was thinking. Delores had said that Nicolette was her only relative; that meant Nicolette stood to inherit whatever estate Delores left. Beth wondered just how much money they were talking about, but there was no way she could ask tactfully.

Of course, tact had never been Lucas's strong suit as a detective, and she had learned from him, after all . . .

Nicolette opened her purse, took out a gold-plated case, shook a cigarette from it. As she lit up, she said, "I've got to be going in a minute. If you want to waste your money on some sort of detective, Aunt Delores, that's your business."

"Yes," Delores said, "it is."

"But I won't be any part of it." Nicolette picked up her stole and looked at Beth. "Don't try to take advantage of my aunt."

"I don't intend to," Beth said.

Nicolette gave a little ladylike snort of disbelief and walked out of the room. A moment later the front door opened and shut.

"I'm sorry, Liz," Delores said. "I wouldn't let anybody else run over me like that, but what the hell, she's family. She and Chester are all I have left."

"I understand," Beth said, although she really didn't, not completely. "Can you keep Chester inside tonight?"

"Well . . . I suppose so. He enjoys his roaming, of course, all cats do, but if you think it's safer . . ."

"I think it would be best. I'll start asking some questions around the neighborhood tomorrow morning. Maybe I can find out something."

"All right. As long as you get results."

"Now, that's something I intend to do," Beth said.

She didn't have any stunt work lined up for the next day. She probably could have scrounged up a gag if she had tried, but at the moment she was more interested in helping Delores Banning. Beth liked the older woman. Like Lucas, Delores was a survivor of another era in Hollywood. This was a town that tended to forget anything older than last week, but Beth had never been that way. She knew that Hollywood never would have grown into what it was without the efforts of Lucas and Delores and thousands more like them.

She figured it might be better to start by talking to the servants who worked in the neighborhood around the Banning house, rather than the owners of the other mansions. By the middle of the morning, she had learned that Chester was a far-ranging little varmint. More than one groundskeeper reacted angrily when Beth mentioned him, and she knew they would have cursed had she not been a woman. She supposed it was pretty annoying to labor over a flower bed for hours and then discover the next morning that not only had the plants been chewed up, but that Chester had left some other little presents to be cleaned up. The cooks looked on the cat more kindly, and a few of them admitted that they fed him scraps.

None of which really helped Beth any, because everyone she talked to seemed surprised when she told them that someone was trying to get rid of Chester. No one had seen or heard anything unusual in the neighborhood. As far as Beth could tell, they were all being truthful. She wished she had her father's ability to read people and know whether or not they were lying. That was something that might take years to develop, though, and she wasn't sure she would ever be investigating another case. Lucas had always tried to keep her at a distance from this part of his work.

She worked her way down one side of DeMille Drive and then back up the other. She was at the house directly opposite the Banning estate when she rang the bell at the servant's entrance and found herself facing a woman who was definitely not a servant.

The woman was wearing a dress that looked expensive enough to have come from one of those swanky shops springing up over on Rodeo Drive since movie stars had moved in droves to Beverly Hills. She was in her mid-forties, with chestnut hair. She was carrying a fluffy, extremely fat white Persian cat. The cat blinked stupidly at Beth.

The woman was anything but stupid. She said, "Yes? Can I help you?"

Beth didn't know what the mistress of this mansion was doing answering the back door, but since she was here, she might as well go ahead and ask her questions. "My name is Elizabeth Hallam. I'm a private detective." That little fib was beginning to sound like the truth to her. "One of your neighbors has been having some trouble, and I've been hired to help her find out about it. Do you know Delores Banning?"

"Of course I do. Delores and I have been friends for years. My husband and I entertained her and Hubert many times. By the way, I'm Carolyn Hawes. Won't you come in, Miss Hallam? I'm afraid it's cook's day off, but I was about to have some coffee. Would you like some?"

"All right. That would be very nice."

Carolyn Hawes seemed like a nice woman, pretty down to earth for somebody who was obviously so rich. She put the cat down carefully on the highly polished floor of the kitchen and gestured for Beth to have a seat at a heavy wooden table. The coffee was already brewed, and it was quite good, Beth discovered as she sipped from a fine china cup that was probably worth more than what she got paid for jumping off cliffs.

"What sort of trouble has Delores been having?" Carolyn Hawes asked as she sat down on the other side of the table with her own cup of coffee.

Beth decided to try a slightly different tack this time. "Do you know anyone who might want to harass or frighten Mrs. Banning?"

"Certainly not. Delores is a lovely person. A bit . . . strange, perhaps, but I can't imagine anyone wanting to cause problems for her."

"Strange?"

"Well . . . she let all her servants go after Hubert died, and there's simply no way she can keep that place up by herself. If you've been there, you've seen for yourself what it's like."

"Maybe she can't afford to pay servants anymore."

Carolyn Hawes shook her head. "I happen to know that Hubert left her very, very well-off. My husband and I use the same law firm, and well, one hears things." She bent down to pet the white Persian, which was rubbing around her ankles and purring. A frown appeared on her face as she went on, "You know, I *can* think of someone who might not be happy with Delores. That niece of hers."

"Nicolette Banning?"

"That's right. Have you met her?"

"Briefly," Beth said.

"That was probably enough for you to know that she's not a very pleasant person. I remember Delores told me that she was upset about the provisions of the will Delores had drawn up."

Beth tried not to look excited as she said, "Will?"

"Yes, that business with Chester." As she spoke the cat's name, Carolyn Hawes grimaced slightly.

"You're talking about Mrs. Banning's cat?"

"Of course. Delores's will leaves—"

Beth jumped the gun. "Everything to the cat!"

Carolyn Hawes stared at her. "Certainly not. That would

be ridiculous, and Delores . . . well, she's a bit dotty, yes, but she's not insane."

Beth felt a little ridiculous herself for having leapt to the wrong conclusion. "I'm afraid I don't understand."

"Delores's will does leave a sizable bequest to be used for Chester's care as long as he lives. That responsibility falls to Nicolette, of course."

"How sizable a bequest are we talking about?"

"A hundred thousand dollars," Carolyn Hawes said off-handedly. "The rest of her estate will be placed in a trust, and Nicolette will earn the income from it until Chester dies, then inherit the entire amount, providing that, in the judgment of Delores's executor, she has taken good care of the cat." Carolyn smiled and shook her head. "Perhaps dotty isn't quite strong enough. Now that I've explained the situation, I'm afraid Delores does sound a bit more than eccentric."

"A bit," Beth said. "But what if something happens to Chester before Delores dies?"

"Then everything goes to Nicolette immediately." Carolyn leaned forward and went on in a conspiratorial tone, "Please don't tell Delores that I've been discussing her affairs. I shouldn't even know these things, of course, but my husband hears gossip from his attorney and from other men at the studio. He and Hubert worked together for years, you know."

Beth nodded. "I won't say anything."

"You never did tell me what sort of trouble Delores has been having. I hope it's nothing serious."

"No, probably not. She was worried enough to hire the agency I work for to check out a few things."

"I understand. You have to be cryptic about the details, of course. Client privilege and all that."

Absently, Beth nodded again. Actually, she was anxious to get out of here now that she had stumbled onto a possible motive for somebody to want Chester dead.

She was about to stand up when the Persian suddenly sprang up into her lap. Beth leaned back in surprise as the cat stuck its face up to hers and sniffed.

Carolyn Hawes beamed. "She likes you," she said. "And you must like cats."

Beth scratched the Persian behind the ears. "Sure."

"Edwina can tell that. All cats can tell when someone likes them. They're quite intelligent, you know. They can tell when someone doesn't like them, too."

Now that Beth thought about it, she supposed Carolyn was right. She owned a few cats over the years, and all of them had taken to her without any trouble. On the other hand, she remembered having friends over who didn't like cats, and the animals had always reacted with either aloofness or outright hostility.

That had nothing to do with her present problem, though. She wanted to talk to Delores Banning again as soon as possible and find out if Nicolette had been around any of the times when Chester's near-fatal mishaps had occurred. Beth would have been willing to bet that Nicolette had been there, all right.

Gently, she lifted the heavy Persian down from her lap. Carolyn Hawes took the cat before Beth could put it on the floor. "She's my precious," Carolyn said. "She's a magnificent creature, don't you think? She's won shows all over the country, and I'm so proud of her."

Beth had never gotten that slobbery over any of her pets, and besides she had to get over to the Banning house as soon as she could. She stood up with a smile and said, "Thank you for talking to me, Mrs. Hawes. You've been a great help."

"I'm not sure how, but if I have, I'm glad. Here, let me show you out."

Beth went straight to her car and sent it down the driveway to the road. It took her several minutes to reach DeMille Drive, then climb the hill on the other side of the road to the Banning estate. That was long enough for her to think through her suspicions. As far as she could see, Nicolette was the only one with a real reason to hurt Chester. Not only would the cat's death increase the estate she would inherit by a hundred grand, but if Chester wasn't around, Nicolette would get the whole thing as soon as

Delores died, rather than having to wait for the cat to die, too. Judging from what Beth had learned this morning about Chester's nocturnal habits—more than one of the servants in the neighborhood had talked about what a feline Lothario the cat was—he was in the prime of his life and might live a long time yet ... if nothing unforeseen happened to him.

And once the cat was dead, who was to say that Nicolette might not try to hurry along Delores's demise, as well?

As Beth pulled up in front of the house, she frowned at the sight of a small, sporty coupe parked there. Even though she hadn't seen what Nicolette was driving the night before, the little car struck Beth as the sort of car the blonde might have. Quickly, Beth got out of the Ford and started toward the door.

Before she got there, the sound of a raised voice drew her to the side of the house. She recognized it as Nicolette's as the blonde called, "Chester! Where are you, damn it?"

Beth's pulse kicked into a higher gear, just as it did before she attempted a risky stunt. She broke into a run, circling the house and spotting movement in an overgrown garden between the mansion and a large pool. Nicolette was there, wearing pants and a silk shirt today, and as Beth approached, she saw Nicolette suddenly lean over and grab at something. She lifted a squirming ball of orange fur by the nape of the neck and said, "Now I've got you!"

Beth left her feet in a flying tackle and crashed into Nicolette before she could wring Chester's neck—or whatever other violent end she had in mind for him. Nicolette yelled in surprise as the impact knocked her off her feet. Beth sprawled on top of her as Chester pulled away and bounded off, disappearing around the front of the house.

Nicolette was still yelling and struggling. Beth got hold of both of her wrists, and with the strength she had developed in her stunt work, she had no trouble pinning the other woman to the ground. "You thought you'd kill Chester so you could inherit everything right away, didn't you?" Beth said, panting for breath from the exertion and from the adrenaline coursing through her.

Nicolette stopped fighting and stared up at Beth in confusion. "What are you talking about?" she demanded.

"I know all about your aunt's will—" Beth began.

Delores Banning's voice said sharply from behind her, "Liz! What the hell are you doing, girl? What's this about my will?"

Beth twisted her head around and saw that Delores had come out of a side door. The older woman was looking on anxiously. Beth said, "I think Nicolette's the one who's been trying to hurt Chester."

"Nonsense! Nicolette adores Chester, just like I do, even if she doesn't always show it."

Delores sounded utterly convinced of that. "I'm afraid you don't know your niece as well as you think you do, Mrs. Banning. Nicolette's the only one with any reason to harm Chester, and just now I saw her grab the cat and try to break his neck!"

"I did no such thing!" Nicolette said. "Chester got out of the house, and Aunt Delores wanted him inside so he'd be safe. She asked me to look for him!"

"That's true," Delores said. "I did ask Nicky to find him. I know she wouldn't hurt him. Why, many's the time I've found Chester curled up in her lap, sleeping peacefully. He only does that with people he can trust."

Beth blinked and tried to make some sense of this. She looked down at Nicolette and said, "Then . . . you *didn't* try to murder Chester . . . ?"

"Of course not!"

"Oh, shoot," Beth said softly.

Between clenched teeth, Nicolette said, "Now will you please *get off of me!*"

Quickly, Beth stood up and helped the other young woman to her feet. "I . . . I'm sorry," she said. "When Carolyn Hawes told me about your aunt's will, I just thought—"

"Carolyn has been gossiping about me again, has she?" Delores cut in. "It's hard to believe that woman was once my best friend."

"She's not anymore?" Beth said.

Delores shook her head. "She's been very cool to me lately, and for the life of me, I can't figure out why. I certainly didn't do anything to offend her, at least not that I know of."

As she brushed off her clothes with curt, angry gestures, Nicolette said, "Mrs. Hawes told you *I* wanted to hurt Chester?"

"Well, not in so many words, but I just thought . . ."

No, she hadn't thought at all, Beth realized suddenly. But she was now, and she turned and ran as hard as she could toward the front of the estate.

Chester had been going in that direction when he fled. Beth had no idea how to go about tracking a cat—Lucas might have been able to do something like that, but she couldn't—but she knew she had to find the animal before something else happened to him. She threw herself into her car, backed around, and took off down the drive. Delores and Nicolette probably thought she had completely lost her mind, but she couldn't take the time to worry about that now.

She headed straight toward the house where she had spoken to Carolyn Hawes, keeping a close eye on the shrubbery on both sides of the drive, watching for a flash of orange fur. By the time she reached the house, she had seen no sign of Chester, but that didn't mean he wasn't over here. As Beth got out of the car, she heard a sudden squall from the other side of the house, loud enough to carry plainly to her ears.

She ran again, her long strides carrying her around the large, sprawling house. She could still hear the squalling. As she rounded the corner of the house, she saw that Carolyn had Chester backed up into a corner of a flagstone patio. The woman didn't look so cool and elegant now as she lifted a croquet mallet over her head and said, "All right, you lecherous little beast! You'll never ruin any more of your betters!"

"Mrs. Hawes!" Beth called, only a little out of breath from her run. "Don't hurt him!"

Chester let out another squall. His fur was puffed up all

over and his teeth were bared in a snarl as he faced the woman he instinctively knew was his enemy .

Carolyn's head jerked around. "Go away!" she said to Beth. "This is none of your business!"

"Yes, it is," Beth insisted, trying to stay calm. "I know what happened now. When are the kittens due?"

"It doesn't matter. I'm going to destroy them immediately, of course. Edwina will be devastated, but it can't be helped." The woman looked at Chester again. "But at least he won't ever force himself on anyone else's precious little darling. He'll be dead!"

"You knew why I was here this morning," Beth said. "You tried to point me at Nicolette Banning by telling me about that will. It almost worked, too. But Delores told me how Chester trusts Nicolette enough to sleep in her lap, and I can see for myself how he reacts to you. He remembers the other times you tried to kill him, doesn't he?"

"He doesn't deserve any less. Now get off of my property, or I'll call the police."

Beth swallowed hard. She didn't know how the police would react to this situation, but she had a hunch they would frown more on her trespassing than they would on Carolyn's attempts to kill Chester. Protecting a cat wouldn't rank high on their list of priorities.

"Let me take Chester with me," she said. "I promise you he won't ever bother Edwina again."

"He certainly won't, the low-bred little monster. I'm going to kill him."

"Maybe I can talk Mrs. Banning into having him fixed." Slowly, Beth moved closer as she continued, "And Edwina will be okay, she really will. Lots of cats have had kittens."

"Not Edwina. She's high-strung. She'll never be the same. She'll never win another show."

Beth kept edging closer, and she was almost near enough to make a grab for that croquet mallet. Then Chester let out a howl and tried to dart past Carolyn. The mallet swept down with surprising speed.

Chester was faster. The mallet smacked against one of the flagstones. Beth leaped toward Carolyn, and the older woman jerked the mallet around, backhanding it at Beth's head. Reflexes honed by stunt work allowed Beth to drop under the swing and lower her shoulder as she ran into Carolyn. Both of them went down.

Out of the corner of her eye, Beth saw Chester taking off toward home.

She wrenched the mallet out of Carolyn's hands, rolled a few feet away, stood up. She flung the mallet off to the side. "That's enough!" Beth said. "I'm going to tell Mrs. Banning everything that's happened, and I hope, if you hurt Chester, that she sues you!"

Carolyn pulled herself up on her knees and glared at Beth. "I told you once to get off my property," she said coldly.

"I'm going. But you'd better remember what I said."

Beth went back to her car, trembling with anger. She had solved the case—such as it was—but she hadn't done anything to protect Chester from further harm. Abruptly, she stopped and turned around, striding around the house to face a still-fuming Carolyn Hawes.

"This whole affair is a secret, isn't it?" Beth said. "Nobody in your fancy cat-show circles even knows that your cat is going to have kittens. Maybe they'd like to hear about it—including who the father is."

The pallor that swept over Carolyn's face told Beth her shot had struck its target. "You wouldn't dare," she said.

"Sure I would. The rivalry in those shows is pretty fierce, isn't it? I'm sure a lot of your so-called friends would love to hear about how Edwina was rutting with Chester like a common alley cat."

For a second, Beth thought Carolyn was going to pick up the croquet mallet and come after her again. But then the woman pointed a shaking finger at her and said, "You just keep your mouth shut. I . . . I won't do anything else about Chester. But tell Delores Banning to keep him away from here!"

"I'll tell her," Beth said. She felt a little better as she went back to her car and drove away from the Hawes estate.

On the way back to the Banning house, she spotted Chester sitting in some flowers and chewing happily on their leaves. She stopped the car and called him, and after a moment's hesitation, he sauntered over to her. His instincts must have identified her as an ally, because he allowed her to pick him up, put him in the car, and drive him back home.

Delores was overjoyed to see him, and even Nicolette seemed happy. The blonde rubbed Chester's ears as Delores held him, and she said to Beth, "My aunt and I don't agree on everything, but I hope you understand now that I would never hurt Chester."

"I know," Beth said. "It was Carolyn Hawes who was after him."

"Carolyn!" Delores said. "But why?"

Beth explained, feeling a little foolish as she did so, and concluded by saying, "Once I realized that Persian cat I saw over there might be pregnant instead of just fat, I figured out what could have happened."

"I should hope so," Nicolette said.

"I mean about why somebody else might want to hurt Chester. It seemed a little far-fetched, but ..."

"You're the detective, Liz," Delores said. "I suppose I'll have to have Chester ... well, fixed so that he won't roam so much."

"I think that would be a good idea."

"I hate to do that. He was just following his instincts, you know. It was second nature to him."

Beth nodded. She thought about how Delores had said she was the detective. Beth liked the sound of that. What Chester had been doing was second nature to him ... and Beth suddenly realized that, just like stunt work, this private eye business might be second nature to her, too.

After all, she was Lucas Hallam's daughter.

For Scruffy

266

Hollywood Considered as a Seal Point in the Sun

•

Bruce Holland Rogers

It shouldn't be a surprise that Hollywood's an illusion. But people still get fooled. The tourists come here expecting to find the place where movies are made, when almost all the real movie business has moved out to the San Fernando Valley. Paramount and Pinnacle are the only studios left. But who knows that, even after they're told? This is Tinseltown. Tourists think the action *must* be here.

They look at the sun-bleached, dusty storefronts, they cruise the supposedly storied intersection of Hollywood and Vine, and there's nothing there. The Brown Derby restaurant *used* to be there, and maybe, in the old days, an occasional movie star really did have dinner in the giant hat. But Hollywood's city limits are not the place to look for celebrities.

But illusions have staying power. Sometimes even after tourists see the real Hollywood, they go on believing that they saw what they expected. Or they believe that it was right around the corner, that they were close, but somehow missed it.

Hollywood is a dreamscape. Everything is transformation and everything is fluid, up until the day when you're discovered. If that big break comes, everything changes. Then you wear the illusion you've made for yourself like armor that's welded on. In Hollywood, you'd better be careful about what you dream.

The illusion I was weaving as I sat in Geoffrey Laska's

office at Pinnacle was a tricky one. I was trying hard not to actually lie, but there were certain turns I didn't want the interview to take. The tactic I settled on was bluster.

"Get this straight," I said. "I don't know any tabloid writers, and I hope to keep it that way." As angrily as I could manage, I ground out a second lipstick-stained cigarette. Unfortunately, the ashtray in Geoffrey Laska's office was the size of a dinner plate, and anything I did to it was going to seem small. "And I resent the implications of your question."

I dug a pack of Trues from my purse.

From behind his enormous desk, Laska smiled very slightly. If I was surprising him, he didn't show it. "All I said, Ms. Hughes, was that I thought you must have some interesting stories to tell about your profession. It wasn't a question at all."

"But it was," I said, pointing a fresh cigarette at him and leaning forward as if my indignation might launch me from the couch and out of Laska's office. In fact, it was going to be a struggle to get to my feet from that overstuffed monstrosity. Everything in Laska's office was king-sized and plush, as if the man needed constant reminders that he was the Big Guy at Pinnacle Studios. Big office, big couch, big desk, and a carpet so deep I was glad I wore flats. Heels on a rug like that would be as tricky as walking a highwire in the Santa Ana winds. I'd have broken an ankle, at least.

The thought echoed in my head for a moment. *Walking a highwire in the Santa Ana winds.* Not a bad line. I should write it down, file it away.

"I was merely commenting—" Laska started to say.

"You were fishing," I told him. "You were asking me whether I'd be willing to spill the details of past cases. What do you think the 'private' in 'private investigator' means? If you doubt my integrity personally, then look at it this way—even a call girl knows better than to part with the secrets of her clients. It dries up business. Or do you ask hookers, too, about their 'interesting stories'?"

His face reddened. If you can make a studio exec blush, that's a real accomplishment. So far, so good. I finally had him off balance, and the conversation would go where I steered it. I still didn't have the job, still didn't even know what the job was, but I hadn't let Laska get to the questions that I didn't want to answer.

"So far, we've done nothing but talk about me," I said. "If you've got some work that needs doing, why don't you spill the beans so I can get started?"

Laska steepled his fingers. We *had* talked entirely about me, and I had said exactly nothing. Would he like that, or would it put him off? Should I change how I was playing this?

No, I thought. Play it as it lays. Only luck could have brought me this interview. The ink was barely dry in my yellow pages ad, and if Laska had done any checking at all, he'd know that. So, obviously, he hadn't checked.

A man like Laska does it all on instinct. He tapped his fingers together, staring at me with a gaze that said, What have we here? Who are you *really*?

Yeah. Who was I?

A country mouse in city rat's clothing. A kid fresh off the bus from Kansas, if you didn't count the year in San Francisco, where I learned how to breathe city air, how to think city thoughts, how to starve writing scripts for ninety-nine-seat theaters. A starving screenwriter looking for up-front money to pay last month's rent. That's who I was. I was exactly what Geoffrey Laska was not looking for to do work so sensitive that even his studio lackeys had been rousted from the office for my interview.

I lit my very last cigarette and pretended Laska wasn't even in the room.

"All right," he said at last. "You'll do." He took out two envelopes and slid them across the desk at me. "It's about Jerry Ellis. We want him found."

I missed the next couple sentences. I was counting the contents of the smaller envelope. Last month's rent, and this month's, and next month's! Grocery money! Gas for the Honda! My mother would never believe it. Supposedly, my older sisters got all the brains. I wanted to throw the bills into the air and laugh.

Instead, I blew a long, slow cloud of smoke.

"Jerry Ellis," I said, nodding soberly.

A year ago, I would have blurted, Not *the* Jerry Ellis! A year ago, I'd have blown everything right there.

The business is just the business. Professionalism is measured by your lack of enthusiasm.

I took another drag on my cigarette. I tried to look like I might fall asleep.

Ellis was a comic actor. I liked his first slapstick cop movies, and I'm picky about comedy. The only reason I hadn't seen anything past the first sequel was that I'm leery of movies with a three or higher in the title.

In the big envelope was a publicity shot of Ellis, along with a few pages of names and addresses. "And what has Mr. Ellis done?"

Laska sighed. "Not a damn thing since *Bullethead 6*. That's the problem."

By the time I got home, I was doing my celebrating out loud. "Selkie!" I called in that high voice reserved for animals and small children, a voice I am careful not to use on the street. "Come on, sweetheart." I pulled a can of gourmet cat food out of the grocery bag. "I brought you the good stuff! I'm a hit! We're in the money!"

I looked around the living room. "Selkie?"

She wasn't on the windowsill, and she wasn't curled among the couch throw pillows or on the little rug in front of the stereo.

"Selkie? Come come, kittikins."

I clicked my tongue, then resorted to popping the can. If she was in the back of the apartment, that should have brought her running into the hallway.

Nothing.

Calling her name, I checked out the bedroom, the bathroom. She wasn't in any of her standard spots.

I checked the living room again, then the bedroom, then the living room a third time. It's not as though I had a big apartment to search. Could she have gotten out?

"Mrrt," she said. I turned toward the sound, and found

270

her standing in plain view between the hallway book-shelves. I must have walked right by her six times. She hadn't moved or made a sound. That's not like her. Like most Siamese, she's a talker.

"Think you're funny, don't you?" I said. "I bring you a treat, and this is my thanks."

"Mrrt," she said again. She looked smug.

I was broiling the first steak I'd had in months when Claire called. "Hey, partner," she said. "The keyboard is getting cold. You were going to call."

"Been busy," I told her.

"Doing what?"

"Surviving."

"So are we going to get cracking on the next script?"

"Soon," I said. "You don't have to wait for me. Why not strike out on your own, do a script by yourself?"

"Because I don't have your flair for dialogue."

"My flair for dialogue hasn't exactly made us rich and famous, or haven't you noticed?"

"It's a matter of time. We're good."

"Claire, everyone in Hollywood is good. Everyone in town is waiting to be discovered. A cop pulled me over this morning. When he found out I was going to a studio meeting, he didn't write me a ticket. He went to the trunk of his cruiser to get the script he drives around all day, just in case he's lucky and bags Geoff Laska running a stop sign."

"You had a meeting and didn't tell me? Who with?"

"It was other business. You know. The investigator thing."

"Who? Who?"

"Could have been anyone," I said. "Maybe it was the janitor. Maybe it *was* Geoff Laska."

"Geoffrey Laska! Maddie! Pinnacle is perfect for *Storm-swept*. Did you take him the script?"

"Did I *say* it was Laska? Anyway, I told you, this was other business."

271

"Tell me you at least pitched the idea. Tell me you didn't go into Laska's office and fail to even pitch."

"Claire, it was other business. For this gig, I'm not a writer."

I opened the oven door wider to check on the steak.

"You're cooking meat," Claire said with disgust.

"What, can you smell it?" I laughed.

"I can hear the grease splattering. What are you doing, frying pork chops? Poor pig. And poor Maddie."

"If you want to grieve, grieve for a cow. I'm broiling a steak, and I'm going to savor every bite."

"In between puffs on your cigarette. Maddie, you know what's holding you back? Impurities. If you would just quit eating animals, quit drinking coffee and alcohol, and stop smoking so many cigarettes—"

"—then I would die," I said. "You've got it backwards, Claire. If you live on poisoned ground, you've got to eat poison, build your resistance. Anyway, beef is good. I was raised on beef."

"Are we doing another script or not?"

"Listen, Claire, I'm out of screenwriting for a while, okay? I've got a new line of work that has a big advantage. It pays."

"So what are you doing for Pinnacle?"

"I shouldn't say."

"I'm like a sister to you."

"My sisters gossip."

"Better than a sister. A best friend. Come on, Maddie. Give. I won't breathe a word of it."

"It's a missing person thing."

"Who?"

"Claire, I can't say, really."

"Somebody's been kidnapped?"

"Sounds like this person kidnapped himself."

"What does *that* mean?"

"He's the invisible man. Returns no calls, hasn't been seen. The servants go in and out at his estate, but money can't buy information they don't have—he's not there. It's not like I'm tracking down a man who has skipped on a contract. There is no contract. The studio just wants to know where he is."

"Why?"

"To beg. They want him to do a movie."

"Must be nice to be wanted."

"You'd think so," I said, taking my steak out of the oven.

"Maybe this guy is just letting the studio guys get desperate as a negotiating ploy."

"My thought exactly," I told her.

"So who is it?"

"I've probably told you too much already."

"You haven't said *anything*!"

"I've said plenty. Not a word to anyone, right? I don't want to turn on the tube tomorrow and find that you've become an inside source for *Entertainment Tonight*."

Claire promised to smoke a cigar if she talked. From her, there couldn't be a more sacred pledge.

The second envelope Laska had given me contained the names and numbers for Jerry Ellis's friend and associates, and there were penciled notes on some of the pages. Apparently, someone at the studio had already tried to track Ellis down.

It was easy to understand why Laska was desperate. He wanted to do another Bullethead movie, but without Jerry Ellis, that'd be like making the next Star Trek movie with stand-ins. Ellis is box office.

That first morning, I made some calls, tried to set up appointments, but the people who'd been spoken to already all sang pretty much the same song. Ellis had been withdrawing from his friends for months, and they had already told the studio that they didn't know where to find him. If I pressed, they hung up on me.

There's no good way to lean on someone over the phone.

On the other hand, these were people who would be tough to just drop in on. Most of them lived in houses with iron gates and dogs on the grounds. I'd have to catch them at work.

Vic Parker was on the list. He was Ellis's tennis partner,

a long-time character actor in the soaps. I called to see if his show was shooting that day, and if he'd be on the set. Then I drove out to the Valley.

The secret to moving around unchallenged in a television studio is this: Walk, don't drive, through the front gates—no one in Southern California knows how to act around a pedestrian. Wear clothes that mean business. Scowl like a prima donna. Prima donnas on a studio lot always look like they belong.

That's exactly how I got to the soundstage where I found Parker doing a sheets scene for his soap.

Simulated sex under bright lights for an audience of cameras, boom mikes and a script girl from Vassar. That's the Hollywood tourists look for. And, like I say, it's not *in* Hollywood.

The scene was pretty hot, but watching Parker and the actress turn it on and off between takes was practically a sermonette in the illusions of love. I've met guys who do that without the bright lights. They're in California, and they're in Kansas, too.

After the last take, Parker came to the sidelines in a robe. He looked as bushed as a prizefighter in the ninth. I guess it takes something out of you, all those scripted clinches.

"I need to talk to you, Mr. Parker," I said. "It's about Jerry Ellis."

He looked at me thoughtfully, then seemed to snap out of a daze. "Jerry?" he said. His pupils were pinpoints of intensity. "Why? What's happened?"

I almost played it straight, but straight lines over the phone had taken me nowhere. Where would the current carry us if I just jumped in? "I think you can guess," I said.

"Who are you?" he said. Before I could answer, he said, "Oh, God. It was the boat, wasn't it? Everybody thought it was such a joke, but I knew, I *knew*!"

I was stymied for a moment, but then I went with the flow. "How could you know? How could anybody?"

"His father," Parker said. "That's how I knew. Jerry made people laugh, but all his life he bore up under that terrible wound. God, this is terrible. Jerry and I were close, so very close. Like brothers."

"So I gather."

Parker scowled. "You aren't a reporter, are you?" The scowl rose to indignation. "How did you get onto this set?"

"I'm not a reporter," I said.

What came next surprised me. In the emotions that crossed Parker's face, I saw the tirade he'd been working up to, the shock at having the rug pulled from under his feet.

"Not, not a reporter?" he said.

And I had thought I was the one performing.

"Then who the hell are you?"

I told him.

He turned his back. It was every bit as final as hanging up a phone. As I walked off the set, I wrote a headline in my head, the one Parker apparently thought I was there to get: 'WE WERE LIKE BROTHERS' ACTOR VIC PARKER LAMENTS.

He was quick on his feet, I had to admit. Unless, of course, he knew for a fact that Jerry Ellis was dead. Then he could have rehearsed those lines for weeks.

At least now I had something to go on. I called the studio's publicity department to ask about Ellis's father.

Later that afternoon, the sound of beery male voices coming from the cabin of the *Watery Grave* made me think I might be getting very close indeed.

I had talked straight with the next few names on my phone list, now that I knew to ask about a boat. Everyone I called could tell me the name of the craft, but it took several tries to find someone who remembered which marina Ellis used.

The hatch at the top of the sailboat's cabin was open. I went aboard.

"Full house, aces and jacks," came a voice from the cabin, and then a deeper, froggy voice bellowed, "You stink! Freddy, you stink!"

"Luck," said the first voice, "and superior intelligence. That's all it is."

A third voice said, "Intelligence my ass."

"Jess, did you drink the last Red Tail?"

"Don't worry about it. After the third or fourth, they all taste the same."

A belch. Laughter. The sounds men make when they think women aren't around.

I stepped down the ladder. The wood creaked too much for a stealthy entrance, and whoever was down there could see my legs before I could see anything at all of them.

"Well hell-o!" said the superior intelligence voice.

Then the frog voice croaked, "Capper, no broads. You know the rule is no broads."

The cigar smoke was like San Francisco fog.

"I didn't invite no one!" Capper was protesting when I could finally see the lot of them. He was the youngest of the bunch, but all of these men were in their sixties, give or take. All the faces were too old to be Jerry Ellis's, though one face, I thought, looked familiar.

"Forgive the interruption," I said.

"This is a private boat and a private party," said frog voice. He had a face to match.

"Jess, where are your manners?" asked superior intelligence.

"I left 'em at home with my wife, Freddy. She can have 'em."

"Yeah," said Capper. "Manners ain't got a thing to do with poker. That's the beauty."

The other two laughed.

"Actually," I said, "I'm looking for the owner of this boat."

"Well, you won't find him here," said Jess.

Freddy stood up, stooping a little under the low ceiling. "What do you want with the owner?"

"Just to talk."

"I smell a newshound," Jess said.

"Seems like I spend my day telling people I'm not a reporter."

Hollywood Considered as a Seal Point in the Sun

The silver-haired man who looked vaguely familiar said, "Do you play poker?" Once I had the voice, I knew him. John VanderZee. He'd had a part in the first Bullethead movie.

"No, no, no!" Jess protested. "Broads on a ship are bad luck, and broads in a poker game are worse!"

"Topside," Freddy told me. "I'll talk to you."

"That's my money you're taking out of the game," Jess said. "Don't you go far without you give me a chance to win it back."

"Jess," said Capper, "ain't you learned that when Freddy's on a streak, you ain't gonna get it back?"

"If you haven't learned that yet, I'll be back," Freddy promised Jess, "to complete your instruction."

At the stern of the boat, Freddy gestured to a seat cushion. I sat, dug out a cigarette, and said, "A little early in the day for a poker game, isn't it?"

"It's one of the advantages of an irregular career," Freddy said. "We get a surprising number of days off. Besides, most of us are semiretired."

"From?"

Freddy smiled. "From work, Miss . . ."

"Ms. Madeline Hughes. Call me Maddie."

"Okay, Maddie. What line of work are *you* in?"

"I asked first."

"Never mind. I think I know. Your clients are pretty hot to talk to him, aren't they?"

"Can you blame them?"

"Sure I can. Bean-counting bastards. But I understand them. Blake Bullethead is a proven commodity, one that only Jerry Ellis can provide."

"Is Ellis just holding out for a better deal?"

"Jerry has been trying to get out from under Bullethead for years, but the only roles he's offered are Bullethead or imitations of Bullethead. He's an actor, Maddie. He could do *Lear*."

"I talked to someone today who thought Ellis might be dead."

"Namely?"

"Vic Parker."

Freddy laughed. "Like he'd have a clue."

"I thought he and Ellis were close?"

"Jerry's too nice to tell flakes to flake off. A tragic flaw. Parker ingratiates himself to anyone who acts in features. He hopes it'll rub off."

"Parker mentioned Ellis's father . . ."

"The tabloids always tried to make a story out of that. There's nothing to it."

"Nothing to his father jumping off a bridge?"

"Jerry was a *baby*. Never knew the guy. Had a great step-dad."

"And the name of this boat?"

"Look, Jerry has that dark streak, it's true. But he's fine. I know he's fine. Scratch that off your list."

"Then where is he?"

"Not sitting at home waiting for an invite to do another Bullethead, believe me."

"You seem to take this business with Pinnacle Studios personally."

"With *Bullethead*, Pinnacle found a formula that worked. There hasn't been a sliver of creativity in those movies since the first one. It's all recycling. That's why none of us worked on the series past number two or three. Recycling. I designed a great set for that first movie. That whole cartoonish style of the buildings and cars, that's all mine. But after that, all they wanted was imitations of what I'd already done. Fulfill the expectations. That's what eats Jerry. I told you. The man can *act*. But the studios won't give him a chance. They figure audiences who see that face on the screen expect to laugh."

"Maybe they're right."

Freddy looked out over the water. "Maybe they are. But Jerry deserves his shot at something else, without interference."

"And what would that something else be, exactly?"

He didn't answer right away. "This boat is private property," he said finally. "You're trespassing."

* * *

Hollywood Considered as a Seal Point in the Sun

I had a good idea of what Jerry Ellis might be doing, but not *where*. Not until I went home to feed Selkie.

It was a replay. I called her, looked for her in all her usual spots. Then I remembered the new place, the bookcases.

There she was, right under my nose.

Right under my nose, and invisible.

In the morning, I made some calls. I ruled out the Ahmanson Theater because of the playbill. The only works in rehearsal were comedies and musicals. On tap for the John Anson Ford Theater were jazz concerts, and a cabaret review. Westwood Playhouse was hosting a Broadway musical; so was the Wilshire. Pantages had closed for remodeling. My best bets were the Doolittle and a whole bunch of smaller theaters. Since the Doolittle was right in the heart of Hollywood, I started there.

And struck out.

There was a play in rehearsal, a brooding drama about despair and unrewarded sacrifice, with a split set that had a living room on one side and a desolate rocky island on the other. What was acted out in the living room was danced symbolically on the island. Very artsy, very dark, and just the sort of vehicle I guessed Ellis would be attracted to, except that it was an all-woman cast.

I stayed to watch more of the rehearsal than I needed to. I mean, I've had days like that. The play spoke to me, at least until it started to annoy me. PMS is hell, but it's not a *raison d'être*. Get a life, girls.

I had ruled out the big theaters, the houses with a thousand seats or more. Now I'd have to try the ninety-nine-seaters. This could take some legwork. There are more tiny theaters in Hollywood and LA than there are farms in Kansas. Then again, I figured Ellis would stay in Hollywood. He'd enjoy the irony.

I tried Theatre/Theater. In two minutes, I spotted Ellis.

The director was walking the cast through their blocking. Ellis had grown a beard and dyed it. His hair was darker, too, with streaks of gray at the temples. Without knowing to look for Jerry Ellis, you might look at that actor and not recognize a familiar face.

"I want you farther downstage when Angelina's speech starts," the director was saying.

"Here? Or back even farther?" said Ellis, and it wasn't the voice I expected at all. It was deeper, richer. I guessed that this voice, not the goofy voice he had cultivated for Bullethead, was his real voice. It reminded me of when I was a kid and had first heard Jim Nabors sing. Gomer Pyle's mouth opened and somebody else's voice came out.

No one paid me any attention as the rehearsal went on. No one, that is, but Jerry Ellis. Since my eyes were on him the whole time, he could scarcely help noticing me. I don't have Selkie's knack for invisibility. When the rehearsal broke for lunch, he headed quickly for the wings. I followed.

"You can run, Mr. E," I called from behind him, "but you can't hide."

He ignored me.

I shouldered my way past other actors. "Do you want to talk to me first," I asked him, "or do I just call the studio and tell them where you are?"

He turned outside a dressing room door, glancing from me to the other cast members. "Are you talking to me?"

For a moment, close up, he almost had me convinced. The voice was so wrong for Jerry Ellis, and the dye job very, very good.

"Maybe we should speak in private," I said, gesturing toward the dressing room. But one of the other actors was already going through that door, and another followed. Theatre/Theater wasn't big enough for a star on the door and privacy, I realized.

He said, "Let's go for a walk."

I followed him up Cahuenga Boulevard in silence. We walked as far as Hollywood Boulevard, then sat on a sunbleached bench at a bus stop. Ellis's shoulders slumped. It's easy to look defeated at the corner of Cahuenga and Hollywood, especially for an actor.

"You didn't use my name," he said morosely. "I suppose I should be grateful."

"Cut the Sad-Sack bit. I'm not buying."

He sat up. "I thought it was a pretty good disguise," he said, "posing as an unknown."

"It would have been perfect," I said, "except for my cat." He gave me a blank stare. "Your cat."

"Selkie."

"A cat named Selkie," he said, warming a little. "Let me guess. She's a seal point."

"You're sharp. Most people don't get that."

"My grandmother was Scottish," he said, watching a bedraggled hooker cross Hollywood. "She used to tell me stories about the seal maidens who stole the hearts of young men."

"Selkie steals no hearts. She's been spayed."

"But she has something to do with your finding me?"

"Selkie has five or six places in my apartment where she likes to sit. Her regular hangouts. I get used to looking for her in those spots. Every once in a while, she changes to a new one. When she does that, I can be looking for her and walk right by and not see her, because she's not in a place where I'm accustomed to seeing the cat. Just like you're in a ninety-nine-seat theater where no one's accustomed to seeing a Name."

"Until someone tells them to look."

A bus went by, kicking up dust.

"My job was to find you for Pinnacle, not blow your cover."

"Geoffrey Laska will have other ideas."

"Why should he care? He just wants you to do another film for him."

"Laska would rather I didn't spend my energies on anything but endless Bullethead films. He'll leak this to the press. I can do the part, but as soon as the attraction is seeing Jerry Ellis in a serious role, I'm caught in the same old web of expectations. I'm stuck with Blake Bullethead."

"Laska would do that? Torpedo you?"

Ellis said, "Not from around here, are you?"

He was right. What a Kansas thing to say.

"When does the play open?"

"Two weeks."

I stood up. "I can give you opening night."

"Why would you do that?"

"Don't ask. I'll get smart and change my mind. But tell me this. How is this going to get you out from under Bullethead?"

He shrugged. "Maybe it won't. The main thing is getting to do a serious role. But I do think that maybe, just maybe, it can be a stepping stone to a serious screen role. If I get some solid reviews . . ."

"You think that would make a difference? Theater reviews?"

"It would be a start."

I said, "Not from around here, are you? It would be zip. The studio buys and sells image and perception. Some critic who loves the serious Jerry Ellis for the *Times* isn't going to change the assumptions of Joe and Jane Moviegoer in Middle America. You haven't thought this out."

That deflated him again.

"Act your ass off," I told him. "You do this play and let me think about the big picture."

In Geoffrey Laska's office, I said, "I'm making headway."

He looked at me over those steepled fingers.

"The guys who hang out on his boat sometimes, they know where he is."

Laska tapped his fingers together.

"We could pass messages through them, maybe. What do you think?"

He let the silence grow. "I had hoped for more."

"More will come," I said. "Trust me."

Claire called.

"Maddie," she said, "if we don't keep something on the front burner, we're going to lose our touch."

"And we have the Midas touch when it comes to scripts, don't we?"

"Don't be a wet blanket. I'm telling you, it's just a matter of time. When we get discovered, we'll want a whole stack of finished scripts to pitch."

"We pitch 'em, and producers knock 'em into the dirt."

"You know what the problem is?"

"Claire, I'm trying to work. I'm *thinking*."

"Red meat. You produce too much bile."

I took in a morning rehearsal at Theatre/Theater. At the lunch break, I cornered Ellis again. We walked to a coffee shop, one that allowed smoking and thinking.

I flipped open a notebook. "Describe the ending you'd want for your ideal vehicle. Give it to me in tone, in mood. Don't sweat the details."

He didn't have time to think about it much. "It's five parts *Lear*, four parts *Hamlet*, and one part *Batman*. Thunder, fire, and rain. Maybe some bodies strewn about."

"Good," I told him. "More."

"Might be a hospital instead of a battleground. Or a cemetery with a fresh grave."

"I'm getting the idea," I said, writing. "Keep it coming."

"What's this for?"

"Jerry, what happens to a seal point Siamese in the sun? Do you know?"

"I haven't the faintest idea what you're talking about."

"I'm talking about burying Blake Bullethead in a way that will count. I'm talking about remaking your career in the eyes of Joe and Jane Moviegoer. I'm talking about an end run around Geoffrey Laska."

Ellis stared at me.

I said, "By the way, it's going to cost."

I named a price.

He didn't flinch.

He said, "You're going to get me into some real trouble, aren't you?"

"That's what I do. I get people into deeper and deeper

trouble. When it can't get worse, it does. Then I get them out."

As soon as I'd said that, I wished I hadn't. Jerry Ellis looked at me and smiled, and I had a feeling that he knew exactly what I meant. Unfortunately.

"I got a message in to him," I told Laska, "and I got one out. He wants to direct. He wants full creative control."

"His agent called with the same news," Laska said from behind his aircraft carrier of a desk. "You're not bringing me much that I can't get less expensively."

"Look," I said, "aren't you getting what you want? He's willing to do another Bullethead movie. He's talking to you, right? You still want him tracked down in the flesh, I'll do that, but it's starting to look like a moot point to me."

Laska could have been carved out of stone.

"Can I ask you a question?"

Laska didn't answer, no doubt waiting to see what sort of a question it would be.

"What's the point of making Bullethead movies if your star's heart isn't in it? Surely the quality suffers."

"Ellis is a pro," Laska said. "He may drag his feet, but when the cameras roll, he acts."

"I guess. But I checked the numbers, Mr. Laska. The first Bullethead was big money. Number two was also a hit. After that, the numbers eroded."

"That's not Ellis's fault. It's the nature of these endless series. You get down to the hardcore fans, no matter what."

"So you'd agree that these aren't the best movies you could make for the money?"

Laska didn't answer that. Too close to home.

"Sequels are safe money," he said. "A Bullethead feature has a ceiling. It also has a floor. It can't bomb completely. Movies are like the stock market, Ms. Hughes. There's a risk-reward ratio. If you put everything into stocks, you can get killed. Bullethead sequels are as safe as CDs."

"And they'll never earn more than five percent."

"But they'll never earn less."

"My advice is to give Ellis what he wants."

"We have a director."

"Cut him loose. Give him another project. Otherwise, you won't get Ellis. Trust me on this. Ellis isn't going to budge."

"And how do you know this?"

I said, "I can feel it."

"That's what I'm paying for? Your feelings?"

"Time and legwork is what you pay for," I said. "What I'm offering right now is advice, and it's free."

"And worth every penny."

"Maybe you don't need a detective anymore, Mr. Laska."

Laska said, "Maybe you're right."

"It's just as well," I told Ellis the afternoon before opening night. "No more divided loyalties. I've got to have *some* ethics."

"My agent called," Ellis said. "Laska rolled. I'm directing, full creative control. I wish you'd tell me how this will do me any good."

I said, "Get me the script."

Opening night, I was in the audience at Theatre/Theater. I laughed. I cried. Ellis was pretty damn good.

The next couple of days, I looked for reviews. The critic for the *Metropolitan* was kind, the LA *Daily Journal* less so. The Hollywood *Citizen News* did a story on recent openings that mentioned the play but passed no judgment. The *Times* had nothing to say at all.

Ellis was doing what he wanted to do, but no more than ninety-nine people a night got to see him do it.

"A contract?" Claire said.

"That's your name there, isn't it?"

She read all the way through. "Maddie, it gives me a screen credit!"

"Second-line credit. Paul Wood gets the first."

"Who's Paul Wood?"

I gave her the title page. It said:

BULLETHEAD 6, PAUL WOOD, FOURTH DRAFT, REVISED.
REVISED BLUE PAGES, JANUARY 5
REVISED PINK PAGES, JANUARY 18
REVISED YELLOW PAGES, FEBRUARY 2

"And where's the script?"

I indicated a short stack of colored pages on my kitchen table. "This is what we're using. The opening is vintage Bullethead, great stuff. And I've pulled some of the funniest scenes, ones that don't depend on a lot of obvious set-up. This is what we keep."

Claire looked at the other, bigger stack, the pages we were throwing out. "I hope I never meet Paul Wood," she said.

"He gets a screen credit."

"Let's hope he still wants it."

"Here's the tone of the ending," I said. I read from the notes I had made with Ellis.

"Brooding. Tragic death. Disease," Claire summarized.

"Yeah. I see it this way. We open with what Wood gives us, a boffo bungled bank heist and hilarious chase. Just what the audience expects. The scene ends, and the camera pulls back to reveal the edges of the set, the cameras in the foreground. Ellis starts stripping off makeup. He talks to one of the other actors. It's the story of the making of a Bullethead movie."

Claire nodded.

"The other actor, the friend of the character played by Ellis—we won't call him Ellis, let's keep some separation—he's dying of something. This is going to be his last movie. Everyone knows it."

"What's he got?"

"I don't know. What's good?"

"Cancer's good."

"Right. Hard to miss with cancer. Okay. Cancer. And he's sort of a father figure to the Ellis actor. John Vander-

Zee, say. While he and Ellis are making this hysterical movie, he's dying. See the existential struggle?"

"Do not go gentle . . ."

"Right, right. Rage against the dying light. And he's a real soldier, facing up to it. A trouper. We can do a lot with the tragic clown motif. Then for a while, it looks like a miracle is in the offing. Things turn hopeful."

"But he won't make it," Claire said with a mixture of sorrow and delight.

"No," I said. "He finishes his role in the Bullethead movie, but those last slapstick scenes are heartbreakers to film. After he's gone, Ellis gets to do his gloom and doom at the cemetery. Or maybe it's a bedside death scene. Anyway, the end will call for some really moody set designed by Freddy Glaver. Do you love it?"

"Where's your supply of green paper?" Claire asked. "That's what we're up to, right? Fifth draft?"

"Unpack your word processor. Let's see those fingers fly!"

"First we open windows," Claire said. "It smells like an ashtray in here."

"Quit complaining," I said. "Are you here to work or to breathe?"

Jerry Ellis read our draft in his living room, while Claire and I watched. His reaction did not exactly reassure me. He read the first pages, the white, blue, pink, and yellow ones of the original draft, in stoic silence. Those were the funny parts.

When he got to the tragic green pages, he started laughing. With every new page he turned to, he laughed that much harder. For sixty pages he read in hysterics.

Claire's face was bone white.

He flipped to the last five pages. As he read the ending, he laughed so hard he couldn't breathe. Then he looked up at me.

"It's brilliant," he said, wiping the corner of his eyes.

"You like it?" said Claire. "You're laughing in all the wrong places!"

"I'm laughing because I keep imagining the look on Geoff Laska's face at the screening."

"Oh," Claire said, not looking very reassured.

"Laska expects to get a safe production for his money," Ellis said. "We'll deliver a blockbuster. And even if we don't, this is just the vehicle I needed. Maddie, you've saved me from years of geriatric Blake Bullethead roles. You were right. You were exactly right about what it would take."

"Thank Claire," I said. "She did the rewrite."

Claire opened her mouth to say something, but I silenced her with a glare.

"A while ago," Ellis said, "you said something about seal points, but you never explained."

"Jerry, before I moved down here, I spent a year in San Francisco. That's where I got Selkie. We had a north-facing apartment, and the steam heat barely worked. It was a cold year. Then I moved down here to an apartment without air conditioning and with south-facing windows. Winter or summer, Selkie basks like a lizard."

"So?"

"So I had pictures of her that I had taken in San Francisco, and pictures I had taken here, and one day I saw some of those pictures side by side and noticed that Selkie's tail, paws, and ears were a lot darker in San Francisco than they are here in LA."

Claire said, "The sun bleached her?"

"Not bleached. I did some reading. It's all a matter of skin temperature. The ears, the feet, the tail, those parts of a cat are colder than the rest of her, so the fur turns darker. But keep a seal point warm, and her next coat will come in lighter everywhere."

"You're making this up."

"I thought it sounded weird, so I asked a vet. He said that if he wraps a bandage around a seal point's tail, that cat's next coat will have a lighter ring where the dressing was."

"I don't see the connection," said Ellis.

"It's this, Jerry. I'd have never seen the change in her

coat without the pictures to compare. That's because I saw her every day, and from day to day, the change wasn't noticeable. That's what we have to do. We grab your usual audience with a promise of the same old same old, then show them a transformation so gradual that it's already over before they notice."

"You're a clever lady."

Claire said, "She knows, she knows."

Ellis dangled the script. "There's room for another name on the screen credit."

Claire looked at me expectantly. I bit my lip. "What makes you think I had anything to do with writing the script?"

"You said so. Remember? You said your specialty was getting people into trouble, making things worse and worse for them, then getting them out. Sounds to me like the job description of a screenwriter."

"He's got you," Claire said.

"So how about it?" said Ellis. "You want your name up in celluloid where everyone can see it?"

Where everyone can see it, I thought.

Studio brass hate writers. They'd never hire a writer to be a PI, not on purpose. They thought it was bad enough that they had to hire writers to write.

"No way." I shook my head.

I knew, even as I said it, that I'd have regrets. This had been an easy case. It wouldn't always be this much fun. I was selling myself an illusion.

What the hell. In Hollywood, at least you know what an illusion is. That's one variety of not being fooled.

Claire looked like she'd just seen me swallow my own nose, but Ellis was smiling. Of course he'd be the one to understand.

"Maddie," he said, "You're shedding."

Remembering its isolation, Tessa wondered if Richard would mind if she buried herself there for a while. Perhaps in the country she could sort things out and grope her way back to the wild freedom she had known all those years ago, before Clarence took her to the city and "housebroke" her, as he'd expressed it in the early years of their marriage.

A cat's terrified yowl caught her attention. She looked up and saw it running along one of the steel girders that stuck out several feet from a higher level of the new building. The cat raced out as if pursued by the three-headed Hound of Hell, and its momentum was too great to stop when it realized the danger.

It soared off the end of the girder and landed with a sickening thump on the terrace awning. With an awkward twist af its furry body, the cat leaped to the terrace floor and cowered under one of the chaises, quivering with panic.

Tessa watched the end of the girder, expecting to see a battle-scarred tom spoiling for a fight. Although cats seldom made it up this high, it was not unusual to see one taking a shortcut across her terrace from one rooftop to another, up and down fire escapes.

When no other cat appeared, Tessa turned her attention to the frightened animal. The night air had roused that touch of arthritis that had begun to bother her this year, and it was an effort to bend down beside the lounge chair. She tried to coax the cat out, but it shrank away from her hand.

"Here, kitty, kitty," she murmured. "It's all right. There's no one chasing you now."

She had always liked cats and, for that reason, refused to own one. It was too easy to let a small animal become a proxy child. She sympathized with Richard's mild disapproval whenever Alison called their dachshund "baby."

Patiently, she waited for the cat to stop trembling and to sniff her outstretched hand; but even though she kept her voice low and soothing, it would not abandon its shelter. Tessa's calcified joints protested against her crouch and creaked as she straightened up and stepped back a few feet.

The cat edged out then, suspiciously poised for flight. From the living-room lamps beyond the glass doors, light fell across it and revealed a young female with crisp black-and-gray markings and white paws. Judging from its leggy thinness, it hadn't eaten in some time.

"You poor thing," Tessa said, moved by its uneasy trust. "I'll bet you're starving."

As if it understood Tessa meant no harm, the cat did not skitter aside when she moved past it into the apartment.

Soon she was back with a saucer of milk and a generous chunk of rare beef which she'd recklessly cut from the heart of their untouched dinner roast. "Better you than a garbage bag, kitty. No one else wants it."

Stiff-legged and wary, the young cat approached the food and sniffed; then, clumsily, it tore at the meat and almost choked in its haste.

"Slow down!" Tessa warned, and bent over heavily to pull the meat into smaller pieces. "You're an odd one. Didn't you ever eat meat before?" She tried to stroke the cat's thin back, but it quivered and slipped away from her plump hand. "Sorry, cat. I was just being friendly."

She sank down onto one of the chaises and watched the animal finish its meal. When the meat was gone, it turned to the saucer of milk and drank messily with much sneezing and shaking of its small head as it inadvertently got milk in its nose.

Tessa was amused but a bit puzzled. She'd never seen a cat so graceless and awkward. It acted almost like a young, untutored kitten; and when it finished eating and sat staring at her, Tessa couldn't help laughing aloud. "Didn't your mother teach you *anything*, silly? You're supposed to wash your paws and whiskers now."

The cat moved from the patch of light where it had sat silhouetted, its face in darkness. With purposeful caution, it circled the chaise until Tessa was between it and the terrace doors. Light from the living room fell full in its eyes there and was caught and reflected with an eerie intensity.

Tessa shivered uneasily as the animal's luminous eyes met her own with unblinking steadiness. "Now I see why cats are always linked with the supernatu—"

Suddenly it was as if she were a rabbit frozen in the middle of a back-country road by the headlights of a speeding car. Those feral eyes bored into her brain with a spiraling vortex of blinding light. A roaring numbness gripped her. Her mind was assaulted—mauled and dragged down and under and through—existence without shape, time without boundaries.

It lasted forever; it was over in an instant; and somewhere amid the splintered, whirling clamor came an awareness of another's existence, a being formless and desperate and terrified beyond sanity.

There was mingling.

Tessa felt the other's panic.

There was passing.

Then fierce exultation.

There was a brief, weird sensation of being unbearably compacted and compressed; the universe seemed to tilt and swirl; then it was over. The light faded to normal city darkness, the roaring stopped, and she knew she was sprawled upon the cool flagstones of the terrace.

She tried to push herself up, but her body responded queerly. Dazed, she looked around and screamed at the madness of a world suddenly magnified in size—a scream which choked off as she caught sight of someone enormous sitting on the now-huge chaise.

A plump, middle-aged, gray-haired woman held her face between trembling hands and moaned, "Thank God! Thank God!"

Shocked, Tessa realized that she was seeing her own face for the first time without the reversing effect of mirror. Her shock intensified as she looked down through slitted eyes and saw neat white paws instead of her own hands. With alien instinct, she felt the ridge of her spine quiver as fur stood on end. She tried to speak and was horrified to hear a feline yowl emerge.

Like footsteps in an empty alley or screams in
the dead of night, cats and mystery fit purr-fectly
together in these collections of cat tales by
modern masters of mystery.

CAT CRIMES
all edited by MARTIN GREENBERG
and ED GORMAN

Published by Ivy Books.
Available in your local bookstore.